CURSE ON THE LAND

A Soulwood Novel

Faith Hunter

ROC
New York

ROC

Published by Berkley

An imprint of Penguin Random House LLC

375 Hudson Street, New York, New York 10014

Copyright © 2016 by Faith Hunter

Excerpt from *Skinwalker* copyright © 2009 by Faith Hunter

Penguin Random House supports copyright. Copyright fuels creativity, encourages diverse voices, promotes free speech, and creates a vibrant culture. Thank you for buying an authorized edition of this book and for complying with copyright laws by not reproducing, scanning, or distributing any part of it in any form without permission. You are supporting writers and allowing Penguin Random House to continue to publish books for every reader.

ROC with its colophon is a registered trademark of Penguin Random House LLC.

ISBN: 9780451473325

First Edition: November 2016

Printed in the United States of America

1   3   5   7   9   10   8   6   4   2

Cover art by Cliff Nielson

Cover design by Katie Anderson

Acknowledgments

David B. Coe for early reading on book one.

Sarah Spieth and MG for more of the info about . . . well, you know.

Mud Mymudes for all the botany corrections, beta-reading for accuracy, and slime mold stuff.

The Beast Claws, best street team ever!

The Hooligans. You know how much I love you. If this book is a success, then you made it happen.

Ltpromos.com. Your work on this series has been amazing. I adore you!

Mike Pruette for website stuff, marketing stuff, and the best T-shirts ever!

Joy Robinson for the artwork on the T-shirt and on the website. LOVE the trees!

Janet Robbins Rosenberg, copyeditor, for cleaning up the . . . everything.

Lucienne Diver, my literary agent with the Knight Agency. You believed in this series even when I had given up on it. Thank you.

Jessica Wade, editor at Penguin Random House. There are no words. Not one of my books is publishable without a developmental editor. Your knowledge and understanding of what a book needs (and your patience) are amazing.

For those who like to find places mentioned in books, the PsyLED offices on Allamena Avenue, off Highway 62, do not exist. Neither does Allamena Avenue.

My thanks to all the wonderful people above. If there are mistakes in this book (and there will be) they are mine alone.

ONE

I pulled up to Soulwood and let the truck lights shine on my house and garden. The trees were leafless, stark branches reaching up to the sky and down to the earth, roots thick and gnarled and digging deep. Leaves were piled against the foundation and against the garden fence. The three acres of grass needed to be cut, despite the time of year. Following on the heels of an early cold spell, the fall had been warmer than usual, and a second growth spurt had left the lawn unkempt and shaggy, the garden full of raggedy weeds and dead plants. I had never let my house and garden go untended for so long. It had been four weeks since I had been home, and then only for a long weekend. Now, the week before Thanksgiving, I was finally home from the training center for the Psychometry Law Enforcement Division of Homeland Security, known to its graduates—which I was one of, though I wouldn't go through formal graduation ceremonies until just before Christmas—as Spook School.

I opened the door of John's old Chevy C10 and the scent of home—rich loam, the creek out back, the tart scent of fall flowers, and the welcoming aroma of a wood fire from somewhere nearby—stopped me. I closed my eyes and simply breathed. The land around Richmond, Virginia, was practically lifeless, the air stank of exhaust, and the traffic roared from everywhere, the constant, distant drone of vehicles. Here, at the end of the dead-end road near the top of a low mountain, it was quiet and alive. The last of the leaves were falling, rustling across the ground, pushed by a steady, light breeze. The creak of the windmill that pumped my water sounded lonely but peaceful.

I left the truck door open and took two steps to the lawn, kicked off my shoes, and let my bare feet settle into the grass. *Oh . . . home. Home, to Soulwood.*

The earth reached up to me, knew me, and took me back into

itself the way a mother hen gathers a chick beneath her wings. I stretched out on the lawn, face and body in contact with the ground, hands extended to my sides, and reached deep into the earth. I spread myself across the life there, rich and fecund and content. I didn't know what I was, not really, not yet, but I knew my land, and it knew me. I was home.

I sensed the new cell tower on the top of the hill between my property and the church. Sensed the turning of the windmill that pumped my water. The presence of the spring that fed the rivulet and the small pool out back. Sensed deer, squirrels, rabbits, and foxes, the fox family having broken up and separated into four overlapping but individual hunting territories.

This was my magic, simple and dark as it was: to read the land that I had claimed, and that had claimed me, to know what it needed. To heal it and be healed by it. And to feed the earth—though I seldom spoke of that part of my gift, that part that felt so good, yet was sinful by every human standard I knew.

But something in Soulwood was wrong, just as wrong as when I'd left to start Spook School. Then, there had been an evil *something* skittering around beneath the ground, a darkness that was my fault, and that I had no idea how to fix. I had hoped the problem would resolve itself, but it was still there, the soul of a cruel, violent man I had fed to the land, a soul that my woods hadn't absorbed, hadn't used, and I didn't know why.

The evil that had been Brother Ephraim was gathered tight on the edge of the woods, a hole in my awareness of the earth, deep and stark and quiet at the moment, somnolent. The foul soul now rested on the border where my property met the compound of God's Cloud of Glory Church, just over the crest of the mountain, the polygamous church I had grown up in.

The church, Brother Ephraim, and his cohorts had shaped, defined, and confined my life and my understanding of myself for every moment until Jane Yellowrock came into it. The rogue-vampire hunter had disrupted everything I was and everything I had by showing me that I could fight back. That I could take a stand.

It was ultimately because of her that I had fought back against the church. Ultimately because of her that I had fed the body and soul of Brother Ephraim to the land. Had taken a job as consultant with the Psychometry Law Enforcement Division of Homeland Security, working with Jane's ex-boyfriend, PsyLED special agent Rick LaFleur. And had later gone to Spook School so I might join PsyLED and fight evil paranormal things. The irony of me being an evil paranormal thing wasn't lost on me.

I still wasn't sure if I hated or loved Jane Yellowrock for all the changes in my life.

I was careful not to make Brother Ephraim aware of me. I had a feeling that his disembodied soul was just as dangerous dead as the churchman himself had been alive. Well, not man. Creature.

To get better contact with my woods, I placed my cheek on the night-cold grass, pressing my palms flat on the ground, reaching deep, communing with my land. I breathed out, searching lower into the earth, listening, feeling the magic that was Soulwood. The old magic of the woods was a strong and profound power, a deep well of energy, strength, and contentment. The power had weight and mass and a greatness that reminded me of God, but wasn't. And a magic that might become self-aware. Despite Ephraim's dark soul, this old power still held sway over Soulwood, and it seemed more alive, more interested, and, maybe, more *conscious* than before I left.

I lay in the grass, eyes closed, arms out, long enough for the mouser cats to find me, one settling onto my back, one curled around my head, the third walking up and down my legs, mewling. My mousers had missed me. I returned my thoughts to the boundary of the woods and to the blot of darkness. It was different from before. It had grown in size, had taken over a larger part of the land. I had to do something about it sooner or later. I knew the land could subsume it. I had seen it happen not that long ago in North Carolina, but I hadn't succeeded with Ephraim. Except for the blot, the land was happy and growing and satisfied. It was good to be back, peaceful, here on my land.

I tracked the energies of the earth out, and saw an odd glow to the east. Shimmering yellow with sparks of red and green and blue. I extended my senses, reaching out for it, but it faded like a candle on a foggy night.

Something trailed across my senses, like a cold, dead hand, smelling like a week-old corpse. Gripping the power of Soulwood, I whipped away from the foul sensation. Jerked myself clear. And saw the evil that was left of Brother Ephraim. It was awake, aware of me. The darkness gathered itself, shaping like an arrowhead, pointing at me. Using the land like a mental rope with knotted handholds, I began to withdraw, pulling myself back to the surface. Easing my way through stone and water and earth.

The malevolent arrowhead shot at me. Pierced me. Wrapped itself through me. Pulling me down. I yanked away, but the malicious soul twisted itself into me, stinking of death and maggots and the grave. Touching me where no one had ever touched me. Opening *me*. My deepest self. Violating *me*.

I couldn't draw a breath, couldn't move. My heart stuttered and missed a beat. Pain spiraled through me. My guts roiled as if the roots that had once grown inside me were twisting and stretching and growing, fast. Something electric sped through me—the awareness of death. I was dying. And I could almost hear the dark soul howling with satisfaction.

An electric spark, hot and flashing, hit me, flowed through me like electric lava. Ripped the evil thing off me, out of me. I wrenched free of the earth and to my feet. Cats tumbled off me, claws catching in my clothing, scraping my skin. Yowling.

I raced to the truck. Heart pounding, I climbed on the hood and sat, hugging my knees, trying to make sense of what had just happened. Shivering. Below the ground, I heard rumbling, as if boulders tumbled and broke in a flood, carried by massive waters. A vibration, like a small earthquake, shook and rocked the land, a battle of great forces.

It was Brother Ephraim and . . . and Soulwood.

Fighting.

Low in my belly, I could feel the clash of wills, a skirmish, a battle. Death and life in one place, occupying the same space, and not enough room there for both. Soulwood was trying to protect me, defend me. The wood had never done that before. I rubbed my palms up and down my icy arms, as if to remove the crawly feel of maggots on my flesh, a sensation that I usually associated with vampires or dead opossum. I sat, waiting. Breath fast, heart pounding.

Belowground, the battle ended as abruptly as it had begun. The darkness of Brother Ephraim yowled and raced away, back to his hole. Curled around himself in the small space he had carved out of the earth at the boundary of the church land. Beneath me, Soulwood settled.

Electric shocks still cascading through me, I bent my legs in a yoga posture, sitting on the warm truck hood like a child. I gulped and caught up on breathing and tried to figure out what had happened. Whatever it was, it was over.

But just in case, I stayed on the truck, trying to calm my mind and my body, both of which had gone into flight-or-fight mode—settling on flight, which seemed cowardly but had kept me alive, so I wasn't complaining. Unwilling to touch the earth with my feet, I sat there long enough for the truck's lights to dim. I was pretty sure it needed a new battery, or maybe a new alternator. It wasn't holding a charge. I had the money and the plans to take it into town this week and get it checked out.

But first I needed to find the courage to get off the truck, get unpacked, and let my family and PsyLED Unit Eighteen know I had made it home safely. The special agents were already established in the brand-new Knoxville PsyLED office, where I had a tiny cubicle waiting on me. But only if I got inside the house. Right. I could do this.

Dropping my arms, I let gravity take me, and I slid off the hood of the Chevy and inside the cab. Grabbed up my shoes and yanked them on, protecting myself from the land with a layer of leather. I cranked over the engine, to let it run a bit and charge up the battery. I was underdressed for the amount of time I had spent in contact with the land, and I was shivering. But at least the maggoty sensation was gone.

Feeling the long drive in my achy muscles, I left the truck running and made trips up the seven steps to the porch, stomping to build up body heat. I carried luggage filled with fall clothing that needed to be washed and mended and I dumped it all in no particular order at the front door, along with my umbrella and raincoat. My potted pansies and sage and chives I carried to the back porch, to be repotted. The soil in the pots had been dug out of Soulwood land, and the plants were in need of fresh soil, though that was as much for me to put my hands in when I was away from Soulwood as anything helpful for the plants. The soil and the contact it provided with my land had kept me sane while I was away for the weeks of training.

My weapons gear came next, from where I had stashed it

behind the cab seat for transport. I had a newly issued service weapon, a Glock 20, locked in the plastic carrying case the weapon had come in, along with two magazines, each loaded with fifteen rounds, and a speed loader. It was a large case. There were also two boxes of ammunition, one standard, one silver-laced hollow points for vampires and were-creatures. My fitted body armor—a Kevlar and Dyneema composite, threaded throughout with a lining of thin silver foil to provide protection against weapons of all kinds, from gunfire to vampire claws to werewolf teeth—went on the porch floor beside the pile of other stuff. *Gear*, not stuff. Talking like a special agent was harder than I had expected. The silver-plated stakes—I couldn't afford solid sterling—and the ash wood stakes in their special sheaths went beside the weapon case, with the two vampire-killers, the fourteen-inch steel blades silver-plated. As a probationary special agent, I was already expected to fight my way out of any paranormal problems with guns and blades and magic. I had the training, the bruises, and the strained muscles to show for it.

I was no longer just a consultant; I had graduated under "special circumstances" at e3/GS 2 grade level. Technically, because I had passed background checks, stringent physicals, and weapons training as well as course work, I was a special agent, with an official title, a badge, and everything. However, because of my speciation classification and because I had no undergraduate degree and only a GED, I would be a probationary employee in PsyLED. If I survived the first full year of my employment in the paranormal branch of law enforcement, I'd move up to permanent employment, a higher pay grade, and access to greater levels of classified material.

To get here, most of my deepest, most private secrets had been released to the world of law enforcement I was now inhabiting. I didn't know if that was a good thing or a bad thing. Not yet.

Now lots of people knew that I wasn't human. I had magic. I was categorized as "nonhuman, paranormal, undifferentiated" by the government medical experts and biologists—undifferentiated because I didn't fit into the most common categories. I wasn't vampire, were-creature, witch, arcenciel, Welsh *gwyllgi*—pronounced something like *gwee-shee*—or even any of the other, lesser-known paranormal creatures that were being identified. So far as the biologists at Spook School knew, my sisters and I were a genetic family singularity, with Mud and me being the most alike and least human. I'd have kept us all a secret if I could have, but a paranormal-hating group called Human Speakers of Truth had outed us. I still hadn't told my family, proving me a bona fide coward. I was putting that off as long as possible.

The new, top-of-the-line psy-meter 2.0 I carried up the stairs all by itself. The device was the newest version, created just for field agents, and was capable of measuring far more than the previous model. They were freakishly expensive. Thirty thousand dollars for the one device. I placed it on the porch floor, carefully. I had been trained in its use and entrusted to bring it to Knoxville, but it wasn't mine. It belonged to Unit Eighteen. The new witchy cuffs—three precharmed pairs for the unit's witch to use—I tucked under the truck's front seat with the strange, silver-toned ballpoint pens in a plastic lock bag. The cuffs and the pens—which scuttlebutt said contained a Spook School–created spell, though no one was talking about them— weren't expensive, but only a witch could activate them.

I debated bringing in the weighty containment vessel that I had been charged to protect and deliver. It might be a top secret part of my job, but it was heavier than a good western saddle and a lot less manageable. Since I would know if anyone took a single step onto my land, there was no way anyone could get to it—short of parachuting in and landing on the Chevy C10, in the dark—without me knowing. With the containment vessel, I left the box full of small handheld psy-meter 1.0s. They were for use in the field when smaller was better than having more specific intel. They were each about the size of a pack of cigarettes and came with wrist or belt straps and locator key fobs, so if one was dropped, the field agent could find it easily.

At my grade level in the government, and not yet graduated, I was mostly a delivery girl.

A delivery girl with full government benefits, but still a mule, even on holidays off.

PsyLED thought my magic made me special enough to train me and give me a chance at a job. They also had offered me the opportunity to go to university on the government's dollar, taking night classes while working full-time. And like other covert and federal law enforcement agencies, I could earn my way up the employment ladder. We'd see. Unlike normal, human American girls, I had grown up thinking I would be a wife and mother, without the opportunity for schooling or a career. Ever. Thanks to an upbringing in God's Cloud of Glory Church, I hadn't conceived of the idea of being a member of law enforcement. I had just hoped to survive and not be burned at the stake for the magic I carried in me. But that magic gave me value in the eyes of PsyLED, value I couldn't help but appreciate.

I locked the truck and entered my house, expecting it to be cold and dank inside. Instead, someone had made a fire in my wood-burning stove, and the house was warm. It smelled of fresh bread and there was a pot of something wonderfully beefy-smelling on the cooker hob. There were also fall flowers—sunflowers and mums—in a bouquet on the kitchen table. I knew who had been here, and I warmed all over. My family relationships were still healing after a youth of misunderstandings and lies, but I recognized Mama's touch in the food and Mindy's in the flowers. Like me, maybe far too much like me, my sister was gifted with plants.

I stowed the gear away fast and checked the pot to find beef stew with barley and vegetables, Mama's secret recipe. I gave kibble to the cats, freshened their water, spooned up the stew, and texted my boss, Rick LaFleur, the senior special agent in charge—or SAC—of Unit Eighteen, to let him know I had made it to Knoxville and had his new equipment.

Duty appeased, I called Mama while I ate. Once greetings had been exchanged and I had described the trip and the roads and the traffic and the weather, all things one did before reaching the heart of a conversation, I said, "You shouldn't have brought me dinner, Mama, but thank you. The stew is wonderful and the house looks beautiful. Tell Mud I love the flowers."

"Of course we should. You'un are our girl and you'un's back after time away. Mindy and I made the stew together. She'uns learnin' right quick-like, and turning out to be quite the cook. Some young man will snatch her up fast, unless I miss my guess. And then we'uns spent the afternoon airing out your house, putting new sheets on that fancy new bed you got, and dusting. Good heavens, those cats of yours are a noisy bunch."

I let the comment about Mud—"Mindy" to Mama—marrying young pass by, but I had no intention of allowing my sister to be married off before she was eighteen. Not happening. If she wanted a life of polygamy, the life espoused by the church, then fine, but it wasn't a decision she would make until she was of legal age.

The phone call ended on a high note, with me promising to come over for lunch tomorrow, lunch with the whole family: Mama, Daddy; Mama Carmel and Mama Grace, Daddy's other two wives; my true sibs and half sibs; and my brother Sam's new wife, according to the church and according to the law of the land, both. A girl I hadn't met. They had been legally married, proving that his wife was of legal age. The legal marriage and the legal age together indicated that things had changed at the church, and hinted that things might be changing even more. I could always hope.

As I washed the single bowl and spoon and put the leftover stew in the refrigerator, my cell trilled out its repeating notes. I'd had exactly seven phone calls on the cell, and it was still exciting when it warbled the notes announcing a call. It was Rick, and instead of responding to my hello, he said, "Can you come into the office?"

My childhood had me automatically trying to say yes, but all the weeks in Spook School had given me better instincts. "I just spent over nine hours on the road in a truck. In a *truck*," I repeated. "It's cold and dark and I am home and staying here."

Rick was silent for so long that I thought we might have lost the connection, but he finally said, "We have a case that fits your special abilities. Unit's on the way to your place. ETA thirty-five, and have my new equipment ready."

"Oh," I said. "Okay." He ended the call and I sighed, not sure if I was sad or eager. A case meant that my long holiday week off was a goner, which was sad, but starting a job, a real job, chasing real paranormal perpetrators would be exciting. Well, most investigations would be predominately paperwork and making deliveries to my coworkers, but sometimes things happened, started moving fast, and that part of the job was undeniably thrilling.

At least the house was clean and dust free, so I wouldn't be embarrassed that guests—coworkers—would see it. I started coffee in the brand-new Bunn coffeemaker, set out small plates, cloth napkins, and spoons, sliced a loaf of Mama's bread, and opened a jar of preserves, since I had nothing else in the kitchen to offer guests. I put the strawberry preserves in a microwaveable bowl to warm when the unit arrived. And I thought about how much my life had changed in the last few months. I had a microwave. It was practically sinful, though I did note that Mama hadn't said anything about my changing and decadent lifestyle—other than my bed, and widder-women often bought new beds—over the phone or in the note on the table. Church-women didn't have microwaves or coffeemakers. Ever.

In the last few minutes of alone time, I unpacked, showered, and dressed in fresh clothes, leaving my feet bare on the chilled floors so I could maintain contact with Soulwood.

Before I left my room, I prepared and crammed a fully kitted-out, four-day overnight gobag with clean undies, toiletries, a faded pink blanket, and two changes of mix-and-match clothes. The personal gear was enough for a four-day trip, and included my passport, extra chargers, battery backups, a bottle of water, and high-energy snack food, for emergencies. If I needed to leave in a hurry on unit business, I would be able to. My large gobag, like all the gobags of the other unit members, would be stored at HQ. I also packed a smaller bag to use in the field, containing minimal gear, two evidence collection kits, field boots, gloves, and one change of clothes for any bloody, wet, muddy, or torn emergency.

When I was as ready as I could make myself and the house, I signed on to the house's Wi-Fi to check my e-mail. Having tech in the house felt surreal. Having a cell phone, a laptop, that fancy-schmancy microwave, and a real coffeemaker instead of the metal percolator I had been content with for years felt almost evil in the blatant consumption of the world's goods. I had lived on the edge for so long that it was taking a lot of time to realize that not all convenience was the devil's hand in the world. Growing up in God's Cloud, and leaving it only to become a junior wife to John Ingram, had given me a skewed view of life, and I was still working through it.

Six minutes before the unit was supposed to arrive, I felt the deep thrum of a four-wheel-drive truck or SUV coming up my mountain. I closed the laptop and added a log to the firebox, warmed the preserves in the new microwave, and checked the solar battery levels on the new gauges at the stairwell wall. The solar cell and battery system had been upgraded while I was at school, thanks to the sale of John's old four-barreled shotgun—which turned out to be an expensive collectible—and I now could run up to three days on full backup power. If I was careful about fuel usage, I could even outlast the lightless days of most ice storms, when I might be trapped on the mountain with only the wood-burning cookstove and the cats for company for a week at a time.

Tossing a shawl over my shoulders, I walked out onto the front porch as the microwave pinged behind me. The SUV came to a stop and Unit Eighteen boiled out of the open doors. JoJo, who had been heard to refer to herself as the unit's token human, also the unit's IT specialist, was wearing a wildly patterned skirt and turban, her braids flinging out around her, the electronic tools of her trade tucked beneath her arms. T. Laine, the moon witch (one with strong earth magic affinities), was dressed in jeans, hiking boots, and a wool jacket with a hood. She moved with a deliberate slowness, as if feeling my land through the soles of her boots, and she carried what looked like two boxes of Krispy Kreme donuts; my mouth started watering. Tandy, the empath, stepped out more slowly, his face wreathed in a smile that faded into something odd in the security lights, but perhaps that was the effect of shadows on the permanent Lichtenberg lines that marked his skin from being struck by lightning three times. Occam, the wereleopard, practically danced up the stairs, and Tandy fell behind as Occam and JoJo grabbed me in a hug.

I patted JoJo's shoulders and, hesitantly, Occam's back, which was solid muscle under his work shirt. I'd only ever hugged family and John, my husband, and he'd been dead for years. Physical contact was not a part of my daily life. The hug by the wereleopard was strong and unexpected and the contact did strange things to my insides. I jerked back a moment too soon for good manners and, at JoJo's surprised expression, I blurted in church-speak, "You'uns come on in. Hospitality and safety while you're here." The formal welcome was an old God's Cloud saying, and though the church and I had parted ways, some things stay with a woman, like accent, hospitality, and a steady hand on the trigger.

"Nell, sugar," Occam said in his strongest Texan accent, "we done missed you something awful."

"What the white boy said," JoJo added. "If you can call a

dude who changes into a leopard a white boy. The jury's still out on that one."

Paka, a native of Gabon in the African Congo region and a black wereleopard, slinked past us and opened the door to snatch up the house cats that raced out. "*I* have not missed you," she said, her black eyes glinting at me in a cat tease, "for I have hunted on your land and eaten of its prey."

Occam play-swatted at Paka—a cat move—as he swept me inside my own home. "The huntin' was nice, I admit, Nell, sugar, and you're a peach to let us hunt here on our moon-called nights."

"Hurry up," JoJo said. "Let me in. It's cold out here for the humans and witches among us. Damn, Nell, look at you in pants!"

Self-conscious, I touched my hips and slid my palms along my thighs. It still felt strange to wear pants. Before I went to Spook School, I had only ever worn pants when working in the garden, and then they had been a pair of Farmer John–style coveralls. I still hadn't worn my first pair of blue jeans yet, but the knit slacks were another step in the direction of becoming a modern woman. "You like?" I asked, my uncertainty clear in my tone.

"I had no idea you had legs that long," T. Laine said. "If I had legs like that, I'd be in pants all the time. Or a short skirt. You look like a model. And you cut your hair again."

"I love the look," JoJo said, reaching out and flipping my short bob. "You took a page out of Lainie's fashion style. Nice cut for a probie. What'd they do, grab you by your hair and force you to the mat during sparring practice?"

"Pretty much," I said. It had been humiliating and I had sworn it would never happen again. I had cut my hair to prevent that hold, and though I'd hit the mat many times afterward, it was never because my hair gave an opponent a handhold.

The group gathered inside, with Rick, Pea on his shoulder, entering last. I kept my mouth shut only by an effort of will. The senior special agent looked as if he had lost ten pounds. Deep lines ran from his nose to his chin, like parentheses cradling his mouth. He was pale. Dark circles marred the flesh beneath his eyes like bruises. Now that I knew his story, I had to wonder if not being able to shift into his werecat was wearing him down. Or maybe the relationship with Paka, which was one-sided in every way, was doing that to him. I knew a lot more about that peculiar relationship now. Paka grabbed Rick's hand and pulled him inside. She was petite but strong, and it appeared that Rick had given up fighting her on anything. He took the seat beside her on the couch, his olive skin looking pale and drab beside her glistening dark skin and curly black hair.

Pea, the unit's grindylow, padded across Rick's shoulders and settled in Paka's lap. The supernatural were-creature killer butted the werecat's hand, demanding to be petted, just like a regular house cat, though Pea was neon green and had hidden steel claws with which she was equipped to kill were-creatures who stepped out of line. Absently Paka petted her judge, jury, and potential executioner.

Paka wasn't a US citizen and was part of PsyLED by way of a complicated liaison agreement between her native country's government and the State Department. I didn't particularly like that Rick was so captivated by her, but Paka wasn't my problem.

The rest of us gathered around the kitchen table, the group asking me questions, all of us talking over one another. It was a great reunion, and it gave me something I hadn't expected. It gave me the feeling of being part of something special. Something important. I had almost gotten that feeling in Spook School, that awareness of significance and value and consequence. As if I was doing something worthwhile with my life instead of hiding on my mountain. I had figured out at Spook School that marriage and a future family were far less important to me than they were to my full and half sibs. I had been born an outsider, and I had finally found a home in PsyLED.

After twenty minutes of homemade bread and preserves, donuts and chatter, Rick cleared his throat. Before he could speak, JoJo said to me, "Ricky Bo's gonna steal your time off. You know that, don'tcha?"

I ducked my head and smiled as I opened my laptop. "I assumed as much."

"Sorry, Nell," Rick said. And he did sound sorry. "I'll make sure you get time with your family. But we have a case, and it falls right into your skill set. However, I don't want to tell you about it until you demonstrate the new psy-meter for us. And you can read your own land as part of the demonstration."

There was something just a bit off in all that, but I drew the psy-meter 2.0 from its carry case. "It's bigger than the incarnation model," I said, "and way bigger than the pocket models. Side switch." I turned on the counter. "Four gauges for the four psysitopes it can read, as opposed to the total psy-value the earlier models had access to."

"Psysitopes?" T. Laine asked.

"That's what the physicists are now calling the energy particles used during magic activities by paranormal creatures. They can be measured, like radiation on a Geiger counter, but unless they're directed, they don't do harm."

I'd studied psysitopes in my Introduction to Paranormal Creatures and Workings class. "Psysitopes are produced both actively and passively—actively by workings, when a were-creature shifts into a different form; passively by being a magical creature. The things we measure on the psy-meter, the psysitopes, are like light, being both particles and waves, but are energies emitting from the paranormal. So far as the physicists studying magic know, there are four psysitopes, each acting a little differently, but the differences are measurable."

The others, including Rick, gathered around. Paka stretched out on the couch with Pea and closed her eyes, looking bored. JoJo watched the werecat with something that might have been disdain in her eyes, but the emotion vanished when she caught me looking. She gave me a bright smile. I had seen fake before, and that smile was fake.

I said, "Like the original model and the smaller units that we had been using in the field, we have to set the device for interference. The werecats and witches will have to compensate for their own background readings, which means that JoJo, Tandy, and I will find it easier to fine-tune the more delicate parts of the device. We now can measure psysitopes one through four, and all four have to be zeroed for ambient magic." I zeroed each level on the device. "Once a day we calibrate for standardized readings of known paranormals. That would be T. Laine for witches, JoJo for humans, and Occam for were." I read each of them—except Rick, who would read differently because of his magical tattoos—and touched the button pads to standards. "Then we take a different known reading for quality control." I aimed the sensor at Paka, and psysitope three rose into the high midrange. Psysitopes one and two rose about half that much, and psysitope four stayed nearly at zero. "Perfect for a werecat," I said. I zeroed it and again extended the sensor to T. Laine. Psysitope one measured higher than the others. "Perfect for a witch."

I set the device down and passed out the handbooks that came with it. "Hard copy for the Luddites among you, provided by Q. I already sent you the e-files."

"Q," T. Laine said. "Ms. Marsters still hate the James Bond nickname?"

"More than ever," I said cheerfully.

"What do *you* read as?" Rick asked.

I shrugged and touched my belly, an instinctive reaction, feeling the rooty sensation beneath my fingers. His question didn't surprise me, but he could have asked me private-like. "I read essentially human, with a little elevation of psysitope four. I can feel the roots, but the medical scans show nothing but thick scar tissue." The roots had grown into me when a tree healed me of gunshot wounds. This was the newest part of my magic, and one I had no idea how to control. "The medical team scanned me top to toe and everything looked perfectly human except the PET scan. On positron emission tomography, my belly is full of inexplicable green energies and red blobs that look like full-blown systemic cancer. Except I'm healthy, as proved by the other tests and scans."

"Poked you full of holes, did they?" T. Laine asked.

"You have no idea." I rubbed my inner left arm where most of the blood draws had taken place. I had been bruised black and blue for two weeks as they worked me over before labeling me street safe. That wasn't the PsyLED term, but it was what I heard the techs call me. Spook School wasn't for the faint of heart or the politically correct. It was more like boot camp for the military, where they insulted you and tested you and studied you and tried to knock you down so they could see what you were made of and if you'd pick yourself back up.

"Okay. Let's see the land, Nell," Rick said.

"Why?" I asked.

"Because our case is about land and a paranormal event. I want readings from all around Knoxville. Here is a good enough place to start as any."

Tandy said, "And besides, we're curious. We all feel something magical on your land."

I frowned at the boss, but I had made a promise to do everything I could to be an equal part of Unit Eighteen, and that meant being open and honest about everything. Well, almost everything. I had been honest about Soulwood being a spiritual, powerful place that I could commune with, but I had never offered information—what was called "full disclosure"—about feeding souls to the land, or my desire for blood. I had just told people that I could kill attackers if I had to.

I had learned to lie by omission. The church taught that that was a sin, but I had never felt bad about the lie. I knew that said something unscrupulous about me, but some things were going to remain my secret. Well, Rick's, Paka's, and mine. We were inextricably tied together with the feeding-the-earth one. Together we had killed a man, who'd turned out to be a Welsh *gwyllgi*, a creature called a dog of darkness—a creature that had been Brother Ephraim, a churchman from God's Cloud of Glory—and I'd fed him to the earth.

This wouldn't be the first time Soulwood had been scanned with a psy-meter, but it was the first time with the newer, more efficient, powerful model. Even I was curious. I didn't have to zero the device between scans, but it didn't hurt, so as we traipsed outside, I aimed at the sky and went through the zero-and-cal process again until I was satisfied that the background readings wouldn't interfere.

Standing on the lowest step, I pointed the device's wand outward, first to the south, then east, then west, as much as I could get from the front of the house. And I was *not* taking a reading from the north, through the backyard, close to where Brother Ephraim and the other man had been fed to Soulwood. That would be foolhardy.

I aimed at the ground and took three readings at the compass points again. When I was done, I climbed the steps, passed through the people, and went back inside, to the heat. "I stored all the data," I said, setting the device on the coffee table and showing them how I had saved it. "Soulwood reads higher than normal woods on all four levels, but not by much." I swiveled the device and the screen at the bottom was now lit, showing the three sets of readings, one atop the other. A normal land reading that had been stored in the apparatus' memory was below for comparison.

Rick said, "Sit, people. JoJo, open a case file for us."

"Black girl always has to play secretary," she griped as she pulled her multitude of braids back in a clasp, but it was now more a wearied complaint without any real heat.

To me, Occam said, "We bought her a cape with the words 'Super Geek' embroidered on it. She won't wear it."

JoJo bit back a smile and her fingers flew over the keys. "It wasn't red. Shoulda been red. Or black. Not that ugly sunshine yellow. No superhero wears sunshine yellow. File's open, boss."

Rick sat back, crossing one ankle over the other knee, and Paka reached over to trap the toe of his boot in her fingers. He tolerated the contact, but his face grew even tighter, as if she sucked all the life and joy out of him with the simple touch. Paka squeezed his boot toe, her eyes on his, as if demanding his attention. Rick took a slow breath, and when he let it out he looked pained but he didn't direct his eyes to Paka.

T. Laine was watching the exchange and she frowned, glancing at Occam, who nodded once at her. It seemed that I wasn't the only one to notice Rick's change and the oddness in the relationship.

"Yesterday," Rick said, "Knox County Sheriff's Department received a report of a flock of radioactive geese on a radioactive pond."

"What does that have to do with us? And how did the info come through? And who took the report?" T. Laine asked.

Rick inclined his head as if she had asked the important questions. "Unknown caller on a burner phone, to the sheriff's nonemergency line."

"No imagination," T. Laine said.

Rick gave her a minute shrug of agreement. "On the surface, it has nothing to do with PsyLED. We don't handle radioactive leaks."

When I looked confused, Rick explained, "Nearby nuclear power plants and government research facilities, in the past, have been known to accidentally release radioactive materials—gas or liquids. Responsibility for the releases or the cleanups were seldom accepted until said accidents reached the public's attention. The resultant media and political blowups usually changed things. The last three times this happened, a whistleblower used a burner phone to report the release. KEMA was quick to respond to the sheriff's report," Rick said.

I typed the initials into my laptop and discovered that KEMA was the Knoxville Emergency Management Agency.

"The pond is about two miles away from Oak Ridge National Laboratory, once known as the Clinton Engineer Works. It's where Uncle Sam made fuel for America's atom bombs during World War II. It also isn't far—as the geese fly—from one of the nuclear power plants run by the Tennessee Valley Authority to make power for the Knoxville area. It makes sense that a radio-active leak could contaminate the geese and a nearby body of water.

"But when KEMA's Haz Mat team showed up, the readings for traditional radioactivity were at normal levels. They assumed it was a prank, but one of the Haz Mat crew thought the geese were acting strange, and took a reading with an old-school psy-meter. It redlined. That was at two p.m. today." Wryly he added, "It took them a few hours to work through channels and get the information to *us*." Regular law enforcement agencies didn't like turning things over to PsyLED.

Rick opened his laptop and showed a sat map of the area. On the satellite map, the pond appeared to be on what remained of an old farm, one likely left from the time in World War II when the government moved in and displaced all the farmers, stealing their land at pennies on the dollar, then throwing them into the cold.

"T. Laine, I want you and Nell to do human and paranor-mal evals at the pond and on the geese after you check in at HQ in the morning. Look for any previous, current, passive, or active magical workings or any paranormal creature that might have used the area. Nell, I'd like you to take the P 2.0 on-site and take readings. And if you will, I'd like you to . . . We need another term," he said. "I'd like you to read the land with your gift as part of the paranormal evaluation. Your help on the last case was invaluable to its resolution, and since this is a land-based, or pond-based, event, I'd like you to see what you can determine."

Discomfort crawled through me. I'd be reading the land in front of the others again. I'd had to do that as a consultant on the previous case, and again at Spook School, and it was difficult. Difficult to get in the proper mind-set, difficult to reach into land that wasn't mine. It had also been difficult to have anything to tell the Spook School people except that the earth near the school was nearly dead, which would lead to eventual desertification. They had been unhappy, and I hadn't enjoyed it. With psysitopes in the ground, this might be even worse. But that was my job now. I said, "Okay. I can do that. Where do you want me and when?"

"Meet us at the new building at seven. You have that address?" he asked.

I nodded. I had been provided the location of the new PsyLED offices.

"Second floor. Door's unmarked. You should have the keypad code as part of HR's packet."

I nodded again. This was really happening. I was going to work with Unit Eighteen. Excitement flashed through me, quickly contained. But Tandy caught my emotional spike and grinned as if he thought I was cute. Like a baby is cute when it first discovers its toes or takes its first steps. I made a face at him and he chuckled.

The meeting devolved into chatter and catching up and somehow we ate all the Krispy Kreme donuts, one full loaf of bread, and the entire jar of preserves. Like friends. Visiting. Feeling on the verge of euphoria, I saw my guests and coworkers out the door and into the night. Outside, a low mist hung two feet off the ground, illuminated by the security light, and bats capered in the glare, chasing the few flying bugs.

I gave and received hugs from most members of the unit, just as when they entered. It was less uncomfortable this time, but only because I kept them all brief, and barely patted Occam's shoulder when he gave me a one-armed hug. Paka walked by without a glance, holding Pea in her arms. The little killer was sleeping.

Tandy hung back, waiting until the others left. Occam glanced back at the empath, some quip on his lips, but he did a classic double take and stopped, let me go, and walked down the steps, his gait suggesting a deliberateness in the face of uncertainty. Odd in every way, but he didn't look back.

"Nell," Tandy said, taking my hands, which was more than the empath usually did.

"Yeees?" I said, uncertain.

His skin held a strange pallor in the porch light, the Lichtenberg lines bright and bloodred in the night. "Whatever is broken in your land, know that I'll help if I can. And you be careful. Okay?"

I started to deny any problem, but Tandy released my hands and took the steps to the ground. Moments later, PsyLED Unit Eighteen was rolling down the mountain.

TWO

I didn't sleep as well as I'd expected, despite the new mattress and the fresh sheets and the cats snuggled all around me. I kept replaying Tandy's last statements to me, and measuring them against the darkness of Brother Ephraim in the earth.

Tandy could feel more than simple emotions in mundane humans. He could resonate with witches, with vamps, and with me. I had known he could feel my land, passively but deeply, from the first moment I met him. Tandy and the werecats could sense the beauty and the magic in the earth of Soulwood. It had been startling and disconcerting that first time, but now I might have to reconsider my own communing with Soulwood. Tandy could feel the malevolence too. Or . . . he picked up my own unhappiness. Perhaps that. The disquiet kept me awake.

A little after two a.m., I rolled over in bed, into a cold place in the sheets, awake, aware of the soft hum of the new, much bigger converter on the second story. Mindful of the cats purring in their sleep. Alert to everything. Except for those vibrations, the house was dim and silent. I slid a leg out of the sheets and down, until the toes and the ball of my left foot touched the cool wood of the floor. The flooring had been cut from the trees of Soulwood before I was born, but the wood knew me, resonated to me. I sent my awareness down through the floor, into the beams and floor joists, down the rocks of the foundation and into the soil. I sent a slow, delicate tendril of my consciousness into the earth.

I was met with a feeling of warmth, of welcome, as if the land was awake now and waiting for me. As if it had expanded, unfolded, yawned, and reached out to welcome me. The land of my woods was deep and wide, usually a huge, slumbering entity, now stirring and wakeful. "Hey there," I said. "Long time, no see."

The energies of Soulwood wrapped around me and held on,

warm and gentle, powerful and content, as if it were a parent holding to a child. And, very oddly, the land felt . . . kind. I didn't know how land could be or feel kind and welcoming, but Soulwood was. I leaned into the welcome, knowing I was protected and safe, and at long last, sleep took me.

Six a.m. came early. There was a time when I'd have been awake long before six, alert, sharp, my day planned out ahead of me, and already with a cup of coffee in my system. Now, with late-night guests and electricity to keep me going long into the night, I was rising closer to dawn. I was a different person, and not sure I liked all the changes, this one included. I stretched, dislodging the cats as I edged upright and turned off the cell alarm.

It didn't take me long to get ready for work. I didn't wear a lot of makeup—mostly lipstick, a swish of blush, and a little eyebrow pencil. My bobbed hair needed only damp fingers with a little goop on them, rubbed through my scalp. Now that I was on active duty, the black slacks and a long, lean white shirt over a black, long-sleeved tee seemed appropriate. I added a belt to hold gear. A warm black jacket. Field boots. No heel. Easy to run in, but classy. That was the evaluation that my Spook School mentor had given of my boot choice. LaLa—more officially known as Linda Pierce—had been proud. And I looked good. Slender but tough. Capable. I clipped my badge to my belt at my waist and carried my service weapon in its oversized box under my arm, keys in the other hand. I was glad I had invested in the field boots, which were sturdy waterproof leather. Goose grease was sticky, nearly impossible to get off shoe soles, and Rick had mentioned geese where I was going.

I shooed the cats out onto the back screened porch, into the dark. They didn't like being out so early, and Torquil hissed his displeasure, following me to the driveway. As I reached the truck I said, "Watch out for the hawks and the foxes. Kill a couple of voles, okay? Kibble when I get home tonight." Giving me a prolonged vocalization, he slid into the shadows.

Within half an hour of waking, I pulled out of the drive onto the road to Knoxville, the address of the new offices of PsyLED Unit Eighteen entered into my cell phone's GPS. Behind me, the woods seemed to sigh with the coming dawn, the sound of owl giving way to hawk, deer prancing across the road in front of me, a six-point buck and two does. A juvenile fox darting in front of me, skulking after the deer, eyes and hunger bigger than his size or abilities.

I took the unlit dirt-and-gravel road down and around the low mountains, or high hills, winding my way toward the Tennessee Valley and Knoxville. Around me, the night grew lighter, a gray-on-charcoal-on-midnight tone that said day was near.

The road merged into a two-lane blacktop tertiary county road and then into a state road. By seven, light was coming over the horizon, and I stopped at a McDonald's for a special-order bacon, egg, and cheese on a bun. With mustard. And a coffee. I could have eaten homemade granola cereal at home. It might have been stale, but it would have been cheaper. But . . . I shook my head. I was clearly not the same person I had been.

The new offices of PsyLED Knoxville were on Allamena Avenue, a new road on a patch of newly developed land off Highway 62, the building ugly as only a government building can be, three stories with the two top levels set aside for PsyLED and for an eventual PsyCSI, whenever the government got around to fully funding the agency. The bottom floor was a deli and a coffee shop. There were no signs to indicate that I was at the right place, but I recognized the oversized SUV from the night before and parked near it. The second-floor lights were on. An unmarked door separated Yoshi's Deli and Coffee's On, with an inconspicuous keypad at the side and a very conspicuous, roving surveillance camera over the door. The security system looked high-end. PsyLED had spared little expense so far.

I hauled my gear, including the witchy cuffs, the zip bag of lightweight, silver-toned pens, and the heavy containment vessel that I had forgotten to give Rick last night, to the door, keyed in the code, and climbed the narrow stairs to another door at the top. There was a keypad there too, but this door didn't respond to my code, so I ran my ID card through the slot and the door *snick*ed open.

The smell of coffee and donuts and stale pizza brought a smile to my face. They might have a fancy new office space with all the electronic bells and whistles that taxpayer money was willing to buy, but the unit was still the unit.

I walked through the door, which automatically latched and

sealed after me, and JoJo pointed out an empty office cubicle by holding out a piece of pizza while talking on speaker on one cell, tapping out a text on another cell, and scanning a file on her laptop, all at once. Multitasking. Not my best skill set, unless it involved plants or farming.

My office space was really a low stall with padded, five-foot-tall half walls, a desk, and two chairs, both looking hard and unforgiving. The government was determined to provide the best of everything except comfort for the employees, not that I cared about comfort. I had a window! It was narrow and faced west, which wasn't the best light, but I could bring plants to work. The dawn light coming through the pane made me want to dance—not that I danced. Not ever. Even the thought made me sick to my stomach. Churchwomen didn't dance. And I'd look like a cross between a kangaroo, a giraffe, and a platypus. Stupid and clumsy and . . . stupid. But I had a window!

I placed the witchy cuffs, pens, and containment vessel on the desk along with my laptop and sealed my weapon into a small gun safe set into my desk, resetting the code to something I could remember easily, but wasn't something anyone else would ever deduce. I put my four-day gobag in the bottom desk drawer and keyed the lock with the keys I found in the middle desk drawer. I inserted one key into my wallet and the other one into the fake plastic tree in the corner. It was a stupid hiding place, and there were probably rules about that kind of thing, but I could move it later as needed.

That hadn't taken long. Everything was in place. My hands were empty. I made one more quick trip to the truck for the box of small handheld psy-meter 1.0s. The newbie/probie had no idea what to do next. Fortunately or not, Rick strode by, looking a lot fresher than only hours before, and waved me to the other side of the building. He was talking on a cell too, and I pocketed my own cell, grabbed up my laptop, the psy-meters, the heavy containment vessel, and followed.

We passed a cleaning closet, a safe room, and a null room— a spelled, sealed room where witches could be held, unable to use their own powers. The room's witchy tech was brand-new; I had heard about it at Spook School. The room was set up so that T. Laine, or anyone else who knew the code, could get in or out. The null room could be used as an interrogation room for magical creatures or a safe room for humans, preventing a takeover attempt by magic users, but once locked inside, it was as if there was no magic. A faint sense of electricity skittered across my flesh as we passed, unpleasant and scratchy.

The conference room was not nearly so comfortable as the hotels where we had met when I was just a consultant. No couches, no slouchy chairs. The décor was totally unlike the colorful offices of TV and film cop shops, and was decorated in beige, gray, brown, and charcoal, dull but serviceable. A sleek, fake wood–and-metal table took up most of the space and more of the uncomfortable-looking chairs ringed it, quickly being filled with unit members. A series of wide video screens were on one wall.

I dropped the box of witchy cuffs and the baggie of pens in front of T. Laine, who made a soft squeal of pleasure. She signed the D&R—delivery and release—forms and slid them to the boss faster than I could set the containment vessel and the box of small psy-meters in front of him. Rick grunted in recognition, and I placed the multiple D&R papers on the desk in front of him too, placing a pen in his hand for his signatures. He grunted again, this time in irritation, but he accepted the pen. As he signed, he ended the call and said, "Problem, people.

"Two of the geese that read high on the psy-meter are dead at the pond site. No visible signs of COD. We need to acquire these geese for necropsy by a veterinary pathologist and see if they're redlining. Our main area of concern is to make certain that the . . . for now, I'm calling it psysitopic contamination . . . stops its spread. Whatever spell or working or creature caused the paranormal readings, it may be ongoing. JoJo?"

JoJo opened a satellite map on the wide screen on the wall of the conference room. "Just before sunset last night," she said, "the county isolated a herd of psysitope-positive deer. They were nowhere near the pond. They were standing in the middle of the road when a delivery truck came around a sharp turn and hit several. Couldn't stop. Killed three. Injured two. Four more just watched the members of the herd die. They were walking in a circle, like they were drugged. Didn't even run when the deputies shot the injured deer. They ordered tox screens on them, but after the geese incident, the deputies called for psy-meter readings too. As Rick said, we need to find the source of the paranormal activity causing this and contain it. Then we need to figure out how the magic is spreading and put a stop to that too."

"That's not the way magic works," T. Laine said. "It doesn't just spread, like an airborne disease. It can't get into the groundwater. It can't spread by touch. It has to be formed and ordered and shaped. It isn't amorphous or contagious, despite what a lot of hardline, witch-hating right-wingers say."

"Okay," Rick said. "Then we need to find the people who are setting workings loose and stop them. Which is why you take lead on this one, Lainie. You and Nell and the psy-meter 2.0."

T. Laine said, "Plugging in the two locations now. But I have to say, again, *this is not the way magic works.* At all."

"Noted. Check it out." Pea jumped on the big conference room table and then off onto the floor to disappear. Catlike.

I had a much higher, upgraded security clearance than I'd had as a consultant, though not as high as the other team members. As a probie, I'd be taking orders, getting coffee, and doing paperwork. And reading the land. I went to the new coffeemaker and started a second pot, remembering the first time I saw such a device and had to figure out how to make it work. This time, I found Rick's special French dark roast Community Coffee and started a pot, as if I had done it all my life. Then I poured coffee for all the unit members while they discussed possibilities of creatures and events that might cause the readings. When I reached Occam's cup, he said, "Nell, sugar. Whatchu doing? Waiting on us?"

I pointed a finger at my chest and said, "Probie. Lowest on the totem pole. Paper pusher and waitress. At least for a while."

"Nell," T. Laine said, with a half smile on her face, teasing. "Make mine to go, milk and sugar."

"Yes, ma'am," I said, pouring us both to-go coffees in metal mugs. "Ummm. Weapons?"

"Special agents do not say *ummm.* Service sidearms should be sufficient," Rick said. "If you find animals that need to be euthanized, call the sheriff's office or animal control. I'm assigning the handheld psy-meters. Record the model and serial numbers and enter them on the paperwork that will be on your desks when you return. You're responsible for them. Take care, people."

I grabbed my coat, a small handheld P 1.0, my laptop, the new psy-meter 2.0, and my service weapon, and followed T. Laine out the door, down the steps, into the day. I got my small everyday gobag out of the Chevy.

"Good God, girl. You still driving that old truck? We'll take my car." T. Laine took the passenger seat of a white Ford Escape. "You can drive a normal car, right?" She waved a key fob at me. "I've got paperwork to do and I always wanted a driver."

I stowed my gear in the back and started the SUV with the push-button start. This was a bottom-of-the-line Escape and had no rearview camera and no electronic upgrades, which relieved me. When I first got the money for John's shotgun, I test-drove a brand-new Escape and was intimidated by the electronics. This one was okay. I adjusted the seat and rearview before driving into the early-morning rush-hour traffic. "I can manage," I said mildly, merging into the flow of vehicles. I had passed the aggressive driving course at Spook School, and it wasn't for the faint of heart.

"Good. Rick can assign you a government-owned vehicle for field use. You can't drive it for personal use, but it'll be better than that truck on city streets."

I didn't know what to say, so I said nothing. I liked my truck. I could haul all sorts of things in the bed. But she had a point about work-related city-street driving. Maybe a small coupe would be better, one with a trunk for locking away my weapons and electronic equipment.

We made good time to the turnoff for the pond, and I drove T. Laine's Escape past the yellow caution tape and parked on the two-rut drive. A pond was visible through the trees, dark water around a bend. Nervous energies tingled under my skin, half worry, half anticipation. This was my first, real, active, ongoing paranormal site. It wasn't a crime site, but it was a big part of what I had trained for.

I let the lead agent handle introductions and the Q and A with the county deputies, while I calmed my mind and went over the protocol for dealing with such sites. Because this was a fresh scene and supposedly no one magical had been on the grounds of the old farm, the first thing I needed to do was use the P 2.0 to determine if there was an active working anywhere near.

I stepped to the back of the vehicle, where I unpacked the device and went through the start-up procedure. I turned the sensor on the closest human to verify human-standard, then on T. Laine to get a good witch reading, and then walked around the bend toward the pond.

It was small, about a hundred feet in diameter, an irregular oval with an open space on the side where I stood, and pine trees on all the others. Kudzu covered dilapidated buildings on the far side. A small shed with farm equipment was to my right. The dew-wet grass beneath my feet had been cut recently and the smell of countryside filled the air.

I was about a hundred feet from the water's edge and didn't expect to get a reading at all. Instead, I got a midline reading on level three and a near twenty-five percent on level-four psysitope. Which was a surprise. Something was still happening here.

T. Laine glanced my way, and I gave her an abbreviated nod. Her eyes went wide for an instant before the cop mask fell back in place.

Because there was no crime, just a quirky reading, I didn't have to take trace matter and blood samples to be held for PsyCSI workup and possible DNA testing. In the event that we discovered culprits or victims, that might change. In that eventuality, I would need to create more than a simple evidentiary record, take psy-meter readings, and gather samples of any elements used in magical workings. I had been trained to collect fingerprints and study blood spatter, but usually in magical crimes, PsyCSI took care of the crime scene workups. Of course, with Knoxville not having a PsyCSI team yet, the techs would have to fly in from another territory. For now, I went back to protocol, starting over with a strictly human evaluation.

I could see what the Haz Mat tech had thought was a problem. The geese were floating . . . No. Slowly *swimming* on the water. In what looked like a perfect circle. Steady, unhurried. But a perfect circle. Geese didn't do that.

Using two different cameras and my cell phone, I took photographs of the pond, the water dark with the tannins of decayed plant matter, the flock of geese slowly swimming in the middle, and the humans watching from the shore. Redundancy in everything kept us from losing evidence that might be valuable at any trial. I got some nifty shots of geese and a few good shots of the morning sky with the pond reflecting golden clouds and the trees that lined it on one side.

I called out to T. Laine, "I'm goin' in for closer readings."

"Copy," she said and turned back to the cops. The dark-haired witch was enjoying being boss. I knew I'd get my share of scut work and paperwork and menial jobs. What no one knew was that I enjoyed this part of the work. According to my coworkers, I had a knack for several things—briefing summations, evidence gathering, and telling the boss what he needed to know, when he didn't want to hear it. And organizing paperwork and files. Scut work.

I documented everything I had done, along with the readings at one hundred feet out, and then tucked my pant legs into my boot tops. Through the high grass, I headed into the seventy-five-foot mark and took readings, then at fifty feet out, then again at twenty-five feet from shore. At that point, the P 2.0 was nearly redlining on all four levels. I went no farther, because if someone had drawn a witch circle for a working big enough to cover the pond and back this far from shore, I didn't want to step on that circle and trigger something. Like a magical bomb. I had seen pics at Spook School, and they had been awful, including shots of humans blown to mincemeat, or with missing limbs, or burned.

If there was an enormous working, then the officer who had taken the reading here, with the older model psy-meter, had been lucky.

Keeping a fairly even twenty-five feet out, I walked around the pond. When I was on the far side of the small body of water, I spotted the first dead goose on the shore. I wasn't sure what had killed it, but scavengers had been eating it postmortem. From the size of the bites and the scattered feathers and body parts, I'd say buzzards and maybe feral cats. If the working was still active, why hadn't the animal activity broken the circle? Assuming there was a circle. I hadn't detected one, and T. Laine was better qualified than the P 2.0 to determine the presence of an active working.

I took photos of the scavenger depredation and continued my circumnavigation of the pond, finding the second goose, this one floating on the water, wings and feathers spread. I couldn't see a cause of death, but there was no visible blood or disfigurement. I took photos and went on around the pond to the car to record everything I had seen and all the readings. T. Laine joined me there when I was done, and she asked, "Finished with the human and tech eval?"

I nodded and closed up the P 2.0. "I stayed outside the redline zone. But there's a couple of dead geese on the far side, with clear scavenger activity at one. If there's an active circle, it didn't break."

"No circle," T. Laine said, her face going pinched, her arms wrapped around her, her hands clasping her arms in a self-hug. "No active working. And I get why someone thought this might be radioactivity. It looks like what Rick said. Contamination. Like someone brought something magical here and dumped it into the pond." She studied the small body of water, its surface placid, mirroring the blue sky. "In a sight working, it's glowing a sickly green gray. I've never seen or heard of anything like this before.

"If it is a working, which I strongly question," T. Laine went on, "it's something new." The moon witch was rubbing her upper arms, the skin of her palms dry and rasping on her jacket, the gesture a worried tic. One-handed, she tucked her too-long black bangs behind an ear. "If this is some magical attack, it'll be a homegrown terrorist group, one utilizing witches. Maybe witches being used against their wills."

I had read about that at Spook School. A full coven in Natchez, Mississippi, had been forced into a working that kept them trapped and slowly killed them as they were forced to keep the magical working going. I put that together with the fact that Congress had still not made a determination about how paranormal beings would be viewed under the law, as equal citizens or something else entirely. If witches had launched some kind of magical weapon, or were even taking part unwillingly, that would likely increase the chance of the government forcing registration of all witches. Throughout history, registration of the populace, or part of the populace, had been a prelude to extermination. Step one of a pogrom.

"We need to report in," she said, "and get Rick involved. Why don't you send him the preliminary psy-meter recording results and I'll have a chat with him. While we talk, I need you to collect the geese and then find a comfortable spot to take readings of your own kind."

Collect the geese. *Ick*. But I had killed my first chicken for the pot before I was ten, so dead birds weren't particularly horrible. Still. *Ick*. I did as I was told and sent the psy-meter recordings to Rick and opened the bulky, fully stocked physical evidence kit in the back of T. Laine's Ford. From it I got gloves, the metal forceps for picking up bigger pieces, small numbered plastic markers, and several sizes of plastic evidence bags, from quart-sized to oversized. The bags were usually paper, to keep bacteria and mold and suchlike from speeding decomposition—*decomp* in PsyLED-speak—but in this case, oversized plastic zip baggies would keep the pond and body fluids from leaking everywhere. I gloved up, took several COC—chain of custody—sheets, sometimes called ERs—evidentiary records—and traipsed clockwise around the pond to the floating bird.

Fortunately it had drifted closer to shore, and I was able to fish it out easily. It didn't have rigor and its wings moved effortlessly as I folded them, tucked the bird into the bag, and sealed it. I recorded the date, time, GPS location, and all the other info I needed to maintain the chain of evidence.

The other bird was dry, if scattered and well gnawed, and had to be gathered in a different manner. I quartered the area and put a numbered marker at each body part. I probably should have tried to preserve the feathers, but they were scattering everywhere on the slight breeze.

I used twelve markers and gathered twelve pieces of birdy evidence. Which stank exactly as it should: like dead meat left out in the elements. I doubted either bird would ever be looked at in an evidentiary manner, but I was following orders, orders that might have been intended for me to practice my new skills.

Paperwork completed, I sealed the birds into a single, extra-large baggie and placed it all in the back of the vehicle. And looked for T. Laine, who was standing, facing the water, both hands to her sides. I knew she was reading the pond in the way of witches. It should have made me uncomfortable, with my churchwoman background, but it didn't. I had learned about witches and their gifts and it wasn't devil worship and they didn't sacrifice goats to Beelzebub. They just had genetically given gifts for the land or the water or the moon or growing things, whatever. With mathematics and geometry, they could harness and use both free energies and those stored in matter to accomplish certain goals.

T. Laine looked okay, so I began my next chore. Reading the land.

She had meant hand-atop-ground reading, the way I did at Soulwood, and the way I had done at other sites when PsyLED was looking for clues in a series of kidnappings. I glanced at the four law enforcement officers standing nearby, watching

T. Laine, two with well-hidden fear, one with amusement, as if
T. Laine was being cute. The other cop, older, graying, looked
on with boredom.

I took a notebook, a pen, a small, square, faded-pink blanket,
and the psy-meter 2.0 with me to the edge of the redlining
border.

I had spent all my life hiding my magics, denying them, so I
could stay alive and not get burned at the stake by the ultrahard-
line elders of God's Glory. And now I was all but flaunting my
tie to the land. As one of my teachers at Spook School had said,
life was weird.

After shaking the blanket open and snapping it to the ground,
I sat in the middle of it with my knees crossed and the notebook
and psy-meter 2.0 in front of me. I synced the device to my cell
and sent the recordings to U-18 HQ. I once again noted the date,
time, and GPS location on the pad. It looked like I was taking
scientific readings. It was utterly a cheat. I studied the land
around me, noted a wildlife cam pointed at the pond, the remains
of the kudzu-buried, tumbledown buildings on one edge of the
property, and spotted the foundations of an old house near them
in the pines across the pond. The brick showed signs of a long-
ago fire. To my right was a better-kept lean-to filled with farm
equipment, a small tractor, and gardening tools, all looking func-
tional and which were secured with massive chains.

Placing my palm on the ground, I took a cleansing breath,
blew it out, and relaxed.

Instantly I could tell that something wasn't right, in a way I
had no immediate name for. The ground was . . . maybe sick,
infested with something, some kind of parasite or illness. The
earth beneath my palm felt cold, icy, not to the touch but to the
spirit, which wasn't something I could easily explain to other
people. It felt sick and murky and restless. As if it was dying,
dying in pain. Alone and afraid.

I sent a soothing pulse of calm into the land, searching
for the cause of the illness. Reaching down into the earth, I
found the water source for the pond, an underground, degraded
concrete pipe that ran along the low hill about halfway to the
crest. The pipe system capped a spring there and collected the
water, sending it down through the pipe and into the pond for
collection, probably for former use by farm animals. It was a

slow trickle of water, and ran off on the far side, through another, smaller pipe, and into a gully. I dove deeper into the land. Below the surface of the hill, near the springhead, was an upthrusting slab of granite angled toward the sky, driven up and broken during some unimaginable earthquake in the far past. It was now shored in place by accumulated layers of shattered rock and compacted soil all around the slab, softening its contours, creating the hillock.

Along the edge of the granite, I caught a thread of . . . something. Not more than a quiver of reaction, perhaps to my presence. It wasn't witch magic in the land. Not exactly. Or not like any witch magic I had studied at Spook School. It wasn't a warmth, like Soulwood, nor an evil like Brother Ephraim. There was no darting, fearful hatred. This was different, more like a vibration of exhilaration, like a trace of scarlet sunlight through the trees in the final moments of sunset. I sought deeper, following the trail of whatever it was.

It led me through the springhead again and dove deep, through the rising current of springwater, following the vein of moisture into the rock where water was under pressure, seeking outlet. And back up to the pool in a loop. The pond wasn't deep, but was full of plant life and microscopic life, parasites and minuscule snails, tiny fish swimming sluggishly, and frogs burrowed into the mud. Decaying leaves and tannins. The richness of life and death on a small scale. I followed the traces of the almost-light sensation up to the surface of the pool, which was still and unmoving, and around the pond, following the vibrating hints of the excitement here and there, hoping to find the source.

I found, instead, the geese. The geese swimming on the surface of the pool. Another one was dead. I pulled up the memory of the pond when I was taking photos. All the geese in the circle had been alive and swimming, looking healthy. Now there was a dead one. And the dead goose floating in the water was different from the live geese; there was a faint, delicate hint of that vibration, that almost-light, brightening the feathered body, tangled around it like glowing thread. The thread dropped, seeming tied to the pond and to the earth deep below the surface. Deeper into the land.

The living geese didn't glow at all. There was no tendril attached to them.

The tendril that tied into the dead goose was something I could follow, deep, deeper, back into the hill and down, along the slab of granite, tracing its broken edges and fractured rim, past roots full of life and reaching for moisture and nutrients. Deep and deep. To a place of bedrock and layers of heavy, dense stone. Soft energies swayed here, bright specks of light in yellow and green and blue, moving among shadows of charcoal and very deep red. Like I sometimes saw when I turned off the lights at night, the energies of my own brain and retinas, sparking. But the colors here reminded me of the glow I had seen last night, just before Ephraim grabbed me, though these were moving and swirling, and last night's hadn't.

Stuff in my brain, the glow, and this were too different to be connected. But now that I remembered them, I cached the vague similarities in the back of my mind, just in case.

I remembered the line of dialogue I had heard at a Star Wars marathon weekend at Spook School, the words uttered by the little green thing, Yoda, "You must feel the Force around you, here, between you, me, the tree, the rock, everywhere, yes." I smiled at the memory, at the image. Or I tried to. But at that moment, the tendril I had been following noted me, and wrapped around my wrist, a silken caress. It tugged, gently, deeper.

I hesitated only a moment before I followed the motion of the shadows and lights, dancing and twining, with no boundaries or limits. It led me down and down, until we touched something else, something bigger, darker, so far down that there was only pressure and heat and a formless, lightless blackness like the deepest night in a sky without moon or stars, a blackness that stretched through the earth, massive and seemingly limitless. A *presence*. Powerful. Profound and somnolent. The gigantic thing, so very deep in the ground, was sleeping.

The lights and shadows twirled across the surface of the deep in the earth, tapping on a layer of . . . something . . . a skin, a thin casing, that kept it separate. A joyful intelligence, happy as a puppy, bounding and pounding its excited paws on its sleeping mother. The lightless presence was the reason the dancing energy had towed me here, the reason for its excitement.

So . . . two inexplicable things. One thing that was energetic and dancing. One sleeping. And the dancing thing sought to

join with, or to interface with, or . . . Yes. To *waken* the sleeping one.

The energy of the blackness was utterly unlike what I felt
while communing with Soulwood, and equally unlike what I felt
from Brother Ephraim. Unlike what I felt from the mutated tree
in the church compound, the one that had put its roots inside me
to heal me not so long ago. More similar to, but individual from,
the huge sentience buried below the mountains in North Carolina. Both were black-as-death, mammoth *things*. Presences.

I let the tendril of puppylike energies spin me around and
into their dance, and lead me far across the somnolent thing, as,
together, we reached deeper. The thing was immense, a presence more so than a being. A sleeping state of consciousness
rather than something composed of matter. It was everywhere I
felt and looked, at this depth, everywhere, and looking for the
end of it was like looking for the end of earth, so much more just
beyond the here and now.

The *presence* was covered with a thin membrane, a barrier.
Or a coating. A microscopic layer of quiet separating it from the
scarlet light-and-shadows dancer. The dancer moved across the
barrier of the sleeping presence, pulsing, reaching down from
the surface in several places, strings of pinpoint energies,
smaller than hairs, power moving up and down the thin byways.

The light-and-shadow energies slid along my mind like
phosphorescence on cave walls, like the warmth of hot springs
and magma far below the surface, like drowsy silk, wrapping
around me and skimming along my mind. Poking and prodding
and petting in their odd little dance. As if learning me.

In the deeps, words began to sound, like a bell ringing, a
vibration so deep it hummed through my bones. "Floooows,
floooows, flows. Pools, pools, pools. Gone, gone, gone." Over and
over. And the movement of the light-and-shadows changed to
match the words, as if the dancing power was evolving. As if the
rhythms of the earth itself were changing it.

The silk that had caressed my wrist tightened, roughened, as
if perceiving more of what it held. As if understanding, becoming aware. Becoming *real*. Or becoming matter, transitioning
from pure energy to something with weight and mass. It slipped
up my arm, twining higher, over my biceps and shoulder and
inside. It paused at my heart, watching. And stroked along my

nerves. It was light and shadow twining with me, dancing inside me. As if capturing me. Taking me over.

Inside of me a spark of fear—my fear—flared in the light-and-shadows. Brightening the blackness. Some of the motes of power were clinging to me, to my heart and nerves. As if already a part of me. I tried to withdraw. To pull away. The energies resisted.

And though it was impossible this far below the surface of the ground, I heard a voice, a human voice speaking in the cadence of a witch working. *Flows, flows, flows. Pools, pools, pools. Gone, gone, gone,* it sang, the cadence like the words to a spell.

The silken shadow-and-light was trying to . . . merge with me. To *capture* me.

I grunted at the realization and jerked. Trying to get away. But it had trapped me.

I heard the sounds of my own fear, moaning. "Eh, eh, eh, eh, eh," with each gasping breath.

In some part of my mind I felt something. I heard slaps, brutal and fierce. I felt pain. Over and over. And then the resonance of my moans in my chest. The hoarseness of my breath. The thundering of my heart, as if I were sprinting, hard and fast, to outrace death itself.

"Nell! Fight! Fight this! I'm cutting you free. Fight!" I knew that voice. *Occam.* He had cut me from the earth once before. I felt things snap and writhe around me. Stinging. Biting. And pulling away in fury. A blast hit my heart. It sped, arrhythmic. Too many thumps in the incorrect order.

I moaned again, the desperate, meaningless sounds. I flailed, but the silk holding me, inside me, mutated, thickened. Strong and scratchy. It was tying me in place. Deep in the dark. I fisted my hands, as I had been taught. Punched. Fought.

"Good, Nell. Keep fighting. Only a few more."

The silk roughened and twisted, reaching through me, reaching for the roots inside me, the roots that the medical scans said weren't there, but that I could feel each time I touched my stomach. I pounded against the restraint. It tightened on me. Pulled me deeper again, along the surface of the presence buried in the earth.

Hibernating, the energies hummed at me, all meaning without words.

And deeper, a human thought: *Get out! Get out! It's mine!*

If I wake the sleeper, I will become . . . free, the dancing energies hummed.

No! Never! the woman screamed. *The sleeping power is mine!*

Yes, I thought. *A woman. Female.*

Before I could tell what species she was, the dancing energies tapped against me again, a torture against my heart, blasts of agony. The light-and-shadow thing was learning too much of me, learning what I was, what my magic did. But I was also learning *it.* And learning the thing it was trying to wake. The silk of its binding coarsened into hemp, creating a shackle, melding into me. The light-and-energy silk/hemp was nothing like what I compared it to, but those concepts were all I had to describe it. It was a new thing, a new construct. *Evolving,* moment by moment, *fast.*

The blacker-than-blackest-night thing below it was old, old, old, beyond old. This one had been here, always, in the land. Sleeping.

Fed by blood and death, the dancer thought at me. *By war and battle and the life-force soaking into the earth for aeons. It has not been fed in many passages.*

I got an impression of humans falling and dying in violence and war. Left to rot on the surface of the land or buried on/in the earth, generation after generation. Energy tendrils rose from the sleeper, touching the surface where each great battle had taken place. Battles between tribal people, between Europeans and tribal peoples, between the gray and the blue. War. Long in the past to my concept of time, but only yesterday to the sleeping consciousness in the earth. It had fed on death. The dancer wanted it to be fed again. Wanted to give it blood, like in those long-ago times of conflict.

What the woman wanted, I didn't know. Was she a witch? Or was she something else?

Pain exploded through me. Shivered through me, stinging and sharp. The light/dark silk/hemp tightened. A blade sliced into me, beneath my flesh, pain that shivered up through my nerves and flesh, flaying me. I heard something cadenced. A woman's voice. T. Laine, chanting. A working, using the energies of life and of the earth. I could see the energies of a tearing, cutting spell, a freedom spell. I had learned about spells in Spook School. Learned not to fear them, not when they were used by people I trusted. Like T. Laine. I reached for the power in the spell even as it reached for me. Words hammered me as steel cut me. The blade cutting me free was silver plated. And coated with my blood.

My blood flowed over my skin and onto the earth. The light/shadow silk/hemp saw my blood and twirled into it, where it spread on the ground.

I was ripped out of the earth and lifted into the air. "I got her. I got her. Nell. Sugar. Talk to me."

It was Occam. I blinked at the sky. Bands of scarlet streaked across the western horizon. Sunset. It was *sunset*. I had been inside the earth for hours. Darkness took me.

THREE

I woke fast, struggling to sit up. Fighting. Trying to get free.

"Nell, sugar. I got you. I'm here. It's okay. You're fine."

"Occam?"

"Yes, Nell, sugar. I'm here. You're okay."

I sobbed and realized that my face was damp with tears and snot and sweat. My short hair clinging to my skin. My heart was racing, and my chest and belly ached. Memory returned. The light-and-shadows dancing in the earth. Evolving to light/shadow-silk/hemp—concepts that almost, but not quite, described what I had seen and felt and experienced.

The blacker-than-night thing so far below, separated from everything by a membrane of . . . I didn't know what.

But the light-shadow dancer had been trying to eat me. Or merge with me. Or become me. My heart rate spiked. I jerked upright, crying out, "Noooo!"

"Nell, sugar!"

"No!" I screamed. I forced my eyes to open. The world outside my head was murky and dim, cloudy as if a fog surrounded me. I tried again to sit up and realized I was tied to a hospital bed. "You'uns lemme up," I shouted. "Lemme up!"

"Panic attack," JoJo said. "Let her loose. The restraints are just making it worse now." A voice murmured something and JoJo said, "You set her free or I'll cut your expensive restraints myself."

And suddenly I was unbound. I scuttle-walked on butt and heels and the pads of my hands to the head of the bed. I was gasping, crying. Sweaty with exhaustion. I wrapped my arms around myself tightly.

The lights in the room were low, medical devices attached to me, beeping, all crazily now, with my awareness. With my fight.

"Nell, sugar?" Occam. His hand was out in front of me, palm up, offering an anchor.

I slipped my hand into his. My whole body shuddered at the contact.

"You're okay, sugar. I gotcha. I gotcha, girl."

"You cut me free," I gasped. "You and T. Laine."

"Yes. You remember."

I fell back on the mattress, the sheets wet with sweat and other bodily fluids. My heart rate and breathing steadied. Slowed. Occam's hand was a sturdy moor, like a piton in a mountain of rock, or an anchor in a stormy sea, though I'd never seen the ocean. "I remember. I remember. I was trapped. You cut me free."

"Yeah. About that. I'm sorry, Nell, sugar. You got some stitches. A lot of stitches."

"You coulda cut off my arm and I'da been good with it. I was trapped." Tears started again and Occam tightened his grip. I placed my other hand over our clasped hands and would have tightened my fingers but for the pain that ratcheted along my flesh.

"Stitches," Occam said again.

"Oh. Ow?"

"Pretty much 'Ow,'" he agreed.

I blinked my eyes clear and asked for water. When someone handed me a Styrofoam cup, I released Occam, drained it all at once, and took another. This one I dumped over my face. The cold felt wonderful on my flushed and sweaty skin. Pea peeked out of Occam's shirt and darted back inside. The wereleopard chuckled at us both and someone dressed in scrubs patted my face dry with a rough towel.

"Where am I?" I asked.

"University of Tennessee Medical Center, the paranormal room of the emergency department," Occam said.

"Why?"

"You weren't breathing right when we got you free. Your heart rate was racing. There was the little matter of the blood. And someone had called an ambulance. Rick said to put you in it. Boss' orders."

"I'm not complaining," I said, again holding his hand as if it were the only stable spot in my universe. "This ain't the first time you cut me free from the earth. Thank you."

"Welcome." There was humor in his tone and I focused on his face. His blondish hair was pulled back in a tail, his eyes amber and gold, the gold of his werecat.

I was suddenly aware of the rank smell that came from my

body and my state of dishabille. My nakedness beneath the thin hospital gown. I almost let go of his hand, but he said, "It's okay, Nell, sugar." And encircled our clasped hands with his other one, his grip tightening. I realized that I felt safe with his hands on mine.

Scrubbing my face with my shoulder, I scuffed my hair back and looked around.

"The gang's all here," Occam said. I nodded to the others. They looked exhausted and frightened. For me. Something lightened inside me, and I felt almost weightless for a moment as I looked from one to another. "It's night," he added. "Ten hours since you first touched the ground. You've been sick as a dog. Now you're exhausted and dehydrated. The doctors want you to stay overnight for observation. You're all the rage with the interns. There've been about twenty in and out all afternoon."

Telling me, in a kind manner, that more and more of my secret was out. That I had magic and it was strange and unknown, as I was myself.

"Not staying here," I said. "No way." University of Tennessee Medical Center was a teaching hospital, and they had one of the few paranormal units and staff in the state. The state's other two paranormal hospitals were in Nashville and clear across the state in Memphis. And their idea of observation might be a lot more invasive and personal than I was willing to undergo so soon after the Spook School examinations.

"Figured as much," Occam said. "Your mama's been callin' you. Rick handled it."

"Oh no. I gotta go. We'uns got family dinner tonight."

"Not tonight," he said. "You took a rain check with your family. Rick told 'em that you came down with a raging case of the flu and that the girls'll take care of you for a few days."

"Oh. Oh, that was a good lie. Okay. Thank you." Feeling steadier, I let go of Occam's hands, pinched the damp hospital gown between two fingers, and let it fall. "Ugh." He was right. Mama would have a conniption if I showed up looking like this and then passed out face-first in my dinner.

"Tonight you'll bunk in with JoJo. We'll all eat and visit and you'll tell us what happened during the hours you were tied to the earth. And we'll inform you what we got. Boss' orders."

I nodded, a knot in my throat. I think I'd have been crying again if I weren't so dehydrated.

"Soon as you sign out, we're going to JoJo's apartment. We'll feed you and update you. Debrief and pizza."

I made a noise of agreement. "Lemme call my mama, though. She's gonna be mighty upset."

But Mama seemed okay, and had nothing but praise for my wonderful boss and all my friends for taking care of me with my sudden influenza. Rick had lied. To my mama. And I had approved. I was sure and certain going to hell, because I followed along and told her that I had to be careful being around the little'uns and the elders, to keep them from getting sick. The flu was a bad one this year. Mama was so fine with my lie that it was almost scary and was certainly shameful of me. But the family dinner was one problem I didn't have to deal with at the moment, and was, in the end, a lot easier to lie about than to try to explain the truth. That must be why lying is such a common sin. It's successful and makes life easier.

Talking to Mama turned out to be much easier than getting my sweat-sticky legs into my pants. After two tries that left me weak as well water, T. Laine brought in my four-day gobag, which she had picked up from HQ, after she'd found my extra key in the fake tree. "Stupid hiding place. Obvious," she said.

I couldn't disagree, but said, "In my own defense, I'm glad you were able to find the extra key." She chuckled as she helped me into an old, elastic-waist skirt and a new sweatshirt, which had both been spooled into a tight roll, the way we were taught at Spook School.

We arrived first and JoJo kicked off her shoes at the door and turned on soft lighting that made the gray, charcoal, and concrete color scheme feel warmer than it might otherwise. I don't know what I had expected JoJo's place to look like, maybe a Bohemian-style cottage, to match her wildly patterned clothing and eccentric personal style. The two-bedroom duplex, with sparse furniture and a sleek modern look, made me rethink everything I thought I knew about her. She had a leather couch, two upholstered chairs, an industrial metal TV stand, and bookshelves in the front room, shelves that also supported a real turntable and speakers placed for quadraphonic sound, something I had read about but never experienced. As if reading my mind, she put on some soft jazz, an instrumental that made my feet want to move. Not that I knew how to dance. Her music collection was enormous and mostly vinyl.

A table made of reclaimed wood with a metal base and six antique Shaker-style chairs sat in the dining space. There were no rugs, just spotless wood floors and a clean scent in the house that reminded me of sage.

I stood in the middle of the living area, my arms weighted down with my gear, feeling totally out of my element. I was shaking with exhaustion when JoJo took my bags from my arms and dumped all but my four-day gobag on the coffee table. She pointed me upstairs. "Come on. Let's get you showered. It'll make you feel better." She shouldered my gobag.

"Are you sure? I feel kinda funny—"

"You offer me hospitality every time I come to your house." She tossed me an exasperated look as, one-handed, she unwound her turban and let her multitude of braids down. "I'm offering you hospitality now. Kick off your boots and come on. I'll get you situated and see that you have any toiletries you need."

She preceded me up the stairs, her bare feet silent. This was surreal. I hadn't showered in a stranger's house in . . . ever. If I hadn't been covered with dried sweat and dried blood and reeking of exhaustion, I might have declined, despite the offer of hospitality. But I stank and I was still so dehydrated that my skin felt as if I had rolled in ground glass.

My boots were still unlaced, so I toed them off as per her orders and followed her up.

Upstairs, the guest room had been turned into an office with a black metal desk and ergonomic chair, and a sofa against the wall that looked like it might pull out into a bed. Across the hall was JoJo's room, centered by a queen-sized four-poster bed with a shiny metal finish. It had a silky comforter on it and lots of pillows. There was a bureau with the shiny metal finish, three candles, and a wooden box with an old-fashioned lock. Minimalist.

I followed her into the bath, which was just as sleek and modern as the rest of the house. "Your house is beautiful," I said, meaning it.

"Home sweet home," she said, with a tone I couldn't place.

"You keep a full travel pack in your gobag?" I nodded. "If you left anything, use what you need. Shampoo and conditioner." She pointed out each item as she spoke. "Bar soap, or there's a pump liquid in the shower. Washcloth and towels. And lotion. Don't forget to put on lotion, girl. Your skin looks a mite pruney, as my gramma might say."

"Thank you," I whispered.

"Anytime. T. Laine is bringing your shoes and dirty clothes and blanket in her car. Shower's hot. Get clean. You'll feel better." JoJo left the room and shut the door.

I had never been in a shower so luxurious. It was like standing in a heated waterfall, one that melted the sweat and blood off my body into a pinkish pool before the drain sucked it down. I had brought my own soaps and toiletries, but once the blood was liquefied and drenched away, I made use of JoJo's gray washcloth, which matched the decorative band of tiles along the bathroom wall.

Her towels were fluffy, so soft they made me want to cry again, when I dried off. And JoJo was right. A shower made a big difference in how I felt.

I smeared moisturizer all over and applied some antibiotic cream from the med pack of my gobag to the stitches. I counted twenty-two on a cut that ran from below my elbow to my middle lower arm, with eight stiches on the outside of my hand, and two more each on two fingers where it looked as if I had been stabbed. They all hurt and showed signs of swelling, so I took two painkillers and smeared on some of my homemade salve. I applied lipstick, adding some to my cheeks and smearing it in, since I looked so pale. I didn't want to hunt for a hair dryer among my friend's things, so I towel-dried my hair and gooped it up more than usual. It would dry fast, now that it was so short. I dressed in clean undies and pulled the pink skirt back on. I managed to pull a fuzzy rose T-shirt over my injured arm, and a soft pink hooded jacket. Not the usual work clothes, but I was glad I had packed the skirt. I looked professional again and not like a body they had pulled out from an underpass, three days dead. When I opened the door, I smelled pizza and heard voices, and the hunger that had been a midlevel complaint now roared and my mouth watered. Pea dashed out to welcome me and then loped back to the living area.

* * *

Pizza and Coke restored my energy levels, and when we were all done eating, Rick said, "Debrief. T. Laine, why don't you start?"

I curled my legs under me on the couch and wrapped my bare toes in my skirt to keep them warm. Sipped Coke as I listened.

"We got to the pond site at zero-seven, forty-two. While Nell did prelim readings, I conferred with the local KEMA techs and local law enforcement, who explained the circumstances of the initial report. As of the last three weeks, there have been two episodes of radioactive wildlife, all reported to the sheriff's office via burner phone. So when the call came in about the hot geese at the pond, the local KEMA techs brought the Haz Mat Geiger counter, which read normal background levels. Fortunately the tech was new on the job, still with a fire in her belly, and decided to try out Haz Mat's old psy-meter. Which redlined. The officer in charge followed protocol, worked his way through the system, and called us. At the site, Nell initiated the human and tech eval while I took reports from the OIC and KEMA techs. Nell, you're up."

I nodded and wiped my fingers on a napkin. "I completed full human/tech eval on the pond, which entailed photos and psy-meter readings at one hundred feet out, seventy-five feet out, fifty feet out, and then twenty-five feet. At one hundred feet, the readings were midline on level three and a near twenty-five percent on the other four psysitopes, which suggested an active working, and I had to consider the possibility that I might set it off like a bomb. At twenty-five feet out, all the levels were redlining, so I stopped there, went no closer to the water at that time, and began a circuit of the pond. I sent the readings to HQ. You should all have them."

"JoJo," Rick said. She pointed her remote at the TV, punched some buttons, and the TV screen came up. "Readings are up."

JoJo had synced her laptop to her TV and pulled my readings up on the wide screen, which was just so cool I couldn't help the "Ohhh. Nice!" Then I took up my narrative. "The first readings you see are from my walk directly toward the pond, with the readings every twenty-five feet. These are the pics that correlate." I pointed. "The next batch of readings starts when I began to walk the circumference of the pond." I pointed. "That GPS is where I found a dead goose showing signs of scavenger activity, which crossed right up to the waterline. That would have disrupted working circles?" I made the line a question to T. Laine.

She said, "Most. Yes. But the presence of scavengers said it was safe for you to cross. But when I did a visual scan working, there was no witch circle, which is why I let you collect goose gobbets."

"Thank you," I said, and everyone laughed. I realized that they thought I was being sarcastic or funny.

I made a mental note to study which witch circles can be crossed and which ones can't. "Here, at this GPS, is where I found the second goose, dead and floating on the surface of the water. I got back to the starting point and saved my info, sending it to you guys. I see a little blip here that I don't remember." I pointed again. "There wasn't anything at this GPS, and I don't know what it meant.

"I collected the dead geese as per orders, but I don't know where they are now." I looked at T. Laine.

"They're in my car. They stink. They're rotting. Thank all that's holy it isn't summer. I'll get them packed and sent to PsyCSI in the morning." PsyCSI was in Richmond, Virginia. T. Laine waggled her fingers at me, and I continued.

"I took a blanket here"—I pointed on a sat map that JoJo pulled up on the TV screen—"for the paranormal eval."

I tried to explain what had happened, and got exasperated when Rick made me repeat, five times, the part about the woman. I finally said, "You can ask me ten more times and I'll say the same thing. Female. Not human. That is *all. I. Know.*"

Rick sat back in his chair, one hand rubbing his chin and the heavy five-o'clock shadow that darkened it, thinking. "Okay," he said finally. "Probie, what do you think the things you felt beneath the ground have to do with psysitopes and magic as we now understand it?"

I pursed my mouth, thinking about magical energy and the light-and-shadow things in the earth. There was something there, just beyond my understanding. Something about the massive thing deep in the ground, sleeping, about the dancer and the woman. And the way energy worked. The way it looked when I was communing with the earth. Something about electrostatic energies, and magical bindings, and maybe even magnetism.

Physics that I had been introduced to in Spook School, but had never really understood.

"I don't know. But physicists in the nineteen sixties speculated that paranormal energy, even magical energy particles, must follow the laws of physics. Psysitopes aren't understood, but they've been qualified and quantified into four subparticles that are capable of working together, and every type of paranormal creature has its own range. Therefore, the things under the ground have to have their own values." Understanding popped into my brain like lightning flashing. "And this is why you wanted me to read land around Knoxville."

"Not bad. Not bad at all."

I blushed at the compliment. Praise was a rarity in my life.

"Summation?"

It was short and probably confusing. "To start out, there were three different . . . let's call them purposes. So, yes, three different purposes belowground at the pond. One that's active and full of movement, and one that's deeper and asleep. Let's call them the dancer and the sleeper for now. And then there was the woman—species unknown, location unknown, purpose unknown, involvement in the pond and deer situation unknown."

But he still wasn't satisfied. Wearing one of those unreadable looks, Rick said, "Fine. The dancer and the sleeper. What are they?"

"I don't know. But I've felt something like one of the sleepers before, in North Carolina, when we rescued the imprisoned vampire in the basement of the Tennessee DIC. It was under his house. Out in his yard. All through the mountains around his place."

Rick stared at me, waiting.

The DIC was the director in charge of the Knoxville FBI office. He had been a Welsh *gwyllgi*, like Brother Ephraim, a shape-shifting devil dog in more ways than just speciation. He had also been a rapist and a cannibal. I had fed him and his buddies to the earth, and good riddance. And despite my God's Cloud upbringing, I didn't feel the least bit of guilt for the deaths. "I don't know," I said again.

"Does your land have one?"

"No. My land has its own soul. It's awake and alert and tied to the moon and the seasons. These things are bigger and deeper and sleeping. Or hibernating. This one today had some thin,

microscopic threads of energies leading to the surface, but I
don't know what they lead to or where, except that they have
something to do with places where large numbers of people died
in the past. The dancer is using some of the threads to go up and
down to the sleeper."

"Is the woman making that happen, or is she a prisoner
being forced to participate?" Rick asked.

"I don't know. It . . . They? Yeah, they, if you count the one
in North Carolina. I got the sense that the sleepers live on the
life and death and blood of war. That this one had been most
active when thousands of humans died at a time, like in the
tribal wars, the tribal-European wars, and the Revolutionary and
Civil wars."

Rick shook his head. "Okay. I'm guessing there's no way to
verify their existence?"

"No idea. One more thing, though. I got a sense that the
active consciousness, the dancer, was trying to wake the sleeper.
Poking on it, metaphysically speaking. It felt like some form of
communication, repeated over and over. I think the dancer recognized me as an intelligence. When it latched onto me, it was
gentle at first, like a silk bracelet. And it learned something
from me. It started a litany of words, in threes. Something like
'Flows, flows, flows. Pools, pools, pools. Gone, gone, gone,'
over and over. And then the woman said the words, but who was
repeating them I don't know."

Rick had sat forward, his eyes focused on the distance, thinking. "Say again."

I repeated the litany of concepts I had taken from the dancer.

"At what point in the reading did the grass try to grow inside
you?" Rick asked. Pea leaped from the floor up into my lap, and
I petted her. Which hurt.

I held up my hand and looked at the unbandaged stitches. "Is
that what happened?" Trying to appear more nonchalant than
the full-blown panic that grabbed at my rib cage and squeezed,
I took another slice of pizza, curled it up in half, and bit down.
I chewed and swallowed, breathing through my nose. Pizza suddenly tasted like dust and ashes and fear.

But roots hadn't attacked me on my own land last night. It
had only happened when I stayed in communication with the
land too long, when I bled onto the land, and when I needed the
land to heal me. So I might be changing, but the earth's reaction

to me was—possibly—predictable. A sense of relief washed through me like a stream down a mountain, and I eased out a breath I hadn't known I was holding.

"I am guessing that started happening when the energies grabbed my wrist and tugged me down. When did you notice that I was getting all grassy?" I asked T. Laine.

"About four hours into not being able to wake you up." She referred to her notes. "At nine forty-two, I came over and tried to talk to you. You were propped on an elbow with one hand in your lap and the other on the ground. When you didn't respond, I decided to give you an hour. At ten twenty, Tandy arrived to pick up the P 2.0. We exchanged info, made some calls, and he left. Then two more sheriff's deputies showed for a face-to-face, to inform me that they had closed the road to the pond because the press had showed up, and that we might expect a low-flying drone from one of the local channels who had a permit."

Oh great. *I was on TV?*

"At noon on the nose, I tried to pull you free for lunch. You didn't wake up when I called your name, and so I . . ." She glanced at Rick. "I patted your face. Not forcefully enough to be called a slap."

I let a small smile onto my lips, remembering the PsyLED *Manual of Administrative Operations*, some twenty pages that covered the rules for touching, though they didn't call it that, given to me by the equivalent of PsyLED HR. Slapping, as well as other forms of forceful or intimidating physical contact, was grounds for disciplinary action.

"You squinted your eyes and frowned at me, so I thought you were okay. Your hand, the one on the ground, was a little gray looking. And you hadn't moved. But you were breathing at four-teen breaths a minute, which is normalish. I called Rick to report in and he said to leave you as is, but that he'd send Occam as soon as he finished with the deer. I couldn't leave you, so I sent one of the deputies to grab me some takeout from Number One Best Chinese, down the road.

"At two p.m. I saw the first roots. I called Occam directly and he showed up in twelve minutes, with a police escort running lights and sirens. Occam." Her tone was strained, which made no sense, but I figured it would soon enough.

Occam wiped his hands on a napkin and sat back in the upholstered chair, lacing his fingers together across his stomach.

He was long and lean, with runner's musculature and the graceful movements of his cat. He spoke to Rick. "It'll be in my
report. Nell had roots, like crabgrass roots, growing into her
hand." With one finger he indicated the hand with the most
stitches. "You were rooted to the ground. I couldn't lift your
hand from the dirt. You wouldn't wake up, Nell."

"So?"

"I patted your cheeks too."

I remembered the sensation of pain. He had slapped me. I
could understand that. I'd have slapped someone too.

T. Laine said, "At which point you fell over and landed with
your forearm on the ground, your palm still flat."

Occam said, "Roots busted up through the ground and
latched onto your arm. I cut you free. I mighta nicked your flesh
a little. You bled. And that seemed to bring more roots."

"They went after you," T. Laine said. "Occam cut you free,
but he made a mess of your skin. You lost a good bit of blood."

"Not enough to compromise your blood levels," Occam said,
"but enough for the paramedics to write up a report."

"Against you?" I asked. He nodded and I said, "I specifically
requested that I be cut free of any prolonged communing with
any land. It's in my exit interview with Spook School."

Occam heaved a relieved breath and let it out. He might have
gotten in trouble for saving me from the deeps. I had to say
something more. "This needs to be entered into my personnel
file. Any time I am connected to the land via plant life, I can be
cut out at the OIC's discretion. Or Occam's discretion."

"So noted," Rick said, a faint smile on his face.

"Thank you, Nell," Occam said. His blondish hair had come
loose from the tail and strands swung forward in the indirect
light, creating shadows and strong planes.

"Okay. Reports from the deer scene," Rick said.

Occam sat forward and punched something on his tablet. A
map appeared on the big screen. "At this GPS, just off twenty-five
west, near Claxton, about here"—he pointed—"was where the
truck driver came around the curve and hit the first deer. The
impact sent him off the road to the left and into the second and
third deer and then into a group of four. By then he had slowed
enough that he injured but did not kill the four deer. He called nine-
one-one. But because the uninjured deer were acting abnormal—
walking around, staring, not running away—the first officer on the

scene called us. Seems word about the geese had made it through unofficial channels to the officers on the streets. By the time I got there, the four injured deer had been euthanized.

"At nine forty-seven, I sent Tandy to get the P 2.0 from Nell. According to records, he arrived on-site with the P 2.0 at ten fifty-five. By eleven fifteen, we had ascertained that we had a paranormal event, with redlining on all four psysitope levels. We needed to get the road clear for traffic, so I took readings in a circular route and found that the earth around the deer wasn't contaminated, only the deer and their trail through the brush. Tandy and I turned the site over to Rick and dressed out in field gear. We hiked through the area, following the readings. We ended up here"—he pointed to the screen—"on twenty-five west. At that point, we were called in to help Nell. We sent up GPS coordinates so we'd know where to start again, and headed out."

"Which is about . . ." Rick drew out the last word, his fingers working across his own personal tablet, "four miles from the site where Nell was." He shook his head, looking tired again. "Too big an area for a witch working. That would make any witch circle so extensive they would have needed hundreds of witches, and we would have noted that, especially here in Knoxville. Or a gathering of the most powerful witch families in the US, which PsyLED would have heard about. So that leaves . . ." His voice trailed off, and he frowned.

"Could it be the magical form of an RED?" I asked into the silence of his hesitation.

"Possibly," Rick said. "We have to at least consider it."

An RED was a radiological exposure device, sometimes called a hidden sealed source. It was a weapon of mass destruction used for terrorism, a device constructed of, or containing, radioactive material. Its purpose was to expose people to radiation without their knowledge. The magical version was called an MED, a magical exposure device. MEDs were postulated weapons. They would be an active or passive working capable of spreading directed and shaped magical energies over a wide area, affecting anyone in the vicinity with a black-magic, curse-based spell-weapon. The working would then spread, just like a plague. Contamination of the populace by terrorists for political aims. But as T. Laine had said, magic didn't work that way, which was why an MED was only a postulated weapon. However, there was a macabre desire among PsyLED agents to be the first to discover one.

I said, "I thought the dancer and the deep presence were responsible for the psysitope readings, whether it was something they were doing or something emanating from them. No one thinks that's the case?"

Rick said, "We don't have enough evidence to rule out anything. We have to consider an MED and the possibility of a weaponized working."

Tandy said, "Back at the accident site, I collected evidence. Rick called PsyCSI and told them they had a transport truck full of contaminated deer on the way."

"I'll bet they were delirious with joy," T. Laine said.

"Not so much," Rick said with an amused tightening of his lips. "They'll be even happier with your decomposing geese. In the morning, Occam and Tandy, follow the psysitope trail of the deer. When you find the origination point, do not enter. Call T. Laine and . . ." He looked at me. "Can you read again?"

"Yes. But let's keep it short, okay?"

"T. Laine and Nell will meet you at whatever location. I also want detailed psysitope readings and evidence collecting if possible. So far no humans are contaminated. We want to contain this situation and apprehend the suspects, assuming that there are some. Meeting adjourned. Oh. Nell."

I looked back at Rick.

"Keep your hands out of the grass and away from the trees."

"Yes, boss," I said.

"Go home, people. Get some sleep. Nell, you staying here?"

"Yes, she is," JoJo said.

"I guess I am. Thanks," I added to JoJo.

FOUR

Things were more normal to me the next morning at HQ, maybe because it was my second day, maybe because my life had been turned upside down so many times in the last few months that *odd* meant *ordinary*. Or maybe because I went in the door and smelled Mickey D's breakfast. Bacon, egg, and cheese biscuits, hotcakes with syrup, those little ovals of potato fries. My hostess had fixed smoothies made of spinach, apples, avocado, and mango. I liked all the foods blended together in the glass, and it was green, my favorite food group, but I was used to protein and carbs for breakfast, a high-calorie meal for a farm woman. I had chowed down on the smoothie, but it wasn't enough, so the high fat and carb content of the smells made my stomach growl with hunger. And coffee. By all that was holy, *coffee*. I poured a cup and grabbed a Mickey D's biscuit on the way to my desk.

Occam and Tandy were already in the field, back at the site where the deer had died, tracking with the smaller, handheld psy-meters. Pecking with two fingers, I completed my reports from yesterday and the equipment paperwork for my P 1.0. I also started the request for a government vehicle. Then I worked on the files of paperwork that had come in via e-mail overnight. Working for the government meant enough paperwork to fill a warehouse every week. Or maybe fill up the iCloud.

When I had the required papers filled out and my reports turned in, and had scanned all the reports that I had missed while I was out cold yesterday, I pulled up the case sat map, or CSM, an interactive satellite map set aside for cases such as this. I was pretty sure the unit had had one on the last case, when I was a consultant, but I'd had no security clearance to speak of then, and I had never seen it. This CSM had the locations of the pond and the deer site and the site where Occam and

Tandy had abandoned the search for the origination site of the deer's paranormal readings.

The deer had meandered through the woods, a long way from where they ended up, which was strange, as herds of deer meant does, and they usually kept to familiar locations, places where water was, and where they had already found grazing areas and grassy spots to bed down at night. Except in rut season. Which it was, but . . . herds didn't run. Only does in heat, chased by bucks to win mating rights, ran.

I marked the site of the deer killings on twenty-five west, then the site where the guys had abandoned the search, four miles away on foot, but only about two as the crow flew. And from there, only a few miles to the pond. Had the deer drunk from the pond?

No one wanted this case to be an MED. MEDs were nightmares for law enforcement, something dreamed up by fiction writers at a think tank in Washington, DC, one created after 9/11 when it was discovered that thriller writers had already come up with scenarios like the bombing of the twin towers. Since then, there had been several possible MEDs but it had been impossible to prove beyond the shadow of a doubt that the magical events were remotely detonated or equipped with magical timed detonation spells. None of the possible MEDs I had studied resulted in slow, encroaching contamination of wildlife or water sources.

I pulled up photos of the deer and noted that they were mostly does and juveniles. No bucks in sight. So why had they run? I texted Tandy, *Look for reason why deer ran four miles. Chased? Dogs? Coywolves?*

I got back a *K*.

Rick had said that a four-mile area was too big for a witch-working, and would have required hundreds of witches. He had said, "We would have noted that. Especially here in Knoxville."

Why especially here in Knoxville? And then I knew. *Secret City.*

Secret City was a set of governmental and military research and development complexes, underground and aboveground, in and around Knoxville. They had a public face, in Oak Ridge National Laboratory, on property where the original atom bomb research was done, and the original uranium was made, for the weapons that had ended World War II. But today the government's

R&D and testing labs had spread out into Knox County, hidden in plain sight and powered by an energy grid that was equal to or better than any other in the country. Today the research was conducted by privately owned, government-subsidized companies that reportedly did energy research, propulsion research and development, radioisotope studies, and other complex studies.

The pond was only a few miles, as the geese flew, from the original lab at Oak Ridge National Laboratory, where . . . where some of the information about psysitopes and the research on them had come from. Rick had to know this already, which meant he was about ten steps ahead of me in thinking that this might be more than a natural event. It was also why he didn't want to consider this an MED until every other possibility had been explored and set aside. Because an MED here could be aimed at the government. Possibly a homegrown terrorist attack.

Then again, if one of the labs had a problem, and it accidentally caused the things we had seen, they might have fixed it already and not want it bandied about. And if the problem was already corrected, then it was unlikely that we'd ever discover who had done it or what had happened. It was also possible that a testing facility had an ongoing problem and it had gotten away from them, in which case they might be trying to keep it quiet so no congressional or military oversight committee started breathing down their necks. Also, if a lab was doing studies on paranormal energies, then it was top secret. And likely not something we would be allowed to continue investigating. Our case would be shut down. I thought about the woman's voice in the deeps. About the dancer prodding the sleeper. If we were shut down, would the woman complete a working that would curse the land? Would the dancer eventually wake the sleeper? Something about that possibility left me cold and shivery inside, as if winter had taken over my soul, freezing my spirit.

Rick was weighing politics against the public good, against possible danger to the populace. At his security level he knew a lot more about what was happening than I did.

I decided to take this directly to Rick, and not trust it to a report unless I had orders to. I got up from my desk cubicle and poured two mugs of fresh coffee, carrying them to Rick's glassed-in office. The doors were shut, but the blinds were open. I was guessing that meant that it was okay to disturb him.

I tapped on the window and went inside when he gave me a come-in gesture. I shut the door, placed his mug in front of him. He looked weary, drawn, the lines on his face deeper. There were gray hairs mixed in with the jet-black, gray that hadn't been there when I met him. Rick was aging fast, which was strange for a were-creature.

I gave him a rundown of my hypotheses. As I spoke, he shook his head, set the half-empty mug on the desk, and leaned back in his desk chair with his eyes closed. I feared I had put him to sleep, but his face relaxed into a ghost of a smile and he asked, "What kind of reasoning led you to all that?"

I had been a smart-aleck about reasoning methods to the director of the FBI not so long ago. I was still being teased about that. "I observed and drew conclusions. Deductive reasoning, which links premises with conclusions or potential conclusions. Or, in this case, brought up more questions and observations leading to multiple potential conclusions. You gonna tell me if I'm right?"

"No. I will neither confirm nor deny your hypothesis regarding policy and potential research and development oversight by any governmental, military, or high-echelon law enforcement talking heads."

Which was spook-speak for *Nail on the head.* There was a fear that we would step on toes of a quasigovernmental operation. That might get us shut down. But Rick didn't tell me to stop digging.

After a silence that went on too long for social propriety, I said, "Thank you." I got up, let myself out of his office, and went back to my desk, looking for government- or military-supported companies that might have research projects going on with energy particles. Or . . . I remembered the way the dancer had leaped and spun, like a puppy. Or a child. So . . . maybe I should look for a working that simulated artificial intelligence mixed with magic. At my security clearance level, I was looking at public domain records and things I could find on the web, on government sites and PsyLED's intranet, and in social media. I wanted to focus on no more than five private and publicly traded companies at this time, but to do that, I needed to get a list of all companies within range of the pond *and* the deer, and then narrow the field by investigation and the process of elimi-

nation. I had been taught the basics of research, and this was a
great time to hone my nascent skills.

I saved the CSM map to my personal file, labeled *CSM-Nell*,
and drew a red circle on the laptop screen, a circle with a diameter that covered five miles, centered around the pond. In the
radius of my circle, I came up with a dozen businesses and companies that might be possible suspects once I eliminated nail
salons and pet stores and anything commercial or industrial.

I went back and made a new circle, same dimensions but
with a green dotted line centered on the place where the deer
were hit by the truck. Then another dotted circle, this one yellow, on the current location of Occam and Tandy, who were still
tracking back along the deer's paranormal trail, in the brush off
Highway Twenty-five. Inside that circle, there were eight potential research companies. All were within ten miles of the Oak
Ridge National Laboratory. I narrowed them to companies that
did medical research, energy research, magical research, and
ones that were black—meaning that the company purpose was
a closely held secret and not available for public consumption.

There were eight such companies in close proximity to Oak
Ridge. Such a close grouping of potential research labs seemed
improbable, but I wasn't going to go by improbability. I was
going to go by facts.

By the time HQ heard back from Occam and Tandy, I had
narrowed the possible R&D companies with possible government contracts in energy or magical research to: Alocam, Inc.,
LuseCo Visions, C-Corp Development, and Kamines Future
Products, Moreare, Inc., and Zelco Corp. I had added in two
companies who were black companies, Rosco J. Moose, Inc.,
and San-Inc.

When Occam and Tandy sent in the GPS location of the site
where the deer had been struck with the working that contaminated them, I added it to *CSM-Nell* and realized that it was
nearly lunchtime. Before I took a food break, I needed to move.
It would take the guys half an hour or more to get back to
debrief us, and I was sore and miserable. I had spent all yesterday in one position with roots in me. Last night in a strange,
albeit comfortable pull-out bed. And today in a desk chair,
stitched fingers tapping on a keyboard. My body ached and my
fingers were sore and swollen. Only a few months past, I'd have

kept myself limber and strong by working in my terribly neglected garden. Now I changed into a pair of warm leggings and running shoes, pulled a thin shirt and a hoodie over me, hiding the ten-millimeter Glock 20 in a spine holster and my badge, and tapped on Rick's door, checking out for a run.

He nodded and flashed his ten fingers at me three times, telling me to get back in thirty minutes, and then he held his thumb and little finger to his head in the universal sign to take my cell phone. I held it up to show I had it, and left the building. I didn't particularly like running. It was bad on the knees. It was bad for feet, even with expensive running shoes to cushion the motion, the landings, and the effect of gravity. But it got me out of the office and it was a socially acceptable form of exercise for law enforcement officers. As I ran, I cataloged the landscaping around the Allamena Avenue building and decided what vegetation I would bring to spruce up the ugly plantings. Then I headed out into the developing area to see what was going up nearby.

At the fifteen-minute mark, I circled around and headed back to HQ via a different route. Moments later I heard a car behind me and then pass me. It could be an unmarked police car, if the stripped-down ugliness was an indicator. Or it could be something less benign. Spook School had made me more paranoid rather than less.

The car stopped. So did I, about twenty feet back. My hand slid behind my back to the service weapon under my hoodie. The passenger door opened. I began to jog backward, seeing three possible escape routes, all without taking my eyes off the vehicle or my hand off the weapon.

Occam got out of the car and my heart rate eased back toward normal. He jogged in place as the car eased away. "Nell, sugar, it's a beautiful day," he called in his Texas twang. "May I join you in your predinner perambulation?"

"Why, I'd be honored, Occam," I said, trying for the same formal tone. "I was just heading back, though."

"All the better. I need a shower and a good tick check," he said as we fell in together, feet slapping sidewalk. He slanted me a quick look, a playful glint in his eyes. "Not that I'm suggesting you do that for me."

"Good thing," I said in a mock-stern, prim tone. Banter was hard, cutting a thin line between flirting, which I didn't know how to do, and sarcasm, which I also didn't know how to do. Most girls grow up teasing with men. I had been affianced at age twelve to keep myself free from Colonel Jackson, the leader of God's Cloud of Glory Church, when the old pervert demanded that I marry him. I had moved in with my fiancé, John Ingram, and his first wife, Leah, who was dying. I never had the chance to meet young men or to flirt.

The Colonel was dead now. I was partly responsible. And I was happy about it. Hell's road was an easy one to tread.

Making my lack of social skills worse, in my background, men and women didn't joke about physical matters until they were married. And often not even then. But I had listened to the joking and teasing and semisexual repartee at Spook School as hormones kicked in and people paired off—not to indulge in sexual experimentation, as that was forbidden and a sure way to get kicked out of the program, but as a form of social interaction. I decided to try a joking response, and raised my nose in the air. "I'm sure that I'm not the tick-checking kinda gal."

Occam chuckled and widened his stride. "I'm pretty sure I can check myself for my ticks. But you can wash my back if you want."

I blushed and Occam's grin, and the small dimple in one cheek, deepened. I said, "I thank you for the offer, but I'll pass on the personal body servant interaction."

Occam sputtered into surprised laughter.

I had no idea what he found amusing. Oddly the sound of his laughter made me feel lighter, freer, like a feather in the wind. I smiled to myself, and Occam's laughter sputtered into deep breathing as he loosened up into the run.

This was . . . interesting. I had made a man laugh. I glanced his way, seeing a blond, golden-eyed man who ran with the grace of his werecat. I had a totally inappropriate thought. I wondered if I could catch the were-taint if Occam and I . . . I wasn't human, so . . . I shook off the deepening blush and pushed the thought away even as I pushed my legs into a sprint. Such thoughts were evil . . . well, maybe not evil, but they were certainly nonproductive and utterly inappropriate for a widder-woman like me.

Back at HQ, sweaty and bothered in ways that had nothing to do with cardio, I grabbed my gobag, disappeared into the locker room for a quick shower, and changed back into my work clothes. I kept remembering the sight of Occam's long legs, sheathed in denim, stretching into a run beside mine. Totally, totally, totally inappropriate.

The unit was gathered in the conference room, salads and soup and sandwiches at each place. I hadn't ordered and didn't know the protocol until Rick said, "I got you a half salad and a half sub from Yoshi's Deli. You owe me seven forty-nine. Receipt is under the bag. For now, eat. Occam, Tandy, update."

I sat and placed my laptop on the table, glad I had brought it, because it looked as if all meals were working meals at PsyLED, whether we were all together in one place or eating alone. Everyone had laptops and tablets and cells at the ready.

Occam dropped into the chair across from me and said, "Tandy, you start?"

Tandy shook his head, his wet reddish hair slapping. "Never go into the woods with a werecat." Drinking soup from a paper bowl, he sent a sideways look at Occam and wiped his mouth. "He kept climbing trees and sticking his nose into disgusting places. I kept waiting for him to spray to mark his territory."

"I was gettin' vantage points," Occam said, sounding fake-wounded. "I was helpful."

"He kept dropping piles of leaves on me. And once a bird's nest. I'm sure it was full of bird mites. I wanted to wash with Clorox, but HQ doesn't have any. You need to talk to the cleaning crew," he added to Rick.

"I'll get right on that," Rick said in the tone that meant, *I'll get right on that, never.*

"We don't have a cleaning crew," T. Laine said.

"Sure we do. Now," Occam said, all innocent sounding.

I narrowed my eyes at him. "I am not keeping up this building. I am not cleaning up behind a dirty, messy, rude, crude man again. Not ever." I lifted my nose into the air. "And I am certainly not sweeping up *cat hair.*"

T. Laine jerked forward and nearly spilled her drink.

Tandy snorted loud and started coughing.

I placed an innocent smile on my face, one worthy of a church-woman to a difficult churchman, and bit into my sandwich.

"Oh, Nell," Occam said, a feral glint in his eye, that even I knew had to be his cat lurking. "You may pay for that one."

"You can *try* to outwit a churchwoman, cat boy. You can *try*."

JoJo said, "Thank God he's got another one to pick on. I was getting tired of proving to him that any woman was a better practical joker than any man."

"Ohhhh. It's on, sugar," Occam said to me. "And as for you"—he pointed at JoJo—"the salt in your coffee was priceless."

"The dead mouse in your desk drawer was perfect, kitty cat. We all heard you go *Eeep*."

"Guys," Rick said. "Back to the report, if you please."

Watching the byplay, I realized that while I had been gone, the individual members of Unit Eighteen had become a team. They teased and played practical jokes on one another. They treated one another the way Occam had treated me on the run. The way my brother Sam and I had treated each other as we grew up.

Most important, they looked after one another. Someone, probably T. Laine, from the way she watched him, had been making sure that Tandy ate. The empath had been far too skinny when I saw him last, his face pale and strained. Now it looked as if he had gained ten pounds and his face was wreathed in a smile. It was a good feeling.

"I sent you all the GPS site where the deer were spelled," Tandy said.

"It was a small wood between two neighborhoods," Occam said. "Lot of scents, animals and people, but not adults or witches, more likely kids, smoking dope or drinking, not casting workings. It should be added to your case CSM."

I opened my laptop and checked the info, adding a circle around the GPS location, the same size as the others I had drawn. I toggled on the touch-screen application and, with my fingers, I adjusted the circles of overlapping territory. The new site fell within the circles of six of the companies I had already earmarked.

"How close is the nearest road?" Rick asked.

"About a quarter-mile hike if you go direct, but it's brambles and mud," Occam said. "Why do you ask?"

"Nell," Rick asked, "are you up to taking a quick reading today, or do you want to wait another day?"

I pretended that my heart didn't race and my breathing didn't wrench painfully in my ribs, and covered by opening my salad and taking a sip of my drink. "How quick of a reading?"

"Just to see if it feels like the same energies you registered at the other site."

It was the last thing I wanted to do, but I didn't fool myself. My ability to read the land was the main reason PsyLED had wanted me, and Rick had said this case *fell right into my skill set.* "I can do that," I said, keeping my tone level so that Tandy wouldn't be affected by my fear spiking.

"I will go with you," Paka said, her catty voice a low vibration. "In my cat form. As protection for you." Paka had been born a black wereleopard, and I had seen her take down a full-grown man on two different occasions. She was feral and utterly without mercy or guilt. I had no doubt that she would make excellent physical protection.

"Who goes with me to cut me loose if the earth has other ideas than letting me go? That's gonna require opposable thumbs and a sharp blade."

"Me," Occam said, his tone forbidding. It was clear he didn't agree with me doing a reading so soon. Well, neither did I.

I didn't look at him. I took a bite of salad and said, "The reading will have to be no longer than half an hour. Not deep enough to touch the sleeper consciousness. Call it a surface scan." Then I added, "I'd hate to end up disabled my first week on the job."

The table fell silent as the unit took that in, several pairs of eyes on my stitched and swollen hand. Which made me angry on some level. So far this had been a fun case to them. For me, not so much. I wanted them to remember that.

"She shouldn't do a reading," T. Laine said. "Not so soon."

"I agree," Tandy said.

"She must," Paka said, her arm moving beneath the table, probably placing her hand on Rick's knee.

I didn't much like Paka, but she was right in this situation. "Rick needs to rule out if this is an accident or a deliberate working," Thinking about our chat, I said, "That's why he wants me to take another reading. Right?"

Rick frowned as if Paka's touch was unwelcome, but he didn't know how to dislodge it. A heartbeat or three too long later, he gave me a scant nod. It was my understanding that Paka had more magic than most werecats. She had been brought to the US by PAW (the Party of African Weres) and IAW (the

International Association of Weres) to help Rick, the United States' first black wereleopard, one changed against his will and left unable to shift because of magic tattooed into his skin. Also against his will. According to the scuttlebutt, Rick had been used and abused most of his life, but he was still standing. That said something about a man, even if he had broken Jane Yellowrock's heart. He and Paka had—not fallen in love. That was too pale a thing for the magnetism between the two. More like they had been mated at first sight, Rick following her like steel to a magical magnet. Their relationship made a lot more sense now that I had heard the Spook School gossip than it had before.

"I'm going too," T. Laine said. "I know what she looks like when she's too deep now. And I worked on a few things during the night that might get her back if something pulls her down against her will." At my questioning look, she said, "Magical things. There's a *wyrd* working called *Break* that severs energies in assault spells. I've been practicing."

"Good," Rick said. "Keep her safe."

I nodded, uncertain about the efficacy of magic against plants sending roots into me, but any kind of backup was good.

JoJo, who had been keying in all the chitchat and decisions into the SODR—the start-of-day report—broke the somber mood with the words, "Attack of the plant people. Got it."

Tandy glanced in her direction, an indication that he caught some emotional shift in her.

JoJo added, "Possibility of pranking philodendrons and sasanqua shenanigans." No one laughed at her lame joke, and she looked around the table. "Tough room. Pass the red pepper flakes; this salad is bland and too sweet."

We pulled over and parked on the side of a neighborhood road, large lots around us. Most of the small houses were unkempt, weeds tall and fall's leaves unraked. There was the rare car up on blocks or buried in brush. A moldy and sun-faded RV listed at an angle. A pit bull on a chain, lying in the sun, watched us with a malevolent eye. Fewer of the houses were meticulously neat, with fall flowers in plantings and pots, the grass groomed. One had iron bars installed over the windows and a rebel flag flying.

I looked away from the passenger window and down at myself. I was wearing my field boots and a pair of jeans with a flannel shirt over a thin sweater. I was now officially out of clean clothes. I either needed a bigger gobag or I had to plan to leave clothes in the locker in the shower room. And I had to wash clothes tonight. And repack. I picked a cat-hair fuzz off my shirt and dropped it on the floor.

"You getting yourself ready or woolgathering, Nell, sugar?"

I let a breath escape and said, "Neither. I'm procrastinating."

"You don't have to do this," T. Laine said from the backseat.

"What the witchy woman said," Occam agreed.

Paka, in her cat form, hissed in displeasure and leaned her big head over the seat to me. She hissed again, showing her teeth.

"I know," I said to her. "I have to do it," I said to the others.

"Because of those thoughts about accident versus deliberate workings you sent to Ricky Bo?" Occam asked. I nodded and he said, "You gonna tell us what you told him?" The werecat slid his back against the door and swiveled in his seat so that his legs spread and one knee came over the console, close to me.

I pressed my lips together. There was nothing in the handbook that said I couldn't tell them. Both of them had higher security clearances than I did. "We all know there's a possibility of an MED here, simply because strange energies are running beneath the ground. Almost as bad as a planned and executed MED would be magical energies *not* in a working like they're supposed to be, but free because of a magical accident or released by means or creatures we don't know about and can't combat."

"An MED," T. Laine said. "I admit that the possibility intrigues me. Always has. Spook School still taking wagers on the first unit to uncover a verifiable MED?" I nodded. "Yeah. Intriguing. Set a working on a timer, maybe tied to the moon's phase or something, and walk away. Later the spell is triggered and spreads the purpose and intent and will of the caster all over. Like a bomb with a delay timer, so no one has to actually set it off. I've been playing with workings to break a curse that sophisticated, but my coven isn't particularly powerful, so, no go so far."

"Procrastinating," I said, opening the car door and stepping out onto the verge of the road. The denim pants felt all wrong, too tight in some places and too loose in others. Other than the long-lasting nature of the cloth they were made from, I didn't understand why the entire world was so enamored of them. I dragged on my pant legs, trying to stretch them into a more comfortable shape, and grabbed up the pinkish blanket and a pad and pen.

T. Laine carried the P 2.0 and a laptop for taking notes and entering data. Occam had two blades, a machete to cut a path through the brambles and a vamp-killer. I didn't think we were likely to meet a vampire in broad daylight, but maybe the silver plating on the blade would be useful for cutting me free from the Attack of the Plant People, which was a real movie, to hear Occam and T. Laine talk. He led the way between two lots, a chain-link fence on one side and the chained pit bull on the other. The pit bull was a mean one, leaping at us, his growls and barks so loud they were a vibration through the air, abrading along my skin.

I kept back from Occam as he cut his way through the overgrown field behind the two houses, the blade rising and hacking down. I was probably better with a machete than he was, being that I used one every year to take down overgrown plantings, but Occam seemed the kind of man who needed to protect the women around him. There were plenty of women who would take him down a peg or two, and fast, on the sparring mat at Spook School, but I didn't have the physical strength to defeat a wereleopard, unless I was sneaky and kicked him in the privates first. I had to admit that he looked good swinging the blade, his jeans shifting with the muscles underneath, his back muscles pulling on his shirt.

And my appreciation was, again, totally, totally, totally unsuitable for a widder-woman.

Had the brush remained so thick, the quarter mile of cutting our way through would have taken Occam over an hour, but the trees took over, at first saplings, and then, quickly, trees that were ten to twenty years old and would provide a tall canopy in summer. There had been a controlled fire back this way at some point, the trunks blackened and the brush thinned out. Rocks appeared and the ground became far more uneven, no longer the level ground of a once-planted field left to go fallow, but the uneven surface of the rocky earth, too stone-filled to plow. We crossed over a rill of water, and Paka stopped to lap at it. I ran my hand through a short drop, where the water ran over stones and fell several inches. "Springwater," I said at the touch of cold. I dried my fingers. Paka chuffed at me, sniffed, and chuffed again, telling me she smelled something on the water. She leaped into the tree nearest and from there to another tree, following her nose.

Occam followed her with his eyes and motioned us forward, on the cat's trail.

"Slight level-one psysitope reading above ambient normal," T. Laine said as we tromped on. A moment later she said, "Level two is coming up. And now three."

We made it to the site where the P 2.0's readings said the paranormal psysitopes had originated, where the deer were contaminated. The P 2.0 was redlining on all four levels. Unlike at the pond, there was nothing here but an open space between trees where wild grasses were rucked up and swirled around, the way deer move grasses as they prepare for the night. There was no pond, no ramshackle building in the distance, no lean-to, no signs of a burned-out farmhouse. No shed. No dead animals. There were no signs of human habitation, and even traffic sounds were scarcely in the audible range.

T. Laine pulled her pocket-sized psy-meter and took a reading to compare by, saying simply, "Still redlining. We shouldn't stay here long."

Occam took my blanket and folded it flat on the ground, which was still damp from the night's dew. I watched him, thinking about T. Laine's comment and everything that had gone wrong. "Did I ask you to look for reasons why a herd of female deer and juveniles might have traveled four miles? Dogs? Coyotes? Coywolves?"

"You did," he said. "I checked with nose and eyes both. No signs of predators, except a few unoccupied tree stands and a pond that away"—he pointed—"with a duck blind."

Human predators. I looked up into the trees and spotted Paka, stretched out on a limb, her golden green eyes on me. Sitting on the folded blanket, I pulled off my boots and socks and set them to the side. I placed my uninjured hand, palm down, on a bare patch of ground, my bare feet flat on the grass, knees bent up under my chin. I closed my eyes. Let my worries go instead of holding on to them. It was so stupid to cradle worries the way I did. I let my fears go. Let myself go. I relaxed and slumped forward over my knees, breathing. And I reached down into the ground.

FIVE

I sank into the dark and instantly heard words, not like a woman's voice, but ringing like bells, vibrations high and deep, humming through my bones. "Flows, flows, flows. Pools, pools, pools." But this time instead of saying "Gone, gone, gone," there were two new lines.

"Dead. All dead. All dead. Forever.

"Dead. All dead. All dead. Forever."

The words no longer had the same cadence as the first two lines. The movement and shape of the shadow-and-light was different too. It had coalesced. Drawn together. It was close to the surface, dancing among roots. The motion I sensed matched the cadence of the words, the power and gloom pirouetting. The light-and-shadow dancer swirled in a figure eight, a form employed by experienced magic users, ones advanced and powerful enough to control the energies and alter their shapes. The shape signified the rhythms of energy, space, and time, something beyond three dimensions.

And then it—they?—saw me.

The silk that had caressed my wrist yesterday slapped around my foot, sliding up my ankle. In an instant it tightened, roughened, pulling me deep.

Once again the dancer had taken my consciousness. Darkness and pressure surrounded me. I lost contact with the ground. With my own body. I was . . . buried alive. I struggled, trying to move, trying to fight. But it was like being wrapped in heavy carpet, around and around. Pulled down and down and around and around.

Wake her. Free me, the dancer hummed at me.

A deeper, human thought slashed at me, *Get out! Get out! You can't have it!*

It was the woman. She— Pain exploded inside me. Pinpoints

of agony. On the surface, my heart stuttered as if a huge hand had squeezed it. The pressure of the deeps. No breath. I struggled. Fought. Desperate. Warmth fled. The part of me that was on the surface, my body, was dying for want of air and heartbeat. Ice froze the blood in my veins. Crystalline, cutting. I was dying. The woman's thoughts said to me, *What are you? What do you want?*

Lost. Dead. Gone, the dancer thought at me. *Flows, flows, flows. Pools, pools, pools. Dead. All de—*

Shut up! the woman screamed. *Shut—*

Something slammed around me, a shattering breaking force, shards of lightning and blue power, cutting through the binding. The dancer screamed. The silk slithered free, shrinking, shrieking. The woman cursed.

I ripped myself out of the deeps. Grabbed hold of the blue brightness. Held on.

I was moving. Then stopped. Enfolded against something heated.

I groaned, the sound like sandpaper over rubber. My stomach rebelled. I pressed away from the warmth. Stopped. I retched, lost my breakfast. The movement began again. I managed to wipe my mouth with some part of me, succeeded in drawing a breath, but I couldn't see. Couldn't open my eyes.

The movement jerked, as if falling a long distance and landing hard. The world swirled and my gorge rose again. The movement stopped. My stomach settled. I tried to control my breathing. My lungs were working hard and fast, as if I had been drowning. Or smothered. Buried. Underground. In the fists of two things, two creatures that each wanted something of me.

Sense returned. I concentrated on slowing my breathing and my heart, which was racing at a tripping, thudding, painful pace. Slowly my body began to achieve a rhythm that felt more normal. A steady tempo that meant I wasn't dead. Wasn't dying.

After what felt like ages, I tried again to open my eyes. I poured all my strength into that single aim. *Open my eyes.* My lids fluttered open.

I was sitting on a rock the size of a small stool, at the rill we had passed on the way in, my feet in the icy water. An icy wet rag was on the back of my neck. Something heated was wrapped around me, something alive, breathing with a deep, shuddering vibration. A bottle of water appeared in the air before me, a hand holding it. My own hands rose and I wrapped my fingers around the bottle. *Oh good. I still control my body.* I blinked slowly, and my eyes felt gluey.

"Drink." *Occam.*

I pulled the bottle to me. I drank. My brain came rushing back at me.

Occam was holding me. He was sitting at my back, my spine against this chest. His arms around me. His legs around me. Holding me upright. I stiffened, and he eased away, taking his warmth with him, and he circled me until he was kneeling in front of me, his heated hands on my shoulders, holding me upright. "Nell, sugar. You okay?"

I nodded. My neck moved like an iron rod had been implanted in my spine. Pain shot up my back, into my head, and exploded. Little lights and fireworks went off, bright in the threatening darkness. I was pretty sure if I moved again my skull would disintegrate.

"We need to know what happened back there," Occam said.

I frowned and blinked until I could look into his gold-flecked eyes. I managed a bare whisper. "Did you carry me out?"

"Yes. Nell? Are you okay?

"I . . . No. I have a headache big enough to drive a tractor into."

He put something in my free hand. Two Tylenol. "Oh," I murmured. "Magic pills. Goodie." I set them on my tongue, finished the bottle of water, and gave him the empty.

Occam breathed out a shaky laugh. "What does she read?"

"Back to normal," T. Laine said. "I think I'll set it to default zero and not the fudged zero I started at." At which point I realized that she had been reading me with the psy-meter 2.0 while I read the earth.

"Fudged zero?" Occam asked.

"With all the redlining, I set the background ambient zero as high as it would go. The way I'd set it if a small coven of witches were getting ready to do a working and I wanted to be able to read the energies of the spell itself over the energies of the witches."

Occam hummed a note that reminded me of a purr. That had been the vibration at my back. Things were beginning to return to me, to make sense. Paka was sitting, front feet together, at my side. She was not purring, but was watching me with a cat stare, the kind a well-fed, bored cat gives a mouse. Alert, interested, but not ready to attack.

"What did I read when I was scanning the land?" I whispered. I looked at T. Laine and the movement of my head made the world swirl and nausea rise. There was a glare everywhere, and my eyeballs ached. I put my hands flat on the rock beneath me. And very deliberately did not allow myself to commune with the deep.

"You redlined," she said shortly. "Even at the higher zero."

Feeling more steady, I lifted my palms and studied them. My fingers were white and quivering, but there was no bleeding, no places where a knife had nicked me, cutting me free. The stitches were clean and neat, the flesh they held together looking far more healed than it should. The ground and the living things in it had attacked. I looked at my feet. No damage except a streak of red. I thought back to the questions Occam had asked me. "I'm okay. I think. Sick to the stomach. A little woozy.

"The smaller consciousness, the dancer . . . recognized me. From yesterday. It . . . didn't grab me, exactly. I was probably only a few feet into the earth when it saw me. It wrapped around me. Yeah. Like a ribbon on my ankle. But not . . . not like it was taking me prisoner." I touched my ankle. The skin was tender, but nothing had penetrated my flesh. "More like it was trying to get my attention. Trying to get me to see something."

A flare of heat from a branding iron pierced through my brain. I breathed slowly, carefully, trying not to throw up. Or *hurl*, as I had learned in Spook School. I pressed a hand to my middle, to the rooty scars that marked me. Nothing felt different. That was good.

"I think . . . I think the dancer was trying to tell me something," I said, "the same thing it told me yesterday. 'Flows, flows, flows. Pools, pools, pools.' But the last lines had changed. It was saying 'Dead. All dead. All dead. Forever.' It was singing the words, like bells. It was dancing in a loose, looped, figure-eight shape. It . . ." I stopped, trying to think what I wanted to say. "It's almost as if it wants to communicate something.

"Then there was another presence. The woman, I think, human or witch. I didn't sense magical energies, so I couldn't tell. She grabbed me and pulled me down. Between them, they were smothering me. Dragging me deeper. The woman seemed to know I wasn't human. So, two presences, one humanoid in its thought processes, one not. Not at all. I need to go back there."

"Not happening," Occam said.

"What cat man said. It took everything I had to *Break* you free."

I squinted up at T. Laine. She flowed with the glare, like an aura surrounding her. *Ah.* I had a migraine. Auras came with migraines. The headache stabbed through my skull. "Owww." I placed one hand to my head, and the stitches on my fingers shocked me. "Owwwie again."

"Nell, sugar?"

"Headache is bad. Maybe a migraine? I never had anything like this before." I squinted through the pain and asked T. Laine, "Was that the blue energies I saw? The *Break*?"

"You could see the energies?"

"Something blue cut straight down through the earth all around me in a circle. It cut through the dancer energies that were holding me. Cut me away from the woman. And I was free."

"Go me." But T. Laine sounded unhappy still and her face was set in a frown so deep it cut lines into her skin, and hair hung in black tangles around her face. She was staring at the small psy-meter in her hands.

Occam, still kneeling at my feet, handed me two things. They were soft and pink. Pretty. "Can you put them on?"

I examined them. Turned them over in my hands. "Oh. Socks."

"Yes. *Socks.*" He sounded amused and improbably gentle. Paka hacked, laughter in the syllable.

"Sure. I can do socks." With motions that sent spikes of pain through my eyeballs, I pulled the socks onto my feet and then pushed my feet into the boots Occam held out for me.

"How we doin', Lainie?" he asked.

"So far, so good."

"What's going on?" I asked, knowing that something was wrong but not knowing what, other than the headache that speared me and the ache that was growing in my hips and knees and shoulders. I tried to unfold my limbs against the discomfort, but I didn't want to move enough to complete the stretch.

"Remember the crabgrass-looking stuff that grew into you yesterday?" T. Laine asked. Before I could reply, she went on. "Well, about three minutes into your scan, we started to see the topsoil move. And at about four minutes, thirty seconds, shoots came up from the ground. Exact same moment the P 2.0 red-lined. They wrapped around your ankle. I dropped the psy-meter and started my *Break*. The moment *Break* hit, Occam picked you up, I grabbed your things, and we hauled ass outta there."

I was reading for only five minutes? That was all? That seemed important, but my headache was getting worse, and I closed my eyes instead of trying to put it all together. My stomach felt as if it would erupt with the slightest movement. "Did Paka sense anything?" I whispered.

"She's shaking her head no," T. Laine said.

The world swirled around me like I was being sucked down a drain.

"Nell? Nell, sugar?"

And then I heard nothing more at all.

I woke when Occam tried to maneuver me into the car. I heard the word *ambulance*.

"No. No ambulance," I mumbled. I was cold and thought that if I started shivering I'd not survive the headache. "Just some aspirin and ibuprofen on top of the Tylenol, a blanket, and a candy bar. I think my sugar bottomed out."

"Nell, you need—"

"I'm okay." I lay my head against the seat back and took a bottle of water from T. Laine. Occam tucked my faded pink blanket around me. "I think . . ." I had to stop and lick my dry, cracked lips. "At Spook School," I whispered, "there was a class on backlash from interrupted magical workings. The usual stuff: fire, explosion, death. But they also said something about physical reactions."

"Backlash," T. Laine said, sounding relieved. "With headaches. Bad ones. Sometimes with auras, both visual and audible. You seeing an aura?"

I mouthed the word *yes*.

The seat dipped, and I felt the presence of someone near. I identified Paka by the sound of her purring breath. She curled in the backseat, leaning against me, her heat like a furnace. As if she knew I was cold, she pressed against me, warming me like a hot fire in a stove. The threat of shivering eased away.

"I didn't interrupt a working," T. Laine said. "While you were getting ready, I drew a circle and prepared *Break*. But I didn't hit *you* with it. I hit the ground with it."

"I was in the ground," I said, not knowing how to explain it any better now than I had in Spook School. I licked my lips again and said haltingly, "If something was full of psysitopes . . . or someone was being attacked by psysitopes . . . by a combative or offensive spell . . ." I breathed, hurting all over, trying to calm myself.

"You," T. Laine said.

I splayed the fingers of my uninjured hand in a *yes* motion. "And I was in the ground, *grounded*, as it were, and the *Break* spell hit, *Break* being a defensive working, that could result in backlash."

"Oh. Presumably yes," T. Laine said, guilt lacing her words, "since the thing that had you was magical. Nell, I am so sorry."

I waved the guilt away. "How about a consciousness or an artificial intelligence program that runs on magical energy?" I said. "Could it be hurt too? 'Cause I gotta tell you'uns. Them things act as if they're alive." The silence that followed was telling. It might have told me more had my eyes been able to focus more than a foot away, but I was doing the best I could.

"No ambulance?" T. Laine asked again.

"No ambulance," I said. "Just OTCs."

"Look at you all medical-talking. Over-the-counters. Nice," T. Laine said. "Allow me to be your street-corner drug dealer. Here's the aspirin and the ibuprofen. Take aspirin now and the ibuprofen in an hour."

"Okay," I said and popped the two aspirin with more water. I barely got them swallowed before I sank into sleep, to wake again only when the car braked at HQ. I swallowed two ibuprofens and tried to get out of the car, but I'd stiffened up and it took both Occam and T. Laine together to get me up the stairs, Paka leading the way. I let them help me because I didn't want to throw up on the stairs. But about halfway up I retched again.

T. Laine said, "You barf on my shoes and I swear I'll make you pay."

"You can barf on my shoes, Nell, sugar."

"No one could tell," T. Laine said.

"True," Occam said.

And then I was lying down on the couch in the break room I hadn't even seen yet, and someone closed the blinds. I felt my blanket being tucked around me as I tunneled down toward sleep and whispered, "Am I getting paid to sleep?"

"Yes," Rick said, his heated hand on my forehead. "Yes, you are."

The last thing I remembered was Paka stretching out beside me on the couch, her leopard warmth so wonderful and amazing that I rolled a little and rested against her.

It was quitting time when I woke, pink sunlight slanting through the side of the blinds. My headache had reduced from a roaring inferno to a campfire suitable for browning marshmallows and roasting hot dogs. Paka was gone, and I was alone on the couch beneath the blanket.

I managed to slit open my eyes and get a fuzzy vision of a table and chairs and two forms sitting there before I took refuge behind my lids again. I had known Occam was in the room. I couldn't say how I had known, but I had. T. Laine sat with him, silent. I also knew they were both feeling bad about letting me scan the earth.

I cleared my voice and whispered, "I think I might live."

"I was hoping you would say that, Nell, sugar. Hauling dead bodies isn't in my job description."

"I need to write the action report," I said, my voice a mite stronger.

"You don't remember much after that headache," T. Laine said.

"I don't?"

"No," Occam said. "Lainie and I wrote reports based on what you told us at the scene. In the morning, if you remember something else, you can write your own report."

From the doorway, outside my line of sight, had I even had my eyes open, Rick said, "I suggest that you read the reports and see if they're accurate." His wry tone said he knew they were covering for me.

"I promise," I said, trying to force my eyes open some more. "I need to go home."

"I'll drive you," Occam asked.

"It's too far out of your way."

Occam said, "Not in my new car. That thing loves an autumn ride in the country."

I felt the tiny pull of muscles at my lips. "You got a government car too?"

He made a cat sound, kinda sneezy and snorty all at once. Derisive. "I am the proud owner of a previously owned 2015 Ford Mustang two-door Fastback GT. That baby purrs."

My lips pulled wider. "I might barf if you take the corners too fast. I might barf if you hit the brakes or speed up too fast. I might barf just to barf, all over your newish car. And that is a terrible word. *Barf*. What's wrong with the word *vomit*?"

"I'll bring you a barf bag, Nell, sugar."

"Whoopie. Okay. Thank you. Will you get my dirty clothes and shoes and laptop and whatever else I need? Oh. Keys. And how will I get back here in the morning?"

"Your friendly neighborhood taxi service. Me," Occam said. "I got a place outside of Oliver Springs, not too far from the foot of your mountain, so don't argue. Piece of cake to pick you up."

I could guess why he had a place so close to my land and the wooded hills owned by the TVA. It allowed him to shift, slip out of his house on the full moon, hunt, and then shift back without needing a place to leave his car. Smart move. "Thank you."

"My pleasure. Be right back."

I heard him leave the room, and I knew I had to fix the other problem. "So," I murmured to T. Laine, "what will it take to make you feel better? Make you stop feeling all awful about the backlash? A foot massage might feel good about now. Or you could wash my clothes. Or put in a couple of hours in my garden this weekend."

"It's not funny," T. Laine muttered. "I could have killed you."

"Could have. Didn't. And I'm pretty sure I would be dead now if you hadn't gotten me free. I was injured by friendly fire, to save me from sure death in the deeps. It happens. I learned something. You learned something. We'll do better next time."

After a moment, while I listened to Rick, Occam, and Tandy bantering down the hall, T. Laine asked, her voice soft, "What did you learn?"

"That when I do a scan, my brain is tied either physically or metaphysically with the ground. What I do doesn't work like X-rays or sound waves, a reading where I might stay in my body and send out something that will take readings. It's more of an out-of-body experience. My consciousness actually leaves my body and goes into the earth. It's what I thought happened, but I could never be certain until now. It makes me wonder what would happen if someone moved my body while I was down there. Would I be able to find myself? Would I just die? Lost in the dark?"

T. Laine made a sound that said she was listening, and added, "Out-of-body experiences have been scientifically proven to be tied into specific brain cell activity, involving parts of the brain that deal with feelings of what brain scientists call 'body ownership,' as well as regions that are involved with spatial orientation. They call them GPS cells. So you really aren't out of your body in an OBE. You just think you are."

I managed a partial smile. "Not in my case. You proved that I'm actually in the ground. *Break* proved it. Had I been getting feedback from the earth and not been actually down there, *Break* wouldn't have harmed me."

"Hoooly . . ."

The word breathed into silence. I could almost feel her brain working on what I had said. "We know something that no one else knows," I said, "about my species, whatever I am. We'll have to experiment on how to use magic without killing me while I'm in the ground."

I heard T. Laine close a laptop and shuffle around. It sounded like she was gathering her things. "Thank you," she said. "For that. And I'm so sorry."

"It isn't a problem, Lainie," I said. "We learned something brand-new. It makes us a better team."

"Are you trying to say you'll let me do a working near you again someday?"

"It's part of the job."

"Next time I'll try not to kill you."

"That would be nice," I whispered, letting the smile curve up my lips and crinkle around my eyes.

"Come on. I'll help you to Occam's chick-magnet car. Did he tell you it's red?"

"Chick magnet," I said, letting her help me slowly into an upright position. "Six months ago I'd have been thinking about getting me some laying hens if you said that. Now I know it means Occam is using the car to get himself a varied sex life."

"Are you two talking about my sexual prowess?" Occam said from the door.

"No," T. Laine said with asperity. "We're talking about how you don't have a sex life without a hot car."

"Ouch," he said, laughing. "Come on, Nell, sugar. Let's get you home and into bed."

My eyes opened fully at that line and I put an I-beg-your-blessed-pardon expression on my face. It was Mama's look when she was getting ready to go to battle.

Occam chuckled. So did T. Laine. And I realized that they were poking fun at me. "Ain't she cute when she looks at us like that? All prim and proper and fulla spunk? Come on, Nell, sugar. Let's get you home. Tomorrow starts early."

It was after eight p.m. when I finished repacking the gobag, washing clothes, and laying them on wooden racks in front of the Waterford cookstove to dry. Finished eating dinner and feeding the cats, who were full of complaints about the fact that I hadn't come home last night. Sleeping outside wasn't a burden on them, but they didn't like being locked out. Long before nine, I crawled between the sheets on my new bed, the cats curled up on top of the coverlet, and we all went to sleep.

When I woke again, it was to cat whiskers tickling my jaw, a cold cat nose nuzzling mine. The night still pressed at the windows. Out back, a barred owl hooted; in the distance, another answered. I realized that I had spent most of the last two days sleeping. It was an unfamiliar feeling, to be so well rested. I hadn't slept so much in—well, ever. I had been the early-to-bed, early (before the crack of dawn)-to-rise person for all of my life in the church and as John Ingram's junior wife, in a life that meant hard physical labor and not much time off from anything. When I left for Spook School, that lifestyle had worked to my benefit, but the hours allotted for sleeping there had been closer to six, not eight, or the ten I sometimes got in winter on the farm. I stretched and checked the time on my cell. It was four a.m. Outside it would be cold and the ground would be hard, if not frozen. Perfect for a little machete work in the garden.

I eased out of bed to not disturb the cats, and dressed in long johns, my overalls, one of John's old flannel shirts, and work boots. Setting a pot of coffee to brew, I got out pancake mixings and checked in on the cats. They slept on, likely thinking that I was insane to go out so early. They might be right. I lifted a big skillet from the warming tray and set it on the stove so it would be ready for use at any time. I took the machete and a pair of leather work gloves from the back porch, set the security light to stay on, and tromped to the garden. I didn't usually wear heavy gloves, but the stitches were in bad places for possible further injury, especially for what I intended.

Entering the garden area, I closed off the rabbit-netting fence, laid out my few tools, and tested the heft of the machete with my uninjured arm. Then I started hacking and slashing with abandon, pulling up the dead stuff and creating a pile of dead, dry, withered vegetation. I also worked up a sweat. It was wonderful. And if I was avoiding doing what I knew I needed to do, well, that was okay. For the short hours until dawn.

When the sun was a faint gray haze in the east, I put away my tools and stared into the blackness of the woods. "Now or never," I said. I went to the trees where I used to sit when John's first wife, Leah, was dying and I was her sole caretaker. To the space between a sycamore and a poplar, where the roots of the two trees had reached out, searching for nutrients, and had intertwined in an interracial arboreal marriage of sorts.

There was nothing here to hurt me. And Soulwood was fine. I knew that. Really I did. Well, with the exception of Brother Ephraim's dark soul polluting the far boundary. But I had seen damaged land, been hurt by something in the earth. I had to see that Soulwood was safe and happy, experience for myself that my woods were undamaged, that Brother Ephraim had done no harm to them. It was the way a mother might feel if she woke in the night with dreams of her child fallen ill or injured or near death. She would rise from bed and rush to her child, consumed by the need to touch and to know.

Dropping to my backside with my feet stretched out before me, I took off the leather gloves. Uncertain, needing this, yet fearing it too, I placed my hands, palms flat, on the ground at my sides, and reached down. And down.

The warmth of Soulwood reached back, a heated and lazy sense of welcoming, a drowsy contentment. The earth of my land was in winter shut-down mode, a time when the roots burrowed deep, the twigs and limbs hibernating, the trees storing starch in their trunks and roots, starches that would be converted to sugar that rises in the sap, sugars in the bark and living wood that brought life to the forest. But it was still active enough

to know me, and I blew out a breath of relief. I didn't search for
Brother Ephraim, but he wasn't in the heart of the land, so I was
satisfied.

I let the land heal the last of my headache, ease the ache in
my joints, and finish the healing of my lacerations. I would need
to remove the stitches this morning or the flesh would start
growing over them.

When I pulled myself up from the deep of the land, I was
chilled, as inflexible as my maw-maw, and she was in her eight-
ies. The sky was pink, and I knew Occam would be here soon. I
raced inside and hurried through a hot shower, dressing in the
pants that had dried in front of the woodstove overnight, layering
on a T-shirt and a clean plaid flannel shirt under a jacket. The
lowering clouds said it was going to get cold tonight, so I put
warm boots at the door and wore wool socks around the house.

I put on the scant amount of makeup I allowed myself to
wear. You can take the churchwoman out of the church but can't
take the church out of the churchwoman, at least not overnight. I
dried my bobbed hair and gooped it up again. Not churchwoman-
ish at all. I liked the look. It was funky. That's what LaLa, my
mentor at Spook School, had called it. Funky. Once I figured out
it wasn't a bad word, I went with it too. Mama was likely to have
a hissy fit when she saw it. But that was a battle for another day.

Once I was presentable, breakfast fixings were out and
warming, and the skillet had been moved to the hottest part of
the stove, I got a pair of sharp scissors from my sewing kit and
started removing the stitches from my arm and hand. As each
one popped, a sensation of electric comfort zipped through me,
and I caught myself sighing with pleasure by the time I finished.
I stretched my fingers and relaxed fully for the first time in
nearly two days.

The moment I felt a car on my road, I added oil to the heated
fry pan and whisked the pancake batter. By the time Occam
knocked on the door, I was dishing up the first stack of pancakes, and I shouted, "The door's open!"

"Nell," he said as he entered, censure in his tone, "I coulda
been anybody. One'a your churchmen here to rape and kill.
Most anything!"

"Nope," I said, not letting him see my face as I poured more
batter into the hot skillet. "I knew when your cute car started up
the mountain. If you hadn'ta been you when you stepped onto

the ground out front, I had plenty of time to get my gun and shoot you." I put down the spatula and picked up the handgun on the cabinet, set it down again, and carried a pancake-laden plate to the table with a cup of strong coffee.

His eyebrows went up, his lips tightened, and he closed the door behind him. "You really know when someone drives onto your road?"

"Pretty much. Drives, walks, or slithers." Ever since I fed Brother Ephraim to the wood, I had known with a far greater certainty. A small silver lining to the big black cloud of Ephraim.

"What's that?" He nodded to the plate I had set on the table.

"Pancakes," I said, as if he was stupid. "Have a seat."

"You made me pancakes for my breakfast," he said, his voice oddly toneless.

"Seemed a mite unhospitable to feed myself while you watched." I flipped the second batch of pancakes over, and brought butter and syrup to the table.

Occam grabbed my hand, turning it over. His flesh was warm, like a fire burned directly beneath the surface. "You healed up right fast, Nell, sugar. Who took out your stitches?"

"I did," I said, surprised. "Who else?"

"A doctor?" He said it like it should have been obvious.

I pulled my hand away and placed the syrup on the table. "Now, that would be a waste of time. Try the syrup." I went back to the stove. "It's real maple. I traded for it. Been thinking I could make my maple trees sap up on really cold winters. I'm kinda hoping we'll have a cold one so's I can try."

Occam scowled at me. "You're gonna make *syrup*? I hate to remind you, Nell, sugar, but you got yourself a job now. You have to work for a living, and time off is precious and scant."

"I aim to try," I said over my shoulder. "Old Man Hodgins on the church compound makes syrup after really cold winters. I thought I might apprentice out to him. The time is less than you might think. Mostly tapping the trees, then cooking the syrup, and both activities are done on Saturdays." I flipped the pancakes out onto my plate and added more batter to the hot skillet.

I joined Occam at the long table. "You like?" Not that I really needed to ask the question. Occam's plate was half-empty.

"I love."

"Good." I flashed him a smile and was startled to see his eyes on me, golden hints of his cat in them. I returned my gaze to my plate, suddenly uncomfortable at the presence of a man in my widder-woman house. It wasn't appropriate or proper.

But Occam was a coworker and a friend. And I'd offered him hospitality.

I shut off the judgmental, condemning part of me, and continued. "You can't tap a tree until it's twelve inches in diameter, and you need in the neighborhood of thirty to fifty gallons of sap to evaporate down to one gallon of syrup. That's why the real stuff is so expensive. I have plenty of maple trees bigger in diameter than twelve inches, and they could take a number of taps. Old Man Hodgins has a large-sized evaporator. The weather isn't cold enough here to get really good sap, but this winter might be cold enough. It happens from time to time." I stopped. I was babbling. Suddenly not wanting to look up into Occam's eyes. So I ate.

When Occam's plate was empty, I got up and brought the last batch of pancakes to him and finished off my own. Then I washed the dishes, cleaned the fry pan, and coated it with a layer of oil so it wouldn't rust. I set the stove to cool burn with summer wood, refilled the water heater—a never-ending process—let the cats into the garden, and gathered my gear.

I felt Occam watching me with every move, and without knowing why, I never let myself look his way even after I gathered up my keys. Not knowing why I was so uncomfortable, I followed Occam to his car. I sat silent all the way into Knoxville, to PsyLED HQ.

When we got to HQ, we were met with an uproar. Our investigation into psysitopes had morphed overnight into something new. As of dawn, humans were now involved.

SIX

"We have three families, two on one street, one on the street just behind them," Rick said. "Their houses form a triangle." He pulled a street map up on the big screen, the three houses marked in red. The triangle was equilateral, all three sides equal.

"That," T. Laine said, pointing, "fits into a witch working. All three internal angles are congruent to one another and are each sixty degrees. Simple, familiar Euclidean geometry, the first maths taught to witches to bind and control the power of the universe. Now we know for sure we're dealing with witches."

Something in that statement didn't feel completely correct, but I kept my partial disagreement to myself. There had been a woman in the earth, a woman who was part of the energies, and yet, who wasn't. Whether she was a witch or not, I hadn't been able to tell, but if Unit Eighteen thought witch, then how was I going to prove her not? Worse, what if I was mistaken? I opened *CSM-Nell* on my laptop, and merged the new GPS coordinates to my own sat map. I drew a slow breath as I absorbed the potential meanings of the locations. In the background, I listened to the unit members discuss the psy-meter readings, the bizarre actions of the humans who had first come to the attention of KEMA, and the multiagency law enforcement involvement that was taking place as of dawn.

"The first family, at what we're calling Point A"—Rick indicated the house with a laser pointer—"was reported by a guy on the way into work. Family of five, all in their yard, walking in a circle. In their nightclothes. Children not wearing shoes. The man buck naked. KEMA techs tested them without interfering and they redlined. Then local LEOs got another report, extended family of seven. That would be Point B. KEMA started driving around, looking for activity, and found the third one. We're calling it Point C, also five adults, some from out of town, visiting.

There haven't been any other reports of suspicious activity. All three families redlined. KEMA set up privacy tents and cordoned off the houses and yards.

"The sheriff deputies are evacuating the nearby families," JoJo said, pulling on three earrings in her left ear. It looked painful, but this wasn't the first time I'd seen her pulling on her earrings. It was a tic, indicating she was mentally occupied and trying to draw correlations from insufficient evidence. "The Red Cross is involved. So are county services, offering support and advice."

Rick leaned forward, his fingertips on the table, taking his weight, a lock of his black-as-midnight hair swinging forward over his forehead. He said, "Since this situation is clearly not contained, and since we don't have a source or explanation for the paranormal activity, the DIC called in the FBI to assist. They are currently acquiring warrants for the houses."

"Did they leave the people walking?" I asked. "In their yards? Undisturbed?"

"No. The victims are being taken to University of Tennessee Medical Center for isolation, testing, and treatment. How do you think this might be relevant to our part of the investigation, Nell?"

"I don't know. How did they take it?" I asked. "The people, I mean. Being taken away."

Rick referred to his notes on his tablet. "No one was responsive until paramedics attempted to remove them from the site where each was found, at which time violent psychosis resulted. As of the last report, all are medicated, on psychotropic meds; no one is coherent as to date, place, or time. Why?"

"I'm not sure. Are the remaining geese still swimming in a circle at the pond site?"

"The geese were swimming in a circle?" Rick asked.

"Yes. It's in my report." I shifted my own maps up onto the main screen, and added in a split screen one of the photos from the pond site. "We had two dead geese at the pond, here and here." I pointed. "You can see the live geese, clearly swimming in a circle. The dead ones were not in the circle. While I was reading the land, a third goose died, and when it did, a line of energy attached it to the deeps." I could see them watching me in my peripheral vision, could feel their interest, but I didn't look up. I pulled up the shots of the accident site where the truck driver had hit the deer. "Were the deer walking in a circle before they were hit and scattered all over by the impacts?"

Rick nodded yes.

"And there are the houses in a triangle with people walking in circles.

"Hmm," I said. "If you look, the three sites for each of the redlining activity—pond geese, deer origination site, and humans, form a second triangle, much bigger. And all the affected beings and creatures were moving in circles. So . . . what if there's a wider circle on the outer limit?" I made a blue circle on the map, one that used the three triangle points to define the circumference.

T. Laine sucked in a breath I could hear in the sudden silence. Despite the fact that the woman in the deeps hadn't been proven to be a witch, we had just discovered complicated witch magic geometries. A working of the highest order.

I went on. "Rick said that there was no way witches set up a working this large. So I started searching for companies that might have been involved in energy research, maybe something using tech to expand a magical working. Specifically paranormal energy research or research into how magic works. Maybe for weaponization. I started out with a simple five-mile diameter from each site. No reason for the five miles," I added. "I had to start somewhere.

"Using the first two sites, I narrowed down the possibilities of companies that might have made a mistake with some kind of paranormal energy and I came up with more than twenty, initially. Now, using the same five-mile-diameter circles, I can eliminate most of the companies. And that leaves six, all of them in the general area of the center of the triangle and proposed witch circle made by the three sites of the disturbances." I punched the names up on the screen.

Rick said softly, "Alocam, Inc., LuseCo Visions, C-Corp Development, Kamines Future Products, Rosco J. Moose, Inc., and San-Inc. Why did you come up with this when we didn't?"

It wasn't the first time he had asked me this. It seemed my brain worked differently from the others'. I shrugged and, after one look at his face, dropped my eyes to my laptop. I had to make this sound professional and smart, and not hokey or stupid. I took a breath to center myself, straightened my spine, and said, "With the exception of T. Laine, who thinks in terms of small workings by witches and about mathematics, the unit thinks about sections of the city, neighborhoods, infrastructure, magical beings, and paranormal crimes committed by magical beings. It's the box you all think in. It's a big box, but it's still a box.

"The box I think in is different. I think in terms of the land, of the earth, of its shapes and hills and valleys and water sites." *And the presences beneath the ground,* I thought. "That's my personal thinking box. So I looked at the proximity of the three sites to the hills, the rivers, and the creeks, and to the energy sources that might affect the actual ground around them." I shrugged again. "The small thing, the dancer, in the ground yesterday and the day before wasn't acting . . . I guess you could say it wasn't acting like I thought it should. It was acting like a kid or a puppy, demanding and playful and temperamental. Because it wasn't acting in what I think of as a natural manner, I considered the possibility that it might be a man-made problem, or have a man-made origination that stimulated a problem with something else."

"Like a working with a built-in AI, capable of self-evolution," Rick murmured. It wasn't the first time artificial intelligence programs had come up.

"And then the woman spoke to me."

"The woman you couldn't positively identify as a witch," T. Laine said, tucking her hair behind her ear.

I thought of offering her some of my hair goop, but there might a social protocol about that, and so I refrained. "I honestly don't know what she was. As to the other stuff, you'uns got lots better ideas in that department."

"I don't know about that," Tandy said. "You just came up with an insight and ideas that we haven't discussed." But I noted that he didn't say that my ideas were totally new, so I was guessing that others had had similar thoughts.

"How about the people who have been to each of the sites?" I asked. "And who had contact with the deer? Any sign of odd psysitope readings?"

"Nothing out of the ordinary," Rick said. "We're thinking that people were hit by a directed working, and these psysitopes dispersed after a time."

I said, "I think I saw a wildlife camera mounted in the trees at the pond site. If we can get access to the footage, that might help us see what happened to the geese who died."

Rick said, "Nell, you and T. Laine go to the pond site and see what's happened to the geese. Get the wildlife cam footage if you can, or find who has it and ask for it. If they refuse, we'll get a warrant. The dead deer were sent to Richmond, to PsyCSI. I expect prelim necropsies back in a few days. The living deer were taken in by the University of Tennessee's Forestry, Wildlife, and Fisheries Department. Assuming things don't change with what you learn at the pond, I'd then like you to swing by the school and see what's happened to the deer."

"I'll get the dead geese sent on too," T. Laine said.

Rick nodded and went on. "JoJo, I'd like you to take Nell's research on the companies and gather everything you can on them, what they do, what their area of research is, employees, financial status, everything you can find out without digging so deeply you ping something and attract the attention of their security systems. If none of these companies are responsible for the psy-contamination, we'll widen our search. But for now, we'll start on Nell's six."

"What about us, boss?" Occam asked, pointing to Tandy and himself.

"I want you to check in with the other PsyLED units. See if they've noted similar readings or unusual human or animal activity. When Nell and T. Laine are finished at the pond, and when Nell feels up to it, I want Occam and T. Laine and Nell back at the DIC's house in North Carolina. I want a reading to see if that site is also affected."

"Boss, that isn't—"

"I know it's not a good idea, Occam. I know Nell could be injured. But it's a long way away. I'm hoping she can read it safely."

I frowned. "What if I can read it from Soulwood? Safer?"

Rick frowned back. His eyes looked blacker, shadows hidden in caverns of bruised-looking flesh. "That's over eighty miles, straight-line measurement."

I started to speak and stopped. Started again. "I bled on that land. My blood in the earth"—I waffled my hands, searching for ways to say something I had no words for—"gives me a tie to it. I can't explain it because I don't understand it myself. I haven't tried what we're talking about, but it might work."

"Try that first, then. If it works, see what you feel from the pond area. You bled there too."

I gave a little hand gesture that meant, *I'll do what I can.*

"Your stitches are gone," Rick said, his attention on my hands in the air. I tucked them beneath the table and said nothing.

"People," Rick said, after a moment. "We have humans redlining from magical workings. This is no longer an information-gathering case. This is an attack of some kind, whether by accident or on purpose. It looks more and more likely that we have an MED."

I didn't feel very happy about it. Not at all. Neither did T. Laine. It had been an easier case, and actually a stressless, pressureless case, despite my run-ins with the dancer shadow-and-light thing, when it only involved a pond and a flock of geese and a few deer. Now it was people who were being hurt. When it hit the media that we had an MED in Knoxville, the news would likely cause severe repercussions against T. Laine's subspecies. This wasn't fun for any of us anymore.

Rick went on. "There is no law or system of laws currently established based on judicial precedent to deal with this sort of situation. Nor are there statutory laws created by legislation to deal with this situation. We are off the legal grid. This is why PsyLED was created: this is our mandate, to deal with problems like this. To stop them. And if people or beings or creatures are responsible, to find them and make sure *they* are stopped." He closed his laptop, picked up his cell, and stood. "Go. Do things. Be smart. Tread carefully. Let's get this solved fast. Forty-eight hours would be good.

"I'll be notifying our upline people at PsyLED and the DOD. A task force will likely be created to deal with the situation if the contamination spreads. And, Nell, welcome to the team. I'd say your first case is well on the way to being something that PsyLED Spook School will study for some time to come."

Rick turned and left the conference room.

"And thank you for the reminder that the first night of the full moon is forty-eight hours away," JoJo said, sarcasm in her tone and her eyes on her screens, fingers tapping keys. "Ain't this gonna be fun with all you people going furry on us."

"I promise I won't bite anyone," Occam said, something sharp and cutting in his tone. "I like my life just fine and got no intention of bleeding out on the floor just for a taste of you people."

"Pea's claws are sharp," JoJo said. "You'd be dead long before you felt a thing."

"Stop it, you two," T. Laine said.

JoJo looked as if she might want to say more on the subject, but instead said, "Nell, your research is good, but you can't get jack in the public domain. I'll dig deeper into our own databases."

"Government-linked sites are likely to be top secret," Tandy said, a thread of relief in his tone at the order for his teammates to stop picking at each other, "locked down on info."

"Yeah, the feds and the spies are stingy suckers. I'll set up an automatic search from a third-party site. And not ping anything." JoJo shook her head. She was wearing her braids swirled up in an enormous bun today, with some strands sticking out like twigs. She looked beautiful, with her tattoos and piercings and her colorful clothes.

Maybe . . . maybe I could pierce my ears when this was over. *Mama would—*

I shut that away. I was a woman grown. I could pierce my ears if I wanted to.

I went to sign out the P 2.0 and get my freshly packed one-day gobag. Case first, lifestyle later.

We arrived at the pond site and parked close to the main road. The pond was still officially locked down by the local LEOs, but they hadn't been back to the site in a while, long enough for people to hike in, circle around the crime scene tape, down the drive, and set up to stay awhile. There were three cars parked out of sight of the road on the curving two-rut drive. "People are fricking insane," T. Laine spat, picking up her pace as we walked the long curve toward the pond. "I hate crowd control." She thumbed on her phone and gave our location to the local LEO dispatch.

"Worse than insane," I murmured, catching her arm and pulling her to a stop. I gestured through the trees to the opening beyond. "They set up tents. Campfires. And I don't hear anyone."

T. Laine went still, listening. There was only the wind and the faint clack of tree branches. The distant hum of traffic. The faint smell of old wood smoke from campfires. T. Laine asked the dispatcher to send three units to her twenty. When she was done, she turned off the ringer and pocketed her cell. I followed her lead until she drew her service weapon.

"Wait," I said, my voice soft, so it didn't carry. I stooped and placed one palm on the ground. Bloodlust slammed into me. Desire so strong it twisted my guts like barbed wire knotting inside me. So much blood . . . I whipped my body back. Nearly fell onto my backside trying to get away. *So much blood . . .*

T. Laine wrenched me up by my armpit. "Are you insane? You could get dragged down—"

"Death," I said, and I wrenched away from the heat and warmth and blood in her veins, just beneath the skin of her hand. I stumbled again. Caught my balance. "A lot of death. And blood." I squeezed my palms into tight fists, fighting the desire to feed the blood to the earth. Not the blood at the pond. Not the blood inside T. Laine. I closed my eyes. *No,* I thought, *No, no, no.* But my mouth went dry and tight and my breath came fast.

T. Laine touched my shoulder with her warm, blood-filled hand and shook me gently. "You okay?"

I backed away, nodding. Lying. *Wanting.* I moistened my lips and said, "Rick said that the directed working dissolved. I don't think this one did. I think it got stronger."

T. Laine gripped her service weapon in a two-hand grip, her finger off the trigger at the slide, the weapon by her thigh as she walked, moving into the edge of the trees. I forced down the desire to feed the land, hard, as if shoving the need into a dark crevice, and followed, but kept my weapon holstered. As far as I had been able to tell, nothing and no one was alive for acres and acres in any direction. Stepping carefully, silently, we moved toward the pond. The trees fell behind as the road opened out into the clearing. More parked cars appeared. Tents in all the colors of the rainbow. A car seat. Bicycles. A keg in a big aluminum bucket full of water. Fires that no longer smoked, but still smelled and felt warm when we passed by. A ladder on the ground. Beach blankets and those webby-seated aluminum chairs, several on their sides.

The pond came into sight. We both stopped.

Bodies floated in the still water. Bodies littered the shore; some on land showed signs of violence, bullet holes in heads, chests, a few with blunt force trauma. I gripped both fists tightly, letting my nails cut into the newly healed flesh, the pain grounding me to the real world, holding off the bloodlust. The yearning to feed the earth with the bodies of the dead grew, the lust stimulated by the death everywhere.

We stepped slowly up to two bodies the farthest from the shore. Two men. One with a death grip on a shotgun. One holding a tire iron. A semiautomatic, the slide locked back, was on the ground, empty, between them. From the looks of things, they had fired through the weapons' ammo at the people in the pool of water and at each other, and then beaten each other to death with the tools once the bullets ran out.

I didn't spend any time looking at them, instead staring at the water. "Look. Look at the bodies. They were swimming in a circle. Idiots went for a swim in the pond. T. Laine?"

She had lowered her weapon so it pointed at the ground, held in the lax fingers of one hand. She took a step toward the pool of water.

"T. Laine?" I said again. She took another step. And another. I called her name, louder. When she didn't turn, training took over. I rushed her. Dropped. Tackled her at the hips. One hand ripping the gun away from her. And to my feet.

She came up swearing, fists swinging, and she shouted, "What the holy hell do you think you're doing? Gimme my gun!"

I held the weapon at her, centered on her chest.

T. Laine's face underwent a series of changes. "What the holy hell. Nell?"

"Are you back in your right mind?"

"Huh?"

"Who is president of the US? Who is the leader of Unit Eighteen?"

She answered both questions, her expression shifting from anger to bewilderment. "What happened?"

I lowered the weapon. Uncurled my finger from the trigger and placed it along the slide. Dropped my shoulders, which had hunched up at the stress of watching T. Laine fall under some weird kind of compulsion from the pond. "You were walking to the water. Just like the other people. So now we are walking away, back to the main road, to warn the local LEOs answering your call that there is an MED here. A big one. Directed or not, it's not disintegrating, but spreading. And people are dying. Do you understand?" She glanced over her shoulder and I shouted, "Do you understand?"

She flinched and ducked. "Yes." She started back down the curved road, away from the pond. "I got it. I hear you. And more, I feel the pull beneath my feet. There's a *come-hither* spell going, or something like it." She brushed off her clothing, where the dust from the ground had mussed her. "I never thought I'd say this on the job, but thank you for tackling me."

"You're welcome."

"You okay? About"—her hand waved back behind us—"all that?"

My eyes followed her waving hand to take in the pond and the dead. There were dead humans . . . adults and teenagers . . . children. In the water. Faces just below the surface. Or floating on their backs, arms out, hair out in spirals. Dead. Dead all around me. I had worked so hard, given up so much, to protect and save children at the church. And here other adults—not churchmen, but regular people—had brought children into a situation and made a party of it. And children had died. And I wasn't feeling a thing that I thought I should. Not a hint of fear. No remorse. Nothing. Except fury that it had happened at all. Anger. A boiling rage that I swallowed back down, acidic and burning.

I released a breath. "No. I'm not. I'm not okay about anything."

T. Laine reached over slowly and took her weapon from my hands, removed the magazine and the round from the chamber, replaced the mag, set the safety, and holstered the weapon, the tiny *snap* telling us both it was seated in the Kydex holster. The sound of sirens coming down the road made her pull her cell and tap on a call. "Rick? Problem. Big-assed major problem."

I shifted my jacket so my badge was showing and got out my ID. I moved ahead of the moon witch and her report to our boss. I signaled to the sheriff deputies as they pulled up, to gather with me, and when I had all three out of their cars, I told them what had happened, all except the holding-a-gun-on-my-partner bit. I kept that to myself. I ended my report with, "We need to make sure all the roads and trails into and out of this entire area are covered. No one in or out. Not even law enforcement."

"Not a problem, in theory," one of the deputies said. "How do we keep the buzzards and rats out? And how do we recover the bodies and how do we ID the bodies? Huh? You got an answer to that?"

I looked at him for the first time and I laughed. The sound was a little shaky and frantic to my own ears, and it must have sounded odd to him too because he backed up two steps before he caught himself. "How?" I repeated his question. "PsyLED has protocols on the books. All kinds of protocols on the books. Someone will figure out what to do." I blinked, and on the lightless flesh of my lids I saw the bodies in the pond. Bodies all in a circle. And only in retrospect did I see the geese. All dead. As if they had swum and swum and swum until they'd died. Okay, maybe I was more shocky than I had thought, but at least the bloodlust was gone. Voice steady now, I said, "Someone will make sure we get the proper paranormal personal protective equipment. Then we can do our jobs."

I stopped and my forehead crinkled at a new thought. T. Laine had felt the pull of the pond. I hadn't. Not even a little. The bloodlust might keep other compulsions at bay. Or maybe my species didn't feel *come-hither* spells. And . . . there was a wildlife camera back at the pond. A camera with all the footage of the last two days on it. "Keep people out," I said, and I turned and headed back along the curved drive, dialing Occam as I went. I passed T. Laine still on the phone. She didn't look up at me.

"Occam," he answered.

"We have a full category-four MED at the pond with multiple casualties. T. Laine was caught in the working, or whatever the heck it was, and I tackled her. Local LEOs are making sure all entrances and exits are covered. I'm going back in to get the camera."

"Nell, what? No."

"Yes. And I need you to talk to me through the whole thing. Keep me centered. I'm putting you on speaker and the phone in my shirt pocket. Talk to me." I dropped the cell into the flannel plaid shirt's chest pocket.

"Nell, do *not* do this."

"Yeah. Like that."

"No. I mean it. Do not enter an MED alone."

"I may be the only one who *can* enter." I remembered T. Laine's slack face, her eyes wandering to the pond, latching on to the sight. And me? The plants had tried to claim me, but the pond had no effect. "You should've seen her. Her face went slack and she headed straight to the pond like she wanted to climb in among the bodies and go for a swim. But I seem to be immune to the spell trap, whatever it is."

"You're doing it, aren't you?"

"Pretty much."

"How many bodies?"

I set my legs into a slow jog and rounded the curve. Death and her dead were spread out all around me. I took a stranglehold on my desire to kill and feed the earth. And though it struggled, it didn't fight free.

"Nell?"

"Counting those I can see on land . . ." I counted aloud as I ran. I reached the ladder I remembered seeing, and said, "That makes twelve total, all on shore. All adults. All dead from gunfire or blunt force trauma. In the water, lemme count." I hefted the ladder up and over a shoulder and returned to jogging, keeping my heart rate high, my mind centered. The ladder was only about six feet long; I hoped it would be enough. "I count ten kids, teens. Two may be younger, all in the water. No sign of physical injury. No blood in the water. Three adults in the water. Ditto on the lack of visible injury. Twelve plus thirteen equals twenty-five victims."

I grunted as I set the ladder against the tree with the camera. Started climbing. It helped that I faced away from the death scene.

"How do you think they died?"

"The ones on land killed each other. The ones in the water? I think they swam to death. Drowned. Just like the geese that are still in the water with them."

"Jesus," Occam breathed.

"I don't think he was here," I said. "The camera looks easy to remove. It's mounted to the tree with a strap, a thumb clip, and a small metal brace to keep it pointed in the right direction. I'll have it down in a jiffy." And I did, narrating my actions to Occam, listening to his angry replies. I climbed down the ladder and put the cell onto video to record the scene as I jogged across the grass, keeping my back to the dead. "I have the camera out and I'm taking video of the scene with my cell as I walk. I'm taking the direct route back to the drive." Which was the only reason I heard the small cry. I stopped. I stopped midsentence, whatever I was saying instantly lost. "Did you hear that?"

Occam said, "Nell? What? What's happening?"

"I think . . ." I turned and jogged to my right, to the baby car seat we had seen on the way in. "There's a baby," I whispered. "I didn't feel it on my scan. Maybe because it's in a car seat on a heavy rubberized frame."

"Don't touch it, Nell. *Do not touch it.* The baby will be contaminated."

"I know." *But that might not matter.* I dropped to a squat at the baby's car seat, both knees up, off the ground, touching the dirt and grass with only my rubberized field boots. The little girl was dressed in pink, and she smelled of dirty diaper and sour milk and tears. She was sunburned, dark-haired, with green-brown eyes. My bloodlust withered and died at the sight of the child. I managed a deep, filling breath and blew it out.

The baby saw me and started squalling. "Can't leave now. She's thirsty. Hungry. Needs changing." I looked around and saw a box of diapers and plastic-bottled formula, and everything I needed. "I can't leave her here alone. And I can't take her with me to contaminate the others. So it looks like I'm staying."

"Stop, Nell. Don't do this."

I laughed, that odd-sounding, near-hysterical laughter that had frightened the deputies. "Too late. Hey there, sweetie. How are you?" I freed the child from the restraints and picked her up. Which made her scream more. "Oh yes. Yes, yes, yes. I know. You'uns been all alone all day, ain'tcha. I got'cha now. Yes I do. Com'ere. Yeeees, you got a load full of the uglies, don'tcha? Let's get you outta the sun and over to the car here. And let's get that diaper off. You still here, Occam?" I added in the same baby-voice tone.

"I'm here," he said, sounding off somehow. Probably spittin' mad at me for going off protocol.

"I'm changing her diaper now. And lemme tell you, it's bad. This little girl hasn't been changed all day. She's sunburned and her bottom is scalded. You'uns miserable, ain'tcha, darlin'? Oh my, there's a load in this thing. Ugh. Here. Let's wipe that messy bottom." She squealed like I'd just stabbed her. "I know that hurts, but I'm almost done. There, sweetie pie. All clean, and a new diaper." I figured out how to use the disposable one, which was a new concept for me, as the church didn't use anything disposable, only cloth diapers, and changed often. "Yes, sweet'ums. Just like that." I sealed the adhesive tabs. "And now let's find you'un a bottle for the formula. Here we go. Your

mama mighta swum herself to death, but up until then she was
mighty organized. Oh yes, baby. That's a good girl. Occam, I'm
sitting in an ancient Toyota station wagon. Tell Rick."

"Oh . . . Nell," Occam breathed.

The Para–Haz Mat van from PsyCSI in Richmond arrived at
long last. It was shaped like a bread truck with a navy-blue-and-
brown paint job in slashes and swirls like an RV and was
equipped for paranormal events. The techs—and there must
have been twenty or more in their POVs—personally owned
vehicles—were dressed out in white null uniforms, paranormal
protective suits each with an orange stripe across the front. The
unis were made with heavy-duty antimagic spells worked into
the fabric, and since no one seemed inclined to go for a swim, I
figured that the unis were effective. The suits had been treated
by the Seattle coven, a full, powerful coven that worked with the
DOD and Homeland Security. The unis were called 3PEs,
which stood for *personal paranormal protective equipment*.
The coven also constructed custom-made armor, but there was
no way I could afford a set of those. The suits resisted all passive spells, to appear to magic itself as though the techs were
nothing more than leaves blowing across the land instead of a
bunch of people tramping. The techs could be attacked by an
active, direct attack spell, but as their feet moved across the land
near the pond, they didn't elicit any attention at all from the thing
beneath the ground.

Farther away from the pond, at a site T. Laine selected by
taking measurements with the psy-meter 2.0, were the PsyCSI
tents, for collecting evidence and ending the active workings
on the bodies. And COD, TOD, and ID, where possible. Cause
of death. Time of death. Closure for the families who wouldn't
see their loved ones alive again.

The tents were white, waterproof, and had been spelled
against workings and magical attack, inside and out. There was
an *inverted hedge of thorns* working on the inside to keep anything magical inside, and a regular *hedge of thorns* outside,
except at the doorway. The three tents were set up, facing away
from the pond so the *come-hither* spell bounced away on the
treated tent walls.

I was the only one not dressed out in the special clothing.

Well, the baby and me. She had eaten and cried and finally fallen asleep in my arms. It had been a while since I'd coddled and cuddled a baby, and though I had no desire to have a young'un myself, it was kinda nice. If I'da been at home, stretched out on the sofa, with a book to read and the Waterford Stanley wood-burning cookstove putting out enough heat to keep me toasty, Soulwood and a sturdy floor between me and the shadow-and-light dancer in the ground, I'da been mighty fine, but Rick had shown no interest in offering me any comfort beyond the basic amenities. Instead of comfort, I was sitting on a webby-aluminum chair, the frame digging into my thighs, and was isolated in one of the antispell tents, just the baby and me.

A single portable toilet booth had been brought in and set up near the trees. A food truck had come by the street several times and provided tacos and hot dogs and burgers at inflated prices. I had been allowed a meal and bottled water and a Coke, which T. Laine had brought in, set on the gurney, and walked out. Without a word, without eye contact. I knew I was in trouble, but I couldn't seem to care. The baby had been without attention long enough to be burned and dehydrated, and no way was I leaving her alone. Period. She had drunk down three bottles of Pedialyte and formula and gone through three diapers. I had found cream to smear on her sunburn and her bottom and she was asleep, finally.

No one was talking to me, but I overheard everything that was spoken nearby, since no one was using their library voices, but rather nearly shouting to be heard between the faceplates they wore as part of the 3PEs. Therefore I knew a lot about what was going on: Access to the entire area had been shut down, with cops on every possible line of entrance. The scene had been set as a no-fly zone, which went for drones and kites, as well as the usual planes and helicopters. The press was gathered on the roadways and conspiracy and antiwitch sentiments were flying in the media.

A senior member of PsyLED HQ had come in to handle the magical incident and talk to the press. Soul, Rick's mentor, was to be the PsyLED PR spokesperson for this magical event.

There were lots of initials in my new life. They called it "alphabet soup," which was funny until I had to actually use the letters in a report.

Anyway, Soul had been in the area—not that any of us had

been aware of that—and she arrived at the site within half an hour of Rick himself, to oversee the investigation.

I had met Soul at Spook School. She was a legend among the graduates, and though she was tiny and curvy and made you want to protect her to your last dying breath, she scared me on some level I didn't have words for. Soul, no last name, just like Occam had no last name, was all of five feet four inches tall, with long platinum-silver hair that she wore loose and down to her hips, as long as I had worn mine, before I'd whacked it off.

I hadn't touched the ground with my boots since the first tent was set up, but I felt Soul enter the site. Or, rather, the land felt something different, and it sucked its presence away from the bottom of the tent I occupied, back to the deeps. I had known that the dancer consciousness was hanging around, aware of me but not able to get to me through the tent's spells, and I was suddenly lighter, an unseen weight gone from my shoulders and rib cage. Quickly, even before I took a single breath, the shadow-and-light was back, fast as a reflection of sunlight on the pond. It . . . *tapped* was as good a word as any, on the bottom of the tent, and raced back to Soul, back and forth between us, like the puppy I had compared it to. But now its greatest attraction was Soul. *Interesting.* The land, especially the puppylike dancer in the land, liked Soul. A lot. The spell could be designed to search for magical energies and creatures and then attack them and take their power for itself. That would require it to have the AI capabilities that had been mentioned. Without letting my feet leave the protection of the tent, I leaned out and watched the legal and CSI goings-on in the acres of cut grass.

Even on a dangerous paranormal crime scene, Soul was wearing only the spelled cloth/paper booties the rest of the LEOs wore. No uni with attached faceplate and gloves. Rather, she still wore her street clothes, a flowing georgette dress that reminded me of the gorgeous clothes worn by Hindu women, this one in shades of lavender and purples and orchid, with jeweled and beaded fringe, sparkling like her eyes. She was gorgeous. But mostly, to the cavorting thing in the land, she was a creature of significance, and its attention to me and the baby continued to lessen as the dancer centered its devotion on Soul.

I took my first deep, easy breath in hours. Not that I had told the others that I was having any problems. No one had asked.

No one had spoken to me. I was learning the hard way that when one bucked the system, one suffered all the consequences.

But even if they fired me, I was glad I had saved the baby.

Unconcerned by the possibility of contamination, Soul walked around the site, talked to people, made decisions. I heard her request that T. Laine contact the Knoxville coven leader, Taryn Lee Faust, and ask her to come down as part of the ongoing paranormal evaluation. T. Laine told her that request had already been issued. Soul told her to reissue it forcefully, and send a police escort from her house to here. I heard Soul ask Rick if protocol had been followed.

His voice muffled behind the spelled uni faceplate, he replied, "Up until the new girl decided to run her own rodeo." They were standing on the side of the tent, not trying to hide the conversation.

"Until then?" Soul asked.

"Day one, she completed the human-sense evaluation, with initial technology, followed by enhanced senses," Rick said, "which went well at first. A few hours in, Nell was attacked by fast-growing grass that Occam had to cut out of her. She received hospital treatment for dehydration and stitches for lacerations."

"More roots? That's interesting."

Rick didn't disagree, nor did he offer more information, which made me feel as if things were not as horrible as I feared, because Rick had been there when tree roots had grown into me not so long ago. He had seen. The fact that I wasn't human wasn't a secret, not anymore, but he wasn't offering up any details that weren't specifically asked for, a gift of privacy that I appreciated.

"Day two?"

"She tried to read the land again at a different site and had to be cut free again. No hospital this time."

"Day three?"

"Far as I can determine, without her filing a report, today she was fine until she got a wild hair to retrieve a wildlife camera in the trees about a hundred fifty feet from where she found the baby. Admittedly I had listed the camera as one of the objectives for the day, but the moment they found dead humans and a spreading contamination, they should have retreated and initiated protocol." They were closer to the tent now and I had to assume that Rick wanted me to hear them, because he kept talking. "From the moment she went after the camera and found the baby, she went rogue, without urgent need and with potential increased danger to herself and her unit. She screwed up."

Soul asked, "If she hadn't gotten the baby and the camera when she did, would the lack of either have compromised the rescue mission or the camera retrieval?"

"No. Camera would still have been there and the baby would likely have survived a few more hours until CSI and null suits got here."

I scowled down at the toes of my leather field boots. I didn't care. I had done the right thing. A baby that might *likely have survived a few more hours* wasn't good enough for me. Even a baby that might be magically contaminated.

"What did we get from the camera?" Soul asked.

"Mind-blowing. JoJo is on-site, downloading the footage to her laptop."

"Hmmm. So she had good instincts about the value of the evidence she broke protocol to attain. And I must say that saving the baby can be spun to excellent PR advantage. Also, it was the right thing to do, correct protocol or no." I blinked and relaxed again, tension that had built as she talked easing away. "Thank you, LaFleur," she said. "That will be all."

On the heels of those words, Soul stepped into the tent and let the unfastened doorway fall closed behind her. She stood in the entrance and studied me, her fingers laced together, draped in front of her hips, white booties the only thing that suggested she was on a magical contamination site. I stared back at her, my face giving nothing away, one hand on the sleeping baby. Beyond the cloth walls, I heard gurneys being rolled away, two by two, into the PsyCSI tents. They had begun to carry the dead from the shore.

Finally Soul smiled, her full lips stretching open and a look of real humor on her face. "When I came to PsyLED, they had no idea what to do with me. I was a singularity at the time, the very first *known* paranormal being in federal law enforcement, a singularity as you are now. A species that humans had no idea existed."

"What are you?"

"That information is above your security clearance," she said easily.

I gave a tiny nod to show that I was listening and, as I always did in the face of authority, took refuge in quotes. I said, "About singularities, 'nature hath framed strange fellows in her time.' And 'nothing can come of nothing.' So you were not, and are not, a singularity, not any more than I am."

Beneath my hand, the baby's leg jerked in her sleep and she made a little popping sound with her lips as she exhaled. Absently I patted her and adjusted the baby blanket. I had spent the first twelve years of my life surrounded by and taking care of young'uns, and I could soothe one in my sleep.

Soul watched and cocked her head to the side. "If you and your sisters are genetic, familial singularities?"

I shrugged as if that wouldn't bother me.

Soul said, "I was nearly fired my first week on the job for not following the rules and regs set down by the people in charge of my unit. I ended up saving a family of four who were being attacked by a werewolf, and this was before the weres were out of the paranormal closet." She smoothed her silver hair from her nape to her waist, curling the tail under. It looked like a self-comforting gesture. "It's an old story, and it proved nothing then or now, except that I have always put doing the right thing before the job."

Which meant that I had done the right thing in Soul's eyes. That was reassuring, not that I would share that either, saying instead, "To thine self be true."

She laughed, and it sounded like wind chimes. Mesmerizing. Like magic. I narrowed my eyes at her and she laughed again. "Shakespeare. They told me you liked to quote things instead of giving a direct answer."

"I always give a direct answer."

"You never give a direct answer." When I didn't reply, she said, "Then tell me what happened here."

"I don't know. But the thing or things under the ground? The shadow-and-light dancer? It likes you. It's been following you since you stepped onto the ground. Which you did without benefit of a car. How did you get here?"

"And you know this how?"

"I bled into the ground and now I know it. Don't ask me how. I don't know how I do what I do, or know what I know. Did you fly?"

"Of course not. This is a no-fly zone." Which sounded utterly irrelevant to the problem beneath our feet, the problem that was moving slowly in a circle, around and around beneath the tent, between us. I could feel the dancer, watching or sensing or whatever the blue blazes it was doing. Soul leaned toward me, and when she spoke there was something in her tone, a magical demand, an influence that burrowed into my skin and pricked my spirit. "How. Did. You. Know. When I stepped onto the land?"

I let a small smile onto my face, speaking with the church accent I had grown up with. "You ain't human, lady, and that ain't a secret anymore. Some secrets are like the wind, blowing where they will, for good or ill."

"More Shakespeare?"

"No. Just me." Before she could question further, I changed the subject. "What are you going to do with the baby?"

"Her name is Lisa Langston-Smith. Her mother and father are at the gate."

My eyes filled with unexpected tears at the sound of the name, and the fact that the baby wasn't an orphan. Another part of me unclenched and eased, a part I hadn't known was tight with worry. I had to wonder how many parts of me there were and how many were still clamped tight.

Soul clasped her hands. "Her aunt brought her here for a party while *babysitting*." Her tone said she wasn't impressed with the aunt's version of babysitting. "Social services has been called. Don't look at me like that. They'll work with the parents and I'm certain that her parents will get her back. Possibly, especially, now that the irresponsible aunt is no longer among the living."

Which was a coldhearted assessment. I crossed my arms over my chest. "When?"

"When will the parents get her back? As soon as social services protocols allow it."

I frowned hard, staring Soul down. In my best, formal, talk-like-a-special-agent voice, I said, "There have always been rumors that PsyLED wants magical beings for their research. Now they have a baby who survived what might prove to be a magical MED event. They'll take her to the labs and do tests first."

"Labs?" She looked amused.

"Government labs. Like all the ones in the Knoxville area. Like one of the ones that possibly contributed to this MED."

"Magic from a laboratory?" Her fingers made a little don't-be-an-idiot gesture. "Conspiracy theories. Foolishness shared by the uninformed and the uneducated."

"'Ignorance is the curse of God; knowledge is the wing wherewith we fly to heaven.' That was a roundabout way of saying that the government needs to prove itself if it wants to be considered among the angels."

Soul tilted her head to me, her eyes sharper than a hunting hawk's, a gesture that suggested I was being tested in ways I didn't understand. "Lisa will be taken to the University of Tennessee Medical Center, the same place you were taken and well cared for. She will receive all the medical care she requires. If a few vials of blood are drawn along the way and a few scans are run, they will not hurt the baby and might help us."

I glared at that.

Soul turned away and stepped out the cloth door.

The shadow-and-light dancer beneath the ground attacked.

SEVEN

The ground threw Soul up and forward; she landed, hard, on her left side. Roots erupted and three vines grabbed her ankle, climbing her leg, faster than my eyes could follow. Soul made a noise I had never heard anyone make before, a wind chime, violin, and wood flute sound all together.

I screamed, "Occam!" and dropped to my knees on the ground beside her. I grabbed the roots and heaved them away from her. But they were faster than I was. Her left leg was wrapped to the knee in vines that were fully leafed, the leaves deep green with black veins and a tarry petiole—the small stem from the bottom of the leaf to the larger stem. Soul's right foot was being pulled into the ground. I tore vines, freeing her right foot. Soul kicked at the ground, trying to crawl away. The roots began growing thorns and between one handful of roots and the next, half-inch-long thorns pierced my skin. My blood splattered on the ground. This was bad.

A white-clad form landed beside me and began hacking at the stems and roots with a vamp-killer, the silver-plated edge catching the light. Through the clear faceplate I recognized Occam. I tore up three vines, but they grew back faster than I could destroy them.

Rick fell beside me, a vamp-killer in his hand. He pushed me out of the way. "Get back inside before it decides you're tasty again too."

I stepped into the tent, but kept the door open, watching. Sucked the blood from my hands. I *felt* the thing in the ground, even through the tent bottom and the protective spells. If it had been a puppy, now it was a wolf, ripping and tearing at Soul's flesh.

The bloodlust I had thought I'd defeated rushed back. I forced it down, fighting the need to take Soul for the earth. The desire was a painful lump in my gut, in the rooty scars. Soul's powerful blood called to me.

The men whacked with their blades, burying the edges in the ground. The vines bled, but in the bright of day, it was a shiny, blackened color, like burned motor oil, cave-black with a hint of iridescent silver when the light hit it just right. The oily black stuff coated their blades and dripped to the ground. Soul was fighting, too, ripping at the vines, and her blood was scarlet, splattering in a wide arc. And everywhere blood landed, roots and vines thrust up from the earth, drinking it down. Searching for her.

Both men were shouting, their voices muffled beneath the suits. Soul's voice was unfettered, however, and she was screaming in that violin–wood flute voice, the pitch rising. Soul's legs began to glow, a pearlized radiance that looked as if they were lit from within.

"No! Soul! Don't!" Rick shouted through his faceplate. "You're almost free!"

But Soul's legs roiled beneath his hands and the men leaped back, both cursing. Light blasted out and Soul . . . twisted. Coiled. Her body shifting into something much larger. Lighter. A nacre-lit brilliance of light and energy, over twenty feet long. Massive back legs. Serpent face with curved and spiraled and spiked horns and opal white teeth and fangs. She swiveled her head to me, her eyes taking in the tent and me and . . . my bloodlust. She screamed in defiance and snapped her fangs at me. I leaped back, into the uncertain safety of the antispell tent. Soul's wings unfurled. She leaped for the sky, trumpeting fury and victory.

A light dragon.

An *arcenciel.*

Soul was an *arcenciel* . . . "Ohhh," I whispered, my mouth falling open.

Rick looked around, his face grim, noting where everyone was. Not one person beyond the radius of us three seemed to have noticed anything. No one came running. No one pointed at the sky where Soul had disappeared in a blast of light. No one had even seen the transformation except Rick, Occam, and me. As soon as I could get my mouth to rehinge, I smiled sweetly at Rick and said, "I guess Occam and me just gained a few points in our security clearances."

Rick cursed again and whacked the ground with his vamp-killer, cutting the vines that were still writhing and thrashing, splattering drops of that oily black stuff. I had to wonder if the silver-plated blades were killing whatever the growing viny thing was. Almost as if in answer to my question, the earth writhed, lifted, fell, and went still. Rick said to us, "This goes no further."

"Yes, boss," Occam said.

I took that as my cue. I picked up Lisa in her baby seat, slid her diaper bag strap over a shoulder, and walked out of the tent, past the men. Both were breathing hard. Neither said a word. Nothing in the ground tried to drag me under. Nothing paid any attention to me at all. On the way out, I paused and read the little girl and myself on a P 1.0. We were not contaminated, the girl reading human-normal, me reading me-normal. The baby hadn't touched the ground or the pond with bare skin, and I seemed to have some immunity to the *come-hither* spell. And when my blood had spilled during Soul's battle with the ground, the dancer hadn't bothered with me. Because Soul's blood was more powerful than mine. Yes.

Social services met me at the front gate. I had planned to give Lisa directly to the Langston-Smiths, in direct opposition to rules and regulations, but the social worker took her from my arms in an action that was so natural it must have looked as if turning her over was my intention all along. Media news vans captured the moment, which meant possibilities of national exposure. I hated the idea of my image being seen everywhere, but there was no stopping it. The child protective agency woman did allow Lisa's parents to hold their baby for a bit before they were all whisked off to UTMC. While the parents cried over their child, the social worker thanked me for being so helpful. And I felt like a traitor to the parents and to Lisa.

I had no faith in the system to do the right thing, despite the recent raid on the compound where I was raised and the removal of over a hundred children for sexual abuse. Some of them had been returned to families who should never have had access to kids. But the system was made up of people, and people made mistakes. They also often tried to do the right thing, so maybe this social worker would see to it that Lisa was returned to her parents. Or maybe not. I had to admit that I was not the person to be making such decisions, but it was still hard to see the weeping parents give their child over to the counselor as armed police looked on.

I should talk to Rick before leaving, I knew that. Proper protocol required that I, a probie who had not followed orders, be censured. I didn't want to hear him fire me. Or put me on desk duty. So I took refuge, as I had done in the past, by leaving. Rick called it running away. I called it going back to work.

I removed gear from T. Laine's car and hitched a ride back to HQ with a deputy who was heading that way. In the parking lot, I repacked my Chevy and drove off. I had done everything Rick had asked me to do except reading the land in North Carolina. That, I wanted to do alone, on Soulwood, and could, fired or not. If I was gonna get sacked or stuck at a desk, it might as well be a punishment I really earned. And since I had gone rogue, I might as well go rogue all the way.

The only person who seemed able to hang around contamination and contaminated people without giving in to it—not that anyone but me seemed to have noticed that yet—was me. That placed me in a unique position to find out things that could take the others days. But first I had to eat a late lunch and talk myself into a rebellion that was normally foreign to me.

I wasn't used to takeout, but I had heard the unit talk about the barbecue at Calhoun's on the River, and I called in an order. Calhoun's was on the Tennessee River, literally on the water, with a wharf for people to motor up to and park their boats. Or maybe dock them. Or moor them. I wasn't sure of the terminology. But the view was wonderful and as I waited for my meal to be packed up, I walked through the place enjoying the ambience. I even had a chance to walk out on the dock, right up to the water. But a sudden feeling of vertigo made me go back inside fast. I marked it to never having been that close to a big body of water, hunger, and the aftereffects of being lunch to the land. I checked my hands, and the slices must have been more superficial than I realized. They had closed already.

I was still getting accustomed to the prices at restaurants, after a lifetime of parsimonious living both on the church compound and as a poor widder-woman, and I gulped at the cost of one meal. I could feed myself for days on the price, which was over ten dollars. But I also had to admit that the hickory-smoked pork barbecue sandwich, which I ate in the parking lot, was as good as anything Daddy had put on the smoker back home. I even put down my cell and stopped reading texts and reports from the other members of the unit just to eat. When I was feeling less peckish, I put the trash in the back of the truck, in the garbage bag I kept there to be dropped off at the dump, and I dialed JoJo on my cell.

"Nell. What?"

"Ummm. T. Laine tried to get in the pond. I didn't. I held the baby and I didn't get weirded out. I think I'm immune to the magical whatever-it-is that's going on."

I could practically hear her mind ticking through the possibilities in the slice of silence between us. "That might keep your ass from getting fired. What do you want to do about it?"

"I want to go talk to the contaminated people at the hospital. And if they can't talk, then suss around a bit. See what I can learn."

There was more silence on the other end as JoJo worked things out. "You called me as second in command because Rick's pissed at you and you think he'd say no just to put you in your place."

"Yes."

"You are sneaky. I like that in a woman. Go to the hospital. Talk to whoever will talk to you. Then go to their houses in the neighborhood and see what you can see. I'll make it right with LaFleur." The call ended. I put the cell on the seat of the truck and thought about what I was about to do. Then I pulled out and into traffic, heading to my next stop. When I remembered to breathe, I smelled pork, but it was a good smell. Far better than the stink of death that clung to me from the pond.

The location of the paranormal unit wasn't listed anywhere on the website for the University of Tennessee Medical Center, and since I hadn't made it there when I was a patient in the emergency department, I had no idea where it might be. I flashed my badge and ID to security at the main emergency entrance and was given printed directions to the paranormal unit, on the other side of the hospital campus.

The paranormal unit wasn't identified as such, for security precautions against paranormal haters and terrorists. It was half of a hallway, sectioned off from a cancer center, via locking doors and security cameras. I showed my ID, made sure my badge was visible, and asked questions that no one wanted to answer. Patient confidentiality, HIPAA rules, and hospital regs stymied me until someone banged on the windowed wall to a patient's room and shouted that she wanted to talk to me. The nurse I was talking to ducked her head and said, "Sorry," before she scuttled away like a dog with its tail between its legs.

The woman in the room was dressed in a uni like PsyLED's, and beyond her, partially visible behind a privacy curtain, was a patient in a bed. The window banger was a family member of one of the contaminated humans, I guessed. And ticked off, if the hammering and the nurse's demeanor were any indication.

Still pounding on the window as she stripped out of the white uni with its orange stripe, the woman left the room and caught my arm. I got just enough of a glimpse inside to see that the patient within was restrained to the bed and that she was restless, struggling weakly.

The woman shook my arm. "What in God's name are my family being held for?" she demanded, her voice hushed but carrying along the hallway.

"Held?" The word sounded clueless, which I was. I wondered if she had been contaminated, some kind of magical psychotic break, and I pulled my arm free, backing away.

"Under arrest?" she said, her voice rising. When I looked blank, she said, "In this hospital? Tied down? I've been trying all day to get my girls free and take them home to South Carolina, to a hospital where I can get some answers and decent treatment. They aren't doing *anything* for my babies here." She leaned in to me, her tear-filled eyes like daggers, and said, "I want them released to me *right now*, or charged for whatever crime they're accused of committing."

I blinked and understood several things at once. One, no one had told the families about the paranormal part of the incident. They must be trying to keep it quiet. Two, I was the first person from PsyLED who had been on scene in the hospital. Three, we needed someone in authority to talk to the families, not me. Four, I shouldn't have called JoJo. I should have asked Rick if it was okay for me to come here. And five, the media hadn't figured out the sick families were connected to the goose pond deaths.

"Oh," I said, stalling. Needing verification, I asked, "No one has talked to you?"

"No. Not to any of us family members. And we're ready to go straight to the media if we don't get answers soon."

"Ummm." *Soul.* Soul was the spox, the spokesperson, the person who should be answering questions. But Soul had been attacked, had transformed and disappeared. I was pretty sure that Soul would have come here after the goose pond, but she had flown away, which wasn't something I could say aloud. "No one's under arrest."

"Then why—"

"Quarantined."

That gave her pause. "For what?"

"We aren't sure yet."

Her tears had dried and her eyes narrowed at me in such a way as to make me need to assure her. "We really, *really* don't know yet, but that's why you have to wear the special white suits when you're in contact with any patient. Truly, they are getting the *very best* care available." That last part might be a lie, because I had no idea if another hospital had better paranormal units and better paranormal specialists than UTMC. But at the moment, assurance was as important as breaking down facts about hospitals.

Comforting people hadn't been a part of the training in Spook School, but it was big part of life in the church. If she had been a churchwoman, I'd have given her a hug and led her to a private place to talk. Instead I said, "Can I buy you a cup of coffee?"

She scratched her fingers through her hair, making it stand up in a faded reddish halo. "Child, I'd kill for a cup." Then, as if hearing her own words to a law enforcement officer, she said, "Not really. I mean not literally."

I smiled at her and said, "I understood. Let's go to the nearest hospital cafeteria or hospital coffee shop. My treat."

"Let me tell the others that I have someone to talk to. Just a sec." The middle-aged woman knocked on one door and then another, talking in hushed tones to family members inside. Then she led the way to the coffee shop nearest, where I got us coffees and we introduced ourselves to each other.

The woman's name was Dougie Howell, pronounced Dug-ee, which was odd but kinda cool. Dougie downed the strong, cheap coffee like she had spent a week in a desert without liquids. She was the mother and grandmother of three of the patients, the grandmother-in-law of two others, and while her hair had dulled down to a strawberry-blondish gray, she still had the take-charge-and-fight-to-the-death qualities of some red-headed churchwomen I knew.

Most important to me, she was willing to talk. Her daughter's name was Alisha Henri, and though she didn't look old enough to be a grandmother in the regular world, Dougie had granddaughters: Kirsten Harrell and Sharon Sayegh. All three had been in Alisha's house, along with one's partner and the other's husband. From Dougie, I learned that her daughter and granddaughters had been hit hard by the . . . the whatever this was. The two others—the ones not blood related—were, oddly, already asymptomatic, mobile, coherent, and demanding release. Dougie's girls were in bad shape, and I wondered if the blood relationship might allow something in the paranormal energies access to them. I had studied blood demons in Spook School. If that was what this was, it was going to be a nasty piece of work.

I bought her a second cup while she adapted to being out of her daughter's room and back in reality. Dougie looked tired and terrified, but was the kind of woman who went to battle when frightened, instead of going into hiding—a warrior instead of a rabbit. When I placed the second paper cup of fresh coffee in front of her, she asked, "What's wrong with my girls? Why is PsyLED interested in them? Why are *you* here?"

I sighed. I really wished I hadn't shown up at the hospital. "I'm here because fools rush in where angels fear to tread?" I said, making it a question. "Honestly there are several agencies involved in the case and I don't know what we're looking for or what we'll learn. Not yet. We're trying to rule out everything right now, from bacterial infection to ancient aliens."

"There aren't really ancient aliens, are there?" she asked, her mouth and tone trying for levity when there was nothing amusing about her situation at all.

I turned my paper coffee cup in a circle on the table and said ruefully, "I hope not, but the world is so crazy it might make better sense if there were." Dougie lifted her eyebrows at me and I grinned at her. "Sure. Ancient aliens. Bigfoot. The Loch Ness Monster. And the chupacabra. Why not?"

She chuckled. "All of those here in Knoxville? Aren't we lucky."

I refrained from humming spooky music, a reaction that came from Spook School but would have been totally inappropriate. Instead I said, "Can you tell me about your daughter and granddaughters?"

"The girls are in town for a Thanksgiving vacation. My house is too small, so they stayed with Alisha, in their old bedrooms. We're going to have Thanksgiving togeth—" She stopped, and appeared to be revising the big holiday plans. Her eyes filled with tears again, but she licked her lips, which were badly chapped, took a slow breath, and started over. "The plan was to have Thanksgiving dinner together at Alisha's. The girls and their spouses got in yesterday evening. I saw them all over dessert, around seven last night. I went home about nine. There was a game on and the spouses had gone upstairs to watch. Alisha, Kirsten, and Sharon were still sitting at the kitchen table over a glass of wine." Dougie was holding the cup of coffee like a lifeline, her eyes staring into a distance that was suddenly full of uncertainty.

I said, "I'm on my way to Alisha's house. Is there anything I should know? Anything you can tell me about what was going on with them in the hours before the . . . event?"

"Warrant?"

"The FBI probably already has one," I said gently. "I'll just be there to do a little paranormal scouting around."

"They're in her house? Who? Alisha would hate that."

"Probably everyone. And just a word to the wise: the house will be a shambles when they finish."

Dougie heaved out a breath that sounded as if it had been held too long. "God. This is a nightmare." She finished off the second cup of coffee and pushed herself away from the table. "Would you lock up when they're done? And call me with what you find?"

"I can call. Locking up depends on what's happening when I leave the house. But I can promise to keep you in the loop to the best of my ability and security clearance level."

Dougie firmed her shoulders and said, "In other words, you may never know what the problem is, any more than I might." I turned my palm up in a that's-the-way-things-are-sometimes gesture. She rocked her head on her neck, communicating frustration and disappointment and a need to stretch or run or hit something. "Go do whatever you want. Just find me some answers, okay?"

"I'll do my best."

On the way, I called Rick and confessed that I had stopped at the hospital—with JoJo's permission. He wasn't happy, made some comments about me going behind his back, rodeoing again, but he ended up agreeing that I should go to Alisha's house and "initiate a prelim eval. Occam just got there. Meet him. He has lead."

"Okay."

"Not just *okay*, Nell. This is your first case. You are *not lead* on this. Understand? You have special talents that make you important to PsyLED, but you are on probationary status. You work with a team, not solo. You will run things by me *before* you do them. Everything. By me."

I thought it through for a moment that stretched too long before saying, "Copy that. How's Soul?"

Rick made a *hunh* noise, followed by his own silence. "Follow orders." He hung up.

I wasn't sure what point I had made, but it must have been a good one.

The neighborhood streets had been cordoned off to the public, the residents had been evacuated, and the media was out in force at the site of what was being called a "possible viral outbreak of unknown origin." I had to park two blocks away, but managed to snag a parking spot near Occam's sporty car. My old Chevy C10 looked out of place, and I dug in my glove box for the small ID card to set in my window to keep from being towed, and picked up the P 2.0. By the time I opened the door, Occam was there, with a quiet "Nell, sugar. This way."

He guided me away from the media vans and the telescopic lenses and the crowd of onlookers, between two houses, and along a back fence, to the house Rick had designated as Point A. I paused to check the GPS and knew it wasn't Alisha's home, and I almost followed Occam inside the one-story house, where he was already dressing in one of the antispell 3PE unis. But the house looked crowded and intense, full of law enforcement personnel: FBI CSI, PsyCSI, uniformed cops, plainclothes detectives, and special agents, all wanting to get a look at the scene. Car-wreck rubberneckers had nothing on law enforcement officers wanting to get in on something interesting.

But the victims of the MED had been discovered in their yards. I motioned to Occam, pointing to myself and then in a circular motion around me, saying that I'd stay outside and look around. He motioned back, bending and placing his palm flat on the ground, then stood and gave me a thumbs-down with both hands, telling me not to put my hand on the ground for a read. I laughed and gave him a thumbs-up. He tossed a uni off the porch in my general direction and disappeared inside.

With the uni draped over a shoulder and the P 2.0 under the same arm, I wandered. The lawn was uninteresting, with boring landscaping plants, recently trimmed and shaped, a fake wishing well, some half-hidden garden gnomes, and dozens of mums. There was also a floorless tent set up on the front lawn and inside were three techs, standing along the walls, each with a handheld psy-meter 1.0, each dressed in a white uni with the ugly orange stripe across the chest.

I stopped outside the door, leaned in, flipped my jacket open to show my badge and held up my ID. I said, "Hi. I'm Special Agent Nell Ingram, with PsyLED."

I stopped. I had never identified myself that way before. The words sent an electric thrill through me, and I grinned uncontrollably, too wide, too excited. I forced my mouth to neutral, ducked my head in embarrassment, and extended the device in my hand. "I have a psy-meter 2.0. Can I do a reading?"

The responses were varied: "Holy shit, yes." "Hi, Nell." And "Thank God, I thought you guys would never get here. Where's your uni?"

I gave a quick shrug and pulled the uni out where they could see it. "Got one. I measured the goose pond. I wanted to measure the newest sites too."

"Goose pond," a female tech repeated. "I hear there's bodies there."

"Lots," I said, instantly seeing the bodies in the pond. On the ground. My chest went tight for a moment. "It was pretty bad." And I realized that I had put my feelings on hold, my thinking about the deaths on hold. Stuffed it all back into some dusky, nameless part of my mind, to deal with later. Much later. Not now.

"Get dressed out and get in here," she said. "I'm Karen Lynne, FBI CSI, and this is my partner, Amanda Gray. We're dying to know what's going on."

I lifted a hand in a half wave.

The man said, "I'm Special Agent Kevin Riley, FBI. I'm not lead, but I'm the only one here who thinks the yard is just as important as the house."

"Of course it is," I said, agreeing. "Lemme get outfitted."

It wasn't like it was portrayed on TV, all solemn and tense or, conversely, full of wisecracking. It was all about the evidence we had seen and cataloged, the tech we were using, and about the victims and what they had in common—which was nothing but the location and bloodlines. It was sharing info, which was unusual in law enforcement, because every agency and every well-established agent wanted the collar, wanted any arrest to be listed under their name and badge number, wanted to be the one on camera at a news conference. But it turned out that we were all newbies, probies, too excited being "on the job," too eager learning and doing to hoard info and data. And because there were no bodies here, we were having too much fun. Not something that TV showed, that the job could be fun. And maybe I needed this after the pond and the hospital.

I showed them the psy-meter 2.0, took readings in the tent and outside in the rest of the front yard, the driveway, and the backyard. I listened to the scuttlebutt that they had overheard from the agents inside. They told me about the violent scene inside that I hadn't heard about until now. There were two bodies inside the house, two twentysomethings, probably killed by the father, who had been naked in the front yard, walking with the rest of his family, covered in blood spatter. The two young men had died from blunt force trauma. I was glad I was outside, not in the house with Occam.

We chatted. I got help setting up a grid in the tent and a bigger one in the yard. I took measurements and they searched for physical evidence.

Just before I finished working up the grounds, I noticed

something about the landscaping that had escaped detection on first glance. Something on the plants.

It was a coating of black mold, crawling up the exposed roots and larger stems of several well-pruned boxwoods, planted between the front porch and the evidence tent. The mold discoloration stopped there, but the shrubs didn't look like they had been treated, so it was likely to spread. Oddly there was no evidence of mold on the boxwoods in the backyard or the other plants or trees in the yard. And it didn't resemble black knot, slime flux, or sooty mold. It was slimy in places, with little antennae-like things in other places, and there were things like fruiting bodies lifting on the slick but pebbled surface. Maybe some form of fungal mycelia, not that I knew much about molds. I never got them like this on my land except on deadwood—fallen limbs or trees, decaying in the shadows. Molds were necessary in decay, and some symbiotic relationships that helped both plants, but there was no decay here, at least aboveground, and this didn't look beneficial to the host plant. Fungal diseases can affect roots, leaves, needles, trunks, and vascular systems of living trees and shrubs. They were a sign that something else was amiss in the environment: the soil, or the water.

If I had to guess, the front boxwoods were dying, yet the leaves were still green, the inside of the stems appeared healthy when I broke one, and when I dug into the soil, there was no indication of deeper root problems. It seemed important, but I couldn't say why, and I was, admittedly, a plant person, not an experienced agent. I was likely to think inside a plant box when none existed.

When I couldn't verbalize why the black mold was important, the other techs wandered away, uninterested in my discovery. And they had a point, summed up by Riley. "What could mold have to do with three families going whacky?"

Molds did a lot of bad stuff, including causing hallucinations, but three families? All at the same time? In exactly the same way? When it wasn't affecting the rest of us? It wasn't likely. I made a note in my tablet—not the easiest thing to do wearing the uni's gloves—took a photo, and, just to be on the safe side, I scraped off some mold into an evidence bag and sealed it. Then I went to get Occam. I wanted to see the other houses.

I wasn't lead agent. I had to check in. I felt tethered. And stubbornly resistant to being tethered. But I remembered something my mama had often said when I was young. *"I may not always like it, but I can work in the system."* For her, "the system" had been church and an extended family and sister-wives and many, *many* children to help raise. For me, the system was law enforcement.

Occam caught my eye at the back door of the house, changing out of his uni, and putting on a new one. His face was set into hard lines, cool and unemotional, and the sight of his expression made me even happier that I had stayed outside. "You okay?" I asked.

"No. This sucks. The kids were beaten in a circular pattern. He used a crowbar. Started at their heads and worked his way around the beds in clock patterns, twelve blows ending back at their heads."

"Clockwise or widdershins?"

"Bloodstains suggest clockwise." Clockwise was a direction used in witch workings. He cursed softly and rubbed his forehead. "I'm glad Rick made Tandy sit this one out at the office. Even the fish in the aquarium are swimming in a circle."

Silent after the terse words, Occam led the way to the next house, both of us wearing clean antimagic unis. The next house was Point B, Alisha Henri's two-story home, with an open, empty double garage and three family cars parked in the drive, two of them from out of state. Occam paused at the driveway and said, "The FBI SAC just spoke with the hospitalist at UTMC. Two people from this house are currently asymptomatic. They don't have a theory yet why only the two from this one house seem to be fully recovered, when the rest of the people from all three houses are still exhibiting psychosis."

The SAC was the special agent in charge, a deliberate reminder that we didn't have true lead on this site. The FBI did. I stuck out my tongue at him and he laughed, the shadows in his eyes vanishing for a moment, the dimple popping into place. "Thanks. I needed that." He lifted a hand in a half wave and went inside Alisha's house. I walked around the yard, taking readings, this time alone and without a tent. The area where the family had been walking in a circle was taped off with crime scene tape and was still redlining. Before I could get more than that accomplished, Occam shouted, "Ingram! In here."

Ingram. Not "Nell, sugar." *Good.* I jogged to the porch and when I entered, found Alisha's place to be much more empty than I expected. Only two middle-aged feds, wearing wrinkled suits, unis zipped open, half off and hanging on their hips, suit-coats sweat-stained, ties pulled loose at their necks, were in the house.

"I want some P 2.0 measurements inside too," Occam said to me. To the two others, he said, "Ingram. Probie. A whiz with the new tech."

The feds grunted without looking up. Occam placed a hand-sketched floor plan into my free fingers. "Read each room and record the results," he instructed, his face less grim than earlier, his eyes holding something I couldn't place.

"Probie work," I muttered, as if it bothered me. Occam snapped his fingers three times, fast, as if telling me to hurry up. "And when you get through, we can chat."

I didn't know what he thought I might find, but I started the readings at the front door, working around the two agents, who were both human. The first floor took less than half an hour, and I ended on the second floor, in what looked like a man cave, with a minikitchen, wide-screen TV, chips in bowls, two colas open on side tables. A cat sat in the corner on a cat climber stand that went to the ceiling, the carpeted leap shelves crossing in front of the window where the cat could stare out at birds by day. As I did the readings, I began to get a feeling that Occam wanted me to pick up on something. And I did. I rechecked the levels on both floors before I found him in the kitchen with the feds, looking over the evidence footage—because without a crime being committed here, they couldn't be called forensic photography or crime scene photos—collected by the first responders. The shots were of Alisha; Kirsten Harrell; her partner, Sally Clements; and Sharon Sayegh, and her husband, Adam Sayegh.

I pushed my way between Occam and a cop and studied the video too. The family all wore nightclothes and were barefoot, walking in a circle. All five had their eyes open, shoulders rounded, stumbling as if sleep-walking. In the vid, police and paramedics approached slowly. The five kept walking. Until a city police officer touched one of the men on the shoulder as if to pull him around. The cop stopped, his back rigid. The man kept walking. Seconds passed. The cop stepped toward the group and tried to join the walkers. Another cop yanked him back, across the yard, and the rest of the officers pulled them both away.

That was interesting. "Is the cop who touched one of them, without a uni, okay?"

"He's okay," the bald guy said. "He'll get a reprimand for being a dumb-ass, but he's okay."

"Ingram," Occam said. "Readings and analysis?"

"Question first. I've seen two houses. Is this the only two-story?"

The bald cop swiveled until he faced me and crossed his arms over his chest. "Yeah. Why?"

"I won't know until I take readings of the other houses, but I have a theory based on the second story and the cat."

"Based on the cat?" The cop laughed as if he thought I was a silly female. He probably thought all females were silly.

I narrowed my eyes at him and went on. "We have redline readings all over the first floor. Upstairs reads in the low normal range on three psysitope levels and only redlines in psysitope level three. Because I know you guys are *unschooled* and *ignorant* about paranormal events, I'll explain."

Occam's mouth quivered with a suppressed smile at my tone. Too bad. I didn't like being talked down to because of my gender.

"Each of the four levels read by the P 2.0 is specific for each creature species. Witches read high in psysitope one. Weres read high in psysitope three, midrange in psysitopes one and two, and psysitope four nearly zero. The upstairs reads like a were-creature. The difference in readings seems significant. The fish at Point A were swimming in circles, but the cat on the second level here is sitting easy.

"Of the five people who were hospitalized from this house, two victims have already gotten better. Upstairs, two colas were open, two recliners were stretched out, two bowls of chips, and the TV was on, though someone had muted it at some point. Having talked to a visitor who was here last night, I confirmed that three blood-related females were in the kitchen drinking wine and two unrelated people were upstairs watching the game.

"I'd say that the contamination, whatever it is, is low to the ground. It's also possible that it's bloodline specific."

The bald-headed cop kept his eyes on me but spoke to Occam. "This the little girl who brought down Benton?"

I felt my cheeks heat at the little-girl comment. Thomas Benton the fourth had been the head of the Knoxville FBI. He had not been human. "Yes, I am," I said, silently adding, *you creepy misogynist.* I smiled sweetly instead, but looked him up and down, head to foot. "He was a Welsh *gwyllgi.* A devil dog. Something you *boys* missed entirely." With that, this *little girl* got out of there. Before I said something that could get me fired.

As I walked out the door, the bald cop asked Occam, "What the hell was that about?"

"You called her 'little girl.'"

"She *is* little. And young enough to be my daughter."

I had a feeling that the bald cop had ongoing gender and age sensitivity issues. Stuff I had learned in a half-day seminar on diversity at Spook School. Behind me, Occam answered, and I slowed to hear.

"You meet her at a church social, you can attempt to address her any way you want, hoss," Occam said, a thread of something I couldn't identify in his tone. "On the job? She's a competent field agent. Learn some professional manners or go home.

"And before you try to make this *your* assessment, I've already documented that Special Agent Ingram offered her professional expertise and conclusions. And I'll be sending that up the line to your boss, the ADIC, Penny Francoeur. And, hey. You call *her* 'little girl' too? How's she like that?"

No one answered. I heard Occam leave the house behind me and I hurried to put some space between me and my bad temper. And my hero. I had seldom been protected in my life; it was nice having someone stand up for me, and I couldn't hide the smile on my face.

The third house, Point C, was easy to find. It was on a triangle from the first two, and it was full of cops. Because here, like at the other single-story house, there were dead inside.

A middle-aged man and two elderly people, a man and woman, had died violently, and the bodies were still on scene while CSI and PsyCSI worked up the site. The specialized team from outside Washington, DC, had sent enough techs to cover multiple sites, the pond, the other houses, and here. Thankfully I wouldn't have to work up this site with the P 2.0. That had already been done, by the DC team with their own 2.0 device, but it didn't stop me from having to see the house and the killing scene.

Occam said, "You need the experience, Nell. If you're gonna remain a PsyLED special agent, you'll see plenty of these scenes."

"Yeah?" I challenged my former (like two minutes past) hero. "How many have *you* seen?"

"Before today? Four. Four scenes with dead bodies. One of them children. After today that brings my total to seven."

I screwed my face up into something worse than a frown, but when Occam stripped out of his dirty uni, I changed out of mine. At the door, we put on fresh 3PEs. I was not looking forward to this. Every time I blinked my eyes, I saw the dead bodies floating in the pond. I never had nightmares, and I wondered if that was about to change.

The house was an open floor plan, tastefully furnished in greens with white cabinetwork, trim, and woodwork. The place smelled of fresh paint and the stink of new furniture. The neutral-toned carpet was brand-new clean, and the furniture was upholstered in a pleasing mix of fabrics. It wasn't a house where young children lived, but looked like the house of empty nesters who had only recently finished redecorating. Maybe just in time for children and parents to come for Thanksgiving. There were three bedrooms in the main part of the house, all showing signs of having been used the night before, and a separate suite in the back that appeared to have been added on. The suite was where the bodies had been found, a bloody track of bare footprints on the new carpet, leading from it.

At the end of the footprint track, a body lay. The middle-aged man had been shot with a handgun about a dozen times. I didn't try to count. In the back suite, an elderly couple had been beaten to death, but unlike the young men in the other one-story house, these two hadn't gone down without a fight. It was clear that the elderly woman had shot her attacker, emptying her weapon into him, but he hadn't died fast enough, not until after he had struck both of the elders in the heads with a baseball bat.

I had seen plenty of killings in my life—hogs, cattle, chickens, sheep, goats. I had been on-site when deer and wild boar were processed. I had studied crime scene photos in Spook School. I might have thought that the blood of those deaths would have inured me to most anything. It hadn't begun to harden me to violent murder scenes. The smells were the unexpected part. At the pond, the air had carried the stench of death away. Here, it was contained and rank. The sickly sweet scent of old blood, the stink of bowels and bladders released in death were all stronger than the fresh-paint smell. The sight of blood in sprays up the soft green walls and soaked into the pale bedding was still fresh—bright and vivid. I feared for a moment that I'd be attacked by bloodlust again, but it didn't happen. I wasn't on Soulwood and the bodies weren't on soil, but on floors, so maybe that was the reason.

I stood in the doorway, doing what I was supposed to do. Getting used to the awfulness of what people did to people. The horror of violence. The utter helplessness of being too late to help, too little to save. I studied each body, teaching my insides not to react, not to feel. Not to throw up.

When I had all I could stand, I left the house, peeling off the uni, throwing everything into the evidence bag at the back door. I went straight to my truck. It hadn't been towed, but a media person had parked herself at my vehicle, and I nearly plowed her down to get past. She was sleek and polished, with long dark hair and enough makeup to make a good Halloween mask. She finally got out of my way and then out of the way of my truck, as I pulled off. If I made the evening news as an uncooperative law enforcement officer, that would be a good way to end my day.

The tears started on the way home. I had to slow down and then pull over so I could cry, snotting and wailing. I don't cry pretty. Never have. But when the misery was cried out, I pulled back into traffic and continued home, with a promise to myself to put some handkerchiefs in the car for next time.

EIGHT

Back at my house, I felt empty and raw, as if my heart and soul were abraded and bleeding. I went directly to the garden, where I picked some spinach that had survived the cold, some late squash, and two pumpkins that were in a protected place and were still good, and dug up a batch of turnips and greens. I carried them inside with me, where I kicked off my boots and washed and cut up veggies, walking the floors in my wool socks, feeling the land through the wood flooring that had once grown here, on Soulwood. I was shaky and mad for reasons I wasn't quite sure of, and the Calhoun's BBQ had worn off long ago. I was sick to the stomach and yet also hungry, which made no sense at all, except as an indication that I was confused and mad and distressed.

Though I hadn't had time to buy groceries since I got back, I had plenty of home-canned goods that I could whip up in a hurry. I should put something together. But my brain wasn't clear enough to know what I wanted to eat.

Moving on instinct and habit, I added wood to the stove and put the greens in a pot to simmer with salt and fatback from the freezer and a few red peppers. I added a couple of whole, unshelled pecans to keep the stink down. The sliced pumpkin went into the oven to roast. I doubted the unit would like turnip greens or roasted pumpkin. Lots of city people didn't, and cats hated the greens. Still antsy and hungry, I stood in front of the pantry and finally chose a Ball jar of spicy field peas. I made some instant rice, and mixed it together with a can of tuna that made the cats come running. It was dinner, tasteless except for the spices in the peas. And I didn't particularly love tuna. But I forced myself to eat, and to not think, not think about anything.

Not about the deaths. Not about the bodies in the pond and on the shore. Not about the bodies in the back suite at the last house. *Not*. But again I couldn't stop the tears. No matter the classes in paranormal crimes and the crime scene photos, this was not what I had expected my job with PsyLED to be about. I didn't know what I had expected, but . . . not this.

Shoveling food in, I kept turning my thoughts away, but it was like herding cats. They kept returning to the blood and the death, just as I kept shooing cats off the long table and away from my tuna, an endless loop of failure. But eventually my belly got full and my shakes decreased. I began to calm and stabilize. Mostly the tuna was gone and the cats wandered away in a snit.

But my eyes were still leaking and my heart felt funny, so I took off my socks and carried a clean, folded quilt made by Leah years ago out to the edge of my woods, to the married trees, put the quilt, still folded, on the ground, and sat down on the pad it made. The weather had turned cold. My bare toes were already frozen. They would be even colder soon.

I rearranged my legs and placed my bare feet onto the earth and my palms flat on the ground beside me, and sank my thoughts into the land. In an instant, Soulwood recognized me and enfolded me. Warmth flooded me, the way a mother hugs a child, reaching all inside me, embracing me. I closed my eyes and breathed out the worry, the fear, and the anger that I had been carrying. The grief. I sank into the dimness and the deep of the land, into the broken stone of the mountain's heart, stone canted up in some massive, ancient earthquake. And I simply breathed. Felt the land fill me, felt it hold me.

Let it tell me that death and life were an endless loop. That life and death were nature's way. That all things, no matter how cruel seeming, were part of living. That I was loved now when I was alive, and I would be loved when I was dust and ashes and my soul was set free.

I relaxed. Let my shoulders droop. Stretched out my legs. I breathed. And breathed. My heart beat. Time passed. When my spirit was soothed and quiet, I remembered Rick's orders, issued so much earlier in the day. I curled my legs up into a modified guru position, icy toes inserted into my inner knees, between my thighs and calves, and thought about what I wanted to do. I reached out and around, reading the land.

In the near distance, twisted into a protective ball, was the evil that was Brother Ephraim. There was nowhere to hide, but he was coiled as far from me as he could get, bowed against the boundary that was Soulwood, against the barrier to the land on the other side of the hill, the church compound. Ephraim had been a churchman before I'd fed him to the earth. I didn't regret killing him. Not at all. Some people just needed killing. But as I studied him, huddled there, as far away as possible, I did wonder, not for the first time, if I had fed him to the land wrongly in some manner. Maybe there was a methodology I had lucked up on the other time I'd fed Welsh *gwyllgi* to the earth. Or maybe *gwyllgi* didn't feed the earth as well as humans, and I had messed up North Carolina too. Or . . . maybe Soulwood was so different from the rest of the Earth that it refused to absorb some foul things. That felt possible. Right, even.

But I didn't know. And I was honestly afraid to find out.

Near Ephraim, something glimmered. I turned my attention to that odd bit of energy, but it was gone as quickly as it had appeared. A moment later it glimmered again. Something that rested within the earth near Brother Ephraim. Something was . . . active. When it sparked, I felt an answering flicker closer to me. Much closer.

Curious. Whatever it was, it wasn't right. Something was different in Soulwood. Something the land didn't recognize as new and altered. Something bad.

The glimmer came again, and I realized there was a precise interval between appearances, like a pulse, beating back along . . . There! It was beating back along a thin, microscopic strand of something. Not the same kind of something that trailed from the surface triangle to the dancer, to the sleeper, but similar. I had no words for what it was. But something was beating from the wickedness that was Ephraim, into my woods. Directly to the place where Brother Ephraim had been absorbed into the earth. And then that energy pulsed back to his shadow. I studied it. It was nothing like the shadow/light dancer. It was a back-and-forth pulsation along a thin thread of . . . something else unknown.

Brother Ephraim had been almost dead when I'd accepted him into my land. Eaten and chewed on by a black wereleopard. By Paka. That crime should have brought her a death sentence. Killing a human, biting a human, always was a death sentence. It was a grindylow's job to mete out justice against were-creatures who broke that cardinal rule. Justice always meant killing were-creatures who bit humans. *Always.* But Pea had been easy to convince otherwise. Pea the grindylow hadn't killed her for it. Later we had learned that Ephraim wasn't human. Pea had known when none of us had.

And maybe that was important here and now.

Pea hadn't been a judge in his death because Brother Ephraim hadn't been human, and therefore two things: he wasn't within her jurisdiction, and he wasn't an acceptable sacrifice to the earth. And perhaps that was also why he was still separate, a discrete energy trapped in Soulwood. Brother Ephraim had been a Welsh *gwyllgi*, and had also been pure evil as a human. Whatever the cause, he had found a way to keep some part of himself from being absorbed into the earth. On some level, he was still self-aware.

And now he was doing . . . something. That pulsing back and forth. And he assumed I didn't see it.

I pulled my consciousness into me and thought through my options. I stood, pulled socks and boots onto my cold feet, got a flashlight, John's old machete, and the limb lopper from the porch, and walked into the shadows, to the place where I feared, where I knew, the pulse was converging. Deep into the shadows of the trees.

Soulwood was composed of trees that had once been standard-sized trees, ordinary twenty-five-year-old trees, the biggest with boles twelves inches or so in diameter. Then I had fed the land the first time, and . . . things had changed. The trees had begun to grow. Now the trunks were big enough that three men holding hands couldn't stretch around most of them. They were the size of four-hundred-year-old trees. Even older. Because of my magic. My evil.

As I came around the massive boles, I could hear the trickle of water from the spring that fed the small clay-bottomed pool. Could hear the chitter of squirrels and the call of birds. Could smell the stench of pond water, full of decaying organic matter. I realized that I hadn't smelled the usual pondish stench at the goose pond. Odd, but not calamitous. On my first visit, I had been excited and possibly missed it. The smell of dead humans had been strong enough to mask it on my second visit.

The flash guiding my way, I stepped high, over a root that was bigger than only a few months past, and into the clearing, setting my eyes on the high branch overhead where the Brother had hung, bleeding out his life. Below that limb, on the ground where I had put my hand to take his dark heart and his life from him, there was a something new. A damp place that smelled of rot. I scanned the entire area with the light.

Around me, leaves that had fallen in the last two months were piled in drifts, against roots and the trunks of trees and in hollows. Everywhere except in this one place. Here, the ground was slimy with something rotten. Here was a mushed, decomposing mass, reddish in color—the color of blood—and in the center of the mushy puddle was a sapling.

It wasn't uncommon for new trees and plants to grow on Soulwood. But this one was unusual.

The young tree was about seven feet tall with two roots rising above the ground before twisting and growing into a slim stalk of trunk. Two branches divided at about five feet high and reached out to the sides and up, bending midway like elbows. It was strangely humanoid shaped, though there was no head, just a slight rise in the trunk, as if a head might someday grow there. The sapling's bark, if it had bark, was a smooth layer the color of blood, a slimy scarlet skin that dripped like blood but stank of tannins and rot.

There were thorns as long as my index finger on the trunk.

Like the other trees at this time of year, the sapling was leafless, but this tree . . . It looked as if it had never grown leaves. As if it never would. It was ugly and stark, a foul thing that simply *felt* evil. A wound growing up from the ground, a blight in the earth, a sin on the perfection of Soulwood, an evil trespassing here. A curse on the land.

I set the flash on a rock and aimed it at the tree. Walked over the mushy dirt, machete in one hand, the lopper in the other, careful to make certain that I didn't sink into the ground, cautious that it was not quicksand or something worse. I set the long-armed loppers down and took a careful stance, a two-hand grip on the machete. I hacked four strong cuts, putting my full body into the swings, trying to cut through the trunk. I knew how to torque my body into the action of a machete or an ax. I cut my own stove wood year round. I cleaned out my garden. But the wood of the thin trunk was too hard, as if it were crimson ironwood, though the scarlet surface of the wood didn't resemble the bark of any of the species called that.

As I whacked, a dozen thorns flew free, but my blade didn't mar the wood of the trunk, so I took up the lopper and pruned off both of the limbs, feeling my muscles clench and strain to cut through. The wood squeaked as I worked, not an unusual sound—metal on wood—but this sounded almost like a kitten crying, a mewling, piteous whimper. I tossed the limbs to the path, to take back with me. On the cut trunk, a bloody sap pooled. It had a tacky, oily consistency, and even in the poor light I could see it was scarlet as mammal blood, but clear, shiny, and thick as syrup.

I didn't know what this meant. I had no idea. But whatever it was, it was bad. Soulwood was wounded. And it was my fault.

I put my hand on the diseased earth and felt down into the land. The diseased part below my hand was partially encapsulated. As if Soulwood had put a wall around it, the way a human body might sometimes encapsulate an infection, making a cyst around it. But the thing that was Ephraim had found a way to link to this spot, along that tiny line that pulsed with faint power.

I reached out along it, following it to the curled presence of Ephraim, who withdrew like a wounded cat, angry and spitting. Mad that I had figured out he was up to something. But the thing I followed didn't end at Ephraim. It wrapped around him, and then continued out on the other side, another line of darkness, down, and . . . into the church compound.

I knew instantly that Ephraim was attached to the tree on the compound, the one that had healed me and had grown roots inside of me, into me, roots that had changed me and mutated the tree. Roots that I could still feel, like ropey scars on my middle. Roots that might be allowing me to sense the earth with greater clarity. Ephraim had found a way to escape Soulwood, to reach out beyond the land. He was back in the church. And if he had found the tree that had healed me, that had grown roots inside me, then he might have found a way into *me*. I withdrew quickly. I had to get to the church.

For the first time in my life, I was afraid of the earth, afraid of a growing, living thing.

I had been wary before, yes. But not afraid. Not until now.

I stood and carried my tools and the lopped branches back to my quilt. I dropped them on the ground several feet away and sat again, worried and discomfited, but still needing to do the readings I had promised Rick. Sundown had darkened the sky from red and purple, a livid bruise on the heavens, to a magenta-streaked black. I wanted to be inside, and soon.

I calmed myself again, and when I could breathe without a hitch, I let my mind reach out to the pond and its dead humans and dead geese. I didn't expect to sense so far.

But I saw the shining shadow/light dancer. After being in contact with Soulwood, I could sense it all better; it was clear now, sharp and easy to discern. The dancer moved in a twisted circle, like . . . like a loosely formed infinity loop. That was what it was called in witch workings. The energies were bright and crisp, a red, blue, yellow, and green ring of light, interspersed with pinpoints of blackness, like the blackness of space, that spun and danced in the earth. I studied it, watching and analyzing. Its shape and course had clarified since the first time I saw it. It was no longer dancing and skipping through the rocks and soil. Now, it followed a specific route, a circle, around an area miles wide, moving fast. Along the circle were these red places in the earth, red as blood, bright as fire. A triangle.

The infinity loop was following the circle that included the triangle points. If I had ever gambled, I'd have put a month's salary on the probability that the three hot spots coincided with the pond, the deer, and the triangle of houses in the neighborhood.

I stretched out my perception of the land, like a hand, long fingers of awareness, reaching.

Far below the triangle and below the dancing infinity's circular course was the sleeping presence. The sleeping power. The infinity energy no longer prodded it or tried to stimulate it, but seemed content to circle above it, not touching, no longer poking it like a playful puppy, to wake it, but sending pulses of power through the threads that moved down to it. It reminded me of feeding tubes, feeding the sleeper. Though in concept, it resembled the shadowy pulsing of Brother Ephraim to the two trees, the reality of it was very different.

I was obscurely glad that the dancer was no longer actively annoying the sleeper. The somnolent presence in the earth disturbed me in ways I had no name for. I withdrew my own awareness, higher in the land, back to the infinity loop.

In the center of the larger triangle, in the center of the circle that the loop raced along, was another location that drew my attention, but it wasn't red or bright or energetic. It glimmered, a soft yellow. I had seen it before, when I first looked at the earth after I returned home, but it hadn't been well defined then, just an amorphous blob of light. Now it glowed like a sun. I studied the yellow glow and I felt its pull, strong and determined, the way the planets in the solar system felt the pull of Sol.

I thought of T. Laine's *come-hither* working. Was this attraction like that? Whatever it was, this was significant. This was . . . I had no idea what it was, but I knew it was important. It might be the single thing that tied the points of the triangle, the circling people, geese, deer, and goldfish, and the outer circle, all together.

And the woman's voice. Perhaps that too.

Altogether, it was a spell, a working. As improbable as it seemed, it was a huge traditional working that covered a massive amount of land, across the surface and down into the earth. Nothing I had learned in Spook School led me to understand what this was or how it had been created. Or why.

Before any of the things I viewed from a distance might see me, I withdrew.

I had sent my awareness too far away, and the warmth of Soulwood hadn't kept up with . . . with whatever it was that I was doing. I was shivering. My stomach was cramping. I needed to eat. Maybe a grilled cheese sandwich on Mama's homemade bread, for the comfort factor. Or a bowl of potato soup.

But Rick had wanted me to check in on the sleeping presence in the North Carolina mountains, and I knew I'd never come back out again if I got full and warm. So I put my palms back on the ground and reached out across the Tennessee River Valley, east of Knoxville, high into the peaks of the Appalachian Mountains.

I felt the presence there, the slumbering consciousness that rested deep. It was far bigger than I remembered, the darkness stretching up and out and high and deep and vast, following the ridges of the earth and the sharp outlines of the broken stone that rose and fell, the spines of the mountains themselves like a coil of massive snakes buried by soil and the life above.

I let myself stretch further, farther, feeling myself thinning, pulling smaller, more constricted. It was cold here, so far away from Soulwood. But the land was fascinating, with contours and boundaries I hadn't expected. Where I had thought there was one huge presence beneath the summits, I realized that there were several buried beneath the ridges of the mountains. All sleeping. They stretched north and south, elevating high along the peaks, and deep into the earth. I had no idea what they were. But I wasn't about to accidentally wake them. I slid silently away, careful not to touch them, not to prod them, even by mishap.

I wished I had someone to ask about the linked presences, but there was no one.

I pulled back inside myself and into the night. The sun had fallen. A cold front had swept in. I had been reading the land for a long time. I sucked in a breath of the frigid air, and it hit me like a punch to the solar plexus. I coughed, a long, wet sound, as if my lungs had not worked while I was scanning the earth this time. As if I had stopped breathing. The coughing went on for a long time, aching through my ribs and lungs, and when my chest finally cleared and I caught up on my oxygen deprivation, I realized that the two severed branches I had tossed to the earth near my feet had dug little rootlets into the ground. Far too fast to be normal rootlets.

I rolled to my knees, feeling brittle as old leather, and picked up the machete. When my hands no longer trembled, I gripped the thin branches and pulled, using the tip of the machete to lift the soil like a shovel, until I had all of the rootlets worked loose. I walked back to my house. Leaving the tools on the back porch, I carried the twigs inside, where the heat slammed into me, despite the thermometer on the wall at the back door, which read fifty-nine. I was hypothermic after reading the land so far away. I'd been sitting in the dropping temps, without enough layers, without enough breath, stretched too far for Soulwood to heat me. I had been foolish.

With the iron eye-lifter, I opened the burn box of the cook-stove. Tossed the scarlet stems onto the burning coals and added a fast-burning winter log, split and splintered, so it would catch instantly and burn hot. The split log caught and so did the hacked-off scarlet stems, the flames licking on the red-slimed bark. There was something erroneous with that, but I was so tired and hungry and worn and empty that nothing came. When the stems were in full flame, I closed the burn-box door.

It was full night, and I was beyond exhausted.

I checked the greens, removed the roasted pumpkin from the oven and set it to cool, and put a pat of butter in my sixteen-inch cast-iron skillet. I stored my skillets on the warming shelf of the

Waterford Stanley, and they were therefore warm anytime there
was a fire inside. When the butter was melted, I added two pieces
of bread and a thick layer of cheddar—once I had cut away the
blue mold that had coated it in my absence. I sprinkled half a
teaspoon of brown sugar on the cheese and closed the sandwich,
setting a smaller, heated skillet on top to hold it down. The smell
of butter, bread, and cheese set my mouth to watering, and it was
all I could do to wait for the cheese to melt and the bread to toast.
I flipped the sandwich, poured yesterday's coffee into a cup and
microwaved it, adding sugar to it too. In minutes, I had me a
king's feast, standing right there at the heated stove.

When I finally stopped shaking and my fingers were no longer an odd, ashy blue, I pulled a chair and a small table close to
the stove, carried over an afghan crocheted by my sister Priss,
and wrapped up. I held my toes close to the stove's warmth as I
logged onto the PsyLED intranet for updates, checked e-mails,
and wrote my reports. All except the things that were happening
along my borders. That was private. Until it wasn't anymore. I
knew I'd have to tell them eventually, but not until I understood
it all. And the case was solved. We had dead adults and dead
children and that took precedence.

I sent reports to Rick and e-mails to the unit about what I
had discovered reading the land, telling them what I sensed
about the triangles made up by the affected sites, and the circle,
and the sun glow at the circle's and the triangle's centers—which
were the same place, GPS-speaking, but could have been any
one of four R&D places on my map. I told them what I understood, and what I was totally confused about. I told them that I'd
be in tomorrow, but that I needed to go by and see my mama first.

What I really wanted to do was go see the tree on the church
compound, the one that had grown roots inside of me, claiming
me, healing me, changing me, even as I claimed and changed it.
Something was wrong with the tree and with the blot that was
Brother Ephraim. It wasn't connected with the problems in the
land at the triangle and circle. It was its own problem. And I had
a dreadful fear that my blood and I had caused it.

I didn't sleep well. The cats were difficult, up half the night,
*mrow*ing and yodeling and walking across the bed, especially
Jezzie, who kept sticking her nose into my ear and breathing. It

wasn't like her. She had never done such a thing before. I got up a little after three a.m. and put them out, but it had snowed unexpectedly during the night and they started caterwauling, so I got back up and let them in. After that, there was no going back to sleep for me. Of course, the cats then curled up on the bed and fell deeply to sleep for the rest of the night. They must have wanted the whole bed for themselves.

The house had chilled down, so I put fresh logs in the Waterford (checking first to make sure the strange branches were still ash—they were), and made coffee. On the couch, in my jammies, robe, wool socks, slippers, and an afghan, I checked e-mails. I discovered that at about two a.m., all the surviving deer from the accident had died. They had been walking in a circle, clockwise, not eating, not drinking, just walking, constantly, at the University of Tennessee's forestry, wildlife, and fisheries department, where the living ones had been taken. Within minutes of each other, near dusk, they had buckled, fallen, and died. Their bodies were still redlining, according to a PsyCSI tech who had been dispatched to the site. The deer were going to receive necropsies and then be cremated ASAP, in case they had something contagious.

Rick had pulled a late-nighter and had replied to my reports with comments and a few questions for clarity, which I answered, and amended my reports to reflect the corrections. Report-speak was a language all its own and had to be searchable, in multiple law enforcement databases, often with their own languages and terms.

Occam had sent a text to ask if I was okay, since I had left the neighborhood scene so quickly, and also because he had seen that I was going to be late tomorrow—well, today, now. I sent back a quick comment that I was fine, and would see the unit soon.

I was dressed for work by five a.m. in a long dull green skirt, leggings, layers, and my dress boots instead of my field boots. Shortly after, I called Mama's number. The Nicholsons were farm people and got up when the roosters started crowing, sometimes by four a.m., so they could make it to morning devotionals, which took place at dawn. Sometimes the family ate breakfast before church, sometimes after. Life on the compound of God's Cloud of Glory Church was both strict and fluid: strict in the sense that everything revolved around church, and church had rigid schedules, and fluid in that families could do what they wanted with their daily schedules, otherwise, so long as they worked at something that supported the church—woodworking, working the fields, sewing, animal husbandry, or whatever needed doing on the land that supported them.

I listened as the call rang. It was still strange to know Mama had a cell phone. It was an old-fashioned one with a flip case, but she knew how to use it.

"Nell?" Mama said, picking up, the sound of Nicholsons loud in the background: a baby wailing, children singing a familiar song about Noah and his animals two by two, skillets and pots banging in the kitchen. Breakfast in such a large clan wasn't usually a single sit-down affair, but was generally done in stages, groups coming and going for a couple of hours. Loud and gregarious and full of energy. The exact opposite of my daily routine, solo and silent.

"Hey, Mama."

"You'un feeling better, honey? You feel good enough to come to breakfast? I'll make you some French toast, just the way you like it."

Right. I had the flu. I was certainly on the road to hell, lying to my mama. "I feel great. I'll be there fast as I can get there."

"Drive safe. I'll alert the guards at the gate to expect you."

"Yes, ma'am. Bye." *Alert the guards at the gate?* I had thought that kind of stuff was done.

I gathered my things, put the cats on the back porch with food, water, and a cat litter box that I kept for very cold weather, tied the old cat blanket from last winter to the hammock, and closed up the house. The cats would spend a few hours getting settled into the hammock, which would be a game, flipping, rotating, and rocking, and then once they settled into it they could sleep away the day.

Out front, the sky was black with a heavy, wet snow falling, and I mushed my way to the truck. The snow slop wasn't truly frozen, and I was able to drive most of the way down the mountain, the tires picking up clods of mud and snow slush. I needed to get a four-wheel-drive vehicle, and that was on my to-buy list as soon as I could afford it, but it would be a while. The upgraded solar panels and batteries had taken a considerable chunk of change from the sale of John's gun, and I wasn't ready to become a truly modern woman and go into debt. Yet.

The guards at the church's twelve-foot-tall gate were carrying shotguns and rifles, but they let me in after I presented my driver's license. Inside, there were dogs and armed men patrolling the grounds, and that sort of thing was supposed to have been finished under the new leadership in the church, but it seemed old habits were too established to let that occur. Or maybe something else had reinforced the old patterns.

Here, there was only a light dusting of snow, and though it was still falling, it was melting even faster. The day was yet too gloomy to see the tree I was interested in, so I drove on to the Nicholson house and parked beside Daddy's red truck. The house was a three-story saltbox-style block of a house, with more rooms up under the eaves, big enough for all three wives and all the children. I cut the engine and pulled a plastic baggie from the glove box. Before I could get out of the Chevy truck, the front door opened and Mud came tearing out at a dead run. She leaped off the porch, yanked open the heavy truck door, and threw herself at me in a hug tight enough to cut off the blood to my lower limbs. I hugged her back just as tight.

"I missed you," she said into my middle. She had grown since I'd been gone. Maybe a whole inch.

"I missed you too," I said softly.

Mud pulled away, backing to the house, jerking on my arm. "Did you'un bring me a present? Mama said I wasn't to ask but—did you?"

"Of course." I held out the baggie and shook it. Mud snatched it from me and said, "Dust?" Then, squealing, "No. *Seeds!*" She turned and raced inside, leaving me climbing the steps to the porch. Mud was whatever I was, species-wise. Nothing was more precious to either of us than living, growing things: seeds, roots, cuttings, flowers, even pollen.

"You spoil that girl."

I flinched and my hands fisted. The result of training and bruises from Spook School self-defense classes. In the same instant, I saw the man sitting in the shadows, on a rocker. Still. Silent.

"Sam?"

There was a shotgun across my brother's knees. He stood and met me halfway, in a hug that surprised me. Sam and I had spent all the years of our childhoods fighting and arguing; hugging had never been part of our relationship. Tentatively, I hugged back.

"You'un gonna steal the bubblegum in my pocket?"

I chuckled into the rough wool of his pea coat. Rather than answer, I reached into his coat pocket and took a piece. "For later," I said. "Thank you." I stuck it in my own.

"We'uns got us a problem, Nellie," he said. "When you'uns done with breakfast, we need to talk about Daddy."

"Okay." Daddy had been shot not long ago. I had seen him on my last visit and he had looked a mite puny but nothing to cause the concerned tone in my brother's voice. Was Daddy sick? Not healing right? Did he have cancer? Heart disease? None of that ran in our family, but I had a bad feeling about it. I couldn't make myself ask, and I hoped it was just a bad guess. Sam opened the front door, like a gentleman, and followed me in. Small talk with Sam had never been easy, but I gave it a go as he closed the door and unwound his scarf, asking, "So, how's married life?"

My brother smiled, showing teeth, his eyes crinkling up. "Better than fine. Finer than frog fur spilt three ways."

"I'm glad. Marriage should be a happy thing," I said, shucking out of my coat.

"I'm sorry yours was bad, Nell."

That stopped me and I shrugged, uncomfortable with the topic of my marriage. I said, "Better the Ingrams than to live with the colonel. Way better, brother of mine."

"*That* is the God's own truth, sister," he agreed.

"What kinda seeds are these?" Mud shouted over the din, a clamor that suddenly crashed down on me. Sam patted my shoulder. "Home sweet home. Come get me when you'uns done with women's talk."

"Okay." I moved through the controlled chaos to the kitchen and hugged Mama. "Love you, Mama."

"Love you too, baby girl. Sit a spell." I did and she dished up breakfast and slid a quart jar of honey to me. "Eat you'uns' French toast," she demanded to all the bodies at the table. "Sam! Daddy's busy. You come on and eat. Give that wife of yours a morning in bed."

"What. Are. The. Seeds!" Mud shouted, jerking my jacket.

"Mindy, you mind your manners!" Mama demanded.

In the living room, three tiny little'uns started resinging the song about Noah and the flood.

"Brighamia," I shouted to my sister, as half a dozen older

little'uns raced through the living room, screaming. I shook my head at the culture shock of being home again. *No. Not that. Just being here.* Loudly I said, "It's a succulent bellflower from Hawaii. The common names are *alula*, *olulu*, or *pu aupaka*. Read up on it. Only plant a few at a time," I cautioned her, and caught her eyes with my own. I added, "You're going to have to *make it grow.*"

Mud's eyes went wide. "Make . . ."

Make. It. Grow, I mouthed. We hadn't talked about her ability with plants. Nor my own. That was a discussion for private places, surrounded by rich soil and clean water and the soul of the earth.

"You . . . you know?"

I gave her a twitch of a smile and said, "I *am*."

Mud sucked in a breath, eyes so wide I feared they'd pop out of her eye sockets. She took off as if her britches were on fire.

"Nell, you let that child get ready for devotionals and eat," Mama said. "You want tea or coffee?"

"Coffee, Mama."

"Coffee for me too, Mama," Sam said.

"Gitchur own cup, Samuel," Mama said briskly. "You ain't a visitor, and I ain'chur maid. If I hear you been making Miss SaraBell get you'un's coffee, I'll tan your bottom."

Sam laughed and got a mug from the cabinet. It was chipped, the lip brown with coffee stains, the enamel cracked and worn, the shine long gone. "I take good care of my wife, Mama."

"You best do. Get a plate, Sam, if'n you want French toast."

Across the room, as the minutes before sunrise arrived, the sister-wives, Mama Carmel and Mama Grace, gathered up all the children still eating and led all the young'uns out of the house, to devotions, all of them waving to me and to Sam and to Mama. They were all dressed for the cold, but didn't stop to talk. Which was strange, as all this morning felt strange. And I realized that Mama was skipping morning devotions to have a cup of coffee with me. Which was incredibly sweet. Or . . . maybe not. If Mama had something to say, she would grab the first opportunity and say it. An impromptu meeting. When I was growing up, such meetings had been a precursor to me getting a good whipping.

Not wanting to start a conversation that I suddenly didn't want to have, I ate Mama's delicious French toast, made with real vanilla, heavy cream, butter, sugar, and her secret ingredient. Whatever that was. No one knew. As I ate, Daddy ambled out of the back. With a cane. Mama watched him, lips tight. Sam watched him, his expression a mirror of hers.

Daddy joined us at the table and sipped on a cup of coffee, his eyes on me. He looked bad. I had been gone only a little while, a couple of months, but Daddy had lost weight, maybe thirty pounds. His face was gray and tight with pain. I wasn't a doctor, but I knew my daddy was in trouble. Yeah. This wasn't just breakfast. It was a meeting, in the odd quiet of the strangely deserted house, just Mama, Sam, Daddy, and me, hastily engineered by Mama when I called.

My French toast gone, I sat back in my kitchen chair, the mismatched spindles pressing into my spine. Mama put on a fresh pot of coffee to percolate, no longer looking at her husband or her son, or even at me—working, keeping busy. Like I did, when there was trouble. I frowned and got up, pouring myself, Mama, and Daddy more coffee from the pot that was ready, and leaving the coffeepot on the table in front of Sam to pour his own. "Daddy?" I asked. "You got a broken leg or something?"

"Jist a bit of digestive upset. Mama Carmel's got me on half a dozen decoctions and infusions. I'll be right as rain again soon. Good to see you, Nell."

"But, Daddy—"

"No. This is not a topic for discussion. You'uns say grace yet? No? This is a Christian household. Sam. Give thanks." Daddy lowered his head, and that ended any chance for me to speak to Daddy's health.

I sighed, the breath little more than a whisper. I had been right. Daddy was sick and was being contrary about seeking medical help.

NINE

In the middle of the nearly unbearable silence of breakfast I finally asked, "How are things? How's the land?" And the most important thing—other than Daddy's lack of health—"How's the . . . the trees?"

Daddy looked up at that, set his fork down, and sipped his coffee, his eyes boring into me, just as they had when I had played hooky from work or lessons when I was a child. Back then Daddy had let silence do his dirty work for him, letting it build until I started crying and confessed. I couldn't help but remember the whippings that followed. My heartbeat sped, my breath came too fast. But I was far too old to get a whipping. And for that matter, I was too old to fall for the silent treatment. So I frowned at my father. And thought about the tree I had fed with my blood and that had healed me and that was now tied to Brother Ephraim. And waited.

"You'un got a specific tree in mind, Nell?" he asked a couple of aeons later.

"Yes. One behind the church. An oak."

"And how would you'un know that a tree was acting strange, Nell?" Daddy asked. "Should we'uns have sent for you'un when it started changing?"

"She'un's *not* a witch," Mama said, her tone strident. "Nell did not curse that tree."

"I did not curse anything," I said calmly, though all I could think of was that if my gift had been made known to the church when I was a child, it was possible that I'd have been burned at the stake. And that I had to protect my sisters from the church finding out. I knew that, yet I had given Mud seeds and told her to make them grow. I was stupid beyond belief. And I had to deal with that soon.

"A little bird told me that there might be problems here," I lied. "Law enforcement officers hear things." The truth in fact, but in context, still a lie. "The tree. Changing how?"

"Some things are best seen in person," Sam said. He pushed back from the table and stood. "Let's drive down." The tree wasn't far. But Daddy couldn't walk that distance. Daddy had cowed the family from doing the right thing for him. But I wasn't part of this family anymore, which gave me lots more leeway to say what needed to be said. *That* was why Mama had arranged this impromptu, intimate breakfast.

I watched as Daddy struggled to his feet and got the cane beneath him to take his weight. "We'uns is talking about your health. Soon," I said.

"You'un getting uppity since you joined the police," Daddy said, affront in his voice.

His hand was white from the stress of standing, his face pale. A slight tremor raced through him, and I thought he might fall. "Sure. That's as good an excuse as any." I stood. "Can you drive, Daddy, or are you too *sick* for that?"

Without a word, Daddy turned and led the way outside, where he got in his truck and drove toward the chapel.

Sam and I followed, wrapping up in warm clothes, my brother chuckling beneath his breath. "Nellie, you'un got big brass ones, that's all I got to say."

I had learned what the saying meant at Spook School, and thought it was silly, as testicles were small, easy to remove, and easily injured. I had seen enough farm animals castrated to know that for a fact, but it sounded like Sam was giving me a compliment, so I just gave him a "Humph" and got in my truck. Sam got in the passenger side.

Oddly, the temperatures had chilled during breakfast and snow fell heavily around us, flakes as big as my fist, drifting down in the still air, settling into a melting white mush on the ground. The sunlight was dim and distant, the world gray and black and white in the headlights. Sam and I drove toward the back of the chapel, the road with a single set of tracks in the layer of white, the porch lights we passed casting glowing circles on the snow.

The headlights of Daddy's truck caught the chapel in the background, painted white against the white snow, trees black and stark. Bright lights fell from the paned windows onto the pristine expanse in arched, pointed shapes. The sound of voices singing muffled through, yet were clear as a childhood memory. The notes of "'Tis Winter Now, the Fallen Snow," seemed proper and appropriate, and for some reason I couldn't explain to myself, felt sad, melancholy. Maybe because I knew something bad was wrong with Daddy.

The headlights stopped on the garden spot where the tree that healed me grew. A few months ago it was just an oak tree, surrounded by plantings I had rooted or seeded there when I was a child. Now it was surrounded by a cement brick fence, gray and dull in the snowy light. The fence was about ten feet on a side and ten feet tall. There were cracks zigzagging up and down through the mortar, and the top wasn't level. The brick-laying looked sloppy, unlike the usual careful work of the churchmen, who tended to take pride in craftsmanship. And then I saw the reason why the bricks were out of plumb. Roots grew up through the ground, pushing high and lifting the foundation, making it appear that the wall had been frozen in motion, a blocky lizard or snake. Branches pressed against the walls and poured over the top, draping down the sides, cracking the mortar even more. Thorns gleamed wetly in the headlights, spikes sharper than needles. The leaves looked wrong. Just wrong. The garden spot, with its beautiful flowers, was no more. This was the tree that had healed me when I'd been shot, had grown inside me. It was also what Brother Ephraim's soul was attached to on the church land.

Daddy sat in his truck, but I turned off the Chevy and Sam and I got out, moving along the line of light to the wall. The roots on this side had been cut through with chainsaws. The draping branches had been clipped and sawn. The tree itself smelled of herbicides and gasoline and soot. Someone had tried to poison it. Burn it. Cut it down. Yet still it grew.

Sam stood in the headlights, his shadow rising up the wall, broad shoulders hunched, hands in his pockets. Staring at the tree. "We'uns had to brick it up," he said.

"Why?" I asked.

"It attacked a little girl. Tried to bury her. Mindy said it wanted blood, but we'uns don't sacrifice to trees." The last part was spoken with humor, as if he was trying to make a joke out of something that wasn't funny.

I stared through the snowflakes at the place where I had been healed not so long ago.

"Is Mindy—"

"I'll take care of Mindy," I said.

"Good. She may need to come live with you'un someday. To keep her safe." When I didn't respond, Sam went on. "The tree. It grew thorns. And the leaves cause a rash, like poison oak. It tries to spread, puts out runners, sends seeds into the air. They come up everywhere. We've found thorned saplings and infants as far away as fifty feet. The Perkinses have a small front-end loader. They bring it in and dig 'em up for us. Then we burn them. The tree keeps coming back, no matter what we do to it. The tree just won't die, not even after we salted the ground."

The song in the church ended, and I heard a man's voice speaking. Prayer, I figured. "What color is the sap?"

"Bloodred. It ain't an oak no more. It's freaky."

My lips trembled into a smile at the modern term coming from my brother's mouth. And I remembered the roots that Occam had cut from my body. They had bled. The sapling on my own land had bled, thorned and bloody. I had changed this one, giving it access to my blood, mutating it during the process of healing. Ephraim had gotten here through the ground in which he was trapped. And had used the tree on the church grounds to learn how to grow his own tree at the site of his death. Maybe to mutate it again, to grow something even more different. I had changed Ephraim too, when I killed him. We were all linked now, somehow. And I needed to find a way to destroy the Brother and his evil trees. "Yeah, I reckon I can see how that might be so," I said, knowing I had fallen back into the church-speak of my youth, and realizing that here, at this time and in this place, it spoke to the bonding of family. Of true sibs. Despite the tree Daddy thought I had cursed. "What's the long-term plan for getting rid of it?"

"We'uns hired Kobert's Earthmovers and Mining to bring in a bulldozer, one of the kind that does top-down mining. We'uns going to drill a hole in the trunk, put a stick of dynamite in, and set it off. Then we'll dig up the roots, haul the whole thing out, every leaf and limb and stick of it. And burn it until nothing's left but ash."

I nodded, remembering the branches I had burned last night, feeling the chill and wet, as oversized snowflakes settled on my head and shoulders and melted onto my scalp, wetting my clothing. "Cut off the branches first so nothing goes flying with the dynamite."

Sam nodded, pursing his lips slightly as he considered why that might be a smart thing to do. "Freaky," he said again.

"Don't leave anything on the ground for long. When you dig up the roots, don't let the rootlets or the cut branches touch the ground. Load every branch and leaf and root up on to something made of metal, maybe a metal-bed truck or dump truck. Cart it to a place that's stone, like the quarry, with no soil or water. And drench it fast with gasoline. Burn it hot until it's nothing but ash. Then make sure you police the grounds here and there twice a day, every day, and dig up and burn anything that looks remotely like it. Fire. Fire will kill it."

Sam nodded, staring at the branch that hung over the wall. It seemed to be growing even as we watched, the leaves, which never fell on a live oak, thick and heavy, a green so deep it appeared to have hints of red in it. "What is it, Nel!?"

"I don't know." I tilted my head to Sam. "But I got a sapling that looks somewhat like it on my property. No leaves, just bare wood. No real bark either. I cut off the branches last night and they bled, and when I left them on the ground for a bit, they rooted. Too fast to be normal. But when I burned them, they burned true. I'll be cutting it down and burning it when I get back."

"You'un need help, you call. I'll bring some gas."

"You always did like fire."

He slid a look my way. "Begging your pardon, Nellie?"

"Um-hummm. That campfire that took off and burned down a field of hay on the Vaughn farm when you was maybe fifteen, sixteen? Even John and Leah and I heard about that event. I always figured that fire for you." When Sam didn't reply I said, "You ever confess?"

"I did. Got my backside tanned right good." He sounded rueful, and at the same time almost proud. "I had to work a whole summer of twelve-hour days to pay the Vaughns for the hay I ruin't."

I shivered hard and knew I couldn't postpone this anymore, so I changed the subject to the important part of my visit. "I need to touch the tree, Sam," I said.

"Why's that, Nellie?"

"You might not want to know the answer to that."

Sam stared at the tree for a while, thinking that over. Likely thinking about Mud and her telling him the tree wanted blood. Looking from the tree to me, his expression told me he was remembering my gifts with growing things when I was a child. How the church wanted to burn me at the stake. Adding in my comment about him being a fire bug when he was a kid. The things sibs knew and accepted and kept quiet about.

The fall of snowflakes thickened and landed on my uncovered head with soft plops. Melted snow dripped down my scalp and neck and into my collar. In spite of the snow and the heavy clouds, the day lightened. I wiped my head, but I didn't move otherwise, giving my brother time to think. This was too important. "You'uns ain't no witch," he said firmly, the syllables steeped in church patois. "The mamas had the townie witches test you."

"They did. I'm not."

"How much does this have to do with you'un making most anything grow? How much does it have to do with the way Mindy can do the same thing?"

My brother had decided to take the bull by the horns, as I had with Daddy. I wasn't sure if I was happy he had grown some or disappointed that he decided to grow now, about this tree and Mud and me. "Can you handle the truth?"

Sam chuckled softly at the movie reference, which he actually got, and shoved down on his fists, buried in his jacket pockets. "After the things I saw with the colonel and his progeny, I reckon I can handle most anything, sister of mine."

"Then yes. I'm not human. Mindy might not be human."

He made a soft *mmmm* sound, not surprised at all. "What about the rest of us?"

"So far as I know you're all mundane and boring."

"Tell that to my SaraBell. She thinks I'm amazing."

"Ick and *eww*. TMI, brother," I said, wondering if he knew that reference.

"TMI. Listen to us culturally aware adults talking in a God's Cloud compound. So. You'un need to touch the tree. What's that all about?"

"I can tell things about plants. Can't explain it." I pointed to myself. "Still not a witch."

Sam said, "I can look at the sky and breathe the air and tell what the weather's gonna do by morning even before the weather report. I can tell when the frost is coming a week before. When we'll have too much rain and risk washing out crops. When we're going to have a drought and how long it'll last. Like that?"

"Yes. Like that." And my heart may have skipped a beat at the acceptance in his tone and the calmness with which he confessed to a paranormal gift that normal, mundane humans didn't have. I said, "You know how the tree attacked the little girl? Well, it might attack me. If it does, I need you to cut me free, even if you have to take some skin."

Sam pulled a small knife from beneath his jacket, a gut-hook knife with a four-inch blade, designed for skinning and gutting deer. I remembered the Christmas he received it. I was still living at home, which would have made him less than fifteen. Even in the gray dawn light I could tell he kept the blade wicked sharp.

I wiped my hand dry inside my pocket and walked closer to the walled tree. I reached up to a branch hanging over the wall. With one finger I touched a single leaf. Nothing happened—no branches grabbed me to yank me over the wall, no roots wrapped my ankles to hold me down. I ran my fingers across the leaf, learning its shape. It felt slippery, thick, like a succulent, and it had faint, spiny ridges on the blade and margin like an aloe leaf. I moved my finger to the petiole, which was thicker, denser, heavier, and more elastic than an oak's. The tree was storing water and nutrients in ways no live oak ever could.

I closed my eyes and sank into the tree. Not a deep read. Not a full scan. Just a brush of awareness across its surface. *Bright. Hot. Spiky. Intense.* My breath felt harsh with fear and with awareness of the thing I touched. *Not a tree. Something else.*

I pulled away and withdrew three steps, looking up at the boughs, which were gnarled and twisted like a live oak, rising into the sky and reaching down over the wall to the ground. The tree was more than it had been. But it hadn't tried to take me down or grow roots into my body or trap my feet in the soil, so that was something.

"Okay?" Sam asked.

"Okay." I heard him close and pocket his knife. "And before you ask, I'm not sure what I felt. I need to think on it a mite."

"All right. You'un seen enough?"

"Yeah." I wiped my hand again inside my pocket where it

was dry. Behind us, Daddy turned his truck and drove away, taking the extra illumination from his headlights and leaving us in the dark. "Tell me about Daddy," I said.

Sam turned and walked back to my truck, his legs cutting through the headlights and snow. I followed and got into the passenger seat. Buckled up. Waited. Sam got in the driver's side and got the engine running, the truck's heater pumping warm air onto my feet. We sat in the dark, not looking at each other. It was church etiquette. When important things needed to be said, eye contact was kept to a minimum, likely a trait gained from multifamily living and the impossibility for real privacy in the homes.

He leaned forward, his arms resting across the steering wheel, staring out at the tree. "Daddy looks bad, don't he?"

"You know he does."

"He won't talk about it. Mama Carmel says it goes back to the shooting and that he needs more surgery to correct what's still messed up in there. She made him see the townie doctor that saved him when he was shot. A general surgeon. He did some tests—X-rays and a scan of some kind. The surgeon agreed with Mama Carmel. Said it was likely one of two things. Scar tissue—fibers holding things together that shouldn't be held together. Or some tiny little bleeder that keeps breaking open and spurting blood inside, causing more damage, though the doctor admitted that he didn't see such a thing on the scan. He wants to go back in and see what's what. Do what he called an *exploratory*."

Sam leaned back and put the C10 into reverse, pulling out across the slushy white carpet of snow. The tracks we had made upon entering were nearly gone, but Daddy's new tracks were dark in the fast-melting snow. My head was completely wet and cold, even with the heater running full blast. This was a wake-up call to put winter supplies into my truck, including a scarf, gloves, a hat, extra socks, a blanket, food, and water. "So when's that?" I asked. "The surgery?"

"Daddy won't have nothing to do with getting cut on again. Says he'll get well or he won't. God's will."

"Daddy ain't right bright, sometimes."

"Love my daddy. Respect him too," Sam said. "But I can't argue with that assessment of the current state of his intellect when it comes to doctors. All the mamas got more brains than him."

"They need to gang up on him. You all do. I'll come back and help. In the real world they call it an intervention."

"Real world?" Sam shook his head at how far I'd fallen away from the church. I could read on his face that he wanted to talk to me about my salvation, but he pushed it away for now, for which I was grateful. I didn't want to fight with my brother about God. "You think an intervention will work?"

"No. But it might get him to thinking." Sam didn't reply. "And if that don't work, sic Sister Erasmus on him."

"Why her?"

"Don't know why, but Daddy respects Sister Erasmus. Even John did, and John didn't respect or listen to nobody except Leah. If Erasmus told Daddy he was cutting the fool, he might listen."

Sam nodded as we pulled back to the house. "You coming in?"

"Not this time. I gotta go to work. Tell Mama I'll let her know when I can make a family dinner. I want to meet the woman who was dumb enough to marry you."

"You'll like SaraBell. She's something else. Redheaded and saucy. Eyes blue like the sky and skin like the finest cream." He thought a minute. "I reckon you know it, but I'll say it anyways. The only way Sara'd agree to marry me was for us'uns to get it done legal. We'uns went to the justice of the peace in Knoxville."

I was proud that my brother had taken him a wife of legal age, according to the law of the land. Something inside me relaxed, what the churchwomen called "heart ease." "Mama told me. Good for SaraBell. And good for you."

"That ain't all, and Mama and Daddy don't know this part, so keep your mouth shut. I had to promise SaraBell, no other wives and no concubines."

I kept the shock off my face with an effort, and my voice neutral, though that was even harder. "How do you feel about that?"

"I'm a man of my word. I love SaraBell to the ends of the earth and back. So it ain't no hardship. Mama won't be happy about not having a passel of grandkids to raise, though. 'Specially with you'un leaving the church, childless and without a husband. And you'un widdered so young." He glanced at me and away. "She wants you to find a good man. She's of a mind to introduce you to one or another fella in the church. Casual-like. As if by accident." A small smile touched his face, telling me he knew how easy that would be to see through.

I put a hand on his arm and tugged his jacket until he looked me in the eye. "I done been married, and for all the wrong reasons. I ain't gonna get married again. Probably not never. The Nicholsons all need to know that. I ain't a churchwoman no more, Sam."

"That right pains my heart, Nell, knowing you done slipped so far from the Lord."

"I never said I slipped from the Lord. I just don't worship him like you'uns do. Not no more."

Sam frowned but nodded and opened the driver door. "I'll think on what you said, Nellie."

"Good. Tell Mama about dinner."

"Will do."

I slid across to the driver's side and heard softly, from the front porch, "I love you, sister mine. I ain't always showed it, but I love you."

"I love you too, Sam. Always have." I closed the Chevy's driver door and pulled away. It was early, but I needed to make some calls, even if it meant waking up some people. I dialed and drove from the church compound as the sun broke through the clouds, and the phone was answered on the other end by a voice that sounded wide-awake.

"Nell! You sleep less than I do!"

"Hey, Jane. I slept, but got up about three. I'm guessing you're still up from last night, what with your vampire job and all."

"Sleep? What's sleep?" We both laughed and she said, "What do you need?"

As if she knew that I'd never call just to chat. Like Jane, who worked 24/7, most everything in my life was about work. Jane Yellowrock was the only rogue-vampire hunter turned Enforcer for a Master of the City in existence. She was also a paranormal creature, and the person who had confirmed for me that I wasn't human, and then told me it wasn't a mortal sin to be what I was born being, that mortal sins were a matter of how we lived, not how we were born. She worked in New Orleans, and kept vampire hours. She was a Cherokee, and she had lived in the Appalachian Mountains for years. If I had a semifriend outside of family and work, Jane would be it. I admired the woman, and while part of me feared her, another part of me aspired to be as strong and self-contained as she was.

Jane knew a lot of things about a lot of paranormal creatures and paranormal events, and she didn't mind being asked questions, as long as she wasn't in the middle of killing something. If she didn't know the answers to my questions, she would find them and call me back.

"You'un heard about the strange things going on up here? People sick? Having psychotic episodes? People drowning? Killing each other?"

"We heard. Sounds like magic."

"You'un ever hear anything like it before?"

"No. But I have people I can talk to, if you want."

She meant vampires. Witches. Maybe even were-creatures, though I had plenty around me who didn't know diddly-squat about this situation, not any more than I did. But I had placed this call and I wasn't one to avoid or waste a potential source. More important, I trusted Jane. So I broke the cardinal rule and said, "Yes. If you would be so kind." With very few misgivings, I told an outsider who had no security clearance what was going on. And asked all my questions. There were a lot of them. Jane hung up and made some calls, asked those questions for me, and called me back far faster than I expected. I was still driving through rush-hour traffic when my cell dinged again. She had indeed found me answers, some in known fact, some in mythos, some in what Jane called "experiential evidence and testimony." Some that were mighty strange.

By the time I got to HQ, the snow had melted and the weather had warmed. And I was worried. Jane Yellowrock had that effect on people.

I brought nothing in with me—no donuts, no coffeehouse coffee, no lunch. But I carried a lot of things that were worrying me, both personally and professionally, things that weighed on me, plucking at my mind and spirit like crows on a dead body. I pushed the personal stuff—the trees and Daddy looking so poorly—to the back of my mind, and mentally ordered and arranged the professional things so I could talk about them. Last, as I swiped my card at the top of the stairs, I pasted a business smile on my face. LaLa had told me it was patently false, but it was the only fake smile I had except a churchwoman smile, and I knew I had never been sweet enough to successfully fake that one.

I might have been up and about for hours, but it was still early and the lights were on energy-saving mode, so I went through and turned them on bright, before taking my one-day gobag to the shower. I dried my hair, gooped it up again, and changed clothes, happy about the mix-and-match possibilities of mostly black with touches of greens and pinks. I hung my wet clothing up to drip-dry in front of the heating vent, hoping the draft would take out the skirt's wrinkles.

The grindylow appeared in the locker room, though the door didn't open. I preferred to think she had found a way in through the ductwork rather than assume she could magically translocate. She sat on the counter at the sink and chittered at me, looking for all the world like a neon green kitten, but one with thumbs, retractable steel claws used to kill were-creatures, and eyes that saw too much. She ducked her head into my gobag like a ferret might, and pulled out my extra bra, holding it up to me. She chittered several times, repeating the sound, a sibilant followed by cracking noises, a bit like, "Shhhhh t-t-t-t-t. Meeoooooee."

"I have no idea what you might be saying, you cute lil' killing machine, other than talking about cow patties."

She said, "Ssssssst-t-t-t-t," followed by a sound like laughter before she dropped my bra onto the bench nearby and went back to trundling through my things. She held up a black tube, waving it in the air.

"Gimme that," I said, snatching my lipstick away. "Mine," I said, shaking it at her.

"Mmmmmmmeeeeeooooooo," she said back, sounding like my cats last night, yodeling to get inside.

I put on lipstick and a bit of blush while Pea studied the buttons on the hair dryer, touching a heated piece of metal on the blower end and looking at her fingertip. "Come on. We'uns got work to do and reports to write." Unexpectedly the grindy leaped from the counter to my shoulder. I froze for half a second and said, "You try to cut my throat and I'll be mighty unhappy with you." Pea made the strange laughter sound again and I opened the door.

I dropped my gobag off in my office cubicle and strapped on my service weapon's shoulder harness, dropping Pea to the desk three times as I worked. I hadn't gotten used to the feel of the harness straps on my back or the rigidity of the Kydex holster beneath my arm. I preferred a spine holster, but the shoulder holster was more regulation. I removed the mag, did a chamber check, and slid the loaded mag back into the weapon. Set the safety. Holstered it. I didn't pull on a jacket, still feeling the hair dryer heat and wanting coffee. Pea leaped back to my shoulder.

Occam was in the break room when I entered, and the grindy pushed off, leaping from my shoulder all the way across the room to land on Occam's. The force of the push shoved me back two steps. The leap was easily twelve feet. It wasn't the first time the grindy had made me think that the laws of physics worked differently for her than for the rest of us.

"Morning, Pea. Nell," Occam said. He handed me a travel mug of coffee and poured another for himself. He looked tired and disheveled, and when he yawned, his jaw cracked. He hadn't shaved today, and the two-day beard looked good on him. I blinked at the thought, as he reached across for sugar packets, his shoulders stretching the plaid shirt and pulling it from his jeans to reveal a slice of flesh, tanned and golden. He tossed the packets on the table between us.

I sweetened my coffee and sipped, my attention now firmly on my mug. I wondered why I felt so out of sorts all of a sudden.

"Nell, sugar, I hope one of us got a good night's sleep."

"Not really. Why didn't you—? Oh. The full moon's close." That explained a lot, including my sudden fascination with an inch of skin. I shook that thought from my head. "Weres don't sleep well before the three days of full moon, do you?" I glanced at Pea. Had she been trying to say *moon*?

Occam drank down half of the coffee in a single gulp and chuffed, a sound more catlike than human. He slid a hand through his hair, pulling it behind his ears, and drawled, "A lot of creatures are moon called, but we weres are the most affected by its phases." His words, the shape of the syllables, were more Texan today, and the lower pitch of his voice sounded more cat than usual. I struggled to remember everything I had studied about weres in the full moon, but all I could think of was the glimpse of golden skin. I clamped down on the thoughts. Were-magics were well documented, even the unintended ones, like sexual allure.

Pea snuggled up under Occam's jaw as if scent-marking him. Occam stroked down her back, the way one might a friendly house cat. "The urge to shift and to hunt waxes strong three days out, abides the three days of, and wanes three days after. Nine nights of pleasure and nine days of hell." It sounded like a quote.

"Are you safe to be around?" I asked, making the words casual, but knowing it might be taken as an insult. I'd had a class in were-manners, but they differed by species, and cats were among the most prickly of them all.

"Not sure that I'm ever *safe*, Nell, sugar." He sipped, his brownish eyes gripping me with the intensity of a cat watching a mouse, and taking on a glow, faint flecks of gold shining in his irises. "'Specially 'round the full moon."

I looked away from his eyes. The color change there was dangerous. Occam had been raised in captivity in his cat shape, from the time he was ten years old, and he had less control than some. I'd learned that a color change or a glow meant that a were-creature was closer to shifting than might be healthy for bystanders.

Few other PsyLED units had were-creatures as members, and in private mentoring sessions, LaLa had warned me that I might have to defend myself on a full moon. LaLa had actually suggested that I keep one weapon loaded with silver, but silver could kill a werecat, and I wasn't interested in that, no matter what happened. Pulling out and sliding into a chair at an angle, the table between us, I asked, "So you're dangerous. Do I need to keep my weapon handy, Occam?"

He chuffed a laugh. "Nell, sugar, the proper response to an out-of-control were-creature is standard ammo, gunfire enough to knock them off course and sway any accidental lapses of control, but lemme guess." Occam's golden eyes went hard. "Privately you were told to use silver. Just in case."

"Pretty much," I said. "Kill you dead, just to be safe."

"Hmmm," he said, his tone lowered, a burr of sound, his eyes so heated that it felt like two torches burning into me. "You got your service weapon in your hand?" He sipped his coffee and waited. When I didn't answer and the silence between us grew heavy, he said, "Safe . . . is overrated. Sometimes it's better to live dangerously." When I still stayed silent—having been reminded of that trick by Daddy—Occam asked, sounding more like himself, "You got a quote for were-creatures?"

I lifted my chin and said, "He's mad that trusts in the tameness of a wolf, a horse's health, a boy's love, or a whore's oath."

"I got no knowledge about the last two, but the first ones I can attest to." He chuckled, the sound a low vibration that quivered along my spine. "But you're more'n safe with me, Nell, sugar. Safer than a running deer or rabbit."

"I ain't never been a rabbit," I said in church-speak. "And I figure Pea right there"—I nodded to his shoulder—"will rip out your'un throat if'n you decide to bite me."

"And you'll pull the trigger before I can get across the table," he drawled. "Right?"

I pulled my weapon, racked back the slide, injecting a round into the chamber, and off-safetied, all in one slick motion. His eyes widened. "I will now," I said. "Because I know when a cat is playing games with me, and I mean to stop it now, once and for all."

Behind me, Rick said, "You playing games with the mouse, my brother?"

His voice was deeper too, and my skin prickled, rising in a tight chill. A faint sweat started, and I knew they could both smell the change on me. Both of them edged closer to me, a minuscule, almost silent shifting of feet on the floor. Was I in danger? I wondered if I'd really have to shoot them.

Over the loudspeakers, music flowed, saxophone and flute and the deep, distant notes of trombone. The melody swelled and fell like waves rolling on an ocean. Pea swiveled her head and stared at me, her eyes as green as her neon coat. The gold in Occam's eyes was snuffed. He shook himself like a cat who had been thrown in a tub full of icy water. Rick shook himself, entered, and went to the coffeemaker. Occam offered Rick a cup of coffee and the boss accepted a mug from him, both guys dipping their heads in that peculiarly male manner of greeting. As if nothing had happened and they were just starting their day.

I blinked, unchambered the round, reset the mag, safetied, and holstered the gun. Because that was what I was supposed to do. But my insides were churning. Fear trickled through my arms and legs and out my boot soles into the floor. I thought to take a breath, and my ribs felt creaky with the motion. I was shaking slightly.

Tandy entered the break room, his ten-mil held at his side, and took a chair beside me. "On the nine days of the full moon," he said softly, "they get antsy. Soon as they do, we start the music playing. Twenty-four-seven. Understand?" Tandy holstered his weapon, no expression on his face.

I said, "Trust me. I will not forget. *Ever.* I'm guessing there's drives with the music on them?"

He placed two in my hand. "One for your cell. Sync it to everything electronic you have. Keep a backup at your house. On the full moon, you keep the music handy and play it continuously."

"Okay. I just got one question. Why didn't Pea do something?"

"Pea?" Tandy, swiveled his head, taking in the entire room, seeing Pea back on Occam's shoulder. His mouth opened slowly and he breathed, "Oh . . . Nell . . ."

"What?"

Before he answered my question, his cell buzzed, and Tandy left the room, his phone to his ear. When I had first known Tandy, he had been this quiet, unassuming, introverted man. Not a man I would think would ever own, much less hold, a gun. Not a man I might consider capable of protecting himself. Not a man I associated with violence, except on the receiving end of it.

I had helped him when we first met, sending him some small bit of strength and power to resist the emotional impressions of the others. Had I sent him more than I knew? Had T. Laine's spells given him access to more assertive, violent personality traits? Had he picked up the aggression from the werecats? Or had Tandy always *been* more than I knew?

Before I could figure out how to address a batch of interlocking situations all at once, the others filed in, sleepy and begging coffee, T. Laine tossing a box of Krispy Kremes on the table. Everyone dug in. Pea jumped to the table and accepted a thimble-sized lump of sugared dough from JoJo. She sat up like a cat on the table and took it in her hands, which had opposable thumbs. I hadn't noticed that until now. Pea nibbled on the donut, her cat eyes watching me, as if entertained.

I stared at the wall, trying to figure out what had just happened.

"Nell?" Rick asked. "Did you ever figure out what the yellow glow in the center of the circle and triangle was?" He swiveled his laptop to me, with the report I had e-mailed last night after I gave myself hypothermia during all my scans.

I said, "I think it's the location of the activity that resulted in the MED."

"Can you pinpoint its GPS?" he asked.

"Not like you mean. Not with an address. Just a general location. I already looked. The yellow glow could be any of several businesses in the center of the circle."

Rick frowned and said, "A typical MED is a *postulated* weapon," he reminded his sleepy crew, "a magical exposure device, a black-magic curse, capable of an active or passive working intended to spread violent, offensive, magical energies over a wide area. Contamination of the populace by a dark-magical weapon for terrorist/political aims. We've considered the possibility of an MED from the get-go, but until we had some evidence for that unsupported theory—physical, material, human, or paranormal—I had no reason to send the hypothesis up the chain of command. After the things we've seen over the last few days, we now have to consider the clear and present danger of an MED. And worse, we may be facing something out of control of the witch or coven who created the working in the first place."

"Out of control?" T. Laine asked.

Rick nodded, his eyes on her. "Something that was and/or is acting independently of its creator."

I sat up. "The infinity loop dancer. Is it acting according to a prearranged, integrated part of the original working, or is it developing its own agenda?"

TEN

Rick looked at me the way a bug lover looked at a strange beetle held down by stickpins. "I've spent the better part of the night online with PsyLED experts in witch workings, *arcenciel* paranormal energies, and a theoretical physicist from MIT," Rick said. "I don't pretend to understand half of what they were talking about, but they narrowed down the problem with magic—as we currently understand it—being used in such a way that the working itself might become stable even after the initial working is completed and the formation energies are used up. Normally whatever energies remain after a working just blow back into the universe, the way a shock wave eventually disperses into the air. But according to the physicists, there is some theoretical possibility that may not always happen, and the energies might remain available, on-site, for other uses. Or take on stability and keep going even after the witch thinks she's closed it down. They postulated mechanisms by which paranormal energies—which they are still calling psysitopes but may alter or add to at any time, because they're scientists and classifications are always changing—can be transformed to become stable. And all of the mechanisms can be accomplished deliberately or by accident."

The others started taking notes. I took a slow, painful breath, fighting a bad feeling in my middle at Rick's words, thinking about my land. Thinking about the dancing infinity loop. Thinking about Soul and the energies I saw her become. A dragon made of light. Thinking about my blood, which might create or hold a trace of psysitopic activity when I commune with the earth. Or when I have roots buried inside me. Like at the pond. Thinking that all these things were disparate, but also interlocking because magic was nothing but energy, and energy was interlocking. $E=MC^2$.

I placed one hand on the break-room table, the other still on my middle where I could easily feel the rooty scars, adding my own thought at the top of Rick's list of possibilities. I might have created a magical something-something when I made roots grow inside, forcing a tree that had once been a live oak to heal me. Because I had to be responsible for that. Me. Not the tree. I might not have wanted to accept that possibility, might have hidden it from my conscious mind, but the knowledge that I had done that had always been there. And if *I* had done one such thing unconsciously, then something similar, or even vastly different, could happen in other ways and places. So, did someone somewhere accidentally release a magical working that caused the effects all around Knoxville, do it and not know they had done so, or did someone somewhere do it on purpose? Either way, what was the infinity loop now?

Around me the moon music swelled, high notes combined with deep, dire low notes of the compositions that kept the werecats from reacting to the moon so much. Music that Rick had provided to PsyLED, so long as no one knew where it came from and so long as PsyLED didn't try to find the air-magic composer. I'd studied that at Spook School too. So much I had learned and was now putting into use in the real world.

"Nell? Where y'at?" Rick asked in the slang of New Orleans. He didn't use it often, but when he did, the odd phrases were comforting on some level. And he might use them more, the closer we got to the full moon.

There was a proper response to the colloquial saying; it swam up from the deeps of my brain. "What it is?" I said slowly, and Rick's eyebrows went up in surprise. "I'm . . . putting it all together. You'uns go on. I'm listening."

"A'ight," Rick said.

A'ight, not *copy* or *okay.* That was odd.

"Idea number one," he said, "is for a working to be so powerful that when a coven is finished with it, the energies don't dissipate. Two is for a nascent magical consciousness to be stimulated by a low leak of mundane nuclear energy and evolve its intellect in the vicinity of the leak. Since none of the sites is located near a currently active energy plant, that idea is on hold.

"Three is for a creature made of energy, like an *arcenciel,* to accidentally stimulate and feed the working, giving dispersing working energies the time to stabilize. PsyLED says that there are no such creatures living in the Appalachians at this time."

I raised my gaze to Rick, let a tiny smile onto my mouth, and raised my eyebrows, saying with my expression, *One visiting. Does that count?* He stared back, not reacting to the meaning in my eyes, almost as if he had no idea what I meant. I had a feeling that Rick was a good actor, or a good liar.

Thomas Jefferson had said, *"He who permits himself to tell a lie once, finds it much easier to do it a second and third time, till at length it becomes habitual; he tells lies without attending to it, and truths without the world's believing him. This falsehood of the tongue leads to that of the heart, and in time depraves all its good dispositions."* Rick LaFleur had learned to lie well and young when he went undercover in New Orleans, and now it was simply part of him. I was pretty sure I didn't like that about him, not that I would ever tell him that to his face. My mama had raised me with manners. Mostly.

"Idea four," he said, turning from my knowing look, "is for the energies of a magical working, in the form of psysitopes, to touch a living creature, perhaps one with nascent magical powers. Perhaps one in the earth. And the . . . let's call it a nascent magical being . . . then evolves a way to perpetuate that energy."

Nascent magical beings, I thought. *Yes.*

"Number five is for a working witch circle to knowingly and deliberately send psysitopic energies into the earth, creating a stable working or stimulating a nascent magical energy intelligence or creature to evolve and stabilize the working. That would be an MED.

"And number five is for a working to track, trap, and release a, so far, theoretical nascent magical energy intelligence or creature and, deliberately or accidentally, stimulate it, to take over the working."

"Like shooting a ground squirrel full of magical power and seeing what it might do?" T. Laine asked. Rick gave her a half nod. "Which one do your specialists think we're looking for?"

"They suggest we search for number two and number three." Rick glanced at me and walked to the coffeepot, pouring himself the last cup in the pot. He put on a fresh pot. The others were busy typing up notes and working to make sense of new ideas. But the ideas weren't new to me. Not really. It felt as if the words were simply expressing what I guessed or knew about life and living and energy and magic, what I had known from the beginning when I first fed Soulwood. More, as if the words hinted at even more understanding, and solutions to my own problems, as well as the problems in Knoxville.

"Number three or number four," I said, my voice quiet. And now I lied, by omission, because there had been two evolution events in the area in the last few months. One was the interconnected one, on my land, involving Brother Ephraim, the sapling behind the house, and the tree in the churchyard. The other I could talk about. "I don't know how many of you read my report, but there are presences deep in the earth. I didn't know what they were. So I made a few early-morning phone calls to some people who know these hills and the mythos surrounding them."

Rick's shoulders hunched and he went still as a hunting cat, the coffeepot in one hand, mug in the other. To him, I said, "You need to call your experts back and tell them about the Old Ones. And they need to understand that they are very, very old, and very, very, *very* dangerous. They are not to be touched or stimulated or . . . or anything. At all."

Rick set down the pot and his mug and pulled his cell. He made a note, not asking who I had talked to. I figured he knew, so I didn't offer, but it would be in my report. What wouldn't be in the report was the fact that I had told Jane Yellowrock everything about the situation up here, even the classified things that no one was supposed to talk about outside of PsyLED. I had only met Jane twice, but she had a good head on her shoulders and knew a lot about paranormal things and creatures. And she was trustworthy with secrets, maybe because she carried her own.

Thomas Jefferson's quote about lying becoming habitual seemed like a mighty truth, and I was clearly racing down that particular road to hell myself. But keeping secrets meant lies, and my job meant keeping secrets. I was trapped in a catch-22 from which there was no escape except back into the life I had lived before. Alone. Or full speed ahead into the life of a liar, with people I liked. There wasn't much contest. At all.

"Old Ones?" Rick asked.

"Old Ones are the name given to . . . let's call them magical intelligences buried deeply in the earth. They live in all sorts of places, from deserts to oceans, but they are most accessible along mountain ranges."

"Old Ones," Tandy said, snapping his fingers as if understanding. "The concept that giant snakes live beneath the earth and when they move that's when we get earthquakes."

"Yes and no," I said. "Some ancient peoples did have a belief system about snakes and earthquakes, but the Cherokee have the concept that the Old Ones are . . . more along the lines of ancient gods, or ancient creation spirits. Jane Yellowrock said it might have something to do with the Hebrew concept of a plural godhead, so that when creation took place it was 'In the beginning, God . . .' and the ancient word for God was Elohim, which was plural. And then 'Let us make man in our own image.' Again plural. And some of the elder Cherokee seem to think that the Old Ones were part of God that was left behind in the earth and that to disturb them will bring about the end of the world. According to Jane, there are other Tribal American explanations and myths for the Old Ones, but . . . they are real. I felt them."

"How likely is it that this MED is related to the Old Ones?" Rick asked.

"I . . . It could be. I don't know."

"Okay. Until we know, we'll continue this investigation as if we are looking for someone or something that deliberately or accidentally caused this working. And try to stop them. And stop the working. Those three things are primary. Find the perpetrator, stop her, and stop the working. Bringing charges has to take a backseat to stopping it. Understand?"

We all nodded and no one commented on the female pronoun. Fewer than one percent of witches were male. And with the woman's voice in the earth, our unknown witch was a female. Rick continued. "JoJo has been working to narrow down the companies that might be capable of an MED. Nell started with six companies. JoJo ended up with three. Jo?"

"Nell started with a couple dozen companies and narrowed it to Alocam, Inc., LuseCo Visions, C-Corp Development, Kamines Future Products, and two 'black companies' who operate within the Paranormal Congressional Oversight Committee, with congressional funds and approval, Rosco J. Moose, Inc., and San-Inc. I ruled out Rosco and San-Inc, two companies under the same ownership umbrella, a single family, both companies working on propulsion devices and R&D for space travel. Neither has interest in psysitopes." JoJo turned her tablet around so we could see. "Then I used Nell's center of the magical circle idea and ruled out two others, leaving us with LuseCo Visions and Kamines Future Products. I put in a few calls up the line and word came back down to visit both, that both companies have witches on payroll or as consultants and both are interested in new energy sources, especially self-perpetuating ones. LuseCo is working on some kind of self-perpetuating energy source, and Kamines is working on something called *Strom*. Not *Storm*. *Strom*. No information available on either research project."

"Nell, can you tell us what to look for?" Rick asked.

"Lainie," I said, using the diminutive of her name, "what do you see when you do a working?"

"Not much. Colors sometimes. Spots of light moving." She sounded surprised at the question. "Well, unless a visual display is part of the working. They didn't teach you that at Spook School?"

"They did, but it isn't true. Jane Yellowrock can see magics. All of the visual and non-human-visual range. She can actually see them working." Rick's breath hitched slightly before smoothing. "Her animal forms can too, which means some animals can see magical energies, normally, just like the werecats can see bodily fluids in the dark, normally, but we can't. And I can see magical energies, at least underground." I frowned. "Could you do something magical, right now, so I can watch?"

"What? Set off a prepared spell? Sure." She tilted her coffee cup and let a few drops splash onto the tabletop, then pulled a carved moonstone disc about the size and shape of a quarter from a pocket and spun it across the table. The coffee disappeared. She snapped up the disc.

I saw nothing. No colored lights, no shadows, nothing, not even the coffee, which disappeared, leaving only a mist hanging above the table. I tuned them out, half hearing them as I thought about what I saw underground when I communed with the land.

"*That*, you pitiful, mundane people," T. Laine said as I thought, "was a little cleanup *evaporate and conceal* spell that I keep handy for when I spill coffee on myself. And before you ask, it's hard to make, time-consuming, and no, I will not make one for you. The only reason I used it now is that it was getting weak and needed to be recharged anyway."

"Getting weak," I said. "The energies dissipate?"

"Totally. Always. A self-perpetuating form of magic, outside of a magical being like an *arenciel*, is an impossibility, just like human life without food and water is an impossibility. The people researching it are wasting man-hours and money."

"Hmmm," I murmured.

"Is there a *conceal* working for blood?" Rick asked, his tone mild.

"Yeah. Ditto on the not making you one."

"Maybe you need to make some *reveal* workings. Just in case someone has access to a blood-hiding spell," he said.

"I can, but there's no need," T. Laine said. "You got cat noses. No matter what we do, witches can't get rid of the lingering scents. The table here?" She pointed. "Still smells of coffee. People may not be able to smell it, but cats can."

"Back on track," Rick said. "Jo, we have LuseCo Visions and Kamines Future Products. What do we know about them?"

"Not much. Both are privately held companies. They do energy research and they are not tied in with TVA, so we can't ask the authority to just go busting in and demand info."

"Everything about energy in Tennessee is tied in with the Tennessee Valley Authority," Rick said.

"Nope. Not these companies. And they got security up the ying-yang."

"Ying-yang?" I asked. "Not yin-yang?"

JoJo did a little back-and-forth head-swivel thing that I could never duplicate in a million years, and said, "Two very different things. Yin-yang is that black-and-white circular thing in Chinese philosophy that means *male* and *female* and *light* and *shadow* and all that."

Tandy said, "Actually yin-yang is an Asian concept that describes how opposite or contrary forces can also be complementary and interconnected."

"Now shut up, you human candy cane. I got the floor."

Human candy cane? Tandy did have white skin and very red Lichtenberg lightning lines sketched across his body, but that term sounded awfully pejorative to me. Except that Tandy blushed. I looked from him to JoJo and back, and I suddenly realized that Tandy and JoJo had a . . . a *thing*. They were involved . . . *romantically*.

My own blush went scarlet. *Wow.* That went against all the rules. If anyone figured it out. Except that there was Rick and Paka . . . and everyone knew about *that*. Maybe Unit Eighteen—which was special among all the PsyLED units because we were composed almost entirely of paranormals—had different rules, rules no one had told me. I had started off without the mandatory policy and guidelines meeting. I hadn't even thought about that until now. Maybe rules for strictly human units didn't apply to a unit made up mostly of paranormal creatures. I shook my head and listened to JoJo who was into a diatribe.

"—*ying-yang* is a hip-hop duo. And it's also the street term for a vagina."

I wished I had not tuned back in so quickly.

"So, *up the ying-yang* make sense to you yet?" She was talking to me.

"Sadly yes," I said. I crossed my arms over my chest and glared at her. "A *great deal* makes sense now."

JoJo flinched the tiniest bit and I smiled in a way that mighta been a tad mean. I decided I needed to get this meeting back on track. I said, "I can see the energies of the working that's affecting all the sites. I thought everyone could. But I guess it's just me."

Rick said, "I thought you were using hyperbolic, metaphorical terms in your reports."

"No. I see the underground energies. I didn't see the energies of T. Laine's tabletop working, but I see the stuff underground. Even T. Laine's *Break* working. Even the Old Ones. So I need to double-check the readings at one of the sites and then do a deep scan on the land on both companies' sites. And even maybe look at the hospital patients to see what I can see there. Today."

"Is that safe?" Occam asked.

I scowled at him. "You wouldn't ask that of him." I pointed to Tandy. "Or of them." I pointed to JoJo and T. Laine. "No. It probably isn't safe. But I need to do it anyway."

"Fine. I'll be with you, Nell, sugar, supporting you all the way." But his tone said he was thinking about ways to make me change my mind.

Rick looked at Occam, then at me. His face softened in an emotion that I didn't understand. "You two"—he pointed at Occam and me—"go. Read some land. And make nice while you're gone. No arguing this close to the full moon. T. Laine, you go referee. And while you're out there, see what magic is doing and try to figure out how to *Break* this working."

"The leader of the Knoxville coven, Taryn Lee Faust, finally agreed to meet with me," T. Laine said. "Me alone. I'll be breaking off from the others for a while."

"Be safe," he ordered. "Keep your cells on. Carry a GPS backup and a stack of 3PE unis. They're in the supply closet

outside my office. You two"—Rick pointed at JoJo and Tandy—
"get the paperwork started on warrants for both businesses. I
want this sitch solved by nightfall. Figure this out, people.
Before more humans die."

"And if it isn't solved by nightfall?" JoJo asked, her tone
steady and uninflected.

"And if it isn't, you're senior agent. You're in charge, JoJo,
just like always."

They were talking about the full moon. It was nearly here.

Antimoon music playing on the fancy sound system, Occam
drove his sporty little car. T. Laine, who had to break away at
some point for her witchy meeting, followed. She called my cell
when we were partway there and offered some advice about
how to do a scan without attracting the attention of the things
below the surface. It was good advice, and I cogitated on ways
to implement her suggestions.

The day had warmed again, proving the old Southern saying,
You don't like the weather? Wait'll tomorrow. Southern weather
seldom lasted more than a few days before shifting into a totally
different pattern. An ice storm, followed by clear skies and
seventy-degree temps. An abnormally warm fall, followed by a
freezing spell with an early snow.

As if reading my mind about the variability of the temperatures, or making small talk, Occam said, "I thought when I
moved up here"—his long legs worked the pedals and the little
car made good time, weaving in and out of traffic—"I'd get
snow and sledding and skiing."

I looked back and saw that T. Laine was a long way behind
us. "You ski?" I asked, my mind occupied elsewhere, less than
half on the conversation. I pulled out my tablet and opened a
new topographical satellite map of the area.

"Not yet. I was hoping to learn. Can't be harder than riding
a horse. You ski?"

"Snow, like a horse, has a mind of its own. Churchwomen
don't ski, so I never learned. And I never saw the point after I
left. You want to ski, you can head east, into the mountains." On
the tablet, I studied the rows of hills west of Knoxville, curving
like a fishhook, row after row.

"You offering to show me the way, Nell, sugar?"

"What? Oh." I pointed to the GPS. "You won't get lost." I twisted in the seat to face him and asked, "You ever hear of the Old Ones?"

"I guess that's a no," he muttered. Louder he said, "Nope. Native American tribes out west got all sorts of legends and myths to explain the world around them. I figure the eastern tribes got much the same.

"You do know that Rick is still hung up on Jane Yellowrock." I nodded and Occam finished with, "It's a very catlike thing you do, Nell, sugar, to keep bringing her up."

I made a *hmmm* sound and slid back into place, my fingers tapping on the tablet. Occam fell silent. Or I blocked him out, thinking. Until the small car pulled off the road and around the crime scene tape, into the entrance of a two-rut road. We were at the pond. I tapped the tablet to sleep and set it in my bag. "Are . . ." My voice sounded reedy and thin, all of a sudden. I cleared it and said, "Are the bodies all gone?"

"Yes. They are, Nell, sugar."

"Okay. That's good." The car rolled slowly around the curve. The turn around the trees opened out and the pond appeared. No cars, no fire pits, no tents, no bodies. I blew out a breath. The grassy area around the small body of water was still churned up. The few snowflakes had wet the ground and the tracks, leaving them damp and softly contoured. The pond itself looked tranquil. When the car stopped at a safe one hundred feet from the pond, we got out and put on unis. Carrying my faded pink communing blanket, I picked out a patch of thick grass in sight of the water and the tree where the camera had been. I sat on the folded blanket, peeled back one inelastic glove, and held my palm gently, carefully, about six inches above the ground. And closed my eyes.

I was going to go slow. Very slow. I was going to do nothing to attract the energies in the land. All I wanted was to observe. Like a hunter in a tree, watching a trail that a deer might take to water. Dropping slowly, I let my fingers extend and point downward, until my index finger touched the dirt. I let my mind ease into the ground a few inches, into the roots of grass and around some root runners that had come from near the lake. None of them seemed to notice my finger or me. Maybe my previous approach had been a lot like a wrecking ball rather than a surgical probe. I pressed a bit deeper. My descent into the earth was like entering a pool of still water so slowly that I left no ripples, leaving no sign that I was here if no one was looking.

That was T. Laine's suggestion. *Go slow.* Hiding just below the surface, I scanned down.

The dancer infinity loop was different now. The rotating lights of its energies were tighter, more compact. It was moving in a regular, unvarying path, like a race track, but perfectly circular. The circle it circumnavigated was clear and concise and seemed to glow a very deep green, right at the edges of what my mind could perceive, marking it as a magical, or psysitopic, energy circle. The green circle was marked with three red-glowing spots of the equilateral triangle, and was centered with a golden glow. The glow was bright and steady, as if the infinity loop had settled into orbit around a false sun.

I hadn't seen all this so clearly before, but then I hadn't thought to drop in and simply watch, like a spy, and not attract attention with looking too hard. Before, I had dropped in fast and looked around, moved around a lot. Been conspicuous. This silent and still observation was much smarter. I eased down even more, a probe instead of a battering ram.

Below all that activity, the Old One slumbered, silent. But from the center of the circle, a faint green trail slid down, deep into the earth, to touch the Old One's presence. Not tapping, not nudging, simply touching. I waited for a pulse of energy as on my land, but this working—whatever it was—wasn't pulsing with anything or doing anything, at least not right now. It simply *was*, a thing in a state of being.

I withdrew to the surface and let go the breath I had been holding too long. Lifted my fingertip away from the ground. There were no vines. No roots. Looking up, my eyes met Occam's, his glowing golden, a vamp-killer in one hand. The blade caught the light of the risen sun. T. Laine stood behind him, watching me, the psy-meter 2.0 open in her hands.

I breathed for a few seconds and then said to them both, "T. Laine, you were right. There was a way to observe and not get caught. I might have a future as a sneaky trespasser."

The moon witch gave me a preoccupied nod and closed up the P 2.0.

Occam sheathed his blade and held down a hand. His eyes bled back to human, but his jaw looked leaner, his expression more fierce. I took his hand and he pulled me to my feet, steadied me with a hand on my waist. His palm was heated, scorching. I stepped gingerly away from him and his hand dropped. "What'd you discover, Nell, sugar?"

"I'm pretty sure that something is emitting psysitopes in a slow, steady release. The dancer, reshaped into an infinity loop of energies, is orbiting it in a circle. Three points of the circle are still bright red with energies that may be getting tighter and smaller, but no dimmer. Let's go to LuseCo and Kamines so I can do a read there."

T. Laine had been looking out over the pond as I spoke, and now she gestured with her chin. "What's that?"

Both Occam and I looked out over the water. It took me a moment to see what she was talking about. Just beneath the pond surface something glistened, something midnight black and oily looking, smooth and round. I took a step that way and Occam grabbed my arm. "Don't," he said.

"Oh. Yeah. That might be dumb." I shook my arm and Occam's fingers slid free again. It was surely my imagination that the touch seemed reluctant to release. "Can we get a camera-mounted drone to make a flyover? Or an RVAC?" RVACs were remote-viewing aircraft, small, quiet, easy to control, and fast. I didn't know if Unit Eighteen possessed one of our own or just had access to one, but we had used them before.

"Tandy's been through the training. We'll see if he can requisition an RVAC and do a flyover out here," Occam said.

Silent, we went back to our cars and drove to Kamines Future Products. The property was gated, a twelve-foot-high brick wall blocking access, a single drive-in, and a security guard in the tiny guardhouse. Occam pulled up and gave his ID to the guard, explaining that we wanted to speak to someone in charge. The guard asked if we had a warrant to which Occam politely said, "I'd rather just ask a few questions of someone in senior management than make this a legal matter. But I can get a paper, sure. It'll be extensive and invasive and disruptive, whereas a little convo might be all we need." I thought he sounded polite and reasoned and the guard and his up-the-line managers must have thought so too because we were granted immediate access.

Kamines was a three-story building with no windows on the sides and a steep roof. It was built of local brick in a beige-brown pattern and the roof was real clay tiles. Occam and T.

Laine went to the front door and inside. I waited in the car, thinking about what I had learned today, about the case and about my abilities to sneak around underground. About my brother and his wife. But mostly about the tree I had mutated. Because I was responsible, and only I could fix it. If it could be fixed at all. I had told my brother how to kill the tree, but I didn't think it would die easily or fast. I thought it would come back again and again, mutating as needed to stay alive. And the fact that Brother Ephraim was in touch with the tree, even through so small a line of energy, suggested that things might be more dire than even I had guessed. What I really needed to know was what the tree wanted. Which was as bizarre a question as I'd ever thought about a tree.

The passenger car door opened, Occam standing there, waiting. The sun was behind his jeans-clad legs, and I saw for the first time that he was wearing Western boots with pointy toes, and his jacket was of a Western design, made of soft leather. I wondered if he had killed and eaten the cow in his cat form, and I smiled. Occam smiled back and stepped out of the way.

"We have permission," he said as I stood from the car and pulled my faded communing blanket out from behind the seat, "for you and T. Laine to search for wayward paranormal energies inside the lobby and in the front yard. According to the spokesperson, Kamines is involved in research for plastics that can withstand the surface condition of Mars, long-term. They said nothing about the energy research JoJo discovered in her deep drill. Lainie's readings inside were ambient normal, and she's ready to take more out here."

"Okay," I said. "I'm ready."

I chose a spot in the sun, on the well-mown lawn, and set my folded blanket so the sun would be at my back. Just as T. Laine left through Kamines' front door and approached, I placed the tips of my fingers on the ground and let the fingers of my consciousness drift beneath the ground. Roots and fertilizer. Grubs and beetles and ants. And then I was below the surface. The building to my side was far bigger than it appeared on the outside. It went down in the earth four stories. There were areas that suggested they had heat-producing machinery down there. Maybe very hot. Like things that would melt plastics. Or kilns for ceramics.

I dropped below the building, into compacted soil and the remains of an ancient riverbed. There were signs of water in the crevices of rocks, and something gemlike, crystalline, but there was no sign of anything golden and glowing below the building. But . . . there was such a thing not far away. I oriented my consciousness for it and pulled back up. "Not here," I said calmly. "That way." I indicated with my thumb toward the east.

"I got only surface readings," T. Laine said. "Nothing anomalous that couldn't be explained by them having witches on payroll to see if magic will work on Mars or if it's an Earth-based-only energy form. So I agree. Not here. Though the spox was a smarmy little woman who somehow made me want to punch her. Despite my calm nature and well-balanced personality."

Occam snorted like a cat in amusement. He offered his palm to me, but I was already rising. I handed him the ratty blanket, which he threw over his shoulder. "We can work up a grid for this site and get lunch before our next stop," he said. "We aren't that far from Tomato Head. I'm in the mood for a beef Cheddar Head."

"You always want meat on full moons," T. Laine said.

"Not me. I'm all about the ladies," Occam said, laughing.

T. Laine shook her head and breathed a single jaded word. *"Men."*

I had no idea what they were talking about, and opened my cell to a compass to orient myself. The golden glow hadn't appeared to be that far away. I marked it on *CSM-Nell*, beginning step two of a PI—paranormal investigation—and drew on my map a grid of the grounds. At my side, T. Laine began to take P 2.0 readings—which were virtually zero. Nada. Kamines Future Products was not involved in the magic working beneath the ground. Overhead, the sun came out and warmed us, making me wish I had brought my sunglasses and a hat. More things to add to my daily gobag.

Tomato Head was fabulous. The beef Cheddar Head had enough meat to fulfill a werecat's protein needs. The lamb sausage and sun-dried tomato pizza we shared satisfied T. Laine's pizza addiction and had me writing out a recipe for a homemade version on a private laptop file. It was totally worth the hour away from the case.

It was after one when we left for LuseCo, and by then JoJo had updated our info on all the companies and what she had found was crucial. I scanned the report, reading the pertinent parts aloud to Occam in a staccato rhythm I had learned in Spook School. "Privately owned business. Government contract. Primary focus is propulsion research. Secondary is energy, doing theoretical and practical experiments on a particle of magic that resulted from an unrelated test in the Hadron Collider in Cern. The lead physicist states: 'The particle was discovered tangentially to particle theory experiments, as the field of study relates to proton-on-proton collisions.' This mean anything to you?"

"Not a lot. Maybe that they were working on atomic particles and found magic," Occam said, "something other than psysitopes, and now they're researching the magic particle they discovered to make it more magical. Or more powerful."

Which sounded dangerous and fit in with some of Rick's theories: for the energies of a magical working to touch and mutate a creature that then evolves a way to use or perpetuate its own magical energy, or more likely, for a working witch circle to knowingly and deliberately or accidentally send psysitopic energies into the earth, and make a working become stable—a working that then begins to do things its creators didn't plan on. At this point both seemed possible. Either one might involve the atomic magic particle and result in an accidental magical release that would look and act like an MED. I wasn't sure which one would be worse.

I continued scanning the summary. "It was later found to be reproduced by a full coven of evenly balanced magic users raising a *hedge of thorns* working. End of summary."

"You know the Collider people had to be pissed," Occam said, "when a group of twelve witches, probably housewives and farmers and artists by trade, with little or no higher education, created the same particle that theoretical and experimental physicists did, without all the fancy equipment."

I laughed softly and checked my cell, sat maps, the GPS, and the compass, and determined that we were headed in the correct direction. The cell rang, and I answered. "Ingram."

"Nell," Rick said. "Just so you know. One of the patients at the UTMC died. Adam Sayegh."

"But he was doing better," I said. "He was likely one of the people in the second story, away from the stronger psysitopes."

"There was an incident overnight. He fell and hit his head, started bleeding, and they couldn't stop it, but the blood was black, not red. After death, his body began redlining psysitopes. PsyCSI took the body for autopsy at the main HQ in Richmond and they said the other remains we sent, some of which had gone through autopsies and necropsies, were beginning to sludge into black goo. The deputy director over at PsyLED and Soul made the decision to cremate all the dead—geese, deer, and now humans, once studies are complete. The medical types don't want to keep them around."

Usually in cases like this, bodies were kept for study and dissection, often for years. The death followed by the decay of the bodies must have been very bad to result in cremation and loss of study subjects.

"We're also getting an additional PsyCSI team on-site later today. The Arizona CSI team will be taking over the third floor of our building, but they have their own entrance, so we may never see them. I've arranged a hotel for them. Tell the others," Rick said. "Are you on the way to LuseCo?"

"Yes. ETA maybe ten minutes," I said.

"Wear your uni. Orders."

The call ended before I could ask what kind of incident caused Adam Sayegh to fall and bleed, redline, and die. And which occurred first, the psysitopes or the dying. Whatever this was, it was evolving fast. I remembered Dougie asking me to save her girls. So far, I was doing a mighty poor job of that. I called T. Laine and gave her, and Occam at the same time, Rick's message.

By the time we got to LuseCo, I had unis for Occam and me out of the space behind the two seats. He sighed but accepted his.

ELEVEN

"There is simply no way that our research or our facility is responsible for the problems you are describing."

I heard the words as I entered the front door after the fastest earth read in my personal history. "Occam. This is it," I said.

"This is what?" the woman demanded.

"This is the site where the . . ." Not having a proper term, I settled on ". . . the contamination originated," I said. "I've notified PsyLED and KEMA. Per Rick, no one in or out."

"This is ridiculous!" the woman said. She was tall and built like a woman weight lifter, all shoulders and almost no waist. She was African-American and something else, maybe Asian or Pacific Islander, and if ever fire steamed from a woman's eyes, this was what it would look like. "You can't come in here and interfere with our research. This is a privately held company. We have rights," she said. "I'm calling legal."

"Makayla, is there a problem?" The voice was melodious and charismatic, and though I was about to head back out, I stopped and listened, standing in the doorway. The speaker was a slender man, about my height, maybe of Swedish extraction. He was blond, that white blond that looks like angel wings, and his skin was the color of fine cream. He took the concept of *gorgeous* to undisputed and dangerous heights, standing with a dancer's grace and a military man's spine, blue eyes flashing. He held a hand out to Occam. "I'm Kurt Daluege, the principal owner and CEO of LuseCo." He took Occam's hand, and both men stopped, still as watching cats, assessing each other. "I will handle this, Makayla," Kurt said.

"Nell?" Occam said, without turning my way.

"KEMA is on the way to seal off the building," I said, "as per standard paranormal quarantine procedures."

Occam nodded and stepped back. "Let's chat," he said to Daluege. I stepped outside, my uni swishing with each step. I had a job to do, and as probie, that meant traffic control. Literally. I'd miss out on all the good stuff.

An hour later, we had LuseCo locked down, the VIPs spitting mad, the employees from the top guy down demanding lawyers, and a certain feeling that we were about to break the case wide-open. I was mostly watching from outside, but the people in charge of LuseCo were brash and angry and seemed perfectly guilty to me.

The entire unit was assembled, deputies at both parking lots and the drive, and Rick and Soul were both on premises and in charge. Everyone was wearing P3E unis, even the LuseCo employees, though theirs were company issued and a silvery gray. Rick had an earbud in one ear, the other hanging down his shirt, the faintest strains of antimagic music audible as he walked up.

"What did your read indicate?" he asked as he crossed the lawn to me.

I had been thinking about how I was going to phrase my report, and how I was going to defend my claim when it was challenged to my face. "We're standing on the epicenter of the activity." I liked the term *epicenter*. It implied energy and destruction and mayhem and specificity. I wanted every single word I used to indicate all that. "If it isn't a deliberate release, then they have a low-level leakage of something hazardous about twenty feet below the surface. The output appears stable, and my scan is backed up by repeated P 2.0 readings and hand-held psy-meter readings. Everything we've seen in the surrounding community reflects this crisis." *Crisis* was a good word too. One of my trainers at Spook School had said, *"Spin is everything."* I rather considered that *context* was everything, but I hadn't argued at the time. "Why? What does the company say?" I asked.

"Kurt Daluege and his CFO, Makayla Lin, finally admitted that they had a problem earlier in the week, but they say they have it under control."

"Problem?" I let the disbelief into my voice.

Rick didn't smile and adjusted the earbud in his ear. "They were using a full coven and a special laser to test part of the collider theory, and the working 'got away' from them. 'Got away' was Kurt's word choice. T. Laine has never heard of paranormal energies 'getting away' from a closed circle."

"Me neither," I said.

"Normally when a company is involved in energy R&D, no paranormals are allowed anywhere near, because mundane energies and psysitopes have been known to either cancel each other out or make them more volatile."

"*Explosive* is a better term," T. Laine said, coming up behind me, her white uni swishing too, "but I'll go with *volatile*." Behind her, Tandy nodded, agreeing.

Rick shielded his eyes from the overhead sun and studied the grounds. "All employees at LuseCo were human until a few months past, when they hired over two dozen witches and got them to form two covens of twelve and sync their energies." Before T. Laine or I could remind him that was not the way covens were formed, he went on. "Money talked and they got two smaller covens to combine. The witches agreed because there's a crossing of two ley lines directly beneath us."

"I don't feel any ley lines . . ." I stopped and started again. "I don't feel any ley lines anywhere," I said. "I didn't sense them . . . Oh. No. Whatever they did wiped out the ley lines below Knoxville."

T. Laine said, "*That's* what I've been feeling. I'd have known it if I had tried any big workings, but . . . And that explains why the Knoxville coven leader, Taryn Lee Faust, keeps putting off meeting with me. She stood up our meeting this morning. Son of a witch on a switch! She knows what's happened to the ley lines and doesn't want to admit it."

Wryly Rick said, "Faust is the leader of the conjoined covens and my money's on them trying to fix it by themselves, off-site and quietly. They haven't been in to work in forty-eight hours."

"That sounds bad," T. Laine said, worried about the repercussions should witches be responsible for this situation. She was always worried about her species, with good reasons. Witch haters were everywhere.

"The energy testing was going according to plan and expectations with each test," Rick said, "on workings that attempted to replicate the particle theory research. But then there was an 'accidental dispersal of the energies'—their words—while raising a working. The testing lab is underground and the witches and the LuseCo techs thought the particles would be simply dispersed into the earth. But there was something different about this working, and by morning, the lab was redlining psysitopes.

"Interpreting their words, reading between the lines, I'd say they shot a fused magical/energy beam into the ground during a working and it didn't dissolve. Instead it evolved and stabilized and is now acting outside of testing parameters. They never expected to need a P 2.0, so all the testing they've done has been on the P 1.0. Lainie, when we finish here, find the head of security and do a reading of the lab."

"Gladly. Idiots. Them, not you," she added.

I extended the P 2.0 to her and watched as she entered the front door, merged with the other people in unis, and disappeared down an elevator.

I said, "The infinity loop dancer belowground talked to me. Either it's using the words of the original spell itself—like Rick's idea of a working that can develop on its own within strict parameters—or it's developed and exhibited some form of intelligence."

"That first one is more likely," Tandy said, his odd reddish eyes sparking with excitement. "The words of the working got caught up in it and took on a life on their own."

That theory made sense to them because it fit into their worldview. But I had seen sentience below the earth—sleeping, powerful sentience. I knew it was possible. "Whatever it was before the testing 'got away' from the combined coven, that dancing thing is the result, whether it noticed the particle and took it for itself, or the particle brought the thing awake and gave it power. I'm now calling it the infinity creature."

Rick looked over my shoulder, into the distance, thinking. The term *creature* changed things from a discovery inquiry to a criminal investigation. It meant that we might have to discover and determine sentience and guilt. His face was drawn and tight, the skin crinkled around his black eyes. Faster-than-normal healing was a standard upgrade for were-creatures, but his inability to shift was aging him. Hurting him. In the background, the moon music played, heard from the dangling earbud.

"Its creation may have been an accident, or something a witch and a LuseCo experimental physicist did on purpose," I said. "But however it was started, the result is a mutation, an evolution. Whatever it was originally has now changed and, on some level, might be aware of its surroundings, and possibly aware of other things around it." Like what I had done with the tree. Mutated it. Changed it. "This could indicate just a very high-level working, or a sign of evolving intelligence."

"Are you suggesting that we protect it?" Rick asked.

I almost nodded but stopped. We killed mosquitoes and termites and roaches and mice as pests, and they had brains and instinct and purpose, far more than this thing might. The infinity might be defined as a pest too. But I didn't want to let it go. What if it was a magical creature? The churchmen wanted to burn me at the stake for being a magical creature. "Ummm. Yes?"

"And how do we do that, Nell?" Rick sounded interested. Maybe a little too polite, which, with senior agents, meant they were feeling anything except polite. "People, humans, are dying. How am I supposed to protect something only you can sense?"

The roots in my belly writhed. "I . . ." I had no way to explain or to bring attention to what I knew in my gut—literally—to be a potential major problem. "I got no idea," I said.

Rick shook his head, dismissing me. My face burned with embarrassment. I had a flash to being a child and seeing the older girls turn away in scorn at ball playing or sewing, because I was such a strange little girl. I hadn't thought about that in ages. My belly ached, and I kneaded the scars there, rolling the hard tissue against my fingers.

I said, "If I know which of the psysitopes is actually redlining, I can do a deeper reading."

"No," Occam said, his voice unyielding.

I scowled at him. I hadn't heard him come up. "I did more than one reading already today, one here while you were inside. I was fine. T. Laine's methodologies are working great at keeping me from being noticed."

"No," he said again, his eyes cat gold.

"Occam," Rick said. "Earbud. Now."

The other werecat growled low in his throat but worked the earbud into his left ear.

Rick said, "It isn't our job to figure out how to deal with the situation on the ground, with the public, with the medical problems, or with media fallout, which is surely coming. KEMA, UTMC, and Soul are here to spearhead that. We have a job. It's problematic for some of us near the full moon, but the job doesn't change. *Focus.* LuseCo's energy experiment went bad. The result is becoming a massive problem, and it's our job to make sure nothing falls between the cracks. So figure out how this happened, who at LuseCo is responsible for the damage and the deaths, and who to charge with a crime, if one was committed. That's it. We have a job, so let's do it."

Rick gestured us to follow and walked into the shade, where he removed his tablet from an oversized uni pocket. Even with gloved fingers, he was able to pull up the case map and highlight the locations of the land where the unusual energy readings were taking place.

He said, "We have a nearly perfect triangle. Triangles and circles are the most basic magical maths, pi and circumference and angles, used in every witch working. And they are the most common ones used in a witch circle when one witch is working solo."

He was giving us Witch Magic 101, which might have been insulting, but I just nodded. *Take it back to basics.* That was the way problem solving was done in school and in the field.

"The most common geometrical configuration when three witches are sitting is the circle and the triangle. Basic triangles are used to channel rising energies in the buildup for a magical working, to contain them as they escalate. So the question arises—is the triangle being used now, by witches or some other magical being, to some purpose? Is some*one* or some*thing* deliberately keeping it going? If so, who? How? And if we accidentally allow the energies to release during the course of our investigation, what happens? If the person who may be keeping the energies going deliberately lets the energies release, what happens?"

And what happens if we shut off the working and kill a sentient being? But I kept that to myself because I knew the answer. It had hurt humans, therefore it would be put down like a rabid dog. I said, "The area first affected was the pond and the geese, and looking at the other sites, that location becomes magnetic north of the working."

Rick lay a finger on the tablet screen and made a strange chuffing sound. "So it is."

"The dancing infinity creature is running on the circle, with those three points maintaining the circle's stability."

"Good," Rick said. "When we're granted access, we'll be looking for previously undetected paranormals, hiding as humans. We will also be looking for witches. For anyone who might have brought in a magical item that interfered with the testing, or any signs of blood magic that might have been added to the testing. Blood would have altered any experimental working. JoJo has already started with company employee records, including upgrading existing background checks. This is new research for them, and to this point no company employees have been routinely monitored for magical energies. So I want every single one rescanned with the P 2.0. We have to look for magical beings who are still in the closet, employed here in hiding. Also, consider things like the possibility of an unknown witch involved tangentially with an employee, who used the relationship to somehow influence the experiment. We need to know about secret love affairs, personality changes, changes in lifestyle, finances, or habits. This is Interview 101 with a twist. Tandy, you will be present on every interview, silent, observational only, unless you sense anything out of the ordinary. At that point, you take over."

Tandy nodded.

"Nell and Occam, your first order of business is to ascertain if these paranormal energies were activated by magic-working terrorists, imported or homegrown. If terrorism is involved, then we have to assume that someone or something will be targeted, and we need to know who and what, fast. I don't expect you to find anything, but if I'm wrong, contact T. Laine, who will turn over the interviews to Tandy and to me, and join you on the info gathering. Second order of business is to detect if the witch circle was sabotaged, for any reason from a lover's spat, to financial concerns, to terrorist activity."

The door opened behind us. Standing there, wearing a gray LuseCo uni with an apricot stripe across it, was Makayla. It conformed to her body far better than our pick-a-size-and-hope-it-fits 3PE unis. "Your unit's *cumulative* security clearance is below the projects taking place here," she said, her eyes still spitting sparks. "However, I have been informed by a *very important person* at DoD that PsyLED's access is confirmed. You have permission to talk to the techs involved in what we now agree may have fallen out of the experiment's paradigm. Not a single tech will stand in your way."

That was an odd way to phrase it—no *tech* will stand in our way—but half the team tramped inside, their unis swishing. Occam and I went to the parking lot, removed our unis, and drove away in his vehicle, not speaking to each other, the anti-moon music playing on his earbuds, hanging around his neck. It wasn't precisely the silent treatment, but it wasn't pleasant either. I figured out what was happening. Occam was acting like an alpha cat, giving me the silent treatment, protecting the pro-bie kitten, not wanting me to do my job. That was not acceptable in any way, shape, or form. I just had to figure out how to tell him that without damaging his cat sensibilities or the unit's cohesiveness. That had been covered in Spook School too, but only for human teams, not in any way that I had been able to utilize or even make sense of for a paranormal unit.

In the multifamily household where I grew up, the silent treatment was an unsuccessful weapon of choice, because in a home with multiple wives, the husband always won in that game. Someone always talked to him, so the silence of one wife was hard to detect unless she resorted to slamming doors or crying, both of which had always been deemed immature. The silence of the husband was ignored totally as the wives were consumed by child rearing and running a home. I had never spent time in a home with adults, watching them work through problems. I'd left home too early. With Leah dying, there had been no cantankerous discussions between John and Leah. Therefore I wasn't really sure what adults did to resolve problems. So this was confusing.

The sun was in my eyes and I pulled down the visor to cut the glare. There was a small mirror there, showing me traffic and more traffic behind us, but my eyes settled on a small green car weaving in and out and back and forth, trying to force its way through the crush. I kept my eyes on it rather than look at Occam. I crossed my arms over my chest, thinking. Finally I said, "I could shoot you."

"What?" There was an alarmed tone in his question.

"I'm not good at playing silly games. You got something to say, say it. Or I could shoot you."

Occam laughed, a spluttering sound that made me want to laugh with him, but I kept my eyes on the road behind us. "That's one of the reasons I like you, Nell, sugar. No nonsense." He slanted his eyes to me and back to the road as he took a right into traffic. "Silver or standard?"

I hid a smile. "Standard. You ain't worth jail time."

Occam chortled. "You do know why I don't want you to do a read, don'tcha, sugar?"

"Tired of dulling your blade on roots?"

He laughed again, his hands visibly relaxing on the wheel. "There is that. But mostly because leaving a woman in bloody pieces is not a way to inspire confidence or to get her to agree to take in a movie."

I dragged my eyes from the green car to him in confusion. "I like movies."

His mouth turned down, puckering in thought. "Chick flick or action?"

"There was a Transformers night at Spook School. I liked that. And the Star Trek marathon."

The green car behind us cut off a driver and passed another, and was suddenly speeding toward us. The windows on both sides came down. Something stuck out the passenger window. "Occam? Are we being followed?"

"See the little green car, do you?"

"And what might be a gun hanging out the passenger window."

Occam took another turn, a hard left, across traffic, without the use of his blinker. Vehicles swerved to avoid us. Horns blew. Traffic on the four-lane road snarled. The green car behind us fishtailed trying to follow our turn.

We were in trouble.

"Call it in."

I tightened my seat belt and pulled out my cell. I punched in 911 and, on the car's computer, I pulled up a map and our GPS location. My heart pounded, my breath came fast and hard, cold as death in my lungs. Hands shaking, I gave the 911 operator our twenty and our situation. I asked for the sheriff's department and the highway patrol. Then I re-called Rick and put him on speaker as it rang. "Rick, we're in trouble," I said as he answered.

The green car was gaining on us, despite the speed of the sportster. To Occam, I said, "Passenger window means they'll shoot you first and take me down after we crash."

"What?" Rick demanded.

Occam took a hard right, tires squealing, slinging me back and forth. I grunted, my breath catching. The seat belt strained my ribs on one side and the door bruised me on the other. On the car's computer screen, the map showed us off into no roads at all. Green screen. And the condition of the street confirmed it. It hadn't been paved in years. Occam put his foot flat to the floor. The small car's engine roared. The road vibrated beneath us. Trees and pasture and a trailer park flew by. We passed a rusted truck so fast it was a blur. Rick was shouting. And suddenly I knew where we were. On a street bordering the property where the pond incident took place, coming at it from the other direction. One turn and we would be at the entrance. Why had Occam brought us here? And then I knew. Woods and hills and places to hide. I opened my one-day gobag and got out gear. Shoved it into pockets, telling Rick what was happening.

In the rearview, the green car followed us, far back, spinning out on the turn, the tires blowing black smoke. Occam cursed, but his eyes were glowing golden. His human half might be unhappy, but his cat was having fun. *The full moon*. We were close to the full moon. He wanted to be in the woods. We took a hard left and he accelerated on the straightaway, the car clearly built for speed. "Rick," he growled and tossed his earbuds to the floor. "Nell, sugar. We'll be running in the woods."

"Woods?" Rick asked, his voice rising. "Where are you?"

"We're at the pond," I shouted to the cell.

Occam took the turn into the two-rut drive hard. The car tilted. Up on two wheels. Bounced back down. The landing hurt. The car made strange sounds. Occam laughed. Tires spat gravel and dust as it fishtailed down the dirt road. The sports car wasn't made for dirt. We raced past the pond, past the tree where the wildlife camera had been mounted. Occam slung the car around the pond on no road at all, through mud I'm pretty sure we skated over, and into a small space behind the old, kudzu-covered buildings I had seen before. He braked so hard the car spun and bounced on its tires. My teeth clacked, and I bit my tongue.

Occam leaned across me to open my door. He stopped, his hand inches from the handle. "Nell?" he growled. His glowing eyes were latched onto my face. I tasted blood.

I whacked him on the head with my cell. He blinked and jerked away. "I bit my tongue, you damn cat. I am not dinner."

Occam blinked again and the gold glow in his eyes began to mist away.

I glanced back and got a good look at the pond. It was different. Its surface was black and oily and . . . not just water. Not anymore. Though what it was I didn't know. In the distance I heard a car coming down the dirt drive. "Out!" I opened my door and slid from the seat belt. "They'll know we had to stop and they'll have to get us fast and get out. Rick. Make sure help is on the way!" I wiped my nose and mouth with a wrist and tucked my cell into a pocket, still connected to Rick. I hoped. I pulled my service weapon.

Leaving the door open, I raced into the woods, full pockets banging on my sides. Occam followed and pulled even with me. Together we leaped a downed tree and sprinted into an area that was all pine, in rows. A false forest of nothing but lumber. The underbrush had been burned out over the summer, the trunks blackened with soot. There was no scrub, no place to hide.

"Nell?" Occam darted ahead and said. "This way. We need to get back to the road."

"Why? What good would that do us? We need a place to hide, where we'uns are protected and they ain't. Where we can shoot from and they can't hit us."

I opened my senses. I stopped and dropped to one knee, and rubbed the mouth blood on my wrist onto the ground. Offering it something of me. Knowing it was stupid, this close to the pond and the circular magics. I would never have done it except we were in danger and I had no time to do anything else. Behind us, the chasing engine roared and tires spun.

Through the smear of my blood, I pushed down. Sent a single tendril of consciousness into the earth. The forest was lazy and spoiled and sleepy, roots narrow and twisted. But blood calls to blood, and I felt the blood of deer, old and dried. Somewhere ahead, several deer had been gutted and the remains left to the forest scavengers. Close by was a boulder rounded up, big and humped and even more massive belowground.

Beneath the earth, something shimmered and shifted toward me. I broke away and stood quickly. "This way." The car braked hard behind us.

We sprinted along an open area between trees, Occam on my trail. A door slammed behind us. Another. They were in the woods. I could feel their feet stomping on the ground as they ran. They would have weapons. Guns. "We have two choices," I said, my voice low and breathy from the run. "A deer stand or some big rocks."

"Three choices," he replied, his voice guttural. I glanced his way to see his eyes were solid gold. There was a golden brown scruff on his cheeks and inch-long whiskers beside his nose. Occam was changing on the run, which I had never heard was even possible.

The rocks were visible just ahead. I aimed my body directly at them. Slowed and bent to pick up a stick. And then pounded up the boulders at a run, the glacier-smoothed stone making it a hard climb, on all fours, though Occam made it look graceful and easy. There was a crevice . . . there.

I halted, dropped flat, and used the stick to reach in and hook a rattler hibernating in the rocks. I threw it at the ground below me. Occam growled at the sight. I threw another one. And the last one. They hissed and spat and slithered away fast for cold snakes. I wiped my mouth again and put my bloodied wrist on the stone. There were no more snakes. I leaped into the crevice, which hid me perfectly, while giving me a good vantage to shoot from, about elbow high. But there was only room for one. "You said we had three choices, and no way am I sharing a hidey-hole with a werecat and me bleeding like a stuck pig."

Occam chuffed. He was shirtless and his shoes were somewhere else, behind us. His feet were paw shaped.

"Guns," I demanded, holding out a hand.

He placed his service weapon in my left hand and I shoved it into my waistband. He lifted his leg, pulled out the tiny ankle-holstered .380, and placed it in my hand. His eyes were slanted, his brow furry, his jaw nothing like a human's. He made a growling, clicking sound and licked his jaw. Then he dropped his pants. I looked away and out into the linear, straight-lined trees. Weapon extended out and steady. As a shooting position it was well anchored, perfect tripod, though I might abrade my wrist on the stone with the recoil of each shot. And my body was protected by rock that I could duck behind when I ran out of ammo. The snakes I had tossed whipped into the trees and disappeared.

Beside me, bones snapped and cracked, breaking and reshaping. A strangled sound of pain, half whine, half growl, came from Occam's throat. And then he leaped past me, into the branches of the nearest tree, a graceful shape of spotted gold and long sleek tail.

I pulled my cell and set it on the stone. "You still there?" I murmured.

"I'm here," Rick said. "We have deputies in two marked units, ETA from the pond about four minutes." In the distance I saw two figures. Racing after us.

"It'll all be over by then," I said. "All but the blood and the mopping up. We have two armed suspects, male." I strained, squinting against the glare. "Carrying indeterminate long guns, heading to my twenty. I'm hidden in some boulders. Occam went furry."

Rick cursed, and there wasn't much I could say in reply. I had said *damn* earlier. I was pretty sure I had never said *damn* in my life until I became part of Unit Eighteen. Of course, I had never been chased like this, or not when off my land. If I took the two humans, I'd claim these woods as my own. And I'd kill two people, though I didn't really care about that since they were hunting me, and not to give me a Publishers Clearing House prize, but to shoot me dead. Here I had only a gun for protection and no chance to pull on the earth or feed the land, because if I did, the infinity loop below the ground would see me. And trap me. And learn from me. *Damn, damn, damn,* I thought, my breath too fast.

"Why did he drive the two of you *there*?" Rick asked, as if that choice was the stupidest thing ever. "Why did he take you to where the magics are strong and you both could be trapped by the land? Did the land make him come there? Did it draw him to itself?"

That was something I had considered, but it would have to wait. I watched, seeing human shapes come nearer, bending, and looking ahead, and I realized they were tracking us by following Occam's discarded clothes. We had been stupid. I could hear their voices now, hissing whispers and mutterings. The *crack* of a stick. They were moving fast, now taking cover, rushing from tree to tree, protected by the trunks. They had some training. But . . . they didn't look up.

"Tell me what's happening," Rick said.

I steadied my aim on the man closest and murmured. "Two males. One Caucasian, under six feet, in jeans, ball cap, and a zipped hoodie. One African-American, well over six feet, in jeans and a Windbreaker-type jacket, hair in multiple braids to his shoulders."

"Who are they? Why are they chasing you, Nell?"

"I don't know. And I don't know. They aren't churchmen." A laugh tittered in the back of my throat, where I smothered it, saying, "That's a first."

Occam perched high, about twenty feet above the ground, as the men maneuvered toward the rounded rock outcropping. Where else could we go, anyway? It was the perfect defensive position and the perfect lure. And Occam's clothes pointed them straight at me.

They came closer. I started to sweat. My vision went blurry and I forced my breathing to slow and blinked my eyes, trying to clear them.

"Stay calm, Nell," Rick said softly, as if he could smell my fear, hear my breathing.

But what he didn't know was that I wasn't afraid of the men stalking me. I was afraid of the land. And its awareness of me. I was standing on stone, surrounded by stone, unmoving. No raw earth touched me. Yet the land was attentive. It knew I was here from the scant reading I had done and the trace of my blood on the dirt. It knew Occam was here, in the trees. It was pulling on me, a slow tug to the pond. Rick was right. The magic of the pond was calling me. I looked to my left. Through the trees I saw the water, calm and still, reflecting back the sun. An oily darkness rested just at the surface.

As we ran, we had somehow circled around and headed back to it. Which meant that it was summoning me. Occam too. And there was nothing I could do about it.

The men had worked their way to within thirty feet of Occam's tree. I had seen a wereleopard leap, and the trajectory was just about right. The werecat tightened his body over the branch. He looked from the men to me and snarled silently, showing teeth so sharp they were like knives. He was trying to tell me something. He looked at the man closest to me, the one my weapon was centered on. Snarled again.

Oh. Right. I shouted, "Stop! PsyLED. Put down your weapons! Put! Down! Your! Weapons!"

Instead the man farther back fired at the rocks. I ducked. Shrapnel flew, bits of rock peppering down on me.

Cover fire.

I lifted my head just high enough to see. The closest man was racing toward me. The long gun was an automatic rifle. With an extended mag. He saw me. Raised his weapon, the barrel coming across his body.

I aimed at him. Squeezed the trigger. Fired. The blast stole the silence from the world.

The shot went wide. But the man ducked and crouched behind a trunk without firing. The other man raced out to the side, as if drawing my fire. Occam leaped from the branch. Landed on the man who had fired at me. I raised up and fired at the man rushing to the side. He returned fire. The sound was thunderous. Rock chips and shrapnel shattered around me. A hail of gunfire. I could do nothing but crouch and wait it out.

The rain of gunfire stopped, and I stood up, spotting the man, hunched over his weapon, half-hidden behind a tree. Changing out the magazine. My only good shot was about three inches of his backside, poking out from behind the tree. I steadied the weapon, breathed in. Out. Held my breath, lungs about three-quarters empty. Squeezed the trigger. Fired. He landed on one knee, his lower leg and foot exposed on one side of the tree, his head on the other. I aimed at the foot and fired twice more. Three shots total. I felt the man's blood hit the ground in two places. Something lightless and empty opened within me.

I could take him for these woods. I could feed him to the earth.

The space inside me was deep and black and starless. And full of longing. It rose within me. Filling me with nothingness. I had his blood. I had his life. He had been trying to take mine. This was my right.

I tried to draw a breath. Tried to breathe past the desire, thick and hot and needing. To take. To kill. To feed the earth. That was my sole gift. To send life into the earth. To nourish it.

I was gasping. Mouth open. My belly cramped, wanting. "No," I whispered. "No. Not gonna . . ." I forced myself upright. The body of the man Occam had taken down was flat. Unmoving. Out cold. There was no sign of Occam.

Movement caught my eyes, and I scanned the trees to see the man I had shot shuffle-running into the standing lumberyard, bent over, holding his backside, limping on a bleeding foot. I'd hit him twice. He was disabled but still moving. Directly toward the pond.

The pond. The working had called the man whose blood landed upon the ground. The magic beneath the ground had snared him. He was nearly at the water, with its glistening blacker-than-night surface.

"Occam!" I screamed, pointing. "That man!"

TWELVE

The cat's ears lifted, swiveling. His head turned toward me, to the man, tracking movement at the pond's edge. The wounded man. Heading toward the water. He leaped up, from tree to tree, covering yards with each bound, faster than any human. Catching up. When he was close, Occam sprang twenty feet to the earth, landed, and dropped his head, shoulders rising. He crouched. On paws and belly, low to the ground, he crawled toward the scant kudzu near his car.

Walking to the lip of the water, the man took one step into the pond.

With a single massive lunge, Occam tackled the man and knocked him away from the pond, banging the shooter's head with the landing. A siren cut through the air, close, pulling along the drive. Flashing lights caught on the trees and reflected blue on the black water. Occam growled at the man beneath him and swiped his prey with his paw, batting hard, but not slashing. Frustrated, Occam slinked away from the pond and the sheriff deputy's bumping, grinding car. Into the brush, where he leaped up into the trees. Vanished in the green needles. I remembered to breathe.

By the time the deputies pulled to a stop, I was in control of myself, mostly, and told Rick to call dispatch and tell the cops to put on 3PEs. I climbed out of the hole in the rocks and got the man Occam had landed on and knocked out safely in handcuffs. He was unconscious, so I didn't Mirandize him, just patted him down and left him where he was.

The deputies had given similar treatment to the man I had shot, and tossed him in the back of the unit before Rick's orders came through, the officers walking the Earth with no problems, seemingly with no desire to go for a swim—yet. The attackers' weapons were confiscated, rounds removed, weapons and equipment were tagged, placed in evidence bags, with heavy rubber straps acting as trigger guards, and stored in the deputies' cars. And somehow, through it all, I controlled the desire to feed the earth the blood of my victim, pressed down on it, smothered it. And remembered to breathe.

KEMA's ETA to the pond was forty minutes. Rick's was only slightly shorter. For now, I was on my own. My partner was at his car, mostly dressed. Missing a shoe, both socks, and his ankle holster. He was dressed in his outer clothes, though his shirt was open to the waist, the tails fluttering in the cold wind, and he seemed to have no desire to button it. His badge and ID were both clipped at his belt, to be seen easily. He was grim-faced, leaner than he had been only an hour before. His beard was half an inch long, scruffy and uneven. His hair had grown out too, a tousled blond tangle. His eyes were mostly their usual amber-brown shade and he seemed moderately in control, once he drank several bottles of water that I found in the trunk of his car. But he wouldn't dress out in proper protective gear, and I knew *his head wasn't on straight yet*—a phrase I had learned in Spook School but had never seen in action until now.

The deputies and I were wearing the requisite antispell white unis with the ugly orange stripe across the chest. I was pretty sick of seeing them by now. I had marked off the crime scene around the boulders with crime scene tape. Brought out the basic crime scene evidence kit. It was my first arrest, my first crime scene, and was something I should have been walked through. Instead, I took it step by step, alone, according to protocol laid out in PsyLED training, because I was the PsySAC, PsyLED special agent charge, until someone with seniority showed up. Or Occam got his head together. This was bizarre.

He wasn't himself. He was silent, unsmiling, and went about making reports in monosyllabic grunts. I had a feeling the reports he was writing were going to be equally terse. But he finally agreed to wear the uni-style booties I gave him, protecting his feet from the magic in the land. He didn't say thank you. Hadn't called me *sugar*. But he kept away from the pond and the men who had attacked us, so I was counting that as a win.

When Rick arrived and took over the scene as SAC, even he noticed Occam's silence, but he did nothing about it, except to find earbuds in the sportster and hold them out to the werecat. Which I should have done. I was Occam's partner for the day, and I should have been thinking for him. Occam had dropped his antimoon music while driving. I should have grabbed the antispell music. I was an idiot.

I said so in my report. All the reports, including the reports I had to fill out for having drawn and fired my service weapon. And the one for having hit a suspect. So much paperwork. There was more paperwork when the ambulance picked up the injured attackers. Neither had ID on them, and it would take a while for AFIS—Automated Fingerprint Identification System—to deliver any fingerprints that might be on file. The car was stolen just this morning, and there might be traffic cam or security cam footage, but everything took longer than on TV and in film fiction. And no one was talking.

Both suspects were taken to quarantine at UTMC where they would be given medical treatment and held against their wills. Interrogated. Background checks. They had fired fully automatic weapons at federal law enforcement. Life wouldn't be easy for them.

Midway through the workup, a deputy found Occam's lost shoe. The werecat took it and walked away, without a thank-you or a comment. His face like a stone.

In the ordinary course of life, I didn't experience guilt about living, didn't overthink what I said or replied or did, didn't agonize about what I should have done. But this was different. I had let my partner down. I had let him shift in a dangerous situation where he might have bitten someone and then might have died at Pea's claws. I should have played the music and forced him to stay human shaped. That was my job. And I had failed at something Unit Eighteen had required of me as the most basic part of my job.

Just before the three days of the full moon.

I couldn't fix what I had done, but I could take Rick's advice and do my job.

Within hours, the site had been worked up and Occam drove off in his car, without a word, with all my gear except my laptop behind the seats. Without me. He was being a typical moon-called werecat, but still. Abandoning me was just mean, no matter where his head was. Once again, I hitched a ride back to HQ with a deputy, where I got in my truck and drove to LuseCo.

Still on the job. Because for some reason, Rick had accepted my gun when I offered it, but hadn't asked for my badge, hadn't pulled me from the field, hadn't sent me home. At best, I was supposed to be deskbound now, until an investigation into the shooting was completed. That hadn't happened. It had to be the effect of the impending full moon, making him forgetful or cranky or something. I knew he would get around to it, but for the moment, I had time to do the job.

I had one innate talent: reading the land. I was going to use it for as long as I could. Wearing my uni, I parked my C10 in the visitor parking lot in front of LuseCo and got out.

I walked out into the center of the lawn, facing the building. It had a gated entrance and was built like a medieval fortress, three stories high with long, narrow windows, and a flat roof with four turret-looking things, one on each corner. There were trees on the roof, and a tentlike awning was visible, possibly a location where employees might take breaks or even work in the sun. The drive split, leading to visitor parking in front and probably to employee parking in back.

The plantings out front were sparse, over- or undertrimmed, underfertilized, and underwatered. There were spindly nandinas that reached for the second-floor windows. The first time I'd driven here, I had barely noted the landscaping around the building. Now I saw that it had been poorly planned, poorly executed, and was uncared for, winter bare, and slowly dying. The grass had been cut so low, so often, that the roots were dying. The nandinas were too tall for the location and in need of trimming. All the plantings needed fertilizer. Mulch. A decent irrigation system. All this I took in without thought, processing it, letting it go.

All in all, the landscape gave off no evil-castle vibes. The place had the look of a moderately profitable small business. I sat down on the dying grass and got as comfortable as possible without the blanket that was still in Occam's car. I took a calming breath and looked up, into the plantings. And stopped. Still as death.

There was a slimy film on the underside of the nandina leaves. Black as tar. Oily. Just like the slime on the plants at one of the victims' houses. Just like what I'd thought I was seeing at the surface of the water at the pond. I got up, went to my truck, and trundled around until I found the evidence bag with the scraping inside. Carrying it away from the Chevy, I knelt on the

concrete parking area. Carefully I opened the envelope. Inside
were scaly, dried strips. Nothing oily. But it had nothing to grow
on either. I thought about dropping them onto the ground, but
that sounded dangerous, and so I resealed the envelope and put
it in a plastic zippered bag, to be on the safe side. I tucked it into
the passenger-side pocket of the C10, and I instantly assigned it
as the evidence collection area. I needed a car with a trunk.

Back in LuseCo's yard, I pulled off my uni's glove, wrenching my wrist trying it get the rigid, plasticized, and spelled fabric off. Next time I'd just cut the glove. I put a single finger on
the ground, as I had recently for reads. I let a wisp of myself coil
down, slowly, beneath the starved and dying grass roots. Into
the soil. I didn't go deep, but stayed near the surface, close to
my body. Beneath me, I could feel the corners of the triangle.
The movement of . . . *something* along the vertices and angles
of the triangle, pooling at the angle points. *Apexes?* The "8"-
shaped infinity loop no longer danced, but raced along the circle, its energies tighter, no shadow between the pinpoints of
light now. And this time I was certain that all of the energies
were tied to the facility in front of me. The glow beneath the
building was brighter, sending out sparkles of sun yellow to the
loop as it traveled.

"Nell?"

I recognized T. Laine's voice, and I pulled myself back to the
surface. Blinked. Remembered to breathe again. I stood and
pulled the uni's glove back on, which involved much twisting
and discomfort.

"You okay?" she asked me. She looked tired, her eyes ringed
with mascara that she had rubbed off. Black hair plastered to
her head from the moisture that collected in the 3PE suit. "You
shouldn't be here," she said.

"I'm okay." I didn't mention that no one had relieved me of
my responsibilities. "Have you done psy-meter readings of all
the employees?"

"About half so far. Nothing's redlining and nothing is above
human normal."

"What about talking to the techs involved with the testing?
The nonwitch techs. And what about the witches themselves?"

"Yes to the techs and clerical staff. All human so far. All
willing to talk about lasers and how they work and how the tests
went. Up to two weeks ago. Then they stopped being so involved

for reasons I haven't discovered yet. Of the employees on-site, not away on vacation or leave, all fall within normal parameters for species. There's no background psysitopes on the premises. No psysitope-active employees."

I pulled the baggie out of my pocket and said, "Would you read this?"

T. Laine shrugged, pulled a handheld unit from her own pocket, and read the baggie. "Nada. Nothing. Why are we doing this?"

"Before I answer, will you read this plant?" I walked to the too-tall nandinas.

T. Laine looked annoyed, but she took a reading. "What the hell?" she said.

I leaned over and saw the results. Total psysitopes were at nearly fifty percent. "Occam drove off with my handheld psy-meter in his car," I said. "May I borrow yours? I want to take some new readings at the houses of the people who were contaminated."

T. Laine put the small unit in my gloved hand. Her face was pulled down in worry, but she didn't explain, saying, "Whatever. It's been a long day. I need to take off this stinky suit, eat a shower—a *donut*—and take some downtime."

Behind her, through the windows, the lights flickered and came back on. I frowned and T. Laine turned to see what had my attention, but the lights inside were back on. "What?"

I told her what I had seen and added, "I thought all these labs and research and development companies were part of the TVA grid administration, on multiple power sources. No electrical outages for them, thanks to the overlapping energy sources." *More than any city in the nation except DC,* I thought. I remembered the itchy, irritated feeling of the ground when I scanned it at one point, though the readings all had run together by now.

"Yeah. I don't know," she said. "Maybe. I'm too tired to give a rat's ass right now." T. Laine walked away from me, pulling her plastic face shield back in place. I wasn't sure what rats had to do with the case, but I shrugged and got back in my truck, stowing the borrowed handheld psy-meter 1.0 in the driver door's side pocket. Sitting in the lot, engine running, I opened up the latest case reports on my tablet and discovered a note to the PsyLED team from someone named Lieutenant Colonel Leann Rettell, which I opened. The e-mail had a *.gov* address and was purported to be from an assistant to General David Schlumberger, asking someone from PsyLED to read the patients at UTMC with a psy-meter.

Since Rettell didn't specifically request the P 2.0. I notified JoJo that I could go by the hospital and provide readings shortly. But would I send them to JoJo and let her send them to the VIPs. I'd rather let a senior investigator handle talks with the military.

In another report, I found that KEMA had ordered a more widespread evacuation of the residential area so they could spray a black mold that started growing there. They would spray around each infected house at the north triangle site with a virulent fungicide. I had to see how bad things were there.

I eased the truck up to two sheriff cars, blocking the way in to the neighborhood where the strange "virus" had struck three families, and up to the armed guards, both wearing white unis, gun holsters belted across the outside and automatic rifles close to hand. I slowed, lowered the windows, and held out my ID. "Hi, guys. Can you update me on what's happened here?" I asked.

"Regular law enforcement to whacko law enforcement?" the older deputy asked. "Sure." His partner winced, letting me know that *whacko law enforcement* was said as a joke but wasn't amusing even to him. The older guy, clearly a self-appointed spokesperson, said, "We got weird tar growing up from the ground. You got any ghosts or goblins who can make that happen, send 'em here. I'll shoot 'em for you."

I didn't bother telling him I was fully capable of shooting my own goblins, should they actually exist, nor that ghosts couldn't be wounded by gunfire. It was a waste of breath to attempt to educate a man whose main professional goal seemed to be being persistently annoying. At which he was clearly successful.

Though he was chiefly a snark, he did know that all the occupants of every house had been evacuated, some by force, to hotels, to shelters, to other family members. "The National Guard brought in lights and chemicals to get rid of the growths. They treated one house and yard so far," he said. "I don't know what kind of lights or treatments, but I can guess that the tree huggers would complain it's bad for the environment." Which he clearly thought was amusing, not knowing or caring that I was a tree hugger. Of sorts. Though not a particularly pacific one.

A chemical stink wafted in through the window and the heater vents, strong and cloying, sticking to the back of my throat like acid glue. I had to agree with the cop's imaginary tree huggers, that whoever ordered the spraying were idiots, contaminating the ground with poison that would harm the residents when they returned. There were other ways to kill mold and plants than poison. But that wasn't my decision or my job.

Which started something tickling at the back of my mind— something important that I should do and know, something scampering across my brain on sticky feet, not alighting long enough for me to identify it. So for now I ignored the sensation of tiny lizard feet and did my job.

I said, "I'd like to enter the area that was evacuated and cordoned off."

"Suit yourself. You have to sign in." He indicated a traditional clipboard with a paper. "I'd suggest you stay on the street," he added. "And when you get back, you'll have to leave your uni here." He pointed to a red biohazard container with an orange stripe across each side and a hinged top.

I left the truck, dressed in a clean uni, and walked down the street alone.

The crime scene tape at the three houses still fluttered, but the tents were gone. The occupants were gone. And the people who should have been in the other houses were gone too. The neighborhood had no cars, no pets, no people beyond the talkative deputy and his silent partner at the entrance, no nothing. Except the dots of black slime that climbed the trees and coated the leaves of grass. I called Rick as I walked, but it went to voice mail. I tried JoJo, and she answered, but only long enough for me to hear her talking to a military person she called Colonel, probably at the DoD, before she hung up.

I remembered one report I had skimmed. According to the feds, the media had been told that the mold was simply an unidentified fungi and was probably normal, but global weather changes, altered rainfall, and acid rain had stimulated it to take over. It was a lot of government nonsense-speak meant to calm the public without telling them anything about the source of the psysitope-active leak. And not tying the mold into the "viral

illness" of the homeowners. Which could be wise, as the source
hadn't been identified and most people panicked easily. I
stopped at the first house and studied the lawn, which was
green, blanketed with a black slime, slick looking, with colorful
little things like buds or antennae sticking up from the tarry
mess. Black also coated the trees.

It was probably stupid, but I needed to read what was happening in and under the ground. I'd made enough waves in
Spook School with my nonhuman self. There was no point in
drawing attention my way again, so soon after getting free,
but . . . I couldn't help myself. I knelt on the street, one knee
down, one up. I peeled back the glove portion of the uni and
placed a single finger on the ground, no more than a foot inside
the grassy area of Point B, Alisha Henri's two-story home, Dougie's daughter's yard. I slid my consciousness into the earth and
back out fast. The land was full of shadows that pulsed with
shifting red and blue lights. It didn't feel like my land. It didn't
feel like any land I had ever touched. The energies were odd
and . . . humming, for lack of a better word. In my experience,
land usually breathed, silent and aware, or slept, like a winter
hibernation. This felt sick. Contaminated. Full of pain. This
was . . . wounded.

I looked out over the lawn again, studying the black, tarry
slime, and wiped my fingertip on my uni pants. This was bad,
and I had no idea what to do about it. Worse, I had a feeling that
the bad things weren't finished for the day.

I walked back to the barricade and stripped off the uni,
depositing it into the biohazard container. Back inside my truck,
I cleaned my finger with a wet wipe and rolled the dirty wipe
back into the foil package, thinking.

I didn't know who to call. Didn't know who to trust to help
me think through this problem. I remembered what Occam had
said, the odd quote-sounding thing. *"The urge to shift and to
hunt waxes strong three days out, abides the three days of, and
wanes three days after. Nine nights of pleasure and nine days
of hell."* So I couldn't talk to Rick, Occam, or Paka, who had
been odd for three days and would be useless starting about
now. Not JoJo, who was busy with research and being lead agent
during the three days of the full moon. Not T. Laine, who was
dealing with the people at LuseCo. That left Tandy. Or someone
higher up. LaLa, at Spook School? Or . . . Soul?

As I sat in the cooling C10, the engine *ting*ing, my cell rang again and the number was JoJo's. "Ingram," I said.

"How fast can you get to UTMC?" she asked. "They've begun advanced life support on two patients, and there's something wrong with them."

Wrong? Other than needing advanced life support? CPR? I thought. But I didn't say that. It might come out as sarcasm and levity, which seemed offensive in the face of a catastrophe I couldn't understand or explain. I didn't ask what was *wrong* with the patients. In a single set of well-choreographed moves, I pulled onto the road and gunned the engine, putting my emergency light in the windshield and flipping the switch on the siren. "God willing and the creek don't rise, ETA of twenty."

"Be safe." The call ended.

I parked in front of the paranormal unit at UTMC and pulled on a clean uni from the pack I had taken from the supply closet at HQ, clipping my badge and ID to the front. I hadn't been wearing a gun for long, but I suddenly felt naked without it. I crossed the parking area, heading straight to the press, all camped out outside, cameras, mics, foldable chairs, and bodies that tried to block my way with all of the above as I tried to get up the steps to the doors. They shouted questions I couldn't answer. I had been taught not to engage, not to react.

"What's going on? Can you tell us what's happening inside?"

"Did one of the patients die?"

"Who died?"

"Why is PsyLED involved? Is there a magic attack on the city?"

"Is it true that witch coven terrorist groups have attacked the city and planted bombs in the hospital and at city offices?"

"Do we have a biological terrorist event in Knoxville?"

That was a new one, and I almost reacted to it. Instead I said, "No comment. No comment. No comment. Excuse me. No comment."

The guards just inside the entrance were off-duty sheriff's deputies, armed with guns and attitude. They stepped out and eased the media people aside, opening a pathway to the entrance for me, and suddenly I was on the other side of the doors and safe inside. "Thanks, y'all," I said.

"No problem, ma'am," the man said.

"I don't guess you know, or will tell us, what's going on?" the woman deputy said, making it a question.

"Sorry. The call said to get over here, that something was wrong. I hope I'll know more on the way out."

"Yeah," she said. "No one tells the county people anything. We'uns are always totally outta the loop."

At the church-speak, my head swiveled around fast. The name on her badge was Hollar, an old church name. "Hollar? God's Cloud?"

Her eyes widened, and I took her in, freckled face, brown hair, short but built sturdy. "A generation back," she said. "My mama, Carla, got away in the middle of the night. She was pregnant with me. May Ree Hollar," she said, looking at my ID and offering her hand. "Good to meet you'un, Miz Ingram."

"Nell," I said. "You too." I shook hands with May Ree.

"Chris Skeeter," the man said. "No church affiliation. And people call me Skeeter."

"Thanks for getting me in here," I said. "I'll say what I can on the way out."

"Appreciate it," May Ree said. "And any precautions . . . ?"

"Unis have been helpful. You got any?"

"Not a one," May Ree said. I tossed her my keys, reciting the plate number, model, and make. "It's my POV, an ugly C10 pickup. Open the door, but be careful as the side pockets are my evidence compartments. My backup weapon is locked in a case behind the driver's seat, just so you know. Unis are behind the passenger seat. Take one each. Lock up when you're done."

"Blessed be," May Ree said.

Which sounded Wiccan, but I said back, "Hospitality and safety."

She grinned at me and headed outside, into the dying sunset.

On the paranormal unit, things were hectic. There were flashing lights, beeping of machines, emergency carts, and people in unis everywhere. Rushing and dodging one another. Ducking through doors before they swished shut. Shouting. The privacy curtains in the glassed-in rooms were pulled. I had no idea where I was going or who was dying. And then I remembered Dougie, and her daughters and their partner and husband. The first death had been the husband, Adam somebody. Fear caught me around me heart and squeezed, bruising and draining.

I followed the noise down the short hallway to the room with the greatest concentration of medical people. On the beds in the room, side by side, were two women, both being administered CPR by uni-wearing hospital personnel. I dressed out in the 3PE and stepped inside, through a purplish blue light that lit me up oddly, and into the room.

Standing at the foot of the beds was Dougie. Tears ran down her face, and she looked beyond exhausted. She was standing with her hands over her mouth, as if to keep in words that wouldn't help. Or screams. Or curses. On the beds were two women. One looked like Dougie, with strawberry blond hair. On the other bed was a woman who . . . oddly reminded me of me, as I had been, with long hair and slender build. The red-haired woman's arm was out. Bloodless and pale. As if she was dying, reaching toward the other woman.

And I knew—I *knew*—the women had to be Kirsten Harrell and her partner, Sally Clements. I stepped to Dougie and tapped her on the shoulder. She turned to me, blinked tears from her eyes, and succeeded in focusing on me. "Nell," she whispered. Over the noise, I didn't hear her, but I saw her lips move. And she slid into my arms as if the shoulder tap had been an invitation. Surprised, I clasped her closer and noted that she towered over me. How had I missed that she was so tall?

I held her, and shifted our bodies so she could see her girls, but that wasn't enough. I felt her grief welling high, and she made a strangled sound, and so I maneuvered closer, our booties sliding on the floor, to the end of the bed. I took her fingers and shifted them until she touched the toes of the redheaded woman. She sobbed, her body growing heavy in my arms.

I held Dougie, and I could tell that the doctor was about to give up. She kept looking at the clock, her face giving away nothing, but her stance tightening, drawing in. One patient suddenly heaved a breath on her own. For a moment, everyone, everything stopped. Dougie stiffened in my arms, not breathing. "What . . . ?" she whispered. The woman on the bed took another breath, her chest moving, the air sounding sticky and thick. Dougie gripped her daughter's feet and squeezed.

The energy of the medical personnel in the room instantly went from controlled methodology to something euphoric. The attending doctor began again administering drugs and ordering tests at a faster pace.

The heart rates of first one patient, then the other, stabilized. The second woman started breathing on her own, and began to thrash, which seemed to be a good sign, from the medical excitement. Dougie held her daughter's toes so tight I thought the woman might never walk again. And Dougie grabbed my arm around her own waist, holding me in place when I thought to step away.

Quickly both patients began to improve, their skin developing a pinkish tint that hadn't been there before. The doctor's stance grew more comfortable, her face relaxing, and something like relief settled there. Another eighteen minutes passed, Dougie and me standing together.

"Okay," the doctor said, at last. "Anybody got any idea what just happened? Other than the new antifungal taking effect in unexpected ways?" She looked around. "Yeah. Me neither. Good work, people. Leave your suits at the door, gloves, shoes, hats, faceplates each in the respective bio waste bins. All needles go in the special needle container. All used and discarded respiratory equipment, IV equipment, and paper wrappers are to be double bagged and placed in the outgoing incinerator trash. All equipment gets a thorough cleaning in the new equipment room, with twelve hours in ultraviolet. Let's keep this contained."

Contained? What needs to be contained? I thought, studying the room with new eyes. And, *Antifungal medication?*

I hadn't recognized it, but the medical people and Dougie were wearing yellow paper from head to toe, not white paranormal unis anymore. The nurses and other people stripped at the door and washed up on the way out, revealing normal hospital scrubs and running shoes. I hadn't even noticed the difference between the medical unis and my personal protective equipment. The room cleared except for four medical personnel who were cleaning up paper and plastic and sheets and the patients themselves.

Dougie let go of me and her daughter's toes, stepping lightly, as fragile as life itself, to her daughter's side, her booties *shush*-ing between the beds. The medical people recognized her as family and stepped back, allowing Dougie to lean over. Gently, through her face mask, she placed a kiss on her daughter's cheek, turned, and kissed Sally's cheek. And then she did something unexpected. She made a shooing motion with her hands and the medical people moved farther out of the way. She took Kirsten's hand, which was still outstretched toward Sally, and she pulled Sally's hand over, between the beds. Dougie slid an elastic strap, what I thought might be a disposable tourniquet, from where it draped on the bed frame. With it, she joined the women's hands, tying them loosely. So they could touch. Even asleep, or unconscious, Kirsten gripped Sally's fingers.

Dougie stepped back, and that was when I saw the black spots on Kirsten's upper arm. Black as tar. Dripping something black onto the floor. It was on the sheets beneath her. Drips spattered the floor. Everywhere. I stepped up and gripped the sheet, lifting it and looking down. "Hey!" a nurse said. "Stop that!" Kirsten's arm and her torso were covered with black spots. Like mold on bread. I checked Sally, who displayed the same spots, only smaller, some appearing to be under the skin, not on top. The mold might be all through them, inside. A systemic mold. *Antifungal medications* . . .

"Nell?" Dougie said, her voice trembling.

I dropped the sheet and saw a box of thick blue plastic ziplock bags to the side. I withdrew one, opened it, and quickly shoved the handheld P 1.0 inside. Working clumsily through the gloves and the heavy plastic, I zeroed the device before taking a reading. Both of the women redlined. So did the sheets. The walls. The entire room.

And that was when it hit me. The black slime might have begun as part of a paranormal event, an accident even, but it was acting like an infection, spreading faster than any mold on Earth as if using the new magical energies in the ground to speed its own growth. So was the mold an unintended side effect of the working? That would make sense, and if so, could give us a way to track the underground working.

I pulled out my cell and stuck it in a baggie too and searched for the word that was hiding in my brain. My fingers tapped out an Internet search through the baggie as my brain kept on working.

So . . . the mold—whatever it was—was a mutated lifeform? An unknown or brand-new mold? I pulled the words out of the Internet ether like a sailor pulling up an anchor. Mycobionts! They were called *mycobionts*, and some varieties made different types of fruiting bodies, or spore-producing structures. It took nutrients and blood, stole its sustenance, from another life-form. And then killed it. I remembered the bumps on the black mold on the shrubs in the neighborhood. The black oily sheen beneath the pond. Was the mold growing inside the earth?

I needed to touch some of the black stuff. With my finger.

I had no idea if I could actually do what I was thinking about doing, but . . . ignoring the nurses, I shoved the P 1.0 onto a shelf at the head of the bed. The psy-meter would need to be cleaned like the doctor had said. This uni was more unyielding and rigid than others, and the gloves were problematic. I spotted a pair of scissors to the side, big clunky things that looked capable of cutting through hard plastic. Using them, I cut the tip off the right finger of my glove and placed the bare skin on Kirsten's face, next to the plastic face mask, on healthy pink skin. And I dropped into her. Like reading the earth.

Heat and sound hit me like a fist wrapped in a wet, steaming-hot wool rug. I was instantly disoriented and dizzy, and I put out a hand. Someone caught me. Held on. I steadied and tried to figure out what I was seeing. This was vastly different from land, from earth, despite the analogy I had always used as to the breath of the earth and the water that ran beneath it and over as blood in veins. So different.

I dropped deeper. Into heat and power and action and life so abundant I had nothing to compare it to, nothing to base an assessment or corollary on. Blood pumped, bright with life, intense and rich. Kirsten's lungs breathed and her heart beat, mighty and powerful. But something shadowed was spreading through the system, a blight, stealing the life from it. The system that was Kirsten. I studied the blight and realized that the darkness was pulsing, ever so slightly, with a dull red light. And after a moment, a dull blue light. Slowly the blight went through the rainbow of colors, just the way the dancer infinity loop had done right at first. But this was darkly and terribly shadowed. I heard a sound with each pulse of light, soft and scratchy. It sounded like, "Aaaaap. Aaaaap." Over and over. Again, I had no idea what it meant. I eased away from the system and back into the hospital room. I remembered to breathe.

"Nell," Dougie whispered. "They've called security. You need to leave now."

I had a feeling about the blight, but it was nebulous, unformed, hovering just out of reach. Something that seemed important. But this was a hospital. They had labs and oncology departments and pathologists. They had already found what the blight was. They *knew*.

I backed away. Silently, I trashed my uni at the door, removing the baggies and dropping them into the garbage, pocketing the handheld psy-meter and my cell. I washed my hands under hot water, with strong soap. As safe as I could make myself, I started to slip from the room, the P 1.0 under an arm, until a nurse stepped in front of me and said, "Hold your ID and electronic equipment to the lights." She pointed up to the bluish lights at the door. "They were outside your 3PEs." I did as instructed, holding them in place until she nodded and said, "You're good to go."

I waved to Dougie, but she had turned her attention to her girls and didn't see. I didn't see security, so I walked the halls and took handheld P 1.0 readings from all the patients. Redlining, or close to it, everywhere.

Down the hall, I spotted the woman I thought was the hospitalist, and a man who might be an intern, and I followed them through the empty nurses' station into a back room. The door swished shut behind me.

"What is the black stuff?" I demanded.

They spun like marionettes to face me.

"The black stuff on them. What is it?" When they didn't answer, I held up my ID and badge and said, "Special Agent Nell Ingram, PsyLED. Is the black stuff a previously unidentified mold? With spores? And is it spreading like . . ." I almost said, *Like cancer?* But I stopped. "Like normal?"

The woman sat, moving as if exhausted, nearly falling into a beat-up old desk chair. The man poured her a cup of coffee from a scorched pot and she took a sip. Made a face. Drank it anyway. "God, this stuff is awful. I can't talk to you about the patients. HIPAA rules."

"I'm not interested in the patients. I'm interested in the black stuff. It has no rights."

The doctor sipped and considered and said, "Okay. I can do that. Yes, it's a spore-forming fungal form, which is why we have a negative pressure unit in each of the rooms and ultraviolet lighting at the doorways, and we're enforcing strict universal precautions, a protocol similar to the one that CDC issued during the Ebola outbreak of 2014 and 2015. But nothing we've tried on the fungi has slowed the progress. The state lab thought at first that it was a *Stachybotrys atra*, because it grows on media with a high cellulose content. But its chemical activity is different from *Stachybotrys*. It also grows on and in the skin, nails, and blood of our patients. And because it's a spore former, it can live through most anything."

"What about anticancer meds?" I asked.

The doctor opened her mouth and closed it, her eyes sharpening on me.

"I'm not a medical person of any kind, but it reads like and feels like something that's been enhanced paranormally. Like a magic cancer attack. It has strange energies."

"Reads? You're not human," she said, making it half question, half statement.

"No," I said. "And the black stuff isn't pure mold."

"I'll pass your suggestion on to the specialists."

I frowned, but that was probably all I was going to get. "Okay. Thank you. Is it contagious? Have any medical workers come down with it?"

"Not so far, but our precautions are stringent."

I backed out of the room and eased away. And as I did, the lights flickered. Steadied. Flickered again. Alarms sounded everywhere. Coincidence was a rare occurrence, and I was beginning to think flickering electrical systems in places where the power was supposed to be stable wasn't coincidence. Things were getting worse.

Back in my car, I called JoJo. When she answered I said, "I've read the patients at UTMC with a P 1.0. I'll put the readings in my report, but mostly they all redline. And they all have mold like the neighborhood does, like the pond does. Suggestion. Send an RVAC over the GPS coordinates where the deer were infected and see if there's mold there. If so, then we might be able to use the mold to track the working."

"Sending a req for a remote-viewing aircraft flyover." I could hear the soft taps of her fingers on the keyboard. "What else you got?"

"Rick hinted that I should read the employees at LuseCo, the same way I read the land, and since I was at the hospital, I tried it on one patient. She felt like a cancer mold, which means nothing to me at all except they're under attack. Do you want me back at LuseCo?"

"LuseCo entrenched and called in lawyers. We're trying to get warrants and full access, but they seem to have protection from people in high places. I've called Soul, but she says they have a state politico on the board. We've been kicked out."

"I thought Homeland Security overrode all the political games."

"That was yesterday." She sounded hard and angry.

I decided not to pursue that topic. "And Rick?" I asked.

"Close to the full moon. Later." She disconnected.

Not sure what I should do now, I drove back toward HQ, stopping only long enough to pick up a few groceries for supper. Reheated roasted pumpkin and greens would only go so far. As I drove, the traffic lights flickered. Traffic began to back up, snarling at intersections, leaving some roads empty while others were full. The last of the sunlight glinted off the power lines in a rainbow hue, shifting from red to blue. It reminded me of the lights underground. Something was seriously wrong.

THIRTEEN

In the break room, I poured a glass of tap water and opened a Subway sandwich, tuna, heavy on the veggies, and started eating. It wasn't Yoshi's, but it was pretty good.

JoJo followed the smell of food and dropped into the chair beside me. "If you tell me one of the sandwiches in that bag is for me, I promise I'll worship you as the goddess of all chicken. Or cattle. Or pig."

I hid my pleasure by taking another bite, and in spite of good manners, answered while I chewed. "I'll pass as a recipient of idolatrous worship, but there's Black Forest ham, sliced beef, meatball, and two chicken breasts, all foot-longs. They had a special."

"Praise Jesus and dance on the head of a pin." She pulled a meatball sandwich out and added, "That's what my gramma used to say, God rest her soul."

I swallowed and said, "What we don't eat today can go into the fridge. And my mawmaw still says things like that."

We ate like ravenous wolves, and were joined by Tandy and T. Laine, who dove onto the sandwiches with just as much fervor, silent, all of us eating and passing around colas, T. Laine griping because beer wasn't allowed while on duty. Not that they followed that rule all the time, I was sure.

I had thought that seven feet of sandwiches would last twenty-four hours at least, but it seemed no one had eaten a real meal all day, just coffee and vending machine donuts and chips and fried-fat snacks and antacids. When I finished, I passed around the cookies. As everyone began to come back to life, thanks to calories and caffeine, I asked JoJo, "Did you get the HVAC flyover of the deer site approved?"

"Rick had already put in for it and we have shots. Slimy mess in all three sites. I'll send them to you after I finish this small bit of Italian heaven."

"Okay, then," I said. "I think I know what's happening. I don't understand *why* it's happening or *how* it's happening, but I think I know *what* is happening."

JoJo wiped her mouth with a paper napkin and took out her dangling earrings, tossing the six pairs on top of the table. As she worked on her jewelry, she said, "God, I'm tired. Go for it, chicky." As if reading her mind, Tandy opened his laptop, signed on, and slid it across the table to Jo, who took the fastest case notes in the group.

When she had wiped her fingers free of greasy tomato sauce and pulled the laptop to her, I said, "We have three hot spots of magic and psysitopes in the city, in a perfect triangle, one point lined up with magnetic north. In every location, peculiar growths have appeared, stuff that looks like black slime to the mundane eye, but that spreads like a cancer. It's attacked—the mold itself, not people acting under the influence of the underground psysitopes—and nearly killed two people from the houses. It may be all or part of what killed the people at the pond. There may be a huge mold at the surface of the water. I've put in a request to KEMA and PsyCSI techs to take samples there. I also called the KEMA forensic pathologists to look for mold in the pond bodies."

"Son of a witch on a switch," T. Laine cursed softly. "It's a good thing Soul is working PR on this case. This thing is gonna need spin like a helicopter blade."

"It gets worse," I said. "I can read the mold, and it isn't mundane. It has strange black shadows in it and red and blue energies just like the infinity loop of early energies, spinning and dancing through the circle. And I think that whatever magical working initially started this is still going, and being altered and changed by someone. I heard syllables, nonsense sounds of *aaaaap, aaaaap*, when I did a reading."

"Describe the loop again," T. Laine said, licking her fingers clean and taking notes one-handed. When I finished describing it, T. Laine said musingly, "I talked this morning with a coven leader in Charlotte, North Carolina. She said her mother, who was the former Charlotte coven leader, talked about energy experiments during World War Two, looking for a sustainable, self-perpetuating energy working that could be weaponized and offered to the US government. It would have meant coming out of the closet, but things were tough, and at the time, the war wasn't going well. They thought it was worth the risk. The search produced some positive results for a witch working for self-perpetuating energy, but it was abandoned after Hiroshima. If someone in the original group picked up the testing . . . and if it worked . . . and if that got away, it might be still active."

"That is a lot of *if*s," Tandy said, speaking what we were all thinking.

I said, "The magic is becoming more cohesive and the molds are spreading beyond the original borders." I stopped as possible conclusions lit up inside my brain, like the release of energy in an explosion. "Oh . . . yes . . . We don't know if one is *part* of the other or a direct or accidental *result* of the other. They may not be the same thing, but they may be working together, or maybe they're in some kind of symbiotic relationship. Like a . . . yeah, like a *symbiont*." I had thought that word before at some point in this investigation. Excitement raced through me, igniting possibilities, as I drew conclusions. I set the last of my sandwich on the table. "What if the energies of the working did two things, one or both by accident? One, creating the infinity energies, and two, mutating an existing mold, and then the mutated mold latched onto the energies . . . yeah. A mutation in the mold might change it into something the hospital can't identify or treat."

"Or *treat*?" Tandy repeated. "Are you saying this the beginning of a pandemic?"

"We're all going to be slimed to death?" JoJo asked, tapping on the tablet. "I thought I'd go out with a bang, not a B-grade movie title."

The empath chuckled, relaxing in JoJo's nonchalant energies.

"Last thing," I said. "The energies may be interfering with, or disrupting, the power grid."

"The brownouts and power shortages?" Tandy asked.

I chewed and swallowed. "We might be looking at problems with community services. And with the Secret City experiments, which all need stable power systems."

"So the company that probably started all this might suffer the results?" T. Laine asked. "Good. I hope they have to call and beg for help. And if they do—"

"You'll get off your butt and go help," JoJo said.

"Yeah." T. Laine tossed a crumpled napkin into the garbage, followed by paper sandwich wrappers, her face as scrunched as the trash she threw. "I know. I'm such a goody-two-shoes witchy woman. Anytime people are dying, there I am, lending a hand. Even if the humans don't freaking deserve it."

"Human here. Be nice." JoJo tapped her chest. Glancing at me, she said, "I got the papers from the office of General David Schlumberger, from Lieutenant Colonel Leann Rettell. I checked her out and she's for real. She asks for something, give it to her. She's a doctor with ties to CDC, as well as being in charge of Schlumberger's medical team."

I drained my drink, letting the caffeine energize my brain. A military doctor might be in a position to get other doctors and researchers to try unusual drugs on the mold, even if just in the lab. The mold had mutated and was growing like a cancer, so why *not* try something new in one of the fancy, supersafe labs? Or if people were dying, why not try it on people? Desperate times call for desperate measures. I put my sandwich down and sent an e-mail to Dr. Rettell. It couldn't hurt. And since I'd be speaking as one underling to another, it might work. Though a lieutenant colonel was not exactly an underling.

"If it's a magical mutation, do you think a magical working might help stop it?" T. Laine asked. "When I finally get in contact with the Knoxville coven leader, I can make her compliance part of any plea bargain. Assuming there are charges leveled against her."

"You still haven't seen her?" I asked.

"No. Once she was fired from LuseCo, she disappeared and has now missed two appointments we've made."

"So you've talked to her?" I clarified.

"If you can call two thirty-second exchanges actual convos, then yes. If you mean anything significant, then no. And her cell's GPS has been disengaged, so I can't ping her. All the witches have nonworking GPS on their phones." T. Laine lifted her sandwich to me in a toast or a salute. "I went with a deputy to her house, which is empty and has been for a week. I put out a BOLO on every single witch. Not one has been seen. They have to have a safe house or two to have dropped so thoroughly below the radar. More coincidence, Nellie. Not."

BOLO—be on the lookout. Spook School cop-lingo class kicking in.

"The local DA will make any charges, but you can certainly get with him in that event," JoJo said. "This case is likely to play havoc with current laws about paranormals." Her cell rang, and JoJo made a little groan when she saw the number. She pasted a fake smile on her face, though the person on the other end couldn't see her, and said, "Soul. What fantastical favor do you need? A pot of gold at a rainbow's end? A solution to turning lead into gold?"

I thought the questions were snide and not particularly appropriate for an underling to say to a VIP, but then, I was raised in the church of God's Cloud, where any female speaking like that to anyone would have been slapped down. Most firmly. And maybe the two had a history I didn't know about.

JoJo leaned back in her desk chair and rubbed her head, eyes closed. "Yeah, yeah, yeah, okay. T. Laine and Nell will be there ASAP."

She ended the call and looked between us. "You're getting your service weapon back," she said to me.

"Okay, but protoc—"

"Protocol is temporarily canned. We need you on this, and I'm making an executive decision. I don't know what's going on, and I want you armed. I also know everyone needs sleep but there's been a major change at UTMC. Gear up and get back there."

"Gear up how?" T. Laine asked.

"As in weapons and unis and the psy-meter 2.0. As in any magical tricks, trinkets, and a magic wand. Take a frigging Quidditch broom if you got one. Soul says someone is flying."

"Flying," T. Laine murmured softly.

We had taken our own vehicles in the hope that when we got done, we'd get to go home, in different directions, though that seemed unlikely as quickly as things were evolving. We had parked one lot over and entered another building, and were taking a pass-through to the back entrance of the paranormal unit, thereby avoiding the press, which was wonderful, and so smart. I had to remember this.

"Freaking *flying*." She sounded as amazed and tired as I felt.

"Like a witch on a switch?" I asked, not smiling, but teasing nonetheless.

"Ha-ha. Not."

Ahead, in the empty hallway, something moved, but when I looked, it was gone. Just the way witches looked when they hid behind an obfuscation spell. "Lainie?"

"I saw," she murmured. "We might have found our missing witches. Be ready."

"For—" Power raked along my skull.

I reached for my Glock.

T. Laine threw up her hands. Shouted, *"Revelabitur!"*

In the same instant someone else shouted, *"Dormio!"*

A sleep spell slammed through me. My eyes closed. I dropped my weapon with a clatter. Hit my knees. Fell to my belly, face to the hospital floor. I blinked, hearing *boom*s and shouted foreign words, feeling the scalding abrasion of magic along my flesh. I was the victim of a magical attack. Was lying on the floor. Grit under my cheek and on the palms on my hands. But not enough to do anything, not without the attacker's blood, and so far she was uninjured. I was useless.

T. Laine stepped across me, one foot to either side, her shoes touching me in a protective stance that kept me within her defensive circle. Something hit the ward she had erected around us, and she shuffled back in reaction, kicking me. I felt the vibration of the curse hitting the wall behind us and through the floor. She fought back. I saw blue and red behind my lids.

T. Laine screamed, "Mortem!" Blackness stole the light. T. Laine fell beside me, heaving breaths, gagging twice, gasping, "Oh God. Oh God," over and over.

Minutes passed like dreams, and she moved away from me, touching me now and again. Finally she said, "Did I kill you?" When I didn't reply, she shook me. "You have a pulse."

When I still didn't reply, she said, *"Suscito."*

Witch energies raced along my nerves and my eyes popped open. "Owwww," I said.

"Sorry. I didn't know what witch workings would do to you, but I needed you awake."

"I'm awake." I pushed myself to a sitting position. "Did you get her?"

"Not a scratch on her. Next time I'll have bigger guns."

I managed a laugh and let the U-18 witch pull me to my feet. The witch energies were zinging through me. I felt pretty good. Like I'd downed a cup of really, *really* strong tea. "I'm good," I said, surprise in my tone. I looked at the moon witch, who looked like a faint breeze would blow her over. "You okay?"

"Good. Well, good enough. I've reported in. Soul is trying to track the energies and follow the witch. We need to check the patients."

"Yeah. I figured." I followed T. Laine down the hallway, wondering why I was still alive. Wondering what effect the *Mortem* working had on the other witch. Because I was pretty sure *mortem* meant *death* in some foreign language.

Outside the sealed doors of the paranormal unit, we identified ourselves to the armed county deputy sitting there. He made a few calls to the unit at his back and nodded us on. Before he could ask, we dressed out in unis and bagged the psy-meter. Then we entered the controlled chaos of the paranormal unit. Which was a madhouse in the most literal way imaginable.

In one room, a young woman was strapped to her bed, arms bleeding, while above her, all the medical equipment was circling, like something out of *The Exorcist*—which I had walked out of one movie night at Spook School. Along the freshly scarred walls was broken equipment and several busted bags of IV medicines. It looked as if they had been smashed against the walls before being dropped. A lone, blue-dressed nurse was trying to bandage the woman's bleeding, blackened arms, stopping the blood flow, from where the IVs had been scratched out. But the equipment overhead kept dipping as if to bash her brains out. The nurse ducked and bobbed and, when she was done, raced through the door and into the hall, between us. She was huffing breaths inside the faceplate and cursing steadily as she rushed past, blond hair stuck to her sweat-damp face in the airless uni.

Without a word, she stripped and redressed before bustling on into the next room, where a child was being held down on the bed by three hefty-sized men. The child kept rising up off the bed, like in a magic act, and it looked as if she wanted to spin in a circle, her body twisting clockwise.

"Patient in room three twenty-one exhibits poltergeist-like activity," T. Laine said into a handheld mic, watching back and forth between the two rooms. I realized she was taking notes while her hands were gloved. That was smart. I needed a microphone recorder. I pulled the P 2.0 and started taking readings, feeding them to her. She stated what was happening in the room and what equipment was flying around, and ended with, "Violent reaction. Patient is covered with black . . . stuff. Looks like mold."

Into the mic, I said, "Redlining on all four levels."

"Patient in room three twenty-two is trying to levitate. Three people, probable combined weight of six hundred pounds, are managing to hold her down. This seems to confound Newton's third law of physics. And gravity. And Einstein's everything. Ditto on the mold."

I said, "Redlining on all four levels."

We walked on and T. Laine kept up a steady commentary as we paused and studied the patients in each room, ignoring any patient confidentiality rules and laws. "Male humans in three twenty-five appear psychotic and hallucinatory, talking about things they see that no one else does. Though they both seem to be discussing the same thing, as if they see into each other's heads. Or into the same alternate reality. One has a moderate amount of mold; the other seems to have little."

"Redlining on all four levels."

"Patients in three twenty-four: One appears to be sleeping or comatose. The sleeping one is moldy. The other one is saying, 'Flows, flows, flows. Pools, pools, pools.' Over and over."

I stopped at the room and covered her mic with one hand, saying, "His words are similar to what I heard deep in the earth, at the triangle sites the first day, the *flows* and *pools* phrases." What I didn't say aloud was my fear that something I had heard below the ground was capable of communicating in human language, maybe just the woman I had heard before. It was probably just parroting back the words of the working, but what if something down there, besides the sleeping Old Ones, was sentient? Mythology offered some unexplainable truths about the life of the ancient world. In my understanding it was Biblical—powers and principalities that humans should fight and guard against. But this felt different from anything I had been warned about in Bible lessons in my childhood in God's Cloud of Glory Church.

T. Laine nodded, and my hand fell from the mic. We moved on, me listening. "A female patient in room three twenty-three is saying, 'Dancing in the earth,' and she's moving as if dancing, even though she's restrained. Double mold. Her skin is nearly tarry all over. Sheets and floor are tarry. There are ultraviolet lights in the room, all on the patient."

I said, "Redlining on all four levels."

As I watched, T. Laine reached the nurses' desk and turned on the toes of one foot, nearly a dance pointe, and moved back up the hallway. She took the P 2.0 out of my hands. I watched as she went into first one room and then another, retaking readings, making notes on the recorder. When she had been in all the rooms we had passed, and taken readings on all the patients, a nurse stopped us and told us that we couldn't enter patient rooms and couldn't be on this floor, and threatened to call security.

Rather than argue or explain, T. Laine and I stripped off our contaminated suits and left, me trailing behind my current partner. She was still muttering into the recorder, "Upon bedside inspection, patients exhibiting poltergeist activity redline in level four but are slightly less than redline on other levels. Patients with the strongest signs of black mold redline on level three and are slightly less on other levels. No idea what this means, if it means anything at all, but a coven of witches might be able to help." She clicked off the recorder.

"You really think a coven could help?" I asked, our voices echoing hollowly along the hallway to the outside.

"No idea. Hope for the hopeless," she said. "I've been at this going on twenty hours. I'm heading home. You?"

"Yes," I said, pushing open the outer door and staring out over the parking lot as we walked to our vehicles. "I think so."

"Well, be careful and don't get bit."

Which seemed a strange comment in every way, until I was closing my truck door on the cold and looked up to see the moon rising over the horizon, full and bloated, as if it had eaten a corpse. This was the first night of the three days of the full moon. The werecats of U-18 would be hunting on my land, as they had on each full moon I was away at school. I wondered if I'd be safe sleeping in my own house. I wondered if I should change out my ammo for silver. I wondered if could kill my friends before they killed me. Of if I'd stand there, frozen in horror, as they tore me to pieces and ate my entrails.

I started the C10, which coughed and spat and got the heater cranking before I checked voice mail, and found one from Soul. It was polite but pointed. "Nell. Soul. Rick has been making progress on his were-shifting predicament. It is not impossible that he might yet shift into his leopard, and if he does, he might be dangerous. Occam has a cage prepared for such an emergency, and it is in the edge of trees, near the graves of your dogs. Stay away from it."

"Well. That stinks," I mumbled through a yawn. "It's hunting season. If the churchmen spot it while hunting, we might have a dead wereleopard."

I pulled out of the parking lot and toward the hills of home, but before the turn to home, I made an illegal U-turn and headed back to the triangle of contaminated houses. I hadn't inspected every house or yard. What if I had missed something?

And I had. Once again, the deputies dressed in unis told me I could go in, but my truck couldn't. I should have thought to bring them a box of coffee and cups. Stakeout nights and traffic guard duty were supposed to be the worst.

I passed through the barricade again. There were landscaping lights on at some houses, the solar-powered kind that came on by themselves. Light-sensing security lights brightened backyards. Two motion-sensor lights came on as I walked down the streets, too sensitive or aimed improperly. My breath hissed and thrummed inside the faceplate of the 3PE uni. My booties *shush*ed softly on the pavement with each step. The absence of humans and pets—of anything alive—made me want to run home and hide, as I walked the gloomy streets alone. The night wrapped itself around me, isolating, insulating, like a freezing, menacing blanket.

I had checked Point B, Alisha Henri's house, so I inspected Point A this time. The black slime was worse here. How could I have missed it before? The mold coated every tree, branch, stem, every blade of grass. In the center of the front yard, a ring of black toadstool-looking things formed a perfect circle, about seven inches tall. Around it trotted four possums, one adult and three small, like a mama and her toddlers, all coated with the slimy tarlike stuff. Their squat bodies glistened with it. As I watched, they went around once, twice, and kept going, clockwise. They were stuck walking in a circle like the geese and humans swimming at the pond, and the humans who had walked here. Like the goldfish in the tank. There was no smell of poison, and I guessed that KEMA hadn't sprayed this yard yet. The possums would die. The possums were dead already, but didn't know it.

In the distance, at the third house, Point C, bluish lights as bright as stadium lighting were shining, illuminating the whole area. I heard a generator running, and voices carried on the faint breeze, along with the stink of poison. Someone was spraying the house and grounds. I stopped midstep and turned around, heading back to the truck. The breeze appeared to fall away, moving no faster than my own feet. Moonlight draped over my shoulder, painting my shadow ahead of me, long and lean, even in the bulky suit. Overhead, movement caught my eye. Limned by silver moonbeams, crows were sitting on a telephone wire. Seven of them, sitting equidistant on the line. Shadows so black they were iridescent. The birds were silent. Awake. Black eyes on the distant lights. I hadn't looked up as I'd passed by the first time. Surely they were perched there then too. I hadn't heard the sound of wings.

I walked closer, my shoes the only near sound, *shush*ing, *shush*ing softly. As one, the crows turned to watch me. Black beaks looking knife pointed and razor sharp. There was something about their regard that was more than simply intelligent, that was also wise and crafty, two murders and a third of tricksters, watching me. Unpredictable as lightning.

One lifted his wings and leaned into a downward glide, off the wire, ahead of me. The others followed, still equidistant, in a floating line of seven, wings outstretched. They glided past the deputies, to my truck, and, one by one, alighted on the hood of the C10, or the roof, fluffed wings, and settled. Stared at me.

The deputies looked from the crows to me and back. The younger one finally found his voice, and asked, "Ma'am, you okay?"

"I'm fine." I came to a stop and peeled off the uni, stuffing it into the biohaz bin.

"What about them?" he asked, tilting his head to the Chevy.

"Those are crows," I said, deliberately obtuse. I opened the truck door and got in. Closed it. One crow walked to the windshield and leaned in, toward me. He pecked there gently. Three times. Three times. Three times, with pauses between each set of three. Like in the Poe story, *"Nevermore, nevermore, nevermore."* Then he flew off, and the others followed, back, I presumed, to their telephone line. I drove away, watching them in the rearview.

* * *

It was after midnight when I finally took the road's last rising curve to home. It had been a long day and I needed rest, my brain needed sleep. But as I pulled into the drive, all I could think was how bedraggled my garden looked in the truck lights. Weedy, even after the attack by machete. The soil had not yet been turned over. The mulch that had been delivered while I was away at school was still in a pile. My garden had suffered from neglect. I was exhausted, but I promised my garden that I'd get up early and work in the land for a few hours in the morning.

So tired my body felt as if it had tripled its weight, I made it to the cold, empty house, turned on lights, added wood to the stove and coaxed it alight, poured kibble into the cat bowls and onto the floor and didn't care that I made a mess. I showered in the tepid water left after the long day with no fresh wood to heat it, added water for morning, crawled into pajamas, and fell into bed, a zombie for sure. But just as I was falling to sleep, I remembered something someone had said about a self-perpetuating energy spell. Which the Department of Energy and the Department of Defense would fight over like angry wolves, an alphabet soup of battles. Fortunately I was able to shove the errant thought aside and slide into dreams.

A scream slashed rents in dreams and sleep. The mouser cats leaped from slumber into acrobatics, including one backflip, off the bed and underneath it. I slapped my hand onto my Glock and racked a round into the chamber, wondering when that muscle memory had formed. Silent, I rolled from the bed to the floor, bare feet on the cold wood, and reached into the earth. Deep and deep, into the warmth and contentment that was Soulwood. There was nothing on Soulwood that didn't belong, except two pools of blood and two carcasses of deer, one in a tree, one in a holler, near the clay-bottomed pool in back. "Ohhh," I whispered.

The cry screamed again, echoing down the hills and through the hollers. Enraged wereleopards. Or . . . a wereleopard in trouble? Hurt? Needing my help? I slid into a pair of slippers, walked through the lightless house, and outside. There were two

wereleopards lying on the grass near the quietly turning windmill. And a naked man in my backyard, near the clothesline.

Rick.

Standing in a pool of moonlight, he saw me, or heard me, or
maybe even scented me, when I left the back door for the porch.
He crouched, his olive skin silvered pale, black hair over his
legs and lower arms, much thicker than what seemed normal.
The hair on his chest was clearly defined, a mat that covered his
pecs and upper abs, and then tapered down into shadows. On
one shoulder, four gold circles shone. I knew they were the eyes
of the magical spell of binding, the only things still recognizable from the black-magic tattooed spell that kept him from
shifting.

He sniffed, his nostrils quivering, and a low growl came
from his throat, guttural and rasping. He wasn't wearing his
moon music, the music spell that helped him to survive the pain
of the full moon, a time when the lunar tides called his body to
shift into his cat form, but his tattoos wouldn't let his human
body go, trapping him in insanity-inducing agony. I had the
music on my tablet. Which I had left in the truck. Which was
stupid.

When I didn't attack or shoot him, Rick stood upright and
glided, catlike, a few feet closer. The pale light softened the
harsh lines of pain on his face. His expression was shaded
with brushstrokes of the night. His hair hung in a black tangled mass, nearly to his waist, far longer than normal. He was
clawed like a leopard, retractile claws on fingers and toes. The
eyes of his cat glowed, greenish and bright in the gloom.
The four golden spheres glowed on his shoulder, the eyes of the
cats in his tattoo, the scar tissue knotting them into an unrecog-
nizable mass of blues and greens and reds. Silver moonlight
caressed his shoulders and stomach and thighs, shadowing
darkly, brushing each muscle, each fissure, with harsh blackness, his body chiseled and slicked with the sweat of a long,
hard run. And he was erect.

I had never seen a real, live naked man. "Ohhh," I said again.

I had been married. I had submitted to my wifely duties with
John. But that was all under covers, in the night, a sweaty, grop-
ing unpleasantness that left me more empty than satisfied. But
this . . . this was lean and muscular, raw and somehow fierce,
despite the stillness of the night, and Rick's unmoving form.

I stepped to the porch door and pushed it open, calling, "Rick?"

He growled again, and snarled at me, hissing, as if showing me cat canines he didn't actually have. He raised his head and words came from his lips. "Bloody tree," he growled, the syllables garbled and slow but recognizable. Cold shivers raced from my spine out through my limbs. As if remembering how to speak he said, faster, "Bloody, bloody, sick tree."

My breath unsteady, I said, "Rick?" I walked out the door, onto the winter-stunted grass, icy on my soles.

The two watching cats rose to their feet. Slowly they paced to me. Hunting stance, eyes on prey. "Um . . . Occam? Paka?"

Both werecats showed me their killing teeth in matching snarls.

"Bloody, bloody," Rick growled. "Bloody dead man sick tree."

"Okay," I said. "You sense the dark thing over there?" I pointed to Brother Ephraim's little niche and back to the place in the woods where he'd died. "And there? Underground?"

Rick grunted. Hunched his shoulders. Raced at me. Inhumanly fast.

In the same instant, the two wereleopards leaped. The black shadow arched for Rick. The spotted leopard leaped at me.

The impact slammed me down. My elbow hit the ground first. My back. Head.

Breath grunted out. Pain shuttered through me, lights flashing in my brain. My weapon spun into the shadows from nerveless fingers. The spotted leopard landed over me. I struggled, but the leopard held me still, front paws on my upper arms, one back paw on my abdomen. I managed to take a single breath and focus on the werecat.

From only a few feet away I heard a catfight. Yowls and grunts and curses. But I didn't look away from the cat on top of me.

His claws were sheathed. Body held off mine, but hunched over me. His eyes glowed a brownish, bright golden yellow. His mouth was slightly open, the glint of teeth in the moonlight. We were nose to nose. I breathed. He breathed. On his breath I smelled the fresh blood and meat of his kill. I wanted to curse, but I had too little air in my lungs to do so. Seconds passed. His whiskers tickled my face. A vibration rumbled through him and into me.

Pea peeked over his shoulder. She had been clutching the pelt on his back and shoulders, hidden in the shadows. The odd little green thing chittered at me and leaped away, into the night. Her lack of interest in what Occam was doing had to mean he wasn't about to bite me, chew me, or snack down on me.

Occam lowered his head and nuzzled my jaw. Rubbing the silky soft pelt that covered the bones of his skull and his coarse whiskers over my face. Rubbing hard against my cheeks and jaws, neck and collarbones.

He's scent-marking me.

He's claiming me.

Like a house cat. Or like a kill.

I tightened in fear reaction. Occam stopped. Eased back. Stared at me. Chuffed into my face. Again nose to nose, he breathed my breath. His chest rose and fell over mine, his weight held off me. Near us, the fighting had stopped, and I heard footsteps sprinting into the woods. Then there was only silence, broken by the creak of the windmill.

Trying for irritation and nonchalance, I said, "Occam. Get offa me, you big ol' dang cat."

He chuffed again and lifted away first one leg, then another, and stepped away from me. But he lay down, belly to the ground, so close I could feel each breath he took. Could feel the heat of his body at my side.

Cold mountain air drifted over me, and I shivered. "If I sit up, you ain't gonna eat me, are you?"

Occam shifted his head left and right, in a human gesture for *no.* It looked odd on his cat body.

"I'm holding you to your word." Which was useless, since he had claws and teeth and fangs and I had two bare hands and Pea was gone. I got my elbows up under me and asked, "I reckon Rick lost his music when he lost his clothes?"

Occam dipped his head and raised it, nodding. The moonlight caught the shaded pelt colorations, lines from eyes to nose, along his jaw. Dark-as-night ear tips and eyelids. Still moving slowly, I sat up straight. "You sure are a pretty thang, ain't ya."

Occam chuffed and butted my side with his head, just like a house cat demanding to be petted. I obliged. He rested his head on my thigh and sighed out a long breath. And he started purring. The vibration was so strong my bones were shaking. I smoothed the hair of his ears and along the back of his skull. I pulled on his ears gently, soothing them. Occam closed his eyes.

"I ain't doing this to your human self, you know," I said. Occam chuffed again and rolled over, exposing his belly to me, like a dog. Or like a cat—testing. "Un-uh. Nope. I ain't rubbing your belly." I stood and looked for my gun, finding it immediately, only feet away. Occam watched me from his upside-down position as I ejected the mag and removed the round from the chamber. "I coulda shot you by accident," I said. Occam said nothing, but he rolled back upright, stretched out in the grass like some ancient god the Egyptians mighta worshiped. He was beautiful, and I had a feeling he knew it.

Suddenly I realized something was missing. "Your gobag. It's gone."

Occam nodded.

"Paka's was gone too. Along with Rick's music."

Occam nodded again and this time he stood, looking into the trees.

I put together the missing gobags, Rick's missing music, his comments about the bloody tree, and the direction of Occam's gaze. "Oh. I have problems, don't I?"

Occam nodded once.

"And my problems contributed to your problems?"

Occam nodded again.

"Is this the classic 'disturbance in the force'?" The Star Wars marathon weekend at Spook School had provided me with a lot of cultural references.

Occam snorted and tilted his big head back at me.

"Lemme get some warm clothes on. And some gardening gear." I dashed to the house, making it about ten feet before I realized I was acting like a rabbit. I stopped dead and looked back. Occam's golden eyes were latched on me. But despite my prey action, Occam didn't pounce on me. I held perfectly still until the wereleopard looked away. I let a held breath go and moved very slowly to the house. I'd been stupid. I had been taught better in Spook School. Rule number one in were-creature class was *"Never run near, around, or from a were-creature. That will get you eaten."* Thank goodness Occam had better control than some weres.

Inside, I pulled on warm outer clothes over my pajamas, added a pair of Farmer John overalls, and tied on sturdy work boots. I put my personal .32 in the bib and made sure the tab was buttoned. The mouser cats were still nowhere to be seen. Little cowards. I tucked my faded pink blanket under my arm and selected two boxes from the kitchen pantry before I left the house for the screened porch. There I piled my load and set the limb lopper on top. I went to the truck for my electronic tablet and the P 2.0. It was getting colder, and the security light illuminated my breath in small clouds.

Carrying the supplies around the rear of the house to the concrete-floored shed beside the porch, I unlocked the door. In the dim light, I set down my load and studied the stored tools, all neatly hung on sixteen-penny nails or resting tidily on shelves. I shook frozen spiders and several years' worth of dirt and filth out of John's old heavy-duty canvas rucksack, tucked the tools I had already gathered into the pockets, and set aside a strong flashlight that turned night to day.

I hefted my husband's old chain saw. It was bulky and heavy, and it was probably unwise to use the thing in the middle of the night in the dark of the woods. I replaced it and picked up the battery-powered chain saw I had bought for myself with part of my consultation check from PsyLED. The teal-and-black, ten-pound, thirty-six-volt, lithium-ion Makita saw would have made John bust a gut laughing, but I had thought it would be fine for most of the things I did around the garden and in the woods. I removed it from the charging block and checked the chain oil reservoir, which was full. I pushed the button to turn it on. The whiny roar split the night exactly like I thought it might. Like a thousand ghosts screeching from the grave. I punched the button off and felt something move behind me. I whirled and found a spotted leopard standing in the doorway, his ears flattened and nose wrinkled in disgust. "Sorry 'bout the noise," I said. Occam tilted his head at me and chuffed, as if he found me amusing. I placed the chain saw in the biggest pocket of the rucksack and cut the overhead light.

I swung the rucksack to my back and palmed the flashlight. Locked the door. In the night, I stopped, feeling the wind in the trees. Hearing the call of a far-off owl. Wood smoke laced through the air, a comforting scent of home. I looked at the moon, hard and cold and bright overhead. I'd get little use of its light in the woods. Even with the trees denuded of leaves, even with the flashlight and its four thousand lumens of raw light power, it would be dark.

Occam butted the back of my knee, as if he could smell me hesitating. Procrastinating. Being silly. Scared of the night. I firmed my resolve and sent my intent into the ground through the leather soles of my work boots. This was *my* woods. Whatever was out there was a trespasser. I would take back what was mine. I felt the land shift, as if my thoughts were dreams that stirred through it.

"Okay," I said to Occam. "Lead the way to whatever made Rick so spooked that he took off his music and his clothes." Glancing up at me once, the spotted wereleopard paced just ahead of me. Walking sedately into the woods, I turned on the flash and followed my guide along an unfamiliar path into the woods.

Trees big around as small houses broke the land into deep shadows and silvered leaf fall. The distant owl fell quiet. The woods were silent in that time of night after the nocturnal predators had killed and eaten their fill and before the diurnal predators had woken. Through the leather soles of my old boots, I felt a small herd of deer over toward the Peay property. Another, slightly larger, group was over toward the Vaughns' place. Rabbits and squirrels were huddling. Rats and mice still raced and trundled along looking for foodstuffs. Two coyotes or coywolves trotted along the border of the land near the Stubbins farm.

Ahead was the clay-lined, spring-fed pool, which was where I had already guessed we were going. Beside it was a black wereleopard, and a man who was more cat than human, crouched, drinking from the cold water. I could feel them through the ground as we drew near, my boots loud in the empty silence. The two drinking werecats—leopard and mostly human shaped—stopped drinking, pivoted their heads to me, and slipped soundlessly into the night.

In the new path, my light caught a glimpse of white—a broken set of earbuds, tangled and torn. A gobag appeared a bit farther on, a woman's skirt and comb on the ground, the fabric slashed by claws and stained by blood. I moved the light back and forth and saw Occam's gobag in bracken. And Rick's cell phone, the screen smashed. A few steps beyond were Rick's clothes, in the bottom of the clay-lined pool. Soaked. The water was pinkish from blood.

We had come this less direct way, I guessed, so I could see the state of the clothing. It looked like things had gotten out of hand—violently so.

I stepped into the small clearing, lifting both legs high over a root that curled above a rock before it found the earth. My flash fell on the sapling.

The small tree had regrown its limbs, slender and more delicate, but longer than before. And more of them. Four limbs. The roots were different now too. Instead of the two roots coiling together, a dozen or so twined and twisted together to form the trunk. The circular place where it was rooted was a bloody mess, empty of natural life. No vines, no leaves, just a bare and bloody-greasy patch of soil. The tree was taller, ten feet or more. Its girth was greater.

Standing back from the sapling, I placed the flash on a boulder and used rocks to position it so its light fell on the tree. In the angle of its glare, I opened John's rucksack and unloaded it.

I plugged in the portable battery backup tablet and set Rick's music playing as loudly as the tablet could. The sounds of wood flute and violin filled the wood grove, and I could feel the interest of the trees. High in the branches, a breeze danced, making a low-pitched sound that seemed to breathe with the music. I angled the tablet into the trees in the direction I felt the werecats and placed all the tools where I could see them in the glare of the flash.

My hands moving with muscle memory, I tested the land with the psy-meter 2.0. All around the sapling, the trees read as they should. But the sapling itself and the ground beneath it read ambient on level one through three, with a little elevation of psysitope four. Exactly like me. And very unlike the sites where black goo toadstools were growing, and unlike the people at the hospital. Whatever was happening in town was different from what was happening at Soulwood, despite Rick's bloody, bloody words. A weight dropped off my shoulders. I turned off the psy-meter.

Less tentatively, I crouched and placed my palm on the

ground away from the red mess. Nothing tried to grab me. Nothing tried to pull me under. The land arched up into me, healing and satiating. Beneath the surface, Soulwood itself was healthy except for the area around the sapling and the area where Brother Ephraim had carved out a place for himself. I followed the pulsing line of shadowed energies from the sapling to Ephraim and then out and down to the tree on the church compound. The trail of energies was no more energetic, no more active than it had been earlier.

The problem in Knoxville was spreading.

But the problem here was contained.

I stood and dusted off my hands.

I had forgotten safety glasses, but I wasn't going back to the house. I took up the chain saw and pressed the button. The awful screaming whine sliced the night like a knife on stone. Occam leaped away, into the trees, and disappeared. Musta really hurt the poor cat's ears. Moving carefully into the small clearing, I stepped onto the bloody earth, carefully making sure it would take my weight. Turning my back to the flash, I stood so the tree caught the light. It trembled, as if in fear. Our shadows fell onto a Soulwood poplar, massive and strong.

Chain saw blaring, I positioned the spinning blade and cut into the small tree. The tree reacted.

Newly grown branches lashed at me. Roots rippled and tried to rise through the soil to grab my feet. I cut up and ripped through the branches, then down and cut into the roots. Something splattered over me, but I didn't care. I cut through the trunk, severing the stump from the roots and the roots from the earth.

Over the whine of the chainsaw, I could hear the tree screaming, the sound coming up through the ground and into my bones. From far away, a twin scream echoed, from the direction of the church compound where I grew up. Still, I didn't stop. I cut it to pieces.

When I was done, I switched off the chain saw and stepped back. The tree was sticks and sawdust. Something trickled down my face. I wiped it and my hand came away red and oily in the flash. The liquid looked like blood, but it was cold and greasy, tacky, like drying glue when I tapped my fingers together.

I opened the two boxes that had come from the pantry and

upended the contents of the first one on the ground, in a three-foot diameter circle around the sapling. The ancients had salted land, rendering it incapable of supporting crops, thereby killing the farmers who depended on nature for food. Monarchs and generals and warriors had used starvation as weapons and punishment for centuries. Maybe for millennia. I scattered the rock salt with my boots. Beneath the layer of crystal, the bloody earth shriveled and curled and moaned in pain. In short order, the moisture would dry out and the land would be a brick. No plant would grow in the three-foot diameter circle for years. Which broke my heart, but not enough to stop. Tears misting into my vision, I smoothed the chunks of rock salt into an even layer.

Then I layered the box of borax on top and stomped it down, my boots making a sucking sound as the wound in the earth bled and the liquid was absorbed by salt and borax. Sam had said that salt hadn't worked against the tree on the church grounds, but this tree was a sapling. Its roots were young, close to the surface. It should work here. The trees nearby would suffer from the rock salt poison too. Everything in the area would unless I sealed it off. So when I was done killing the tree, I scuffed my boots clean and walked to the nearest patch of healthy ground. I placed my hand on the earth and willed the land to seal off the wound, keeping it separate from the rest of the area. Willed it to seal away water and nutrients and to let the tree die. I didn't know how Soulwood would manage that, but the land had done more amazing things even without my help.

Hand on the earth, I thought about the long strand that draped through the ground to the huddled form of Ephraim. I imagined snipping it in two with loppers. Nothing happened, but it made me feel better. And maybe the land would smother the line of energy now that the sapling was dying.

Finished, I gathered up the severed parts of the tree and tucked them under my arm. I left the blanket beside the tablet, which I left playing, and repacked my gear. I checked the area to make sure I had left no branches, no rootlets, nothing that might root or sprout. And I walked away. Ahead of me on the path, a giant cat dropped from the trees overhead and looked at me. The flash caught his golden eyes and the spots and striations in his pelt. Occam turned away and padded before me, as if leading me once again. I understood that Occam had appointed himself my protector. It was sweet, if unnecessary. "You trying to make up for being catty rude at the pond today?" I asked him.

He glanced back, slant eyed, and I couldn't have said why, but I got the impression that Occam was amused at the thought of a cat being called to task for rudeness.

Back at the house, I replaced the tools, checked to make certain that rootlets hadn't sprouted on any of the chipped-up bits of sapling, and stopped at the marriage trees. One knee on the ground, I put a palm on the twined roots, intending to do a light surface scan. What I got was a lot more. The land around Brother Ephraim's little bolt-hole was churning with anxiety. And Ephraim himself was roiling with fury, sparkling with black lights that had even blacker centers.

If I were using my eyes to see his reaction, I'd have seen nothing, but since I was just sensing his feelings with my brain, the black on black made sense, an indication of fury. As I studied him, I realized that his tenuous connection to the place where he died—the thin strand of energies—was gone. I had broken it without magic, with purely mundane and human things. Power tools and ice cream salt. I chuckled, and it wasn't a nice chuckle. It was mean sounding. I didn't care if Ephraim knew it or not.

Pride goeth before a fall and all that kinda thing.

The energy that was Ephraim heard me. Or felt me. Or saw me. And he lanced at me like a spear launched from an atlatl—a spear-thrower. I tore myself up from the ground and leaped away. I landed hard, and the dirt and roots where I had knelt roiled for a moment as if an earthquake rattled the earth. Then it fell still and I felt Ephraim as he raced back to his hidey-hole. "Last time I laugh at you," I said.

From the back door, Occam snorted, the discharge of air an interrogative.

"Never you mind," I said to him. "This is not a problem you need to deal with. It's my problem. And yes, I'll ask for help if I need it."

When I got back to the house, I locked Occam outside, much to his amusement, and put the tree pieces in the still-hot stove to burn. They lit up instantly, a bright red flame. I showered the bloody tree stuff off me. It had grown sticky as it dried, like tree sap, which was interesting but not overly helpful.

As I dried off, I discovered a voice mail on my cell phone from my brother Sam, which had come in only seconds past. It was short and pointed. "Nell. We'uns got trouble at the church grounds. I'd look kindly upon a visit from you. As soon as possible. Sooner, maybe."

FOURTEEN

"Can you meet me at the entrance to the church?"

T. Laine knew what I meant by the words "the church," though there were dozens of churches in Knoxville.

"Why?" she asked, talking and yawning at the same time. "You got black mold growing there too?"

"No. Well, I hope not," I added quickly. "Remember that tree that grew roots into me?"

T. Laine grunted. I feared she was already halfway back asleep.

"Well, it's going crazy. Growing thorns. Attacking children. It's put on a couple thousand pounds of wood over the last few months."

"Attacking . . . That sucks. But . . . what can *I* do to stop that?" she grouched. "We've already got a case." I didn't blame her. We were overworked and tired, and here I was asking her to help with something personal.

"You can tell me if a witching will kill it."

"Witches don't kill."

"According to PsyLED files, a death witch can kill with her magic."

"Death witches don't use magic; they use curses."

"Whatever," I said, trying out the word and the attitude that went with it. It must not have come out the way I wanted, because T. Laine laughed, though not unkindly.

"I wanted to sleep in till at least six a.m.," she said.

"I wanted to sleep in till four."

"Four? Well, hell. I guess if you can burn the midnight oil, I can at least help. ETA forty-five. But you owe me breakfast."

"Eggs, bacon, biscuits, grits, and pancakes or waffles?"

"God, yes."

"See you then," I said, not feeling the least bit guilty that I would be foisting my family off on her with breakfast at the Nicholson place. Not in the least.

T. Laine's car followed me in, the witch driving, Tandy in the passenger seat, sipping on coffee-shop coffee. I could see the logo through the window. I was glad to see the empath looking so hearty, and also happy to see that he and T. Laine were so friendly. Tandy needed someone stable in his life, someone other than a romantic interest. But I hadn't expected him to be here. I was suddenly worried what effect the massed emotions of the church and my family would have on him.

It was after dawn, and the church was finished with devotionals, the members walking and driving away, each and every one making a wide detour around the tree in its cement-block prison. Mostly because the walls around the tree were far more cracked and broken than before. One whole section was rubble.

To the side of the crumbled wall, a gleam of yellow utility paint could be glimpsed beneath a mound of vines that hadn't been there yesterday. The vines originated up in the tree, as if the tree had decided to grow finger vines and attack. Deep inside the vines, I could see a bulldozer's external tracked extensions—grousers. It looked as if a heavy-duty bulldozer had taken on the walls and the tree and had lost.

In the early light, the tree was massive, curling limbs and twisting roots in shapes a live oak attained after centuries, not decades. Today it was mostly leafless. The trunk and branches, the cement walls, and the ground for ten feet around it were blackened by fire. Where the fire had missed a section of the tree, a scarlet blaze brightened the bark. The branches there were covered with thorns as long as my fingers. The few leaves remaining were deepest green with crimson veins and scarlet stems.

The tree had started mutating when it had access to my blood. At the time, I had wondered if the mutation was mutual and if I would be changed as much by the tree as it was by me. Now that fear had waned. Though I had scars, I was otherwise unchanged. The tree, however, was an alien mutant ninja oak. I didn't know what to do with it.

I got out of my truck and heard T. Laine's vehicle doors

closing. My brother walked up, leaving the chapel, the pointed-arched windows casting diffused light onto the ground. Sam had been in line to take over the leadership of the church, a contentious decision, but I had been too busy, and too thoughtless, to ask what had happened with the elders' decision.

Sam walked closer, dressed in green camo pants and green camo shirt, with a matching camo coat over it and a camo ball cap. His boots were brown. "We tried what you suggested," he called over the short distance.

"What happened to the bulldozer?" I asked.

"We think the tree ate it." Which was what I had thought. I smiled at my true sibling as he continued. "Driver got away clean." He stuck his hand out to T. Laine and then to Tandy, saying, "We met before. Sam Nicholson. Nell's full sib." Sam surprised me that he didn't address all his actions and comments to the man first. My brother went up a notch in my estimation. The special agents gave their names, and together we approached the tree, stark in the headlights I had left burning. We stopped about twenty feet out, beyond the drip line.

Sam said to the others, "We cut off the branches, poured herbicide on it, and burned it. It kept coming back. Last night we tried to knock it down. It ate our bulldozer."

"Mean-assed tree," T. Laine said thoughtfully.

My brother coughed and laughed at the same time, surprised by the language. T. Laine looked at him, an innocent expression on her face. I just shook my head. "A dog nibbled the lichen last evening," Sam said, his face going hard.

"Dogs'll eat anything," T. Laine said.

"This one died," Sam replied. His voice was even, but something in his stance suggested he was not at ease at all. And then I realized what had happened.

"Oh. Sam," I whispered. "Tell me it wasn't one of Chrystal's grandbabies."

My brother scowled and hunched his shoulders. Chrystal had been his best hunting dog, a liver, white, and tan springer spaniel who could sniff out a bird at a hundred paces. I had heard she had passed while I was at Spook School due to a sudden-onset cancer. She had been fine one day and died the next. Sam hunched his shoulders tighter in the dawn light and said, "It was Tally. That tree's dangerous."

Tandy placed a hand on Sam's shoulder, the first time I had seen him voluntarily touch another human in . . . ever. Sam looked at Tandy and controlled his double take at the up-close sight of Tandy's Lichtenberg lines. A sense of pride opened in me like the lift of a hot air balloon. My brother was more open-minded than I had expected.

Mama walked up, her long skirts swaying in the headlights, a heavy scarf around her shoulders. "You'un gonna curse this tree, Nell? Lordy. I swear it's a devil tree. It ate that behemoth yonder"—she gestured to the vine shrouded bulldozer—"and then it tried to eat Mindy."

"Curse—? I'm not sure how to curse anything, Mama." Mindy—Mud—was my true sib in more ways than genetics and parenting. Mud was a nonhuman creature like me. Whatever I was. And had it tried to eat her or incorporate her? They were very different things. Ultimately the same result, but different intents.

"Kill it," Mama said. "Kill the damnable thing."

I blinked. And blinked again. Mama cussing? I resisted looking at the sky to see if Jesus had come.

"Mama speaks from a position of power," Sam said, his tone carefully modulated to demonstrate no emotion at all. "She and Sister Erasmus are the newly selected deaconesses, in charge of women and women's complaints. And the women want it gone."

Deaconess? Mama and the outspoken Sister Erasmus? Women with positions of power in the church? God's Cloud was about to face trouble with a capital *T.* A chortle bubbled in my throat, but I forced it down, deciding to not respond to Sam's comments. "Any chance there might be breakfast for guests?" I asked Mama instead. And the thought that I was a coward flashed through me.

"Always, baby girl. I'll see you and your friends at the kitchen table in half an hour."

"We'll be there," I said.

Mama and her sister-wife Mama Carmel moved away, trailing my true and half sibs. Other attendees to the morning devotionals made their way home, and in every case, avoided the tree.

When the last church member was gone and it was just Sam

and my coworkers standing in the brightening daylight, T. Laine murmured, "Is the tree like the things growing at the pond and the neighborhood?"

"I don't think so," I said. "They read differently on the psymeter 2.0. They have a different color."

"They?" T. Laine asked.

Ouch. I had forgotten that I hadn't told them about the tree on Soulwood. But now that Rick and company were running around naked and pelted on my land it wasn't much of a secret. Quietly I told them about the newly butchered tree. "What I did to it isn't a curse. And the two trees we're seeing are not the same things as the other odd growths. But they might be connected in some way to the sleeping"—I made a little circular gesture with my hand, trying to find a word for what I felt when I communed deeply—"entities . . . ? In the earth? The Old Ones. The things we aren't supposed to disturb."

"We have to take your word for that," T. Laine said.

And there was nothing to reply to that truth. But Sam wasn't so complaisant. Voice hard as stone against stone, he said, "My sister don't lie. Not when she was a little'un, and not now."

A warm glow lit me from within, and I said, "She's talking empirical evidence, Sam. Not trust." At least I hoped so.

"Trust we have in plenty," T. Laine said. A tension I hadn't noticed eased from my brother's shoulders. Protective. My brother was *protective* of *me*. It brought a silly smile to my face.

"PsyCSI could rule out that the two things are the same," Tandy said quietly.

The tension hunched me up again. But he had a point.

"If you break off a thorn and a leaf and scrape up some of the red stuff, that should be sufficient," he said. And even softer, he added, "I can do it for you."

I looked up from the study of my toes. "You think the tree will let you?"

"I think I can convince it to let me."

I was seeing all kinds of confidence from the empath, and not a one I had expected.

"I have evidence bags and some plastic baggies in the car," T. Laine said as she opened the passenger door.

Tandy took the baggies and the paper evidence bags from her

and moved slowly toward the tree. No roots sprang from the ground. No branches whipped at him. I walked to the side so I could watch him, see his face. Tandy looked calm, peaceful, as if he was meditating, his odd white skin shining pale, and the Lichtenberg lines bright in the morning light.

T. Laine was holding the psy-meter 2.0, taking a continuous reading as Tandy slowly, step by step, approached the tree. The mutant oak still didn't do anything. T. Laine murmured, "The levels read like plant . . . Wait," she announced to Tandy. The empath stopped. Her voice modulating into calm again, she said, "There's a little spike in psysitope four." She glanced at me. That was what I read on the P 2.0.

I said nothing, studying Sam's expression. My brother was interested in how Tandy could get so close to the tree without it grabbing him. Like the way some people might walk right up to a deer. Or a wolf . . .

"Okay," T. Laine said. "Levels are back to tree-ish."

Tandy took the last three steps and reached out a hand. His fingertips brushed the soot-blackened bark of one branch. I realized he was reading the tree the same way he read people's emotions. Carefully he traced his fingers up the branch to a thorn and snapped it off. The tree did nothing. He broke off two more thorns and dropped them into a plastic baggie. He opened another baggie and snapped off several leaves. The break sites began to bleed. The tree quivered.

Over T. Laine's shoulder, I checked the P 2.0 and it spiked on psysitope four for three or four seconds. Tandy placed his palm on the tree and closed his eyes as if meditating, and the levels settled back to . . . normal. Not *me*-normal. *Tree*-normal. Tandy had calmed the tree. Restrained it maybe?

"This may sound weird," I said, "but . . . is the tree sentient?" Tandy cocked his head, his eyes opening and coming back from far away to focus on me, but he didn't answer. "And if it is, can you suggest, or maybe nudge it to do something?"

"What do you have in mind, Nell?" he asked, his tone was relaxed and peaceful.

"Put it to work." I studied the tree. "It clearly wants to do something, become something. So . . . give it a job?" I raised my brows at Sam, who tried not to respond to me talking about the tree like it was a working dog. "What do you think?" I asked my brother. "Guard duty at the gate?"

I watched as Sam's brain tried to wrap itself around my questions. He asked. "You think it would let us transplant it?"

"Not so much that as tell it to send runners or roots underground to the gate." I looked at the tree and at Tandy. "It's a long way. Nearly half a mile. But if it had a job maybe it would stop being so rascally."

Tandy closed his eyes again and his breathing slowed. Minutes passed.

Slowly Tandy drew his hand away and walked back to us. My brother's mouth was pursed and he was nodding.

"Tandy?" I asked when he got back to us, my thoughts racing and rolling over one another like squirrels playing.

"I asked it to move itself to the gate. It's willing if it gets some kind of nourishment. This spot has the best . . ." He stopped abruptly and his face screwed up with confusion. "I can only think of the word *compost* to interpret its needs. This is the best spot in the entire compound."

My mouth managed to stay closed. To heal from gunshots, I had fed the tree my blood. "We'll think of something," I said. "Will you come back later and attempt to encourage it to move? If I can make the other place more palatable to it?"

Tandy gave me a full smile, eyes crinkling, his Lichtenberg-cracked teeth showing back to the molars. A full smile was so rare I had ever only seen the one. "Palatable. Yes. I'll come back."

T. Laine's cell *ding*ed and she said, "Text from JoJo. We'll have to take a rain check on breakfast. Duty calls."

Sam grabbed me. Hugged me. I stopped all movement, as still and stiff as a board in his arms. There was a definite one Mississippi, two Mississippi before I patted his shoulder and he backed away. "I'll tell Mama you can't stay," he said. "Pity, as my wife will be there and you two still ain't met."

I nodded and searched his face for the reason for the hug. Sam chuckled wryly, shaking his head, as if he understood my reaction and wasn't happy about it. He lifted a hand in farewell to the others. "Don't be a stranger, sis." His boots clomped into the day, and my eyes tracked his retreating back.

Wordless, I drove to the gate and I pulled over. T. Laine and Tandy followed, our vehicle lights bright. I got a single piece of equipment out from behind the passenger seat, walked to the twelve-foot-tall fence, and stood there for a moment. Standing in the headlights, I pulled a vamp-killer from its leather sheath. I didn't have any alcohol wipes, but I could worry about infection later. With the well-honed steel edge, I nicked the pad of my thumb and hissed with the pain. Then I squeezed out several drops on the ground.

The earth of the compound reached up to me, hungry, interested, the way a flower turns to the sun. I deliberately did not claim the land. Deliberately kept my mind blank.

I walked back and forth, squeezed out more drops. Then I went to the truck, wrapped my thumb in a handkerchief I found in the glovebox, and cleaned and put away the weapon. I felt, more than heard, Tandy approach. He took my hand and pulled the stained cloth away. He dabbed a bit of ointment from a tube onto the laceration and wrapped a self-adhesive bandage around it. "Keep it clean," he said, before leaving for T. Laine's Escape.

While I had worked, T. Laine had texted the address and I followed them out of the compound. As I drove, it occurred to me that using death magics on the mold in the slimed neighborhood might be counterproductive. It seemed as if there was a curse on the land already. So maybe the working that started all this mess might have been a blood-magic curse, not a working, and we needed to bless the land. Or something. But I was too tired to figure out what I should do about that little germ of an idea.

We stopped at the neighborhood and parked at the police barricade, where we all dressed out in the ugly unis with the orange stripes. I was beginning to hate the sight of them, but after seeing the man run toward the pond as if to dive in, I understood how important they were.

We were running low on the contamination suits and T. Laine sent a text to JoJo to order more while Tandy and I chatted with two new deputies. T. Laine got back a snarky comment that our monthly budget was not going to be happy. The rest of us ignored that one. When we were all in the paranormal personal protection equipment (3PEs), we walked down the road, through the neighborhood, taking the same route I had last night.

The residents had been gone only a few days, but their land was eerie, silent, lifeless. Bicycles and cars lay abandoned in driveways, the occasional child's toy lay in a yard, already dusty and unused. Odd, low-lying *things* were spread across flower beds; plantlike things in colors of yellow, purple, orange, pink, and black were everywhere. Some had strange flowers a few inches high, blooms that were purplish or black with a reddish tinge and sharp, pointed, curling petals, red stamens and pollen the same color. The flowers seemed to move, as if breathing, or crawling, a slow and nearly invisible motion, but my eyes kept tracking it, like a long, low ripple in the various beds.

Either the black lichen stuff was changing as it spread and grew, or we now had a bunch of other things growing up with it. Or it was crawling.

Strange growths were clustered on tree trunks and up in the limbs, hanging like mistletoe, but bizarre colors of rust and red and yellow and purple, with the slimy black undercoat beneath, attaching one bed of bizarre-ity to another. Among it all, there were dead animals—several possums in a circle in the yard where they had run the night before, and twelve dead crows, all lying in a circle in the middle of the street. A dead cat seeming to lie where it dropped, as if it had crashed while chasing its tail.

Tandy, our self-appointed evidence collector, gathered samples and sealed them in bags. The broken stems bled black tarry stuff onto the fingers of his gloves. The crows slimed into the bottom of their plastic evidence bag. The cat's tail fell off. When he handed the baggies to me, I compared them to the samples from the church tree, and though both sets were bizarre, they were unalike. The psy-meter readings were different from the ones on the church tree too. Every bit of evidence we collected told me that my problem on Soulwood and on the church land was different from the problem in Knoxville. But nothing told us what the Knoxville problem was or what to do about it.

All I could think about was the voice I had first heard in the land. The woman's voice.

We probably needed to take more samples and do a dedicated search of the entire neighborhood, but T. Laine got another text sending us back to UTMC. Again ping-ponging us all over. But this time it wasn't to collect information. Two of the patients had died—the woman who had been making her medical equipment fly around the room and the levitating child. Mother and daughter. Something shattered within me. Cracked and split and fell inside, crushed and plunging like splintered glass, cutting, drawing my blood. *Children*. I had saved some at God's Cloud of Glory Church. I was losing children here.

Things were hectic when we got to the hospital. It turned out that the moment the girl flatlined, the equipment in the entire paranormal ICU department died. Every single piece was shorted out. It shouldn't have happened. Battery backups and extensive surge protectors were standard on every single medical device. There was backup power available, generators that were tested on a regular basis. But even the lights had gone out, including the ultraviolet lights that were being used to impede or kill the fungi. Including the heat. And life-support machines. Medical people, nurses probably, were breathing for some of the patients with bulbous blue bags that they squeezed and released, over and over.

There were blue-suited electricians checking lines and sockets and other electrical stuff that was unfamiliar to me. The hospital managers were among the mix, getting in the way of the maintenance workers, the techs, and the medical types, demanding answers that no one had. Everyone was still grappling with how to get power restored, how to get new equipment transported in, what to do about the ruined, contaminated equipment, and where to send the patients if the situation remained this grim.

And there were military people too, camo showing beneath 3PE white unis like ours, guns slung at the ready. I assumed they were here in case this turned out to be a terrorist situation. Or a mob of fearful residents attacked with pitchforks and torches. Or perhaps in case someone needed to do something dire like nuke the building. The air was cold, but I started sweating beneath the uni at that thought.

No one checked my ID beyond glancing at the white uni. If I had been that elusive terrorist and I had killed the agent dressing in the uni, stolen his or her suit, and walked in like I owned the place, I could have done so undetected. I went through the doors into the paranormal department and began checking psymeter readings. It took maybe ten minutes to discern that the entire ward was on total redline. And that the same black slime was evolving and growing in here as well as in the neighborhood. It had taken root in the cracks at walls and ceiling, on the window glass and ledges, in the bathrooms. The mold was black, red, yellow, and occasionally bright purple, with bulges that suggested it was about to flower. Molds didn't flower. This was something new. Something different, no matter what it had started out being.

Back outside the department's doors, I nearly bumped into Soul, who was talking to two people, a young man wearing army olive drab under his white uni, carrying a clipboard, and a woman in the same fabric, with some metallic doodads high on her collar. I knew that meant she was an important army somebody, but I couldn't remember what the designation was. Standing close enough to eavesdrop, I recorded the P 2.0 readings and learned that the military and PsyLED were now working hand in hand to bring in massive generators and racks of ultraviolet lights to "kill the funguses," as the woman's assistant said.

That made the army woman almost smile. "Fungi," she said, "is the plural. And this isn't technically fungus. It's a new species—or multiple new species—of slime mold."

I pocketed the P 2.0 and pulled my cell, which was protected in a plastic baggie. I punched the words *slime mold* into a search engine. I had never heard of it. Which was strange enough on its own.

According to the almighty Internet, the stuff was weird, with a lot of words I had no idea how to pronounce mixed with things I understood well. Slime molds were neither fungi nor lichen, but were spore-forming protists, whatever that was, eukaryotic (another word to look up later) creature things with their DNA enclosed in a nucleus inside each cell. I went to another site, hunting protists, which were not plants, not animals, not fungi, though they acted enough like all of them that scientists believed protists had paved the way for the evolution of most forms of life. Protists fell into four general subgroups: single-celled algae, protozoa, water molds, and slime molds.

Slime molds were one of nature's wild cards. They could move from place to place; change shape, color, and texture; and they were smart. One species, whose name I couldn't pronounce, had a cartoon character named after it. The SpongeBob SquarePants slime could solve mazes and copy the layout of man-made transportation networks as it moved, all without muscles, tendons, bones, or brains. It could choose the healthiest food from a diverse menu in nature, without noses, ears, eyes, brains, or nervous systems.

That made sense and fit the evidence I had seen in the cursed neighborhood. The sense of movement I had detected. *The slime could crawl.* Attack of the Black Mold. It seemed as if a B-grade movie was being made after all, in real life.

There was movement nearby, and Soul snapped her fingers. She wasn't looking at me, but I'd been summoned before. I knew what it felt like. I ended my search and moved up to her, my shoes *shush*ing on the floor because I wasn't picking up my feet. T. Laine and Tandy approached on her other side. I had a feeling that Lainie had been eavesdropping too, and that Tandy had been reading Soul and the army types. "Yes, ma'am?" T. Laine said.

Soul held up a finger, imperious, until the army woman and her toady, both of whom had moved away, started talking to another man. Beneath the faceplate and hood, Soul's platinum hair caught the light in a nimbus of rainbows, just like her native form. Which I wasn't supposed to know about. That didn't stop me from looking her over carefully, trying to see if I could catch glimmers of her rainbow dragon form. I couldn't. At least not beneath the uni.

"Get back to LuseCo," Soul said, her mouth holding in a smile, her eyes glittering like onyx. I figured she knew that we had been eavesdropping. "The CEO of LuseCo has a problem that political favors can't fix. The company that does the groundskeeping told the manager that their grass is leaking black ink and there are molds and fungi everywhere. All of the plants look diseased. The LuseCo techs came out and started collecting the stuff, looking as if they were trying to hide it, but the deputy on duty had been to the neighborhood, and he recognized the slime. As of ten minutes past, I've quarantined the grounds, the employees, and the groundskeeping crew. Nobody's happy." Except for Soul, who sounded delighted, if a bit evil.

Her smile spread, pitiless and vicious, looking as if she was sucking on a mouthful of lemon candy. She said, "However, don't think this will be easy just because Kurt Daluege suddenly needs us. They have totally different lawyers on the grounds now, ones to limit liability, so there will be just as much difficulty, but of a different sort. I expect you to play your cards right and get what you need, which is PsyLED inside checking out every single room and every single employee with all the skills, equipment, and gifts at your disposal. And find those witches," she said to T. Laine.

"Yes, ma'am," T. Laine said.

"If you discover something that points to a crime, bring them all in for questioning. If they have slime mold on them, notify me. Lieutenant Colonel Rettell will be setting up some decontamination tents at all the sites and here as well. Stick anyone who is contaminated into a tent, put a guard on them, and e-mail the lieutenant colonel."

"Yes, ma'am," T. Laine said again.

T. Laine pinched the sleeve of my 3PE in two fingers and pulled me backward. As we stripped and decontaminated, she said, "JoJo found another line on Taryn Lee Faust, the coven leader, and two of the witches who were working for LuseCo, not far from the company building. I'm going after Faust. Can you and Tandy handle LuseCo for a bit? The CEO, Daluege, and his right hand, the CFO, Makayla, are pieces of work and a hot mess of attitude."

"I can handle them," I said, hoping I was right.

"Tandy was there for the initial questioning of the employees, and he'll take lead."

Which was enormously relieving. "Okay," I said.

We stuffed the suits into the biohazard bins, and I ran my fingers through my sweaty bob as Tandy shook out his reddish ringlets and we headed to my truck. Tandy and I were supposed to handle a CEO, a CFO, and maybe a COO with secrets to hide and lawyers to help hide them. At least we could get food and coffee on the way.

The National Guard and the Army MedCom had parked troop transport–type trucks in front of the LuseCo driveway. There was a twenty-by-twenty-foot white decontamination tent to the side with ultraviolet lights blasting away, looking hot in the daylight. Human forms were moving in and out and all over, all in unis, and not one getting off the property. I figured that the same thing was happening at the neighborhood and the pond and in the woods where the deer had been. We provided ID and waited around for phone calls that verified our purpose at the company, but eventually we made it around the National Guard truck and onto the grounds.

Tandy and I stopped dead.

The weird slime mold was covering the entire front lawn of LuseCo. It moved as if breathing and even as I watched, tiny buds pushed up on tiny stalks and opened. "I thought the groundskeeper crew said it was a black mold," Tandy said, his voice muffled through the plastic faceplate.

"They mowed some." I pointed to the place where the mower had stopped. It was still in the middle of the lawn. "Maybe cutting it released the slime mold to a new state of . . . whatever this is."

Tandy followed me single file to the front doors where a 3PE-suited National Guardswoman allowed us entry to the lobby and told us to dispose of our suits that had been outside and put on fresh suits for inside. She was stone faced and not talkative. Just pointed with her weapon to a door. I hoped the safety was well set, and leaned away from the weapon, just in case. "Change in there," she said. "When you get dressed out, the asshat CEO's office is down that hallway"—again she pointed with her weapon, but deeper into the building, past a receptionist's desk where a perky, petite woman sat, the gatekeeper of the VIP kingdom—"to the left. The CFO's office is on the right, and the COO is at the end, across from the conference room. Daveed Petulengo is on leave in the Alps somewhere, but the CFO is in. Have fun." Her tone said we wouldn't.

We entered the changing room, leaving behind the laconic guard. "Tandy?" I asked while we were changing out of dirty suits and into clean ones. These weren't the ugly white suites with orange stripes PsyLED wore, but slim, trim, silver gray, the fabric coated with something that felt slick beneath my fingers. The gloves were elastic, like built-in nitrile gloves worn at crime scenes, but they felt slicker, and my fingers slid into them easily. "What's a CEO, CFO, and a COO?"

He didn't smile, an unexpected strain showing on his face. He turned his back as he pulled the booties on, and answered, grunting a little. "Chief executive officer, chief financial officer, and chief operations officer."

"Let's start with the financial one. I have a feeling about the infinity loop dancing in the ground."

He didn't reply, and was standing facing away from me, shoulders hunched up slightly.

"Tandy? What's happening?"

"Someone in this place is . . . sick. In his head. Or her head."

"Mentally unbalanced?" I had learned in Spook School not to say *crazy* or *insane*. The terms were politically incorrect and also not descriptive enough. Proper medical terms had to be used in professional conversations, especially where agents might be overheard or taped. To say *psychosis* was okay. To say *nutso* or *batty* wasn't.

Tandy shook his head, not in negation, but as if he wasn't sure how to say what he was picking up on. Then, "Howling. There's howling. Inside his head. It's . . . loud. It hurts."

"Okay. Breathe. And if you need, take my hand." I reached around him at his elbow and Tandy looked down at my hand. Slowly he slid his into it. And he let a breath go. "Better?"

"Yes. Thank you. So how do you want to handle this?"

"I'll play bad cop and you read the emotional responses." Tandy nodded and I said, "Okay. Let's do this."

The receptionist's desk was empty, so Tandy and I walked past it, down the hallway. We reached the COO's office, and I opened the door and peeked inside. The office was decorated in leather and browns, and there were animal heads on one wall, rams, big-horned goats, moose, and elk. There were photos with him standing over the kills of three spotted big-cats. The COO was a hunter and wanted people to know that he could kill an animal from a long distance with a big gun. Big whoop. I closed the door and went on to the office marked CHIEF FINANCIAL OFFI-CER. We didn't knock and the woman behind the desk didn't look up when we entered, so we stopped in the open doorway, Tandy releasing my hand, taking a reading of her. Clearly she wasn't the source of the crazy vibes he had picked up. She wasn't howling at the moon or spitting foam like a rabid dog.

The CFO was Makayla Lin, the tall, intimating woman I had met the first time we came here. Her office temperature had been set at a crisp sixty-eight, according to the thermostat at the door, and the bronze, silver, and copper metal décor matched the temps with an icy intensity. There was no other exit door, and the only windows were up high, near the ceiling, about three feet by three feet square. The floors were walnut-stained wood, and the upholstery on the couch and guest chairs were copper-colored cloth.

Makayla was wearing a sleeveless black dress, even in the cold, and her hair was cut scalp short, worn plastered to her head with some sort of solid, hard goop. Silver and copper hoops hung from her ears, a single set, one copper bangle per wrist, and a single copper and gold ring per hand, each ring set with a black stone, as if she had accessorized for the interior design. There was no splashy bling for the CFO. She looked like she might have walked directly from a fashion magazine to the black leather desk chair and sleek laptop. It was bronze too.

I turned on my best God's Cloud of Glory accent and said, "I'da thought an operations officer woulda been wearing a T-shirt with a tool belt weighing down his jeans to show his butt crack. Instead he's got dead animals hanging on his walls. And the CFO's office would be stacked with money around the walls. But here it's just cold as Hades with an ice queen sitting behind a desk."

Makayla didn't even look up from her laptop. She lifted a hand away and pressed a button on a small box beside her and said, "Shonda, call security. We have intruders."

"Shonda ain't at her desk," I said. "And since I'm the cops, maybe you might want to show a little smiley face and cooperation, okay, Makayla?"

She swiveled her head and narrowed her eyes at me. I gave her my best Sunday-dinner grin as I crossed the space to her, holding my ID and badge out for view. "We ain't been properly introduced as I recall. I'm PsyLED Special Agent Nell Ingram, and this here's my partner, Special Agent Thom Andrew Dyson."

Tandy did a little double take at my introduction of him by his full name. It was the first time I'd used it, and I right liked the sound of it. He held out his ID too.

"I hope you don't mind, but I won't be shaking your hand." I put away the badge and ID in a pocket in the front of the gray suit. "See, somebody's done let loose a magical working for self-perpetuating energy, into the earth. There's odd growths in the city and a few peculiar deaths and we haven't ruled out it being contagious. And that spell? We got proof that it come from here."

Makayla tightened all over in shock. And I knew I had her.

"But then you'un know all about that, right? Being as how LuseCo was the ones who let it loose in the first place? Tandy? How'm I doing?"

"You're bowling strikes, Nell," he said, his accent a little more crisp, Seattle, maybe. I wasn't much good with accents, having never been anywhere or met many people, but there had been a guy from Seattle at Spook School.

"Strikes? Is that like a touchdown, Tandy? I ain't never been bowling. What's the name of the *wyrd* spell, Makayla? And where's the witches who let it loose?"

Makayla's slight tell was gone and she reached to pick up her desk phone. I leaned in, putting one hand over it, my weight supported on her desk, only inches from the laptop. Where I could see the screen in my side vision, clear as a bell, even without focusing on it.

"We can talk about this here'n the frigid confines of your office or we'uns can go down to PsyLED HQ and do it with the lawyers and maybe an FBI or CIA VIP present. What's it gonna be?"

"Is my client under arrest?" a cool voice said from the door.

Makayla closed her laptop with a soft *snap*. I stood upright and let my happy smile slip away as I faced the man in the very expensive suit, and no uni. There were two men behind him, wearing unis that made them look as though their shoulders were going to pop right out at the slightest movement. Bodybuilders for sure, hired for bulk and given guns.

"A lawyer and two musclemen to back him up," I said to Tandy. "Are you'un feelin' intimidated?"

"No, Nell, but I am feeling a great many other things," Tandy said. Which sounded positive.

"Me too." I dug a little lower into the church-speak and addressed the lawyer. "Your'un client here can tell me about a self-perpetuating energy spell or she can tell her lies to the federal prosecutors while she's wearing a truly tacky orange jumpsuit. There ain't a lot of laws on the books to control witches, because they'uns tend to control themselves, but there are laws on the books that cover harm to the general population by individuals and corporations. And wrongful death lawsuits, and involvement by the Environmental Protection Agency, and OSHA, and the DOE and DOD, and fines, and all sorts of things that can plague a body and a company into legal and financial ruin."

The suit said, "LuseCo has nothing to do with the problems seen—"

"We know better, bubba. People have died, thanks to the *wyrd* curse this company let loose into the ground, maybe combined with a laser, maybe with blood magic. Now, somebody's gonna talk to me."

Tandy fought a smile at my words.

"How's my bad cop?" I asked him.

"Delightful. And she knows all about the spell that got away. But her lawyer doesn't."

"Ohhh, bad girl," I said to her. "Lying to your lawyer."

The lawyer said, "Miz Lin?"

"I'd like a moment with my lawyer," she said. "Then we can talk."

I looked around the room, double-checking that there were no exits, and I nodded.

In the hallway, Tandy said, "Nell. You were . . . unexpected. And brilliant."

I grinned happily. "I was, wasn't I? I reckon growing up in the church and watching so many debates between factions and near factions twisted my mind into a semilegal bent. And watching so much TV and movies when I was at Spook School mighta helped with my interrogation techniques."

Tandy laughed softly. "I think we created a monster."

"Why, thank you, Tandy. This monster needs to text JoJo to get a warrant for anything related to a working called *Infinitio*. I saw it on her laptop. And she was also online, inside the TVA. That woman is in this up to her plastered scalp." I pulled my cell and sent JoJo a quick text.

Twenty minutes later, the well-dressed and calm lawyer appeared in the hallway, where we had staked out a place on an uncomfortable bench-seat couch to prevent exodus by any of the company officials. He stopped in front of us, and Tandy made as if to rise. I thought at him, *Sit*. He did. Which might be quite scary, when I had time to think about it.

The lawyer said, "It is my client's understanding that you wish to see and test the lab in the basement. She has agreed to open it to you." *Basement*—singular, not plural. She didn't know I knew about the subbasement.

"And the witches?"

"There have been no contract witches on the premises for over seventy-two hours, at which time they were summarily sacked. My client Ms. Lin, and LuseCo itself, have no idea what the witches were working on beyond their assigned duties, and bear no responsibility for anything said witches might have done while on premises, behind the backs of their supervisors."

"Blaming the witches. Ain't that always the way. And yet, speaking of witches, we have a magical working that came from this location, and got free into the environment just like an MED. You ever heard of an MED, Mr. Lawyer Man? Look it up. And just after the MED, them witches were fired," I purred, "from a job that gave them access to things beyond their 'assigned duties.' I don't believe in coincidence—it goes against most of what I perceive as rational, and LuseCo's got coincidence piled on coincidence like a stack of coins that's ripe for spilling over. So I want all contact info and personnel records on the fired employees. If I get them by the time I'm done with my little trek into the *two basements*, I'll be happy and leave without ordering up Makayla a pretty orange jumpsuit. Okay, Mr. Lawyer Man?"

The lawyer's face altered just a bit. More important, my partner sat up straight. "My name is Brad Maxwell. Not Mr. Lawyer Man."

"Your client is still keeping secrets, Mr. Lawyer Man-well."

"Maxwell. Brad Maxwell."

"I want access to *both* lower basements within the hour, and I'd like to get it without calling Washington, and with LuseCo's complete and generous assistance. But I'll start at the first basement. For now." The lawyer turned and entered the office of the CEO and shut the door quietly. I had a feeling that he was trying to deal with the semithreats and unexpected information I had tossed his way.

I sent a text to JoJo telling her where we were going and led the way to the elevator. Not improbably, there was only one basement button on the elevator's control panel. That meant the lower basement was a big secret, with a secret elevator or—I put my finger on three key openings on the control panel—a secret keyed access. *Interesting.* I pushed a button, and the doors closed on the two of us.

FIFTEEN

I waited until we were alone in the first basement hallway to pull the P 2.0. I zeroed it and then read the hallway, which read high on level one—the witch reading.

As I worked, Tandy murmured, "You should have been a lawyer, Nell. That was spectacular."

"I'll admit it gave me a peculiar and forceful sense of power. I also admit that this could become addicting. You best promise to slap me down hard if I overstep my bounds."

Tandy slid me a sideways look and said, "Somehow I think you'll know when to pull back."

"Hmmm. Maybe. Maybe not. That was fun. And nothing at all like what a churchwoman would be able to do in similar circumstances."

Tandy chuckled, sounding entertained and, again, a bit more self-confident than he usually did. I assumed it was because he was picking up on my own emotions. I had to be careful where I might be headed with this new attitude. It was one thing to race headlong down a road to some kinda insolent arrogance, for which I might someday pay a price I hadn't considered yet. It was another thing entirely to drag Tandy with me.

"Which office first?" I asked him.

Tandy tilted his head a little to the side as if hearing a distant melody. "This one, I think." He pointed. "I watched T. Laine interview her and she kept secrets. Nothing we could pin down, but secrets nonetheless." We entered the office of Colleen Shee MacDonald, who looked as Irish or Scottish as her name implied. A blond woman about my age, but with a calm, self-confident worldliness and a sharp intellect in her blue-eyed stare that instantly left me feeling outclassed, outsmarted, and out-gunned. "May I be of some help to you?" she asked with a burr of an accent that went along with the name. And in my hands, the psy-meter 2.0 redlined on level one. This was a powerful and capable witch.

LuseCo was keeping secrets. Lots of secrets. Or . . . they didn't know that they had a witch employed here? Oh . . .

I might not have been told a lie exactly, but I hadn't been told the truth either. I had to wonder what other partial truths were at work here.

I decided that the chatty hillbilly talk wouldn't work with Colleen, so I flipped open my ID, stepped forward, introduced myself again, and said, "Tandy? Did Colleen deny she was a witch during your first interview with her?"

"Yes," Tandy said slowly. "She did."

"Did she read as a witch on the psy-meter?"

"No. Which means she knows a working that will hide what she is."

"Interesting," I said. "You wanna tell me about that working?" I asked her.

The elevator door opened again and Mr. Lawyer Man stepped out.

I started to speak to him when Tandy grabbed my shoulders. Threw me at the floor. I jerked out my hands to catch my fall. Tandy landed on top of me. The floor smashed into me with a *whoomp,* a vibration like a bass drum, deep and low. Bone shattering.

It took us over fifteen minutes to sort ourselves out and get some of our hearing back, but we had missed the worst of the blast, thanks to Tandy knowing someone intended us ill will. It wasn't the first time the empath had saved us.

By the time we could sit up amidst the debris field, we had security, Makayla, the CEO, whose name I couldn't remember, and two white-suited military VIPs standing in the small elevator area with us. And by then, Colleen was gone.

T. Laine showed up moments later and was able to tell us that Colleen had set off a small, short-range, locally contained acoustic knockout bomb. The sonic blast had left Tandy and me with terrible headaches, but because we were on the floor when it detonated, that was the extent of our troubles. Mr. Lawyer Man/Brad Maxwell had a headache, busted eardrums with complete but temporary loss of hearing, and the need to spend an inordinate amount of time in the bathroom.

The magical sonic bomb was an evil weapon spell, one that targeted the brains, ears, and bowels of the victims. T. Laine said it was something left over from a vampire war in Europe over a thousand years ago. I could only imagine vampires lined up to use the Dark Ages' equivalent of a portable toilet to rid themselves of the day's blood. Or their blood-meals leaning on trees in the woods, so sick there was no way for the vampires to feed.

As my hearing returned, I put myself together, running my hands through my stiff hair until it popped like Rice Krispies, rearranging my clothes, checking my equipment. I picked up the thirty-thousand-dollar psy-meter from the floor. The P 2.0 was broken. While in the hands of the probie. I'd be in trouble once Rick came back from his moon-called crazies.

More important, Tandy had lost (briefly, I hoped) his empathic abilities. He was sitting, a beatific smile on his face, in a corner, totally alone inside his own emotions for the first time in years. He looked like a happy drunk, inebriated on the emotional silence. I asked him—three times—for his P 1.0 and he finally understood what I wanted. He pulled it from his pocket and extended it in my general direction. A very happy drunk.

The sonic attack on federal law enforcement officers was exactly what law enforcement needed for all the agencies to walk in and take over. That and the fact that Colleen's office redlined on the P 1.0. That was the nail in LuseCo's legal defense. Whether deliberately or by accident, we had been lied to about a threat to the populace, a magical weapon of mass destruction.

With the absconding of Colleen, Mr. Lawyer Man counseled Makayla (from the bathroom, yelling through the stall walls as his hearing returned) to share a good deal more information with us, and we discovered that, contrary to the account given to the feds earlier, there was a LuseCo employee missing. Aleta Turner, a specialist in particle physics, had dual citizenship in the US and in South Africa, and she hadn't been to work in three days. Her mother, Wendy Cornwall, and her aunt, Rivera Cornwall, were both among the fired contract witches, powerful

witches who could trace their ancestry back to Salem, Massa-
chusetts. Aleta's father was not in the picture and hadn't been in
twenty years, having traveled back to a tiny South African
township and the pub he owned there. Aleta wasn't a witch. But
she had contacts through her mother and aunt. All this was info
we should have had access to the minute we started working
with LuseCo. The deluge now was more than suspicious, the
kind of thing a guilty party might provide to shift attention
away from itself.

I was provided the electronic files on all the fired contract
witch employees, which I sent off to JoJo during a quick trip to
the surface level, and I got offers to look at the security footage,
to search all the offices of the missing people and the lab where
they had worked, and nearly obsequious attention from Mr.
Lawyer, whose name I couldn't remember since the explosion.

Leaving Tandy where he sat in silent bliss, I reentered the
busted office where Colleen had disappeared. The walls were
scored with cracks and scrapes. The ceiling was pitted. Her
work laptop was missing and her personal things were gone. Her
desk was covered with dust and debris, and the plastic-and-metal
base of her chair was split as if it had been hit with an ax. I
moved her desk chair, the wheels squeaky on the tile flooring. It
seemed to be otherwise intact and so I sat in it and went through
the drawers. All empty. Except the bottom drawer, which had
four dead plants in it. They looked like succulents that hadn't
been watered in years: brown, dried husks; leaves lying limp
over the sides. But in the soil of each plant, black spots were
growing. Slime mold.

Each slime had a different type of reproductive body fruiting. One had several yellow, vaguely bell-shaped buds. One
flower—though I used the term loosely—was black and shaped
like a tulip. One was orange and looked like something my cats
might leave on the kitchen floor. One was in the midst of
crawling—at microspeeds I couldn't actually focus on—over
the lip of the pot and into the bottom of the drawer. It had
reached the corner and was spreading up the sides. Perilously
close to a tiny micro–thumb drive memory device. I was pretty
sure we had both probable cause and a warrant by now and so I
took the thumb drive, which was shaped like a jade leaf, a
heavy, deep green, like a charm for a bracelet. I dropped it into
an evidence bag, added date, time, and my initials to the bag,

and started an evidentiary chain of custody form to indicate where I had found the item, what it was, and its evidence number. I left the next line blank, which would be for the person who opened the bag and worked with the microdrive. It would likely be me. I was pretty sure I was going to hate COC forms before the day was out. I tucked the bag into my uni pocket.

I removed the drawer and spotted Mr. Lawyer Man—Brad Maxwell, that was his name—in the hallway, between bathroom visits. He looked a mite clammy and pale, entering Makayla's office. I followed before the door could close and offered him the drawer. He took it, looked inside, and blanched even more. To Makayla I said, "You will now give us all the access we need. Are we clear?" I asked.

"What happened to the accent?" she asked, as the lawyer placed the yucky drawer on top of the desk, moving as if it might explode in his hands.

I thought about that for a moment before answering truthfully. "I'm done using cute"—*and my childhood*—"to look harmless. So, again. Are. We. Clear?"

"Abundantly," she said, flinging a heated glance at the lawyer as he rushed back to the men's room. "The security footage is ready. Would you care to view it now?"

"We would," T. Laine said from behind me. "And as Special Agent Ingram has just implied, any further hindrance to our investigation will be viewed as accessory after the fact, if not collusion, in what might be considered by the federal prosecutor as homegrown terrorism. Now. Are *we* clear?"

"Yes," Makayla said. "This way."

The footage was set up in security, and I watched as the hallway camera showed Tandy throwing me down, landing on me, and the debris shooting out. The lawyer falling back against the wall and sliding down to the floor. Colleen walking out of her office and later out the front door.

At that point, the video, which was all digital, went on the blink as she wrapped a witchy working around herself and walked through the advancing military crew as if they couldn't see her. And they couldn't because the spell made them not want to see her. It was called an *obfuscation* spell, and it worked like a doozy. She was gone.

I left T. Laine studying the footage, discussing various sections with JoJo at HQ, and walked back to the first basement. Something seemed off, but I couldn't put my finger on what. So I did what agents were good at. I was very nosy. I looked into the kitchen and the bathrooms and the labs. There was a short-order cook in the kitchen, who kept breakfast foods, coffee, tea, salads, and sandwiches available all the time. I discovered that groceries and other supplies had been delivered to the front door since LuseCo had gone on lockdown. The bathrooms were set up with schedules. There were showers in the labs, also with schedules. There were three coffee lounges and sleeping areas with folding cots.

As no one had been allowed to leave, the employees had been given cots and had claimed different parts of the building for sleeping in shifts. The employees with no assistance for child care had been given subsidies, and LuseCo had hired a bevy of part-time nannies to care for the children at the employees' homes. For a company that might be involved in an attack on Knoxville, they were taking really good care of their personnel.

I found the cot used by Colleen. She hadn't taken the time to clean out her sleeping area, and it was full of personal belongings—which meant information. There was also a tiny spiral notebook, inside of which was contact info on all the witches in Knoxville, intelligence that was much more comprehensive than that given me by the HR department. I photographed and sent everything to Jo and Lainie, and again, the density of the records took time. Back in Colleen's office, I did the same thing with the electronic data. And with the info from human resources. To be on the safe side, I also copied it all to a micro–thumb drive, which I hung on my key chain.

As I worked, I tried to think, but I wasn't having a lot of luck with that. How did an investigator get a clue when she didn't know what the instigating incident was? Or who it was aimed at? Or even if there was a deliberate crime, with motive and intent, or just an accident? But someone had shot at Occam and me a while ago, so someone wanted us out of the way. And Colleen had sent a bomb our way. I wandered back up to the main level, thinking.

While I was pondering the uselessness of my brain, there was a strangled scream close by. It was Shonda, who was standing in the open doorway of the office of the CEO, Kurt Daluege.

I wasn't the first to arrive, but joined a small group to see the CEO, who was standing on his desk, buck naked, facing the outside window, orating about going to space and seeking out the final frontiers for the fatherland. It was all psychotic-sounding gibberish until he said, "Pools and flows and dies in the land." That was vitally important to the case.

He shifted his feet to the side, his body following as he turned around in a circle, slowly, slowly, his bare feet shoving papers and desk equipment to the floor while saying things about energy for all people, mumbling the name Midas, several times, and saying, "All the gold in the land will be mine." Very strange things.

I got a good look at Kurt's naked body, which was blotched with black spots, just like the patients in the hospital. Just like the neighborhood land and the hospital walls and the drawer in the office downstairs.

Kurt faced the doorway once more and his tone softened as he seemed to focus on our growing group. He held out his hands in a blessing and said, "It was lost to us, but it is ours again. Flows, flows, flows. Pools, pools, pools. Dead. All dead. All dead. Forever . . ."

I pushed my way inside, wondering what about this job and my life was making me see so much naked male flesh. But that was a discussion with the Almighty, if I decided to talk to him again someday, and with Soulwood—all for later. For now, I read Kurt with the P 1.0 and he was redlining. I called JoJo who sent in the military medics and carted him off, not telling me where they were taking him.

I rounded on Makayla. "Talk to me. *Now.* What was being tested. What was *Infinitio*? And for the love of God, what went on? Or I swear by all that I hold holy, I will place you under arrest and this place will be locked down and under quarantine until the devil builds igloos in hell or the government nukes the place."

The conference room was well appointed, with padded walls, a carpeted floor, and a table big enough to seat twenty easily. Makayla was sitting in the center of the table, a place she had migrated to without thinking, as if it was her assigned space at meeting time. She sat slumped, resting her weight on her elbows, and stirred the mug of coffee placed at her left by Shonda. I reined in my impatience and waited.

Eventually Makayla said, "Kurt and I had been working on energy and propulsion research and were making headway on a quantum vacuum plasma thruster. Real headway." She met my eyes as if to convince me, which instantly left me unconvinced. "But Harold White and his team at the Johnson Space Center beat us to the first US working model. NASA showed interest in their design. We lost our funding.

"We were on the verge of closing our doors when Kurt's grandmother died and he came upon some old papers in her attic. When he translated them, they proved to be the research notes of a coven in Germany, circa World War Two, testing a self-perpetuating magical energy device. With a little research, and interviews with the local coven, he discovered that covens all over the world had been testing similar workings before the end of the war, with special success in Britain and the US."

"Witches weren't out of the closet in World War Two," I said, feeling a little muzzy headed from the blast. I sat across from Makayla and propped myself on my elbows.

The CFO sat back in her chair. "Long before they came out of the closet, witches all over the world were in contact. Had been for centuries, via private couriers, almost since the concept of writing. The SS in Germany discovered the existence of witches and covens during their early paranormal studies, long before the war even started, and they captured every witch they could find and eventually put them to work, including the powerful Rosencrantz family." She waved a negligent hand as if it was ancient history and didn't matter.

"Following a trail of coded letters, Kurt managed to acquire notes about self-perpetuating energy workings from eight covens from around the world, from the same time period, and he and Daveed Petulengo, our COO, hired Aleta to get us an interview with the local coven leader, Taryn Lee Faust. Together, Kurt and Daveed convinced the local coven to help with our research into a revolutionary energy source. The working is called *Infinitio*."

That was a lot of information to process, but even with my dazed head I got some important things out of it. Kurt had a lot of ancient research papers. A self-perpetuation energy device would totally revolutionize energy as we now understood it. A lot of rich people would lose everything if and when it became available. And a lot of less-rich people would get *really* rich. All were reasons to help or hinder the research, depending on where people stood on the financial benefit/detriment line. Shonda brought me a cup of herbal tea, something red and aromatic and sugary. I thanked the woman. She was so sweet. They *all* were. Which seemed odd for just a moment, before that thought slid away as unimportant. I stirred my tea and remembered what I wanted to ask. "How?" I asked. "How did he convince the local coven to help him?"

"Money. Lots of money that he was able to raise in South America and Europe, using the notes as bait. Initially the money was paid to the coven itself, as if hiring a subcontractor. He provided them a place to work that was totally safe and insulated from the outside world. He offered them shared patents, if they could make *Infinitio* actually work, and ten percent of the energy company they would form together if they were successful." She shrugged and giggled. *"Money."* Her tone suggested that nothing else had any value.

I needed to talk to Kurt, but I had let the military cart him off. That was stupid of me. The CEO had started this stuff. The workings had been his idea. Now I needed to figure out why and how. "What happened next?" I asked, not thinking that there would be more, but Makayla was amazingly forthcoming.

"In the papers from Germany, Kurt found a similar working to *Infinitio*, a version stronger and more promising than *Infinitio* alone. The working was called *Unendlich*. It was supposed to be more than an energy working," she said, "and we knew that the DOD would jump on it. But we needed the research to show promise fast, and that meant some form of testing that pointed to a possible successful weaponization of the workings, to garner some of the Defense Department's budget. Those pockets are so deep they have no bottom. Not anywhere.

"Our team started research and testing on both workings." She stopped and picked up her coffee mug, cradling it, her long, brown fingers striking against the white glaze of the stoneware.

"I'm confused," I said. "I thought you were looking for energy sources, not weapons."

Lazily Makayla waved away my statement. "We would never have turned over a weapon to them. We just wanted their money to keep LuseCo going until the research was complete. And as the two workings were similar," she said, "it was supposed to be a two-pronged research project with two covens meeting on opposite days of the week to keep them from overlapping magically. Then on the new moon last week, there was an . . . incident."

"Tell me about the incident," Tandy said.

I nearly jerked. I hadn't heard him come in. But . . . I was feeling very mellow, as if I'd had some of the wine made by Sister Erasmus in the church. Makayla's expression was placid, as amiable as I felt myself. Which made something inside me sit up and take notice, the mellow sensation beginning to drift apart. "Tandy . . . ?" He didn't look my way. And I realized that Tandy had learned a new trick . . . or found it after the sonic explosion. He not only could read the emotions of others, he had learned how to alter our emotions to his needs. He had gained his empathy gift after being struck by lightning. Had another bit of likely brain damage caused an alteration in his gift? "Tandy?" I asked again. He lifted his hand at me. The mellow sensation flooded back, though Tandy looked strained and he was sweating. I had never seen the empath sweat before. His skin was pale, the Lichtenberg lines standing out, scarlet on his pallid, ashen skin. I sipped my tea. It was delicious. And I was so glad that Tandy was trustworthy.

I blinked and frowned. Tandy . . . trustworthy. The mellowness dried up and blew away like chaff in my mind. Tandy was projecting at me. I pushed the last of the equanimity away and narrowed my eyes at him. Tandy was abusing his gift. On Makayla. And *me* . . .

Makayla yawned in lazy leisure. "On the night of the new moon, there was an explosion in the second basement lab. It disrupted everything." She stretched, moving like a dancer, limber and graceful.

"Where is the key to the second basement elevator?" Tandy asked.

Makayla pulled a chain out from her cleavage. On the end was a round key. It would fit perfectly into the elevator keyhole I had noticed.

"You want to give it to me," Tandy said.

Makayla held it out to him. Tandy accepted the key and handed it to T. Laine. The PsyLED witch took the key and turned away, but not before I saw her face. T. Laine was troubled. She knew what he had been doing. And she let him. There was a quote about that. George Orwell had said something about power not being a means to an end. He said that power *was* the end. I stared at Tandy, who ignored me. He looked exhausted, his reddish eyes bloodshot, his fingers, laced on the table, trembling. This—whatever he was doing—was painful. Good. I hoped it hurt so bad he never did it again. I pushed my empty teacup away.

Tandy said, "Originally, before you hired the witches, how did Kurt find Aleta?"

"He and Daveed Petulengo and Colleen worked on it for weeks, trying to find someone who could give us access to a coven. Mostly social media research and ancestry and genealogical research sites." Makayla stretched again, twisting like one of my mousers. "Colleen hit pay dirt. She discovered a promising young physicist at Stanford, Aleta Turner. Her grandmother had been part of a Scottish coven working on a form of *Infinitio*, outside of Glasgow, in the last two years of World War Two. They were very close to achieving success with it, and only terminated the research when the war ended. The witches disbanded, scattering across various parts of the globe." A faint smiled crossed Makayla's face. She picked up her mug again, wrapping long fingers around it. "Aleta's grandmother had passed on after immigrating, but her mother, Wendy Cornwall, and her aunt Rivera Cornwall had the notes on *Infinitio* from the war research. Both were practicing witches, here in the States. Aleta accepted a position here, a very lucrative one for a physicist still working on her thesis. Once here, Aleta convinced Wendy and her twin sister, Rivera, to move to Knoxville to work with the local coven on a contract basis."

"And was the research into *Infinitio* successful?" Tandy asked, his voice beguiling.

"Beyond our wildest dreams. Up until the night of the new moon. When everything was ruined." She set the mug on the table and hung her head over it. "Ruined. Three dead. *Ruined*. All our plans ruined."

"Who died?" Tandy asked.

"Three techs. We were able to cover it up, so none of the others knew about the failure, but we think Aleta had heard rumors about *Unendlich*, and the witches in Germany. We think she and Colleen found that they were working on Hitler's paranormal research and sabotaged the tests."

"Why would Aleta and Colleen ruin it after they worked so hard to put it all together?" Tandy asked, his voice growing hoarse with the effort of doing whatever he was doing.

"They had *morals,*" Makayla said, softly scathing. "Aleta went to HR about the *morality* of a working that might *possibly* affect the structure of atoms or degrade biological cells or damage matter nearby. The *morality* of re-creating a weapon that the German witches had died to protect. When there was so much money waiting for us if we pulled it off."

"Wait," I said, sitting up fast. "The German witches *died*?"

Makayla frowned and shut her mouth, her eyes going narrow and accusing. She turned to Tandy, stunned, recognition dawning that she had spoken her company secrets aloud. Tandy reached over and took the CFO's hand. The accusation on her face melted away and she smiled again. Patted Tandy's hand. T. Laine, who had been tapping on her laptop at the head of the table, said, "I've been looking through Kurt's electronic files and I found a summary that explains a lot. "The German coven was close to a finished *Infinitio.* But they knew Hitler was going to weaponize it and turn it on the world. They created a death spell and set it over themselves. It was too late for Hitler's SS to re-create the research and save the war effort. The witches destroyed everything, except one copy of the notes, which was smuggled out of Germany by the wife of an SS officer and her children. The notes were recovered by Kurt at his grandmother's. The notes mention *Unendlich,* a similar working but with the ability to store immense amounts of energy and then direct it to other uses. Like the weapon he envisioned."

"And you think Aleta discovered all this?" I asked. "Maybe after she introduced the coven to Kurt? And felt responsible for setting them up, for releasing *Infinitio* and *Unendlich* on the world?"

"She was afraid of *Infinitio* being combined with *Unendlich* and weaponized," Makayla said, sounding sleepy again. "That wasn't a big part of what Kurt was looking for. Hoping for." Makayla sipped her coffee and made a face. It must have grown cold. "That was what the DOD wanted. A weapon that no one would expect, that could be set off with a single spoken word. That needed nothing to make it work but the will of the witch and the air she breathed to speak. A thing of deadly beauty."

"God bless quantum mechanics and psysitopes," Tandy said, his voice hoarse. He had sweated through his clothes and I could smell him from across the table. His skin looked sallow, a dull yellow as if his liver had stopped working weeks ago and he was dying. I hated what Tandy was doing, but . . . he looked so bad that he might really *be* dying. I looked at T. Laine, but she refused to acknowledge my stare.

Makayla laughed softly. "Exactly. But we would never have given such a thing over to them."

"So why are you still in business?" T. Laine asked.

"Because of the success of *Unendlich*. And the money that came in from the Department of Defense. *So. Much. Money.* Initial testing suggested that we were closer to an end product on the energy research than we expected. And then the readings started going haywire. The growths started. Our power grid kept going down. We knew we had been sabotaged, but we weren't sure who on our team was responsible. We had been able to keep it from the DOD and our backers, until you showed up on our doorstep."

"Unendlich?" Tandy rasped. "What does that mean?"

"Unending," Makayla said. "Unending power." She closed her eyes, some mixture of anger, despair, and exhaustion. "All the power. Everywhere. It . . ." She stopped, and her eyes moved behind her closed lids as if she was dreaming or thinking very fast. "It may have gotten loose and . . . caused a problem. And now we can't stop it."

I blinked. The dancing infinity loop—*Infinitio*—had been created by LuseCo's coven, and it was trying to wake an Old One. How the slime and deaths related to the Old Ones, I didn't yet know. Except that magic is power, and power has to come from somewhere, despite people's hunt for a self-perpetuating energy device. Were the Old Ones part of the power they were trying to tap and use?

"You will walk us to the lower basement. Now," Tandy said.

"Of course," Makayla said, leading the way to the elevator, Tandy's trembling hand in hers. Moments later, we were standing in the bottom of the building, and staring at the twenty-foot circle scorched into the floor. The burn marks indicated that the flames from the broken working had climbed up the walls and even trailed across the ceiling. There were cracks in the concrete, and moisture had already begun to seep through. At the cracks, black mold blossomed, all one form, with bloodred bulbs on the ends of tall stalks. They looked ready to explode, which would spread the spores everywhere.

"Get out! Get everyone out!" I shouted.

I pushed Tandy and Makayla and three others back into the elevator and shut the doors between us and the lower basement.

"Get military medical people down here," I said. "We need ultraviolet lights and fungicides. Fast."

Makayla had regained her own mind and will, eyes flashing, mouth spewing cussing I had never heard, even in Spook School. She was in a cold fury, demanding her attorneys and threatening lawsuits for a magical attack. I blocked out her verbal rampage and, as the elevator rose to ground level, I stared at Tandy, letting thoughts of disappointment and betrayal fill my mind. Tandy caught my gaze and his eyes closed. He slid to the floor of the elevator, his head against the back wall. I knelt beside him and checked his pulse. He was icy-cold and his pulse was fluttery. His breath was ragged. He was also out cold. The doors opened.

The next minutes were little but the frenzied action of a paramedic team taking care of Tandy and putting him on a stretcher. Of men and women in unis, carrying equipment down the elevator. I didn't stay and watch. I had things I needed to attend to. And though Tandy was down, I couldn't feel sorry for him. I knew he had gotten information that we would have gotten no other way—or certainly not this fast—but . . . but Tandy had violated my will. Makayla's will. He had taken control over us. T. Laine had sat far away at the conference room table, out of the way of his control. She had known what he was going to do and she had let him. She hadn't warned me to sit on the far end of the table too. I didn't want to be close to the empath or the moon witch. Not just now.

I had been in the CEO's office for hours. Alone. Once I left the elevator, I didn't want Tandy anywhere near me. He had made us happy and talkative and taken away all our barriers. He had nudged Makayla to speak the truth. It was something like hypnotism and mind control, and he had used it on us. It was a betrayal and a violation and so unlike him that part of me wanted to find out who had forced him to do it to us. But according to T. Laine, Tandy had done it all on his own. He was nursing a massive headache and flulike symptoms with fever and dehydration. I had no sympathy for him at all.

I wasn't speaking to either of them. I wasn't letting the empath within five feet of me, which was about his range, according to T. Laine.

I had reported the change in the empath to JoJo, who was talking to Soul about it. We had problems in Unit Eighteen. Big problems. Missing werecat leader. Two other missing werecats. And none of them had come to work after they shifted back to human at daylight. Power-hungry empath. Moon witch who had allowed her partner to employ questionable methods to obtain information. So the door was shut and I was reading through Kurt's timeline of the experiments. Something about the research and experimental work seemed out of sequence from what Makayla had been told.

According to his personal files, Kurt had known about *Infinitio* and *Unendlich* long before he had talked about them to his partners and the board of LuseCo. And he had known of a problematic outcome long before he turned the papers over to his witch team. I scanned through the papers and his personal notes and discovered a notation that said there had been no problems with *Infinitio* in the rest of the world. Only in Germany, when *Infinitio* had been paired with *Unendlich*.

How had Daluege determined that? He wasn't from a known witch family, yet he had known that the German coven committed mass suicide before they could turn over the weapon to the SS of the Third Reich.

What could have been so bad that an entire coven killed themselves rather than releasing the spell? Or . . . had it been something else? Had the results been even more powerful than the SS or Hitler had hoped? A doomsday working the witches feared he would use? Or . . . had it mutated the vegetation around the working there too? Was *Unendlich* a radiation-type weapon? The first calls to the cops had been about radioactive geese . . . Had the WWII witches all gotten a disease and killed themselves because of that? All I knew was that the questions were making my sonic-blast-induced headache worse, and I had no idea how to answer a single one except to keep digging through LuseCo's files, headache or no.

I sent the translations of the coven's notes to JoJo, along with a list of the witches who had participated in each working, a schedule of each working. There were twenty-seven witches altogether, involved in some capacity with LuseCo, all female.

There was Aleta's family, Wendy Cornwall and Rivera Cornwall, twins, of the Cornwall witches.

Irene Rosencrantz, of the Rosencrantz witches, listed as a recessive-gened witch, which usually meant a witch of little power, but the Rosencrantz witches were different, especially when working together. And Irene's sister Lidia Rosencrantz. Colleen Shee MacDonald of the Shee witches. Taryn Lee Faust of the Lee witches, and the leader of the coven. Theresa Anderson-Kentner, of the Anderson witches, and Suzanne Richardson-White, of the Richardson witches. Barbara Traywick Hasebe of the Traywicks. And eighteen more, though none of the rest were from famous witch family lines. Several of the witch families had emigrated to the US after World War Two, including the Rosencrantzes, mentioned by Makayla; the Cornwall family; and Colleen's family, the Shee witches. It seemed odd that so many powerful witch families had ended up in Tennessee, but in a cursory search nothing stood out as suspicious. Maybe they had written letters and come to a similar part of the country. No matter how it had happened, there were too many possible suspects.

I turned my attention to what Kurt himself had done. The CEO had divided his witches into two groups and melded them into distinct and strong covens. He had given each coven one working to concentrate on. And he had given three orders to each coven. One: test mathematics on the new moon. Two: test workings on the full moon. Three: do not switch the two dates.

Makayla had said the problem occurred during a test on the new moon. Had the coven deliberately disobeyed the orders? If so, why? Sleep deprived, I couldn't see an answer to any of the questions. I sent the timeline to JoJo and to myself for later study.

I left the CEO's office, and to keep myself awake, over the course of the next two hours, I walked through the complex, taking readings everywhere and listing them on the building plans. There were a total of eight employees whose office spaces redlined. All were techs except for the office of the CEO, Aleta's office, and Colleen's office. None of the employees on-site exhibited signs of slime mold, but one stood up in the middle of our discussion and said, "Flows, flows, flows . . ." She was turned over to the Army MedCom and whisked away.

I was beyond exhausted and confused and had no idea what to do next, so I checked in with T. Laine, who was back to interviewing people, Tandy beside her. I didn't like it. But I wasn't in charge. I also called JoJo to report in, and left the building, walking into the chilled night. I was hungry. Sleepy. Too exhausted to drive just yet. Hoping the cold night air would wake me.

Someone had stuck something to my truck. I peeled off a blue marker that was taped to my driver window, loaded my gear inside, climbed in, and closed the cab door. Turned the engine on to let the heater warm. I didn't know what to do about the marker or what it was for. I slumped into the seat and yawned to try to pop my damaged ears. Checked my cell for messages, finding over seventy e-mails and texts that related to the multiple cases. I'd never get a chance to sleep. Holding the blue marker, I sat in the harsh artificial lighting outside of Luse-Co's parking lot, paying no attention to the uni-dressed people rushing around me, and read the day's correspondence. Well, scanned it. I was too tired to read it all.

At Spook School, only one person had ever mentioned the exhaustion of a multiorganization case, or the mental confusion that set in, or the sheer mind-boggling-ness of it all. I clipped my cell to the steering wheel and blocked out all the action around me as I went through the correspondence, the research and evidentiary chains, the back-and-forth on . . . way too much stuff. But as I read, a picture of the day and the case began to form.

PsyLED was conscripting people from other units and sending them to help, both in-person investigators and online analysts. Soul had requested a medical team from Tulane University to help treat the people in UTMC and in the Army's MedCom site. The nurses that had arrived were all witches, and two vampire physicians had been transported in, one to work at the hospital to see if vamp blood would help the sick and dying, one to the MedCom site, which was set up outside of LuseCo.

LuseCo. Where I was.

I looked around me and focused on the dozens of people wearing white with orange stripes, all rushing here and there. They had figured out how to differentiate themselves. Doctors

and medical people had added a medical staff design on the left
side of their chests and on the back, the snake and staff in red
marker. Military had insignia drawn green. PsyLED had a blue
starburst. Hence the blue marker taped to my window. I got it.

There was an update on the patients. The black lichen was still
progressing. Doctors were discussing telomeres, whatever they
were, previously unseen cancers, cancer-fighting medicines,
because the fungicides had stopped working. Witch nurses had set
block workings to stop the paranormal activity on and by the
patients, making them easier to treat medically. Doctors and biologists were discussing transformations and species mutations.

Soul had taken a hotel room in Knoxville and would be at
HQ in the morning for a meeting with all members of Unit
Eighteen. Eight a.m. sharp. I did not want to attend that meeting
and be around when she discovered that her protégé Rick hadn't
been to work for two days in the middle of a crisis.

And I knew that I should—must—commune with the land
around LuseCo again to understand and hopefully find a way to
stop whatever was happening. But I was afraid. And lack of rest
had made me muzzy headed. When I was done with the day's
deluge of information and queries, I drove from the parking lot
and headed home.

SIXTEEN

The security light came on as I drove up, illuminating parts of the house and yard and not others. The three mouser cats were on the porch, mewling and crying, tails straight up, walking in circles—not in a line like the possums in the neighborhood, but with each cat going its own way. They were acting very strange, almost the way cats acted when in heat, but all my cats had been spayed or fixed prior to me taking off for Spook School. No kittens for me.

I turned off the truck, gathered up my gear, and opened the door, letting the icy air of night sweep in. It carried in a noise that had never belonged here, on Soulwood, a purring, chuffing sound, in and out, two sets of them. As if breathing out of sequence.

Wereleopards. Close by.

A scream slit the night, powerful and petrifying. Not an African lion roar, but the dark of jungle nights, half shriek, half rumble, a hacking, growling reverberation that spoke of blood and threat and death. Close. Too close.

I twisted, searching for the sound, still in the protection of the truck body. I dropped everything onto the passenger seat. Drew my weapon and a flashlight. Placed my feet to the ground. The rumbling noise was from the roof of the house. I trained the powerful flash high. On the roofline, at the crest, were two leopards, a black leopard and a spotted one—Paka and Occam. Their eyes were trained on me, one greenish gold in a black coat, the other the amber shade of old gold, in a spotted coat.

For a moment, I knew what it felt like to be prey, a prickly, enervating weakness, as if all the blood had already drained from my body. The cats were crouched, showing fangs, white in the flash.

Pea was between them and me, on the edge of the roof, facing them, her neon green fur standing out all over. Her impossible

steel claws were out, catching the flash in silver slashes of illumination. She was spitting with rage, and when Paka shifted her
paws, Pea yowled with fury, louder than the weres, the sound full
of warning. The mouser cats bolted to the ground and under the
front porch. Paka seemed to rethink whatever it was she'd wanted
to do and settled back, belly to the crest of the roof.

I stayed where I was too, protected by the body of the truck,
and shined the flash around. I spotted Rick on the porch, curled
into a ball in the shadows of the swing. I trailed the strong beam
over him. He was a mess. Bleeding from what looked like claw
slashes and fang bites. Paka's bites? Rick was a were stuck in his
human form, unable to shift into his cat form, spending the
three days of the full moon each month in torture. But from the
black hair covering him from head to foot, it looked like Rick
was now part cat, partway through the shift into his black leopard form, which he had never achieved before. The tats on his
shoulder were four glowing golden discs, so bright that they
looked heated. As if reacting to the burn of the tats, Rick tightened the muscles of his arm and gripped it with the clawed hand
of the other. Cat claws. He mewled, clearly in agony.

I eased back into the cab and shut and locked the door. And
though I didn't want to, I punched up Soul's cell number. Rick
was in trouble, and this werecat stuff was out of my sphere of
knowledge. Rick leaped off the porch and landed on the ground,
on all fours, crouched in the shadows cast by the security light.
Rick. Fur covered. Naked, otherwise. Things I did not need to
see. The cell rang.

Rick set his belly to the ground. Elbows and hips high.
Began crawling toward me. Fast. So fast. *Ring two.* Rick leaped
to the hood of the truck.

The Chevy rocked with the weight. His paws made little
curved dents in the hood. His paws, clawed, trying to grip the
metal. His shadow cut across the hood in stark lines. Soul's line
rang a third time. Rick leaned in to the windshield and snarled
at me, showing leopard teeth.

My breath stopped in my throat. Rick was half cat, half
human. Partially furred. His face was cat jawed with human-
shaped forehead and eyes, irises glowing greenish gold. Ears
pointed, high on his head. Fanged. Nose wrinkled as he scented
me. His tats glowed like heated gold.

He snarled again, eyes on me. Licked his jaw.

I was . . . *prey.* Dinner. *Oh . . . God.*

A flash of green swept across the hood of the truck. Pea. Landing between Rick and the windshield. Between Rick and me. She growled, spit, and launched herself at Rick. Steel flashing.

I screamed, "Pea! No!"

Rick and Pea rolled off the hood, into the shadows beside the cab. Screaming and yowling. Blood splattered across the windshield. Three drops splatted onto the land of Soulwood.

The earth woke up, alive and hungry. I could feel it without even standing on it. *Bloodlust.* The land was hungry. Waiting.

Rick screamed, a cat scream. Piercing, shocking, this close. I flinched away from the door. Rebounded off the seat. Blood splashed and sprayed, landing in wide arcs that I could feel even though I wasn't touching the ground. Soulwood sucked it up, waiting for me to feed it. Hunger gripped my rooty belly.

A black leopard landed in Rick's place, Paka, paws touching down lightly before she leaped off and into the fray. The cats rolled into the yard, into the brightness of the security light. The roof over my head dented. Popped back in place, dented again.

There was a werecat on top of the cab. *Occam.*

This was . . . not good. I stifled a hysterical giggle, pulling my sidearm from its case. I removed the magazine full of standard rounds and slammed the new magazine home. Silver hollow points. The gestures calmed me. My breath came easier. Steadied my need to feed the land.

Soul's voice said, "Where are you? Are you in danger?"

I had dropped the cell. I fished it from the crevice of the seat. My fingers weren't shaking. The barrel of the gun was rock steady. The need for blood eased away a bit more. And when I spoke, my voice didn't carry the hysterical laughter of only moments before. "I'm in my truck at the house. Danger looks possible. Rick and Pea and Paka are in a catfight to end all catfights."

"So I hear." Soul sounded calm and wry. "I heard you prepare your weapon. Silver ammo?"

"Yes, ma'am. Hollow points. But I really don't want to kill them." Not that I needed hollow points. All I needed was to take the lovely, lovely blood and feed them to the earth. I was in no danger. But my friends *were.*

"Try to avoid brains and hearts and they might survive. But save yourself first," Soul said.

From the roof, a paw appeared at the top of the windshield.

Another. A long, catty chest and belly. Occam was walking down to the hood. Just like one of my mouser cats might. Before he might show me far too much of his catty parts, he leaped to the hood, denting it deeper than Rick had.

When all four paws were on the flat surface, the werecat turned and looked at me, then back at the fray. He lay belly down on the still-warm hood. I had a feeling that Occam was guarding me. Maybe so he could eat me later. My laughter escaped in a judder of lips. Occam turned to me and snorted before looking back at the battle.

The fight was bad, bloody. Rick was covered in bites.

I asked, "Why are they biting him?"

"They hope to force a shift on Rick."

"Oh. Well, I'd say he's half cat now." And he was. He had a cat jaw. Were-fangs. Clawed paws. Human hips, knobby legs bent the cat way, human shoulders, and cat elbows, his joints not fitting together in any useful way. There was nothing human left in his eyes at all. And far too much werecat blood all over my land. I swallowed, just thinking about all that heated, powerful blood sinking in. But only a moment had passed, and I finished with, "Maybe more than half cat."

Even over the fight, I heard Soul draw a breath. "I'll be there in a few moments."

Two minutes later, Soul was walking down the driveway, her gauzy clothing waving in the breeze of her passage. Rick had a tail. And there was a lot more blood on the soil and grass. A *lot* . . . of blood. I was moderately in control, but I was afraid that if I stepped onto the land, connected with it, I'd kill my friends by accident.

Soul walked up to the fighting cats, who were now on the far edge of the grassed lawn, near the graves of my dogs. She waded into the fracas, yanked Paka up by the scruff of her neck. And threw the spitting-mad cat into the woods on the far side of the road. Paka rolled in the brush and slid into the ditch before reappearing, all teeth and flying black cat hair.

Pea did an impossible high jump and landed in a tree, twenty feet above Paka. Then she dropped onto the werecat and their fight continued.

Rick . . . Rick had a tail. And a long, sleek body. His cat eyes were green with hints of gold. He was lying on the earth, panting. Tongue hanging out the side of his mouth like a hound.

Steam gusted with each breath. He was healed. He had shifted. Rick was a huge black leopard. Occam stood and dropped to the ground, approaching Rick slowly, head down, tail high, a posture of neither aggression nor of submission. More like . . . curiosity.

Rick snarled, stood, and showed teeth. Occam stopped, standing still as a stuffed cat. Soul said something to them, the words lost over the distance. She swatted Rick's ears. He growled at her and she made a fist. Faster than I could follow, Soul socked Rick in the jaw.

He flew up from the earth, landed, rolled into the ditch, and came up growling, snarling. Soul was on him and she said something else, her voice less than a murmur. She swatted his ear tips again. Rick showed his teeth, but he lay down on the ground in front of her, belly low in what looked like some odd form of submission. Occam was lying on the ground near him. Both cats facing at an angle from me. Occam belly-crawled to Rick and washed his face with his tongue. Rick didn't look happy at the contact, but he allowed it.

The biting and fighting had forced a shift on Rick. I hoped he didn't have to be bitten by a human before he could change back to human form. I chuckled quietly, the sound shaky.

My desire for blood had eased as the residue from the fight sank into the ground. I put away the cell and gathered up my gear in my left hand and arm, keeping the Glock in my right. Silently I slid cross the seat and opened the passenger door. Keeping the truck between the tableau and me as much as possible, I slipped through the shadows to the stairs and up. And inside. The mouser cats bounded back to the porch and raced in at my feet. I locked the door and set my gear on the desk. And remembered to breathe.

I stood so I couldn't be seen from outside and stared through the window, my breath fogging a little circle. All three werecats and Pea were now on the lawn, rolling in play. Batting, swiping, grooming one another. Soul stood to the side, still talking to them, her body language stern. Behind me, the mousers were yowling for kibble. My need to kill my friends had subsided to manageable.

Moving through the shadowed house, I left the window and brought in wood from the back porch. With icy-numb fingers, I built a fire in the cold Waterford Stanley. Topped off the water in the water heater with the hand pump. Got leftover soup out of the fridge and set the pot on the stove, foil-wrapped roasted pumpkin nearby. Found my winter flannel jammies. Closed the door to the second story to keep any stove heat downstairs. And heard the knock on the front door. I padded back down and met Soul with the business end of my shotgun.

The petite woman lifted her eyebrows at it, as if she found the gun and me comical. With ill grace, I stood aside and she entered, rubbing her arms as if at the cold weather, but I had seen her in her true form, and I doubted a dragon made of light felt the cold like I did. Shotgun hanging in my arms, I shut and relocked the door. Set the gun on the table where I kept it, within easy reach. Not that I needed it much these days, with the church less interested in me or my land, but old habits died hard.

Soul, who had never been into my home, turned on the lights, walking through the house to the kitchen as if she lived there, and started a pot of coffee. I frowned at her. Hard. But she ignored me. I guessed anyone who had just broken up a fight between two wereleopards and a grindylow could ignore my scowl pretty easily. As she worked she said, "We have a great deal to discuss." She lifted the lid on the soup pot and sniffed appreciatively, then pulled the cut loaf of bread from the bread bag and hunted a bread knife. I had Wüsthof knives, which she admired before she started slicing the loaf. And I decided that nothing I did was going to send her packing. I had company for supper.

Dinner was actually pleasant, though Soul stopped eating several times, got up, went to one door or the other, and listened to things I couldn't hear. She seemed alternately satisfied and concerned, but not enough of either to go back outside. As the cookstove warmed the house, I turned on the overhead fans to distribute the heat. And finally Soul turned to me, her eyes piercing. They looked black in some light, crystal in others. I figured they could look any way she wanted them to.

"I've read your reports. Thorough. Detailed. Succinct."

"Uh-hunh." *How's that for succinct?* I thought.

Soul trilled a laugh. "You remind me of Jane when she is in a snit."

"I'm no skinwalker."

"She told you what she is. Interesting. What are *you*?"

"You read the reports on me at Spook School. You know what I know."

"No. This land sings with magic. It claims you are much more."

I shrugged, not lowering my eyes or looking away. Not altering my expression. Remembering my body's reaction to the were-blood on my land and the way that I had had to compel myself not to take it. Forcing my breath to stay slow and easy, I asked in return, "What are you? No. Never mind. You're an *arcenciel*. Light dragon."

Soul tipped her head in acknowledgment. Got up and poured us each a cup of coffee. It looked as if we were going to drink the whole pot. Thank goodness she had made decaf. I didn't think I could make it through another night on little to no sleep. I accepted my cup and added cream and sugar.

"You didn't answer what you are," Soul said.

"Don't know what I am."

"The researchers at PsyLED suggest that you know more of what you are than you have said." I didn't reply and after several sips of the coffee, my eyes on her, Soul went on. "The land says you're ancient. The land speaks of old times and primeval ways."

"I'm twenty-three. Not so antiquated. Aunts and sister-wives were present when I was born. I tested not witchy when I was eleven or twelve."

"So you have said. Yet the land—"

A scream rent the charged air. I didn't see Soul stand, but she was suddenly simply flowing to the front door. She unlocked and opened it and called, "I told you to go play. *Hunt*." Her voice deepened, and she added, *"Go!"* I felt the land respond at the command in her tone and knew that the cats had turned and raced off. Even with my bare feet off the floor, I could follow their progress. Soul shut the door and came back.

"You wanted to talk. I assume it isn't about species," I said, sounding grumpy. "I'm tired and need to go to bed."

"I found something in your research. You need to look at it again."

"I found something and you want me to find it again? I'm not in school with some info to put together for a training exercise." My grouchy tone was growing, not at all subservient, like a good probie should sound. "You know what it is, so tell me."

"I know what it might be. Look at the World War Two information. Especially the photographs. The names." She stood and set down her mug. "The cats are quiet now. I'll check on them as I leave." And she walked back to the door and out. And disappeared in a flash of light. I locked up again and put the dishes in the sink to soak, took the fastest shower ever, and climbed into the cold sheets, my oven-warmed cast-iron frying pan at my feet, wrapped in towels. The cats piled on the bed with me, Jezzie climbing under the sheets to cuddle with me. I was asleep instantly.

I woke when my cell beeped at five a.m. and crawled out of bed feeling rested and wide-awake, despite the scant hours I had been allowed. The house was still cold, so I made a hot fire in the stove, took a hot shower, added more water to the water heater—a never-ending process, as letting the boiler go empty meant melting the seams, an expensive repair—and dressed for the day in layers. I was wearing navy pants today, with a navy tee and button-up shirt, and a black jacket and shoes. It was the first time I'd worn the new outfit, and I had to figure out how to position my shoulder harness over the shirts and under my suit jacket to make it fit right.

Outside, it had sleeted, and the ground was treacherous, so I texted JoJo that I'd be late to the eight-a.m.-sharp meeting, and went back inside. I opened my laptop and pulled up the witches' names, Kurt's timeline, and a summary on the research on World War Two, all from Kurt's computer.

I found something. A Kurt Daluege had been executed in the postwar trials.

A frisson of certainty heated its way through me. Below the ground, Soulwood reacted to my interest with a clatter of tree limbs in the wind. I poured a cup of coffee and returned to my open files.

The original Kurt Daluege had been an SS officer of some kind, tangentially associated with paranormal research. And had been hung in the trials as a war criminal. His wife and children had survived, and some of the children immigrated to various countries. I did an ancestry search of Kurt Daluege and quickly discovered that Kurt was named after his grandfather. Who had been in Hitler's Schutzstaffel, or Protective Squadron in WWII. My heart rate sped and the roots in my belly went tight.

One of the local witches was Irene Rosencrantz, who traced her Jewish lineage to a witch who died near the end of the war. There was a Rosencrantz listed among the witches who'd died of suicide rather than give their weapon to the SS officers and Hitler's war machine. Now we had two Rosencrantz witches and a Daluege in Knoxville. Impossible coincidence. Three coincidences in a row stopped being flukes. It became enemy action, according to Ian Fleming in a James Bond film. I had to agree.

According to a police report, at two a.m. Irene Rosencrantz's car had gone off the Gay Street Bridge into the Tennessee River. Which was ridiculous. I had driven that bridge, and there were thick concrete curbs about two feet high on either side of the lanes and a walkway with an iron handrail beyond both curbs for walkers. The bridge area allotted to cars was narrow, and it would be difficult if not impossible to get up enough speed to go over the impediments and into the water. But her car had done just that. According to news reports, divers were in the water and had found the car.

I studied the police reports. I wasn't a traffic accident investigator—there were people specially trained for that—but the photos looked staged. There was a lack of tire skid marks. No damage to the curbs beyond . . . a single skid mark on the *top* of the curb.

This wasn't an accident. Something else had happened. I kept reading and discovered that the investigative officer had called in his supervisor. So I wasn't the only one who thought things looked off.

There had to be a connection between Germany in World War Two, with its slime molds, and this accident. With Kurt being the grandson of a Nazi. Witches from all over the world in Knoxville, Tennessee, including some that sounded Germanic. A witch working here that made no sense. Attacking slime molds here. People drowning and killing each other at a pond here. *Enemy action.*

I sat back to find a cat had settled in behind me. I picked up Torquil and placed him on my lap, where he started purring. *An accident in the twenty-first century that traced back to World War II?*

I marked the list of witch names and the accident report to

come back to. Had both of the Rosencrantz and the Daluege grandparents or great-grands lived in Germany? Had they worked opposite sides of a war that was mostly about *ethnic cleansing*?

On a hunch, I began a search on odd growths in Germany during the war. And I struck pay dirt. At the end of the war, outside of Kassel, Germany, an entire small town had been overtaken with four forms of distinctive, disgusting, and dangerous fungi.

Bleeding tooth fungus, which was repulsive, looking like rotten, bleeding teeth and gums. The fungus was capable of absorbing cesium-137 from the environment, a radioactive isotope that could be toxic at sufficient levels.

Doll's eye fungus, which looked like dolls' eyeballs on the end of scarlet stalks. This fungus was deadly.

False morels, also deadly.

And . . . black slime mold.

There were photographs of the slime covering buildings, budding in rainbow hues of ugly, spore-forming, fruiting bodies, looking like fantastically shaped flowers. Soooo . . . I stroked Torquil, and the former mouser cat rolled over and exposed his belly for me to rub, batting my hand when I was too slow. There was a connection between Knoxville's slime, the pond, the deer, the dancing infinity loop, Germany in World War Two, and the accident on the bridge at South Gay Street. Even I knew that sounded bizarre. My whole body on alert, I went back to my research.

The Allied bombing of Kassel had ended the attack of the slime molds and toxic fungi. Similar slime mold attacks hadn't been documented anywhere else, even during the war. But . . . now we had the slime mold and the presence of two Rosencrantz witches and the great-grandson of Kurt Daluege in the same place. There *was* a connection. I just didn't know what it was. I thought about Tandy and his ability to force info out of Makayla. I wondered if he could get Kurt to talk, once Kurt was back in his right mind. And that thought left a bad taste in my mouth. I'd do this the human way—research.

According to Makayla, Kurt had tracked down the covens from the war. So maybe he had also specifically traced the Rosencrantz witches. Maybe he had set up his business here in this city, with the intention of using a Rosencrantz to re-create the spell that the witches had died to hide. Maybe a Rosencrantz was necessary to the workings.

My fingers tapped nervously on the edge of my tablet. Torquil batted my fingers, this time with a bit of claw, and I went back to stroking him.

Blood was an integral part of blood magic. A blood sacrifice was needed in most black-magic ceremonies. Maybe Rosencrantz blood was necessary to make the spell work. Maybe the working was a blood-magic curse and not just a working. And maybe Kurt hadn't told the coven that. If so, then maybe Kurt had gotten Aleta and her mother to move here under false pretenses. And gotten them to bring their own family's research notes. That sounded plausible. Maybe the Knoxville coven had been successful this time. And maybe the success had resulted in black slime, death, and destruction. And a faked accident. Maybe the death of a Rosencrantz. The sisters were missing, along with the other witches. Where were the Rosencrantzes? Had they been sacrificed, their blood used in the working? I opened a file and looked at the photos of the sisters, both gray haired and stern faced.

And were Aleta and her family safe? *Where were the witches?* A knock came at my door right at dawn, and I grabbed my shotgun. I spotted Occam—human shaped, dressed in his thin gobag clothes—on the porch, leaning against the front wall, eyes closed. He looked exhausted, skin pasty instead of its usual golden tone, scruffy beard, hair too long and unkempt. But he looked as if he was in his right mind. I opened the door, aiming the same shotgun at him that I had leveled at Soul. "You thinking of doing me harm, Occam?"

"Nell, sugar, I'm so tired you could beat me with a wet noodle and I'd cry uncle."

Paka was climbing up the stairs, also dressed in the too-thin clothing, her curly black hair in a mass. "You will shoot us?" she asked, pausing at the top. There was something odd in her eyes that I didn't like but didn't know how to describe or name.

"Only if you try to eat me for breakfast."

"Breakfast sounds wonderful," Occam said, pushing away from the wall and stumbling inside. "Eggs? Bacon?"

"Fresh out," I said.

"Cereal? Coffee strong enough to stand up a fork and peel the bark offa tree?"

I gave the two werecats a half smile and allowed Pea past as well. The grindy walked, neon green tail down, to the master bedroom and jumped to the made bed with the mousers, Torquil trailing behind. Not seeing a human-shaped Rick, I shut the door behind them and placed the shotgun down. "I reckon I can fix you something to stick to your ribs. Where's Rick?"

"He is caged," Paka said, a hint of pitiless satisfaction in her voice. "He did not shift back."

He had to be in the cage that had been delivered. I didn't know what to say to that, but it bothered me almost as much as Paka's expression. I picked up my service weapon and snapped it into its Kydex holster, beneath my left arm, making sure the sound was loud enough for my guests to know I was armed. There were tales about werecats on the full moon. They weren't quite human, and establishing that I was queen in this ever-expanding clowder seemed like an important task. I moved to the kitchen and started a fresh, strong pot of coffee. Paka was still watching me like I was a mouse and she was hunting. "He *will not* shift back," she said. "He is leopard."

"That sounds bad," I said as I measured out grounds.

"It is, Nell, sugar. Very bad. Any chance you'd let me shower?" Occam asked. "I can pay you on Tuesday."

"Short shower," I said. "I don't have a very big hot water tank, but what I got's free. Clean towels on the shelf. Home-made soap too."

Occam grunted, made his way to the bathroom, and closed the door. A moment later, I heard the water come on, and I hoped he had remembered to take off his clothes before he climbed under the spray.

Paka, looking cold in her thin clothing and flip-flops, curled up on the couch and pulled the afghan over her. I hit the START button on the coffeemaker and went to the pantry, returning with the homemade organic granola cereal I had traded dried beans for at the market two months ago. It might not be stale. Milk, cold from the fridge, brought by the team the night I got back. Bowls and spoons and mugs went on the table. Paka watched me as I worked, not offering to help.

"You got something to say?" I asked, without looking up. Avoiding eye contact, a leftover habit from my youth in a large polygamous family, was sometimes helpful.

"I do not like the cold."

"I'm not too fond of it myself sometimes." I leaned a hip against the kitchen counter, now meeting her predatory gaze. Maybe she had stayed too long in cat form and my movements looked too much like prey. I stretched slightly, adjusting the shoulder rig, drawing attention to it.

"Why do you stay here?" she asked.

"This is my land." It seemed obvious to me.

"You could claim land anywhere," Paka said, her body relaxing from whatever hunting instincts she had been experiencing. She pulled a comb from a pocket and started to untangle her tight curls.

I didn't let the surprise show on my face. I could? And if I could . . . could I—

"You could come with me to Gabon, in Africa, and claim the land. We could share it."

This was a bizarre conversation. "No. Thank you. I like it here. Besides, why would you want to go? Your mate is here."

"My mate no longer. I was given to him by Raymond Micheika of the Party of African Weres, that my magic might enchant him and force a change upon him. I have done everything that I was tasked to do. Rick is cat. He is trapped in human form no longer. More, I have freed him from my enchantment. I will go home now. Today."

"You will?" Occam sounded surprised and a little angry. He was standing in the doorway and had clearly been eavesdropping. He was barefooted from the shower, his thin pants hanging low on his hips, his chest glistening with water droplets, his blondish hair straggly and dripping. I politely turned my head away, but it wasn't an easy thing to do. Occam was a mighty pretty man, in cat or human form. From the corner of my eye, I saw him smooth a towel over his head, but he didn't take his gaze off Paka. The way a cat watches something it's about to pounce on. "But who's gonna help him change back?" he asked.

"That is not my concern," she said, wrapping a long curl around a finger and sliding the finger free. "That was not part of my task."

"*Exactly* what *was* your *task*?" Occam asked. And I remembered the strange story of how Paka and Rick met and came together, the night Paka stole him from Jane Yellowrock.

"I was paid by Raymond Micheika to enspell the man and find a way to bring him to his cat. That is all. It is done." But there was something in her expression that suggested there was more, and that she was looking for an excuse to tell us more. To gloat?

"And Soul knew this?" Occam demanded. "That you would leave?"

"I do not know what the dragon knew. I do not care what the dragon knows. I have completed my task, and I will return to my home. Today."

Occam's mouth pulled down, his face hard, unyielding.

Paka knew Soul was a dragon. Interesting.

"What does that mean?" I asked him. "That Paka will go home?"

"Something's still wrong with Rick. His tattoos are still glowing gold. He's in pain. And he's still in his leopard form. He should have shifted back to human slicker than owl snot this morning, and he didn't. And she knows why." He gestured to Paka.

She said slyly, "I have magic and that magic called to him. It bound him, and my bites helped him to change. Now he has become his cat and I have withdrawn my magic." Paka smiled, catlike. "I have completed my task. He is free."

Occam took one long stride toward the couch, growling out the next words. "And if Raymond Micheika, the were-ambassador to the US, the leader of the International Association of Weres, and the leader of the Party of African Weres, asks you to stay?"

Though I'd never met the man, I knew the name from paranormal poli-sci class at Spook School. Micheika was a rare African werelion and the most politically powerful were-creature on the face of the planet.

"I will still go home."

"Why?" he snarled.

"Because that was the arrangement between Kemnebi and my family."

"Who is Kemnebi?" Occam asked.

Paka stood slowly, her eyes lighting at the question. This was what she wanted us to know. "The husband of the woman Rick slept with in New Orleans. The husband of the black wereleopard female who bit and turned Rick. The husband of the woman killed by the mother of Pea for passing on to him the were-taint. The vengeance of Kemnebi is now complete."

I went still. So did Occam for a minuscule instant before he dove across the room. To Paka. Were-fast. He was holding her by the throat. His hands clawed. Paka laughed as if she thought Occam was amusing. He growled, lifted her from the sofa with one hand. "Vengeance? You were sent here for *revenge*?"

I shook my head, trying to understand what was happening.

The backs of Paka's hands grew black hair. Retractile cat claws spread, pricking Occam's skin where they touched. Occam shook her slightly, his grip tightening. Her husky voice went deeper, scratchier at the pain of his hand. But she didn't fight. She seemed happy to talk. And maybe she was. Paka had been silent and undercover inside PsyLED for months. "Ohhh," I whispered.

The cat-woman wrapped one slender hand around Occam's wrist and tilted her head up to him. Her black hair spilled across his hand, sticking to his damp chest. "Kemnebi, the leader of my people, brought money to my mother and father and secured my services. This was long before Micheika came to find me, for Kem knew that Raymond would seek me out. Among my people, I and my magic are rare and valuable, and I alone might free LaFleur from his torture."

Her cat smile stretched to reveal cat teeth, pointed and sharp. "Long before PAW or the IAW communicated with me, to bring me here to *help* LaFleur, my father and Kemnebi contracted together for me to do four things. To bind the wife stealer to me. To gain vengeance upon the American policeman who seduced Safia and led her into dishonor. To see that LaFleur achieved his cat form. And to leave him as cat. I have done all that Kem paid me to do and all that Micheika demanded. It has taken long, but my magic has accomplished all my tasks."

"What? No . . . ," I whispered. "You have to help him change back."

Paka pushed away from Occam, and he let her go, backing away. "No. I do not. I have broken no laws of these United States of America. I have broken no laws of my people. I have avenged the death of Kemnebi's wife, Safia, who was killed by grindy-low claws for infecting Rick. I have helped Rick to achieve his leopard form. I am done here. I go home."

I didn't see Pea leap, or even leave the bedroom, but she landed on Paka with a one-two *thump* of sound. Blood sprayed across the room, and then they were all outside, faster than I could follow, leaving the door open, the morning chill sweeping the house's heat outside. I raced across the house and shut the door, locked it, leaned against it, wondering what all this meant to my life, to the case, to Rick, and to Unit Eighteen. I looked out the front windows, but they were gone.

I could have forced Paka to stay in the U.S. I had claimed her months ago, when I fed Brother Ephraim to the land, claimed her to keep her safe, to keep Soulwood from rejecting her. But free will was important. Forcing her to stay seemed wrong.

Not sure what else to do, I cleaned up the were-blood with lots of Clorox and paper towels and sent a group text to Soul and the unit, explaining what Paka had said. They were horrified, and a dozen texts came back demanding more information, but I had no more to share.

SEVENTEEN

Instead I asked JoJo to send traffic cam footage from anywhere near the accident on the Gay Street Bridge. I also asked for someone to take readings with a psy-meter at the accident scene and the vehicle once it was recovered from the river. Then I copied the first text I had sent and my fingers hovered over the cell, trying to decide if I should send the message. In the end, I decided that she should know about Paka's deceit, and what she did with the info was up to her. I hit SEND, the message winging to Jane Yellowrock. Then I put away the phone and the food, packed up my gobag, and prepared the house for a day away.

There was blood on my front porch. It might be part of a crime scene if Occam and Pea killed Paka. I rinsed off the porch and the grass nearby with the hose, and felt the land soak up the blood as if it was an offering. And I realized that I hadn't fallen into bloodlust at the fight, the fear of the combatants, or the blood spray. Maybe I was getting some control over my desire to kill my friends and feed the land. That would be nice. I locked the door and drove away.

I was halfway down the mountain when I got a text from an unknown number. It was short and sweet. *The witches you search for are at a witch safe house.* An address appeared in the box below that. I pulled over and sent the number and text to JoJo to check out, and programmed the address into my GPS. JoJo sent back the information that the number was a burner phone, which meant several things. One, someone who knew my number had bought or used a burner to send me the note. Two, I might be walking into a trap. Three, it was my job to go anyway.

I remembered the female voice beneath the ground. A witch? Someone who had orchestrated all this magical contamination in Knoxville? Had killed women and children and men to some political end? A true MED?

According to sat maps, the address was an older, vinyl-sided ranch house on Airport Road in Oliver Springs. I'd have to travel within a mile or so of the address anyway. I might as well check it out. I motored slowly down the low mountain to the river valley below.

I parked my truck on the street and approached the house, my badge on my belt and ID in my hand. About fifteen feet from the door, I felt magics tingle across my skin. I stopped. The house was protected by a ward, and instantly I wanted to take off my shoes and read the land to see the magics, but not without backup to watch over me. One thing I knew, even without a read, was that the working wasn't a kill-intruders-on-sight ward, but a someone-is-here ward. Because I was still breathing. I knocked on the ward. The magics buzzed under my knuckles, and a soft gong sounded inside, like an alarm. A small dog started a shrill barking, that of a house yapper, not the baying of a hunting dog. A moment later I heard a woman's voice and I called out, "I'm Special Agent Nell Ingram. I'd like to talk to talk to you about LuseCo, *Infinitio*, and *Unendlich*. And maybe Germany and World War Two."

The dog went wilder, barking as if he had sighted a dragon. Or a mailman. Until it fell abruptly silent. When no one spoke, I said, "I don't mean to make your situation worse. But you need to know that the workings at LuseCo might have contributed to the illness and deaths of several humans."

A moment later, the ward fell with a tinkle of almost-sound and a faint breeze across my skin, and then a second one that covered just the house itself. That one was likely the kill-on-sight ward. A young woman opened the door, and I recognized her from the employee photos. This was Aleta Turner, the young physicist who had—inadvertently or not—set all this in motion. A woman stepped up beside and behind her: her mother, Wendy Cornwall. In the corner, as far from the door as possible, stood Rivera, Wendy's twin sister. The witch twins weren't identical, though both were strawberry blond and freckled.

"How did you find us?" Aleta asked.

"Tip from a burner phone," I said.

"Betcha twenty bucks it was Shonda," Aleta said. "She always did hate witches. Or Irene."

They didn't know about the accident on the bridge. "Irene's missing," I said carefully, watching their faces.

The Witches seemed to take a collective breath. "That's . . . not good," Aleta said.

"Lidia," Wendy said. "Well, now we know, at least. Though what good it does us, I don't know. Come on in." She pushed the door wide. "We need to put the ward back up. We've had death threats."

I stepped closer, asking, "Did you know that *Infinitio* and *Unendlich* would drain the ley lines?"

Wendy sighed, pushing the door wider in invitation. "No. We had no idea. Not until it was too late."

At which point Wendy fell back. A rifle shot echoed, ricocheting down the road. Rivera screamed, "Nooooooo!" Part of the doorframe splintered into the air. A second shot sounded.

"Down!" I shouted, diving over the spot where the outer ward had been. Landing hard. A skidding scrape. The door still hung open. I rolled upright, raced up the front stoop. Dove again, this time inside. A lamp exploded. A third shot sounded. "Raise the ward!" I shouted.

The ward went back up with a sizzling heat, and I realized that I was holding my service weapon in a two-hand grip at my right leg. Breath heaving, I slammed the door. Flipped off the lights. Crawled over to the two women close to the door. On the floor. One was bleeding. She held a pillow over her waist. I hesitated, but my need to feed the land didn't rise. Maybe being shot at inside a house held it at bay. A titter of hysteria tickled the back of my throat. I swallowed it down.

"Where are you hit?" I asked as the ward gonged twice like a bell. It had been hit with rifle rounds. Someone was shooting with a high-powered weapon. Without the ward, it likely would have penetrated the brick even though the shots came from far enough away that the sound was a heartbeat later than the damage. Again, and once more, it was hit and gonged in a vibration I could feel. I placed my weapon on the floor beside me and pulled a striped throw off the couch nearby, wrapping it around the woman's waist and the pillow, applying pressure. Rivera crawled over and pressed her hands on her sister's side, still moaning, "No. Noooo."

A gun was pushed into my face. It had been there for a while, but I hadn't seen it until the cold barrel touched my forehead. My mouth went open. The barrel looked about four feet long and bigger around than a cola can.

"Move and you die." Aleta wasn't a witch. But she clearly wasn't powerless.

"Ummm . . . not moving." I could try to grab my ten-mil and fire. I could roll away and hope she missed. I could swat the gun and likely get a head shot for my trouble. I was on my backside. No way to kick or hit or run. With two fingers, moving slowly, I pushed my service weapon toward her. And held up my hands.

Outside, the firing had stopped. In the distance I heard sirens. Well, this was gonna be a mess and a peck.

"How did you find us?!" Aleta demanded, knowing the answer, her tone calling me dimwitted and dangerous.

My mouth opened slowly. "Ooooh. I'm an idiot." Someone who wanted a chance to kill the women, but who knew they were hiding behind a ward, had sent me the address. Then waited with a high-powered rifle for the ward to be dropped while both women stood in the open doorway because a stupid law enforcement probie had shown up. "Cell text. Address. Turned out to be a burner phone, but I thought I should check it anyway."

"Is your name *Stupid*?"

"It is today." I sighed. With the same two fingers, I removed my badge and ID and slid them across the floor to Aleta. "I'll call in a GSW. Okay?" I pulled my cell phone and called JoJo. After that, things got a lot more hectic.

I got the chance to ask Aleta and her mom questions before the ambulance pulled away, but it turned out I learned little I didn't know, except that the COO at LuseCo, Daveed Petulengo, had a mother who was a Romney witch out of the Petulengo family. And there had been a Petulengo clan witch at the German research and development site in World War Two, working under duress to keep her family alive. I texted JoJo to run a check and see if Daveed was back in the country.

Moments later, she called me. "Wouldn't you know," she said. "He's been back in town for a week."

"Military training?" I asked.

"Sniper," she said quietly.

I remembered the animal heads on his office wall. There was

a man who knew how to shoot a high-powered rifle. A high-powered rifle had been used against Aleta and her family. A strange, itchy heat buzzed in my palms and through my chest. "He texted me the address. But why would he wait to shoot them now, when he could have killed them anytime at the company?"

JoJo said. "He really was out of the country, so maybe he had no idea things were going bad."

"The Cornwall witches seemed to think that Shonda or Irene sent me the burner text with this address. And when I told them that Irene was missing, Wendy said something like *Lidia. Well, now we know. Though I don't know what good it does us.*"

"I don't know what good it does us either," JoJo said, "but I'm running a deeper background on Irene, Lidia, and their families and finances."

"Interesting that Daveed Petulengo has been out of town this whole time," I said. "What do *his* finances look like?" I heard tapping in the background, JoJo's faster-than-light fingers working on her keyboard.

"More than strained," she said. "Bank records came in overnight, and he's strapped, in debt up to his eyeballs."

"Follow the money," I murmured, quoting the Spook School lessons.

"On it," JoJo said. "I'll try to have something on Petulengo and the Rosencrantzes by the time you get to HQ." She disconnected.

I got to work minutes late, my mind full of worries, all as ugly as one of the slime mold blooms. JoJo met me at the top of the stairs with the words, "Daveed Petulengo just received an infusion of money. Fifty thousand into his account routed through the Caymans."

"How is Wendy Cornwall?" I asked.

"In the emergency department. They're still trying to decide if she needs surgery. Where's Paka? And Soul?" Jo asked.

I closed the door on the narrow stairs, and Jo followed me to my cubicle. "I left Paka and Pea and Occam fighting in my front yard. I haven't seen Soul since she took off just before the big revelation about Paka's goal in the US. Maybe an hour, an hour and twenty minutes ago."

"Soul was *here* when your text came in. No way was she with you then."

I blinked. "Okay. I must be mistaken about the time." But I wasn't. Soul had traveled to HQ by other than mechanized means. She had . . . flown? Right. Dragons have wings.

JoJo continued. "When she heard about Paka's little job, she cursed, words I never heard her use before, and took off like her tail was on fire."

"Hmmm." I put my gobag and weapon away.

"Before that, though, Soul said to tell you that we've been getting little earthquakes, registering zero-point-two to zero-point-three on the Richter scale, for the last hour. That's too low for a human to feel, but she said you'd be interested." JoJo did a one-eighty and left my cubicle. She was wearing gray and black clothing, not bright and vivid hues. That was different.

Probie scut work was supposed to be paperwork, research, and errands, so I went to work on the Germany/World War Two/Kurt Daluege/Rosencrantz/Daveed Petulengo relationship. I was done with the Internet and history research by lunch and had JoJo's deep background information on file. I was still not used to electronic methods and so I printed off the background on the Rosencrantzes and sat at the conference table, where I could spread out my papers. The first thing I noted was that the Rosencrantz sisters had received financial infusions in multiple small batches of $2,500 each. This was well below the limit that would make a bank inform the US government about large deposits, but the total added up to well over a hundred thousand dollars over the last year. Each deposit had come from a bank in the Caymans, the same one that provided Daveed Petulengo's windfall.

Someone was paying three members of LuseCo to do . . . something. So . . . maybe this was . . . The thought worked up through my subconscious like a seed sprouting. What if this was evidence of corporate espionage? I did a search on the finances of the other company involved in magical propulsion systems, Kamines Future Products, the company that was LuseCo's foremost competitor in energy R&D. Surprise, surprise. Their company's financial holdings were in the Caymans. That one key unlocked others. Sometimes being the probie put on scut-work research paid off.

I put my thoughts into a report that included the witches in the workings at LuseCo and their relationships to covens involved in World War Two energy experiments. There was a considerable overlap.

Then I went looking for T. Laine, U-18's resident witch. I had feelings about what T. Laine and Tandy had done to Makayla and to me, but that could wait until the Old One was safe. JoJo mumbled something about Lainie interviewing more LuseCo employees, so I needed to drive to the company. Again. My driving patterns were ping-pong-ball specific, but I had an idea and needed to toss it around with the moon witch. It might be nothing. But it might be something. It might fix some things. Or ruin them. It was that kind of idea. Worrisome. Problematic. But an idea all the same. Before I left, I gave JoJo my report and said, "Check out the Rosencrantz info first. If you find them and send someone to pick them up, make sure it's a mixed bag of paranormals, with as many witches on the team as you can get."

"We've got exactly one witch on payroll. Where you think I'm gonna get 'some' witches?" Her eyes flashed, and she looked at me like I was ridiculous. "How many are *some*? Three? Five? A full coven's worth?" JoJo was tired. With Rick gone, she had been sleeping in the office, grabbing catnaps when she could, pulling back-to-back twenty-four-hour shifts. Her colorful clothing had made way for comfy sweats, and her healthy eating habits had been replaced by delivery—pizza and burgers, and takeout from Yoshi's Deli and Coffee's On, downstairs.

"You'll figure it out," I said. "That's why we call you Diamond Drill behind Rick's back."

JoJo spluttered with laughter. "Really?" I nodded and she glared at me. "You even know what Diamond Drill means?"

I leaned over her desk. There was a pile of earrings on the surface, and I realized that JoJo had no jewelry on, and no makeup either. "It means you were a hacker of the highest order, able to drill into any website or secure computer system, before you were recruited by PsyLED. Which means you can do anything." I tapped her keyboard. "Anything." I turned for the door. "If you need a dozen witches with really big magical mojo, you'll find them, I'm sure. I'll be back at LuseCo. Again. I feel like I live there."

"Cry me a river," JoJo grouched as I headed down the hall. Then she shouted, "Wait!"

I stuck my head back into her cubicle. JoJo was speed-reading my report. "The Rosencrantzes and Daveed Petulengo were all three being paid off to sabotage LuseCo's R&D?"

"The rule says, *'Follow the money.'* That's what the money said."

"But that doesn't make sense. They all three stood to make a lot more money when LuseCo was successful."

"Petulengo needed money now. The sisters had reason to want revenge on Kurt and his family for what their own family suffered in the war." I hesitated, thinking about Paka and vengeance and her being paid to hurt Rick. "Maybe revenge was enough all by itself. Maybe the money was just the tipping point. Maybe we don't have all the answers or know all the motivations yet."

"So why is the working in a triangle? Why is it generating slimes?"

"Not sure. Except that *Infinitio* was being tested all over the world during World War Two. But in one place it was being combined with *Unendlich*. And in that place it grew molds. And the witches died."

"They committed suicide," JoJo said.

"Before or after they grew molds on their bodies?"

JoJo grunted softly, her eyes growing wide, but she didn't answer. She was already fact-checking my report, muttering, "That's it. The two workings together. That's the tie." She pulled on her earlobes, her smile cutting through the exhaustion. "If we know what started it, we can stop it."

I wasn't sure I believed it was all so simple, but I didn't argue. I said, "There are two ley lines that cross under Kassel, the town in Germany where the witches worked. Just like here. Ley lines in both places."

JoJo added, "If you find the LuseCo witches, bring them in for questioning." She whirled in her chair to her printer and whipped a single sheet off the tray. "Here. Here's molds in a triangle." She slid the sheet, which was a color photograph taken from the air, across her desk to me. "That weird stuff is growing everywhere, from the pond to the deer spot to the three houses in the neighborhood."

"They seem to be spreading out in the surrounding area."

"What odds you gonna give me that they'll eventually fill in to form a circle? That slime mold is indicative of a working that's going haywire. I'm sending this to the unit and up the line to DC, to PsyLED central. Figure this out and get it stopped before one of those wingnuts in the government decides to nuke the place."

I got gas in the truck, checked the tires, and ogled spanking-new cars in a Ford dealership while stuck in traffic on the way to LuseCo. I figured it was my fifteen-minute break for the day. At LuseCo, the uni-wearing cop checked my ID and sent me to basement level one, without asking me who I wanted to see. Which was interesting. On the way down on the elevator, I checked my messages, found some noteworthy tidbits of info, and mentally added them to the image I was building as I wandered the halls seeing what might need to be seen.

My phone dinged with a text just as I rounded a hallway corner and spotted the U-18 witch in a lounge with four other women. I could make out two of the faces through blinds that partially covered a window between hallway and room. It was two of the LuseCo witches. I hugged the wall and put my cell on vibrate. They were sitting around a small table with T. Laine. There were papers, silver-toned pens, and two laptops on the table, along with cells and brightly colored tablets. It looked like a business meeting.

I was alone in the hallway, and I moved closer to the open door, listening. The smell of stale coffee and old food clouded the doorway. Two vending machines were in the back, and a microwave sat on top of a minifridge. A small cabinet held a bar-sized sink beside an overflowing garbage can.

I wasn't certain whether to go in or not, hearing the words though the partially open door. "It's not our fault," one of the women said. "It was Daveed's fault. We warned him and he didn't care."

The voice. It was the voice I had heard underground. The woman had short black-dyed hair, but her back was to the door and I had no clue who she was. Except that she was a witch and she had done all this. Somehow, she had spoken *Infinitio* and *Unendlich* into life, with dangerous consequences.

T. Laine asked calmly, "What did you warn him about?"

"That using both workings in a confined space, even on separate days, would result in poisoning the land," the woman said. "In the growth of strange fungi and molds. In . . . other problems. Just like in Germany."

"And you didn't think to tell *us*?" another woman demanded. Her I could see. Taryn Lee Faust, the Knoxville coven leader. "You let *us* harm the earth? You *bitch*!" Power streamed from the room, a gathering of magic that raised the hairs along my arms and up the back of my neck.

"How do we stop it?" Taryn asked, her blue eyes blazing. If the itchy feeling on the air was any hint, she was powerful and livid.

"It's too late to stop it," the dark-haired woman said, her tone exhausted.

My cell buzzed, the vibration unexpectedly loud.

"Who's out there?" a third woman demanded.

The hum of magic through the partly open door strengthened. Thinking T. Laine might need help, and knowing I was discovered, I entered. T. Laine had been working to locate the witches involved in the LuseCo workings and get them together to tell us what was going on with the testing. From the photographs in the LuseCo consultants' records, she had succeeded. She had found four of the witches. And unless our exhausted Diamond Drill had somehow forgotten to tell me that, Lainie hadn't told anyone. "I'm Special Agent Nell Ingram."

The power in the room spiked. I looked at the black-haired woman and felt my insides crawl. Black eyes glared at me. In her photos she had long gray hair. Now it was black-dyed, cut short, and stood out in a dark corona as if she had spent hours scraping her fingers through it. This was the face to go with the female voice beneath the ground.

I glanced at T. Laine, looking for a cue as to what I should say. Her eyes were wide, full of speculation, darting from one witch to the other. She gave me a single hard look and a minuscule nod that seemed to tell me to talk. I wasn't sure what I was supposed to do about it now that I had interrupted the meeting, so I turned on church-speak and manners I had learned at Mama's knee, in the same instant that Spook School training kicked in. I stepped into the doorway, blocking their only way out.

My cell buzzed again. Ignored. Tucking it into a pocket, I said, "Suzanne Richardson-White, of the Richardson witch family. Theresa Anderson-Kentner, of the Anderson witches." I stared at the third woman. "And I believe you must be the long-lost Knoxville witch coven leader, Taryn Lee Faust, of the Lee witch clan." To the fifth woman, I said softly, "And Lidia Rosencrantz of the German Rosencrantz witches.

"You'uns talking about World War Two and a city that came under attack by fungi and molds? And resulted in the suicides of a full coven of conscripted witches working against their wills for the *der Fürher*?" I paused for half a beat and finished with, "And about the Romney witch whose last name was Petulengo?"

Lidia's shoulders hunched.

"You, I recognize from the curse on the land," I said. "I'm not sure why you're here, unless you're under arrest for crimes against humanity, including releasing a weapon of mass destruction on the city of Knoxville."

Lidia raised her hands off the table, her power lifting her crown of hair like black fire. The other LuseCo witches realized we had a problem and they lifted their hands, some already holding amulets with pre-formed spells. This was going badly, and fast. Power filled the small lounge, burning and pricking my skin.

"It's not my fault," Lidia said, magic sparking the air. "And I won't pay for this. I won't spend time in a null." Her hands fisted. The air crackled with electric power. Lidia started to speak again.

T. Laine threw a ballpoint pen at her and said, *"Contineantur."*

The flames of Lidia's working snuffed out. Before Lidia could react, T. Laine said, *"Finis,"* and threw her entire body across the table. In a power roll, she slammed into Lidia and dragged her to the floor. Faster than I could follow, T. Laine snapped witchy cuffs on her prisoner and set a ward, repeating the *wyrd* spell, *"Contineantur."*

Good Lord a Moses, I cursed internally. Lainie was *fast.* She held the other witch facedown, one of the silver-toned pens I had brought from Spook School on Lidia's back. It was temporarily blocking or draining her magics. It was a small version of a null working, but clearly a directional one, because Lainie herself wasn't affected by it. *Lordy baby Moses and all the water in the Nile,* I swore to myself. Lidia moaned in pain.

The other witches were staring openmouthed, their power dissipating, their amulets unused and unnecessary. "Lidia? Nooo . . . ," Faust said, sounding tired. "Why?"

"Lidia and probably her sister Irene," I said. "Just after I got here, I saw an updated report on the single-car accident at the Gay Street Bridge. The accident was magically enhanced, according to psysitope readings. Magic sent the car over the curb and railing and into the river. With Colleen Shee MacDonald inside. She's dead."

Taryn closed her eyes, her face crumpling as if someone had crushed her in an immense fist. "You killed Colleen . . . ," she murmured.

T. Laine yanked Lidia up by the cuffs and a shoulder and shoved her into a chair. The witch had begun to cry, and tears gleamed on her face, but her lips were tight, mulish, and her eyes focused on the near distance, with quick back-and-forth motions, as if she was trying to figure out what to do next. Or was trying to cast a working while in witchy cuffs, which was not going to happen. The last of the painful spears of magic in the air died away.

"What just happened?" Soul's voice rang in the room from a laptop on the table. I closed my eyes. Soul had been part of this meeting of witches. I had gone all rodeo again, as Rick had said. I was likely to be fired.

"I think our probie didn't get the text," JoJo said, "and interrupted our conference call."

"Conference call?" I tapped my cell screen and saw that the texts I hadn't looked at were both from JoJo, saying not to interrupt T. Laine's conference call at LuseCo. My face flamed. "Oh."

"T. Laine," Soul said, sounding exasperated and spent, "update."

"Lidia Rosencrantz attacked and is in cuffs," Laine said, "under arrest, which I'm sure everyone back at HQ heard."

To the room in general, Soul said, "The police have BOLOs out for Irene and Petulengo and are staking out all the private and commercial airports for a hundred miles."

With a knee, T. Laine nudged Lidia's bound hands and leaned close to the witch's ear. Gently she said, "You know. Because of the tickets we discovered to the Marshall Islands, a country the US has no extradition treaty with."

Lidia closed her eyes at the words. "Vacation," she said, wiping her nose and cheeks on her shoulder.

"Right," T. Laine said. To the other witches she added, "Yes. Both Rosencrantzes and Petulengo are part of the problem with the workings and with the fungi and the pond and the deaths.

We believe they knew that activating both workings in one locale would result in problems and strange growths and attacks on wildlife, and they did it anyway."

"Did you know it would harm humans?" Taryn ask Lidia softly.

Lidia's mouth went even harder, but her head tilted to the side in what might have been shame. Or not. I find it difficult to tell real shame from faked shame.

"Oh, Lidia," Taryn Lee Faust said in a drawn-out sigh. "They'll blame witches for these deaths. *All* witches." She put her fingers over her eyes and pressed gently as if her eyeballs ached. "It will bring all the racial and species tensions back to the surface. We'll have to start over to be accepted here."

T. Laine asked Lidia, "Where is Daveed Petulengo? Where is your sister?"

Lidia glared at the table, silence her only answer.

A knock sounded in the room and two male deputies stood at the door, one Caucasian, the other African-American. Both stood with their hands free, ready to draw their weapons if needed. I stepped out of their way, my childhood in God's Cloud of Glory making me see cops as the enemy, even though I was one of them now.

T. Laine pocketed the pens and pulled Lidia Rosencrantz to her feet. The U-18 witch looked cool and in control, and I remembered telling JoJo to send multiple witches to arrest Lidia. But it hadn't been necessary, not when we had Lainie and her new equipment. Lainie, who was a . . . moon witch, during the height of the full moon. My mouth formed an O of understanding.

Lidia looked scared, her breath coming in pained gasps. "The cuffs will hold her," T. Laine said to the men. "I'd appreciate it if you would take her to PsyLED HQ. We have a holding cell there that will negate her magic."

At the word *magic*, the human males' mouths pulled down. Neither was happy to be dealing with witches, and I got the idea that they would rather drown her in the river than transport her anywhere. But they both nodded.

Lidia growled and tried to jerk away, clanking her cuffs. "Fools. Every one of you! I curse you and the land you walk on."

"You ever wish you had duct tape?" I asked T. Laine.

The darker-skinned man chuckled and the two carted Lidia away, down LuseCo's hallways.

I tried to think what kind of problems could result if law enforcement, or worse, the general public, got their hands on the silver-toned null pens or reverse-engineered the witchy cuffs. I tried to think what effect the pens might have on me. Neither was a happy thought.

I said, "Ummm . . ."

T. Laine looked at me and her eyebrows went up. A half smile touched her face, and she tucked a strand of black hair behind an ear. "Talk to me, Green Thumb. Tell me interesting possibilities."

I had told her about my childhood nickname, but it sounded peculiar coming from her. I started to cross my arms over my chest but resisted that protective instinct and stuck my nervous hands in the pockets of my jacket, fists dragging down on the heavy cloth, saying, "Not to change the temper of the room and not to step beyond the purview of PsyLED's responsibilities, but I have an idea. If it works, the Knoxville witches can be the heroes." The wide-eyed witches still sitting in their chairs raised their gazes to me. "All it'll take is for a full coven of the Knoxville witches to try a dangerous *Break* spell mixed with some nonwitch magic, and swear a blood oath that you'll keep my own little secret."

After an uncomfortable silence, during which the witches exchanged meaningful stares that I couldn't interpret, Taryn said, "Talk to me."

I watched T. Laine as she retook her seat. Lainie had a speculative look on her face and she gave me a wait-a-minute gesture with one hand as she pulled an elastic and tucked her hair up in a tail to keep it out of the way.

From the tablet's speaker, Soul asked, "Do I need to be part of this?"

"Beats me," T. Laine said. "But deniability is always helpful."

"Indeed. In that case, I'll handle the questioning of our powerful Rosencrantz suspect in the null room. Keep me informed of anything you think pertinent. Soul out."

"Me too," JoJo said. "By the way, we just got a hit on Daveed Petulengo. Local LEOs picked him up at a private airport outside of town. He's in custody and on the way to FBI headquarters for questioning and processing. Call me if you need me." T. Laine closed her tablet and turned it over on the small table.

I said. "Remember when we first met and you said you might be able to route a spell through me?"

"A *working*. Not *spell*," she said. "*Spell* is pejorative."

"Okay. Fine. Do you remember?"

T. Laine gave me an abbreviated nod. The other witches were watching, puzzled but attentive.

"The slime molds move, almost like magic. Well, what if they are actually being powered by the working? If so, then they can be stopped by a working. And do you remember the *Break* sp—working you used to cut me loose from the site where the deer were caught up in *Infinitio*?"

T. Laine frowned as she put two and two together and came up with the same idea I had. Her eyes lit up. "What if witches can direct a *Break* working to sever the connection between *Infinitio* and *Unendlich*," she suggested. "Instead of trying to stop the workings, we just separate them and then shut them down one at a time."

"That would prevent backlash," Taryn said.

"Even if *Infinitio* has some kind of self-aware AI programming, it should work," I said, finally taking a place at the table.

"It would take twelve of us—a full coven," Lainie said. "But if we time it right we can—"

"Destroy the circle and triangle," I interrupted, not wanting to say certain things—about the Old Ones—in front of the others. If they didn't know, I wasn't going to tell.

"Right. And if we can't *contain* the *Infinitio/Unendlich* energies, we can at least break them up and dissipate them safely." T. Laine gave me a smile that was mostly guile, emphasizing the word *contain*. She was thinking about the containment vessel I had brought from Spook School, though neither of us could say that aloud. Containment vessels were created in the R&D department of a company PsyLED paid to create antimagic weapons for the sole purpose of protecting humans from magic and magic users. Meaning witches, among others. Fortunately that company was in Silicon Valley, not in Knoxville.

I shrugged and tilted my head in agreement.

"We'd have to test it first. And then"—she pulled her cell phone and checked the time—"get it done tonight, before dawn."

"Why before dawn?" I asked Lainie.

"Because according to Taryn, this working was sabotaged.

The altered working has been building for the last half of the lunar cycle, and is set to complete at the end of the cycle at dawn tomorrow."

"Complete?"

Carefully T. Laine said, "The working was supposed to pull energy from deep in the earth from a well or reservoir of some kind of *ancient magical energy*."

"Ley lines?" I asked.

"That's what they say." T. Laine didn't look at me, but I realized she was talking about more than just ley lines. She too was hinting at the Old Ones, but not saying the name.

Taryn sat forward in her folding chair, concentrating on Lainie and me. "Before we try anything you need to know what was going on. All of it and not the bits and pieces that LuseCo told you and that you figured out yourselves. Our tests of *Infinitio* and *Unendlich* were supposed to provide enough power to meet all of Knoxville's energy needs for a year, tying into and unifying the grid for seamless, available power, not weaponization, as you indicated earlier. We didn't know it would damage the ley lines. There was nothing in the notes about that ever being a possibility."

"You were monkeying with the power grid. That's why the lights have been flashing," I said. Then, remembering a screen on Makayla's computer, I added, "Using a back door into the TVA. You hacked the TVA to test your theories."

"Not us, but maybe someone at LuseCo," Taryn said. "And if the Rosencrantzes didn't know that LuseCo was tinkering with the grid, then there's no telling what will happen when the sabotaged working completes."

T. Laine said, "Worst-case scenario is a fear that the energies will explode and send a psysitopic backdraft through the empty ley lines, scattering the energies everywhere and shorting them out."

I thought about that, remembering the fact that the ley lines, early on, had felt empty, almost gone. "Why? To what purpose? There's no motivation for any of this."

"Soul and JoJo think that it's a matter of everyone having different motivations and keeping them all secret from each other," T. Laine said, "including you and the other witches."

Taryn sighed and rubbed her eyes again. "Fine," she said, sounding weary and beaten. "We went to work for LuseCo for two reasons. To make money and to stop them from doing anything with *Infinitio*. We knew the working wouldn't do what they wanted. It wasn't intended to make a self-perpetuating energy device. *Infinitio*'s original purpose was to take ley line power and dedicate all of it to human use."

Suzanne Richardson-White, who had been silent until now, said, "Harvesting ley line power would have given them exactly what they wanted—a permanent and secure energy source."

Theresa Anderson-Kentner spoke, possibly emboldened by Suzanne's comment. Her words had a Great Lakes accent, some place up north. "It would have resulted in a socioeconomic and political upheaval worse than the invention of steam, and with as many negative consequences to the environment. Worse, it would have put major economic power in the hands of three people."

"Sooo . . . ," I said. "We got it wrong? The Rosencrantzes didn't sabotage the working. *You* guys sabotaged it?"

Taryn stood, looking innocuous in jeans and leather jacket, her long hair, pulled back from a widow's peak, caught in a clip. "We weren't a real coven. A real coven is a group of witches working together for common goals. We were put together and given money to do a job. We all had different goals and different concerns that the larger group didn't address, which forced us apart. We split into small groups, each with a different aim. Between us, we all sabotaged the workings."

"And if the Rosencrantz sisters had other aims," Suzanne said, "to steal the workings for another company, then they just made what we did worse. Beyond dangerous." She looked to the other witches, communicating something with her eyes that Lainie and I weren't part of.

"I guess it's time to tell everyone what we discovered below the lower basement," Theresa said. "There's something else down there. Belowground." The tension in the room went up, and she stopped, uncertain.

Taryn said, "We think the Rosencrantz sisters and Petulengo discovered something else below the ground. A power source."

"An entity so vast, so amazing," I said, "that it dwarfs the imagination?"

Taryn's eyes went wide. The other witches in the Knoxville coven froze. And without a word or a sigh, they began to draw power. The barbs of magic that had died spiked again, hot and piercing on my skin.

T. Laine clicked a silver-toned pen and said softly, *"Contineantur."*

The magic in the room shattered and fell with a sound like a dozen vases crashing to the floor. The witches gaped at Lainie. So did I. She said softly, "Don't make me hurt you."

The Old Ones were not a secret in this room. I had nothing to protect. "It's call an *Old One*," I said. "And while you may be correct in LuseCo's motivations, and those of the three in custody, the sabotaged working has done unexpected things. The workings have gathered all the ley line power, power that keeps nature in its boundaries, and wrapped it all around the Old One, like a membrane. Not just in preparation for using the ley lines. But in preparation for stealing the Old One's power too. Which might wake it." I took a breath that hurt my rooty middle. "According to ancient Cherokee tradition, the Old Ones are sentient."

"Holy shit. And if they wake it?" T. Laine asked, quickly opening her laptop and starting a report.

"Earthquakes? Rousing dead volcanoes? A complete slippage of Earth's crust?" I made a helpless gesture. "All hell may break loose. No one knows what might happen. Even if no one intended it, the consequences of the sabotage might be deadly."

"But back to the *Break*?" I said to the Knoxville witches. "If I help you, a full coven, one working together, might be able to *Break* the working."

And I might be able to capture the energies in the containment vessel.

EIGHTEEN

The witch circle was bigger than anything I had seen at Spook School, and it had been constructed by the witches themselves, on a fresh acre of land, one previously planted with soybeans and never used for a ritual. The flat area was high on a flat hilltop that looked down into the city of Knoxville. It was also above a drained ley line, one big enough and stable enough to handle a colossal backlash of power. We hoped.

The four-inch-deep circle had been dug from the winter-bare earth with brand-new steel shovels and backbreaking work, aligned to magnetic north with a compass, with the center of the working at LuseCo directly to our south. There was no pentagram or pentacle, which relieved the schoolgirl fears I'd secretly harbored ever since I'd come up with this harebrained experiment. The circle's trough had been filled in with a peculiar mixture of rocks, leaves, live plants, and, oddly, salt, which the witches claimed would help them control the spell. The working.

That *I* had come up with. Of all the strange things in this case, that one made my skin crawl.

There were fifteen of us present on the patch of farmland outside of Knoxville. Thirteen of us were witches, twelve sitting in the circle. T. Laine sat outside it with Soul, who seemed to have the most autonomy of any person I had met in PsyLED. And me. I was in the middle of a witch circle, right where the churchmen had always said I would end up. I was not going to be telling my mother one single thing about this event, whether it worked or not.

The four most powerful witches in the covens sat at cardinal points. Taryn, an earth witch, sat at north. Barbara Traywick Hasebe, a moon witch, and arguably the most powerful witch present, at least during the three days of the full moon, sat at east. Suzanne Richardson-White, an air witch, sat at south. And

Theresa Anderson-Kentner, water witch, sat at west. The other witches were placed in between, the positioning determined by specialty and power levels in a mathematical negotiation that involved way too many numbers and too much geometry for me. The locations for the moon witches were the most important mathematically, thanks to the lunar cycle and the moon witches' overwhelming power for these three days.

I recognized all of them from the photos provided by LuseCo. Some looked nervous. Two looked angry. They would all lose the money coming to them from LuseCo for the experiment they were about to *Break*. The rest looked tired or resigned. They had all been part of an experiment that had killed innocent humans. Odd how things of the soul reflected on the faces.

With the exception of Taryn, we were all sitting in our places, cross-legged, each of us on a blanket, and each witch had an object, a focal for her power, at her knees: feathers, stones, a small live plant, a stick of wood, a bowl of water from the nearby creek—whatever element signified their power and would hold a measure of that power to steer into the working. I had two things in front of me: a tiny empty silver bowl and a fire burning in an iron brazier.

Carrying a wooden tray, Taryn walked to Soul, placed it on the ground, and, with long-practiced dexterity, opened an alcohol packet and a sterile lancet. She removed the lavender top from a small plastic blood collection tube. "The anticoagulant will keep the blood from clotting. It will do nothing to keep the antibody-antigen reaction from taking place, so we still have to work quickly, but we'll have a few minutes to work before the collected blood goes bad," Taryn said.

Soul lifted her eyebrows, the evening sunlight catching in her silver hair. She was smaller than Taryn, a diminutive figure, but she seemed bigger than life, her flesh glowing in the reddish sunset. She hadn't told them what she was, but she wasn't hiding her power from the witches, which seemed odd and maybe a little scary. "Science and magic? Together?"

"Power evolves as the people who use it evolve."

Soul gave her an abbreviated nod and cleaned her left thumb with the alcohol pad. Pricked her thumb with the lancet. The *arcenciel* allowed three drops to fall into the tube. She dropped her paper waste into a grocery bag and the lancet into a small metal sharps container. Taryn reapplied the lavender top and mixed the blood with the clear stuff inside the tube, three complete movements of the tube: upside down, right-side up, upside down, right-side up, upside down, right-side up, in what looked like a ritual.

As she rotated the tube, she said, "This is our oath. That we will not hint or suggest, speak, write, or sing of the Old Ones. That we will not hint or suggest, speak, write, or sing of the working that breaks *Infinitio* and *Unendlich* from its attack on the Old One. That we will not hint or suggest, speak, write, or sing of Nell's part in the ritual, despite the untruth of the lack of full disclosure. Do you so swear?"

"I so swear," Soul said, her flesh brightening.

Taryn gathered up her equipment and the garbage, and carried the tray to T. Laine, who repeated the procedure. Then Taryn carried the equipment to her place in the circle, but still outside the mixed-element ring. She turned to her left and took three steps, clockwise, to the witch sitting there, where she repeated the process. And then to the next. And the next. As she moved, the breeze came up and the wood burning in the brazier smoked and blazed, getting into my eyes. I had to blink against the smoke and lean back and forth to keep it out of my face, but I succeeded in seeing every part of the ceremony. Each part of the collection process was done in threes, deliberately but not slowly. It took about twenty minutes, which I thought was fast, for every person in the clearing to donate three drops of blood to the small tube and swear the oath, including Taryn herself.

Lastly Taryn came to me and sat before me. Moving awkwardly, I cleaned my left thumb and squeezed the thumb pad with the fingers of my left hand. I stuck it with a sterile lancet. The pain shocked through me, unexpected, despite my knowing it was coming. Clumsily I added three drops to the tube. Taryn topped it and inverted the tube three times. Then she poured the contents of the tube into the small silver bowl. As she had promised, the blood hadn't clotted, but there were minuscule clumps in it. Three drops from every person present.

Sitting with the brazier between us, Taryn said, "This is our oath. That we will not hint or suggest, speak, write, or sing of the Old Ones. That we will not hint or suggest, speak, write, or sing of the working that breaks *Infinitio* and *Unendlich* from its attack on the Old One. That we will not hint or suggest, speak, write, or sing of Nell's part in the ritual, despite the untruth of the lack of full disclosure. Do you accept this oath and agree that you will never speak of your part in it?"

This meant that I couldn't write or file a final report for PsyLED. That T. Laine couldn't. That Soul couldn't. The after-reports from this case would be interesting. "I so swear," I said.

"You do understand that you will be given credit for the *idea* of the working only? And you accept the consequences, should there be such, from the lack of full disclosure to the authorities?"

"I do. I so swear."

The breeze seemed to strengthen as I spoke the final words, and the smoke from the brazier whipped around me. More important, I felt Soulwood awaken, not so very far away, sleepy but aware. The wood reached to me, through the ground, through the earth, a long underground stream of power. It filled me. Restful and heated, deep and full. Like water filling a vase, higher and higher. It was getting hard to breathe. Or perhaps *unnecessary* to breathe. I struggled to force breath after breath, holding on to whatever it was in me that was still human, that still needed air. And still the power filled me, making my palms itch and ache. I felt as if my skin would stretch and burst, and I gasped, mentally pushing the flow of Soulwood away. Back to its place.

The flow tapered off. Stopped. And Soulwood withdrew. Surprise flashed through me. I swallowed. My breath came more easily. That was an interesting reaction to blood vows. And important. Because *Break* might damage my wood. I had been afraid—

"Nell?" Taryn said.

I nodded that I was okay. Opened my eyes. Blinked against the smoke until I focused. Into the fire that burned at my knee, I poured out the blood from the silver bowl. Then, following the ritual as it had been explained to me, I upended the silver bowl and placed it into the center of the fire so the flames could lick and cook the last remnants clean. Taryn overturned the container of lancets into the flames. Then she opened a small bottle and I smelled alcohol, the drinking kind, not the sterilization kind, and she poured it into the plastic tube, swirled it to get all the blood free, and emptied it into the small tub that had held the lancets. She dumped the mixture into the fire. Flames leaped high and we both leaned away from the blaze. She dropped the tub and tube into the trash with the alcohol pads and trash paper.

"This is our oath," she said again. "That we will not hint or suggest, speak, write, or sing of the Old Ones. That we will not hint or suggest, speak, write, or sing of the working that breaks *Infinitio* and *Unendlich* from its attack on the Old Ones. That we will not hint or suggest, speak, write, or sing of Nell's part in the ritual, despite the untruth of the lack of full disclosure to those in authority over her. We so swear."

I felt something heated, icy, arid as a desert, moving like a stream, coil through my body and into the ground. If I'd ever had doubts that witch magic would work on me, they were gone with that nearly electric sensation.

The witches and Soul and I all said the same words, "We do so swear."

Taryn got up, gathering the trash, flipping the silver bowl over with a stick, and into the cooler coals at the side. The bowl had begun to glow a dull gray color, and the stink of burning silver was acrid on the air. Leaving the brazier burning, she took her place at cardinal north, tapped the circle, and said, *"Aperire finis."*

Together, the eleven other witches said, *"Aperire finis."*

I felt the circle close, and I closed my eyes again, feeling the power around me, but not reacting to it.

Taryn said, *"Aperta pro fractura."* The witches repeated her words. The power grew.

From below us, in the river valley, came the echoes of explosions as transformers blew. The night grew darker, then brighter, as the entire electric grid guttered several times, and went down. Several heartbeats later, the part of the city that had backup on the secondary grid flickered on, the city of Knoxville like a patchwork quilt of light and dark. Sirens began to sound.

I had one job to do. Only one. I closed out the sound of the witches. And I put my palms onto the ground, flat to the earth. And I began to scan.

The *Infinitio* was circling, spinning, so fast that if I'd seen it only now, I would think it a ball of color and light, not the infinity symbol whirling like a dervish. It felt important, that I know what it was as it spun around the circle of the huge working. From the center of the working at LuseCo, the light blazed like a sun, a warm glow that seemed to have its own gravity. A power stolen from the ley lines just below it. From all around the circumference of the circle, lines dropped down upon the

Old One, the consciousness buried in the earth. The lines of power spread across the sleeper tapped and drilled and bounced on the consciousness. Which . . . shivered in its sleep.

A slight waveform rolled across the surface of the Old One, the membrane created from the magic stolen from the ley lines. I remembered the Richter scale readings, too slight to register as earthquakes but too great to be missed by seismologists. This had to be the cause of the mini earthquakes that JoJo had been talking about, the microquakes of zero-point-two and -three. The Old One was being *annoyed* awake. As a child, I had seen my father annoyed awake. I had seen my husband, John, annoyed awake by a dog wanting to go outside. Neither awakening had ended well, and I had a feeling that this awakening would end no better. In fact, far worse.

Around me, above me, as deep into the soil as the four-inch-deep circle, the power of the witch circle was growing.

The night was cold and I hadn't brought a winter coat into the circle with me. Just prior to full-on night, I pulled the blanket out from under me, unfolded it, wrapped part of it around my shoulders and body, and pushed a portion back under my backside. I wasn't warm, but I wasn't quite as miserable. I looked over at T. Laine and Soul, who were on a flat-topped boulder, sitting on blankets or towels or foam pads of their own. Watching. I felt safer knowing that they were here, PsyLED guards. Rick had once said that no PsyLED agent ever went into anything alone. Had I doubted, this proved his truth.

The energies of the working whirled over us, behind us, around the witches, blue, green, lavender, yellow, red. It was like being stuck inside a spinning multicolored ball—a little nauseating. But the witches had completed *aperire finis* and were close to the final part of *aperta pro fractura*. Which was a Latin *wyrd* working for a *Break* spell. That was the part where I came in. I had been waiting. And waiting. And just when I started shivering again, as badly as the Old One beneath me, Taryn whispered, "Nell. Now."

I set my palms back onto the cold surface of the ground and *reached*. Sent my energies down and down and stopping, just above the surface of the Old One. The vibrations on its thin skin, the almost-not-there overlay of ley line energies, had grown bigger, higher, more profound. The sensation reverberated through the ground and up into me. My shivers altered, shifted, and slid into the rhythm, matching the vibration that attacked the ancient presence. My magics matched the tempo and cadence. Blended into it without making it stronger.

My body was shaking so madly I had to clench my jaw to keep from biting my tongue. Holding the beat of power, I *reached* back up to the circle, where I sat and . . . tapped the energy of the witch circle's underside. A different kind of power reached out to me. Witch power. And it let me take it in my hands. The energies were hot and cold, the movement of falling water, the massive strength of tides, the pull of the moon, airless and merciless. The might of stone. The cold of glaciers. The green, green, intense *green* of living things. The heartbeat of all life. Keeping my place in the rhythm of *Infinitio*, I pulled the magic that had been gathered in the circle down and down and over. And out. Like a net. A trap. A cage.

When I had the witch's circle centered, I opened my mouth to tell them I was ready.

Something grabbed me. Yanked me down.

Into the dark. Cold. Breathless, deathless, nothingness.

On the surface of the earth, something followed my own energies up and broke through the ground. Slid and slipped, wrapping around my wrists, pinning my palms flat to the earth. Slithered around my ankles and knees, gluey, sliming, adhering to me. And twisting into my skin. Tighter. Pulling. Wrenching me down. My skin split. Blood hit the ground, just above the witch circle. And slime mold sprouted from the earth. Slid over me. Over my head and eyes. Down over my nose and mouth. As if it was trying to drown me.

A heartbeat later, the ground beneath each witch in the circle erupted. Dark stems of slime pushed up and through. And over them. Entangling them. Holding them still. Pinned. Trapped. All but one.

The slime slithered down my cheeks. I couldn't get my eyes open to see who was still safe from attack. And therefore who was most likely involved with the culprits we already had in custody.

I took what might be my last breath.

And heard the overlapping words, as if from a distance, "Now, now, now, now!" *T. Laine*. Panicked. Afraid. Though she and Soul were on a rock, safe.

In the yawning, profound lightless below me, I felt the vibration on the ley line–based thin skin of the Old One increase, a bass drum of might and command. *Infinitio* and *Unendlich*. Waking the Old One.

The two workings were no longer separate. Whatever the multiple sabotages had begun as, they were one, a blended magic so seamless I hadn't perceived it until now. Deep in the earth, the blended working of the *Infinitio/Unendlich* had become a curse, and the curse sensed me. Faster than lightning, it blasted out and caught me, twisting my own magic. Seizing my magic for itself.

Fighting the witch magic all around me. Knotting witch circle power against them. *Infinitio* adding it to the working that had become its own purpose.

On the surface, the slime was trying to cover me, to pull me into the ground. Me, and the witches as well. All of us. Or were trying to cut us to slivers so they could have my blood and the witches' power. And my power to feed the earth. *Oh . . . yes. That is what* Infinitio *wants. What it was designed to do. To take and use and store power. More power than anything ever in the history of humans or witches.* And *Unendlich* had melded in, the two becoming one. Not two workings with a *Break*able joining, but one seamless spell.

I heard the words, "Son of a witch on a switch. We're going to have to do this the hard way." Taryn, realizing what had happened with the melding of the workings.

The sabotage had given the working focus, a single-mindedness that was almost alive. It would take all power, all life, for itself. Around me I felt the grass wither and die and crumble into ash. The trees at the edge of the field died and fell apart. My magic to feed the land was under the control of another force. The fields on the other side of the ridge died. Below on the downhill slope. They died.

The tremor beating on the Old One grew harder. Faster. My power was being directed down, adding to the vigorous pounding, fierce and brutal, onto the Old One. I wrenched my body, trying to free myself. Twisted. Pulled. Pain beat at me, distanced by the muffling of the earth. My blood spread through

the ground, life-giving. Potent. A sacrifice taken by the conjoined working.

Infinitio/Unendlich knew my blood, knew it from the pond
and the piney trees, and . . . it wanted my blood. Wanted me.
Because my magic could make it more than it was now. My
magic could give it true life.

I couldn't breathe.

A new vibration reached me, bright and blue and shining,
yellow as the sun, silver like the moon, the tones of the rainbow
against a storm-tossed sky. *"Aperta."* The words sang into my
bones and blood. So much blood pooling into the ground.

Break. This was the *Break* spell.

The vibration grew and grew. Dozens of slimes spilled over
me. Mutated. Dug into my belly, tearing my skin. My blood
splattered. My abdomen ruptured, the roots from within me
erupting out. Fighting the power of *Infinitio*. Fighting being
pulled into the earth. Battling against the slime from the
ground. But slime was genetically different from other plants,
much more mutagenic. Easily melding with and being altered
by other life-forms. Like me . . .

The *Infinitio/Unendlich* were using the slime molds to
explore the world above. To find the form they would take on
the surface.

Flows, flows, flows. Pools, pools, pools. The power pushed
into me.

I could sense the original working circle created by the
witches at LuseCo. The triangle of power below the ground,
across the city. The infinity loop that sang the words of the
working created by the witches, dancing, singing of its purpose.
Flows, flows, flows. Pools, pools, pools. To create its own life.
To *be*.

". . . Fractura." *Break* slammed down, down, down. Disrupting. Tearing. Shattering. *Ending*.

I screamed.

The circle of *Infinitio/Unendlich* lost cohesiveness. Shadows
appeared. The mutating working . . . tilted. The three bright triangle points on its surface shook and slid to the side. They
slammed together. As if released by a slingshot, the triangle of
power whirled into the distance. Far, far, and far away, deep in
the earth, I felt/saw their combined energies skip across a froth-
ing pool of liquid stone, *magma*, heat inconceivable. Skip. Skip.

Like a stone on a volcanic lake. The last skip spun them up, directly into the empty ley line. They hit. Slid inside. Ricocheted through the empty pathways. A blast of energies detonated, erupting. The ley lines sparked and snapped like a whip. Power roiled through them. The magnetic-electro-magical energies of the Earth cracked like lightning, stretched, and settled.

My pain quivered through the earth and back at me. *"Aperta pro fractura."* The vibrations of the words beat against me.

The absorption of the power trembled through me, through the slimes. *Aperta pro fractura* sliced through the earth. *Breaking. Ending. Infinitio* screamed in . . . horror. Shock. Fear. *Fractura* smashed through the nascent life below us, the roots and veins and trunks of life that had been damaged by our working. Through the bodies of the molds and fungi and slimes and their odd, malleable, genetic structures.

Ending everything that was not meant to be.

Beneath me, within me.

Within the patients in the hospital.

I could see *Fractura* halt and tear, shredding and dissipating into the earth. Into the *Earth.*

The slimes that had grown over me . . . died. Crumbled. Ashes to ashes, dust to dust.

The slimes on the ground withered and died. The slimes on the witches followed, dying, feeding the earth.

The roots inside my belly twisted and went still.

I gulped in a breath. Another. Shaking. Crying.

The heart of *Infinitio/Unendlich,* the infinity loop, spun out of the circle that no longer was. Like a train off the track, hard, out and away. Flung free. Where it could wreak havoc on its own. But, freed from the slimes, I was able to shift my own energies out and slip the smallest part of me through the loop. Catching it. It spun around me, uncertain. I gave it the tiniest of tugs.

"Nellllllll," it called, the sound of its voice like bells ringing, calling, charming.

It's alive. "Yessss," I whispered back. Towing gently. Drawing it toward me.

It wrapped itself around me, holding on. It *knew me.* It was *aware.* And it burned. Every part of my magics it touched *burned.* The last of the ley line energy that had been siphoned off, stored. It scorched my body and my soul, burning, burning,

burning. I dragged in a breath to fight the torture. It didn't help. It just made me more aware.

Ignoring the pain, the rapidly growing agony, I gripped the *Infinitio* loop where it gripped me. As if I had taken its hand in welcome. *"Nelllll,"* it trilled.

I slung it up out of the earth.

Into the containment vessel held by Soul.

"Betraaaayyyyeeerrrr," it screamed, just as Soul closed the lid on the jar. Sealing it within.

The last threads of the working broke, shockingly. Magics sluiced over me, lifting my hair, burning, stinking like magical fire, chemical and astringent, like something Tesla might have imagined had he indulged in drugged dreams. I gasped, realized I was flat on my back, my hands buried, burned in the coarse soil, lumps and clumps raised up where the slime blooms had come through and then died. I pushed against the earth to sit upright, muscles pinging with pain. The dead slime molds around me crumbled. Dust on the breeze. My skin was slicked with my blood, fresh, liquid, and chilling over older blood that was cold and tacky to the touch. All the witches were covered in the gleam of power, bright in the night. All were bleeding. Some were crying. Others angry. The soil around them was disturbed. All this I took in with a sweeping glance as the world swirled around me and my gorge rose.

My head swam. My mouth was dry. I couldn't hear.

The witches were screaming, some standing, some lying on the ground. The working had fallen, taking some of them with it, the backlash knocking them out.

Hopefully not dead.

At the south point on the twelve-place witch working, a woman stood. Rivera Cornwall. The witch from the safe house. Before I could make sense of what I was seeing, she pointed at me. Fire seemed to weave through her fingers.

When I went to the safe house, Rivera had said one word over and over, "No." She had gone with Wendy, her twin, to the hospital, by an ambulance, for what was later revealed to be a through-and-through wound, involving only fatty tissue. Rivera had then bolted and disappeared. Had the shooter even meant to shoot Wendy at all? Or had the superficial resemblance between the twins meant that the shot had been intended for Rivera? She was crafting a working, and all the other witches were on the ground, still affected by the molds and the ley line backlash, all except T. Laine, who was carrying the containment vessel back down to the cars.

I didn't know if Rivera was guilty or not, but I couldn't let her get away.

"Soul," I croaked. And pointed at the witch. Just as Rivera threw her hands out, directing a *shatter* working toward Lainie.

There was a blast of light. And Soul disappeared, taking with her the containment vessel. And all the power of Rivera Cornwall's curse.

T. Laine whirled. Saw Rivera. Raced to her, tackled the witch, and took her down. Banged her head hard on the ground, so hard I felt it through the soles of my shoes. Lainie slapped a pair of witchy cuffs on her, and said, *"Tu dormies."* Rivera's eyes closed and instantly she was asleep.

"Stupid witch," T. Laine said.

My palms on the earth told me that the earth was calming. The vibrations were stopping. The Old One shifted and stilled. Sleeping. It was over.

I woke in a hospital, being sewn up. The doctor leaning over me said, "You're awake. Good. Some of us were worried."

I focused on him, a blurry image of an overweight, balding, out-of-shape man who stank of tobacco and Mexican spices. Leaning over me, around him, were four others, all in white laboratory coats, all looking on with interest. Two were witches. I could see the magics swirling around them, one set of energies green and verdant, the other magics dimmer, slower, brown with red tints, hard as stone. Interns in the University of Tennessee Medical Center's paranormal emergency department. I could see their magics. This was new.

"Be glad your friends were so insistent," the older doctor said. "Any other patient would have been stapled closed."

"Metal might have interfered with her healing," a voice said.

I blinked a dozen times, clearing my eyes, and tilted my head. Occam was standing at my right side. He was wearing his gobag clothes, thin and insufficient to the cold, but his hand holding mine was feverish, heated with the warmth of his cat. His face was inflexible, as if he held tightly to himself and his emotions. His eyes contained some feeling I couldn't name, an intractable, obstinate, purely pigheaded something. And in his eyes was both a knotty problem and a stubborn solution. I could read all of that and more. I could see his cat energies, a boiling, golden overlay of power, like a tornado, whirling and spinning, forceful, dominating, violent, and yet controlled, like a tornado made of sunlight. The energies were something beyond my understanding, but were harnessed to him. Part of his skin and bones and, perhaps, even his soul.

To his side stood T. Laine and Soul. T. Laine looked like moonlight on frozen tree branches, her witch energies sparkling and deadly, far more deadly than I expected. A moon witch on the last day of the full moon.

Soul . . . Soul was a blazing dragon, light and movement and intensity, with glistening scales and horns and claws, wings tightly furled to her. As I watched, the dragon saw me looking and swiveled its head on its neck to look back at me. Eyes the colors of moonlight on ice clouds, the tints of moonbows, focused and pierced me.

"You can see me," Soul said.

"Yes," I said.

"That is unfortunate."

"I don't think it'll last."

"One hopes not."

Beside me, the doctor said, "Now that you're awake, we'll need to administer lidocaine to close the larger lacerations. This will pinch."

It didn't pinch. It *hurt*.

I had to hobble to the van. Had to be helped inside. Occam had to belt me in before he slid in beside me. He buttoned my coat. And made sure the faded pink blanket was arranged carefully over me. I let him do all that because I had one hundred eleven tear lacerations on my body. Some were small, needing only a single stitch to close them and help them heal. A dozen needed ten or more. Some looked burned. All of them were in bruised and damaged flesh.

But mostly I let Occam take care of me because he needed to do something for me. And because my hands were bandaged. There was that small problem. Of the overall damage, my hands and wrists had taken the brunt of the attack. They were in pretty bad shape, with twenty-two lacerations on the left and twenty-seven on the right. They hurt. Even the smallest movement hurt. The van making a turn onto the main road hurt. Breathing hurt.

I needed to sit in my yard and commune with Soulwood. That would help me heal. I hoped.

If Soulwood had been protected from the *Break* spell.

If the witch magic hadn't killed it.

I didn't know.

Because I couldn't feel my woods right now.

Soul climbed into the van with Unit Eighteen. Well, the unit as it existed now, without Paka and with Rick in a cage on my land. Soul said, "You missed the case summary."

I turned to study her. She was dressed in new clothes, silver gauzy stuff that caught the slightest breeze. Her platinum hair was swirled into a long curl that rested over her shoulder and down to her lap. She no longer wore her dragon form, the effect of *Break* having worn off, thankfully. Occam started the unit's van and pulled away from the hospital. I had seen entirely too much of UTMC over the last few months and I was more than happy to see it vanish behind us.

"All through Knoxville, the molds fell apart and dusted away," Soul said. "We don't know why or by what mechanism. The patients in the paranormal unit are, one and all, making swift and amazing recoveries."

"Oh. Okay. I guess," I said, knowing that I sounded as if I was hiding something. Which I was. "Um. What about Rivera?"

"Rivera Cornwall is in custody at PsyLED. Lidia Rosencrantz is now at FBI, awaiting further interrogation. Irene and Lidia Rosencrantz and Daveed Petulengo confessed to working with Kamines Future Products to be paid for stealing the research and development. At this point they are each blaming the other for the murder of Colleen Shee MacDonald."

At my blank look, Soul added, "JoJo said you told her to follow the money. She traced additional wire deposits from the Cayman Islands to Rivera Cornwall. All the witches' money originated from the same account as the funds that were wired to the COO, Daveed Petulengo. And when JoJo did some tracking back, she discovered that the account was owned by Kamines Future Products. While corporate espionage wasn't the sole reason for this fiasco, it played a large part. I understand that Kamines was on your short list of companies interested in self-perpetuating energy?"

I nodded, trying to figure out what I had missed. Where this was going.

T. Laine said, "The Rosencrantzes were working under the table for the CEO of Kamines to gain access to and control of the testing results. So were Rivera Cornwall and Petulengo. Kamines was hedging its bets. The Cayman accounts payed for the assassins who shot at you and Occam at the pond, and Petulengo himself was responsible for the shooting at the Cornwalls, hoping to hit Rivera, who had changed her mind about being part of the conspiracy."

"Not crime? Not terrorism?" I asked.

"No. Wendy and Aleta figured out that the German coven's working had created slime molds, secondary to *Infinitio and Unendlich*, and they feared the working might injure the earth, so they sabotaged it. Taryn and her coven began a different form of sabotage to keep the working from success. The two opposing forms of sabotage twisted the working, and the result caused the workings to turn against the Old One, trying to drain the power of the earth."

"What will happen to them all?" I asked, though I knew, in a general way, what witches did to their own who were caught misusing magic.

Occam said, "There are several null sites, run by the National Conclave, where witches can be kept sealed away from their magic. The Rosencrantzes took money to turn on their coven. They'll be transported to Virginia for confinement for as long as they live."

"And Rivera Cornwall?"

"She's fine. A little wigged out by it all," T. Laine said. "She'll serve a jail term but not nearly so long or arduous as the ones the Rosencrantzes will serve."

"Daveed Petulengo?" I asked.

"Will be tried in a human court of law," Soul said. "Not our circus. Not our flying monkey."

Which made no sense to me at all, but I nodded. "Kamines Future Products?"

T. Laine gave me a smile that belonged on the devil himself. "They got notes on the workings. The moment they try to use them, I'll know. And they will be stopped. Permanently."

"Okay," I said, digesting their words. "Sooo . . . Irene and Lidia deliberately took a job . . . ," I said, feeling out what I had learned and sensed in the circle, ". . . related to the witch working that cost them their family to the Holocaust, and their great-grandmother to suicide, trying to keep that curse out of Hitler's hands. They wanted to remake and sell that curse?"

"Money spoke to them," Soul said. "They were . . . misguided. The Rosencrantz clan has agreed to the punishment. Lidia and Irene will be incarcerated for the rest of their lives, their magic stripped from them. Rivera's magics will be stripped for a period of twenty years. All will remain under lock and key in null sites with no opportunity of parole."

"And *Infinitio*?" I asked, remembering the scream as the vessel was closed. *Betrayer* . . . "They helped make it. Helped keep it going. It had achieved some sort of sentience. What happens to it now?"

The silence in the van was acute except for the hum of tires on the highway.

"It will remain locked away with other things that are too dangerous to be allowed into the world." Soul looked around the van. "Nell needs assistance tonight," Soul said. "It will be hard for her to get around with bandaged hands."

"I'll stay," Occam said. "My leopard can take care of Rick and hunt anything that comes onto the land."

"I'll stay," T. Laine said. "I can cook. And I can spot a magical attack before any of the rest of you."

"Why do you need to be able to spot a magical attack?" Soul asked, ever the teacher. "Why would Nell be attacked?"

"If Rosencrantz had an outside witch accomplice," T. Laine said, "There might be repercussions for today and tonight."

"I need to talk to Rick," JoJo said, "assuming he can understand English at this point, so I'll stay too."

Talk to a black leopard? I thought. But I didn't speak the words.

Tandy, who had been silent until now, opened his mouth, but before he could speak, Soul said, "Tandy and I will write up the reports, then. Agreed, Tandy?"

"That's not what you want," Tandy said, his voice still raspy from the use of his power. "Or . . . it's what you want, but not ultimately what you're trying to accomplish."

"Allow me my foibles," Soul said to him, sounding tired but

tranquil. "You and I need to talk about what happened to you when you were hit by the sonic-blast working. The alteration and enhancement of your empath gifts is gone and you are back to normal now, yes?"

"Yes," Tandy said, sounding tired, disgruntled, and resigned.

"We will do paperwork. We will talk. The others will take care of Nell."

"Pizza," Tandy said. "I've pulled sixty hours on this case in the last three days. I haven't slept. I haven't eaten. I want pizza. And you to pay."

I turned in my seat to stare at the empath Tandy, who had started in Unit Eighteen as the one least likely to take care of himself, had just stood up to a VIP of PsyLED. He had changed. I wasn't sure it was a good thing.

Soul raised her eyebrows but smiled when she said, "Pushy for an empath. Working with Eighteen has been beneficial for you. I like this part. Done.

"And you"—she pointed at me—"what do you see of me now?"

"Normal human you," I said.

"That is fortunate. Sleep."

I did, and woke only when T. Laine nudged me awake at the house.

NINETEEN

I pushed open the door, banging it against the inside wall of the cold house. The mouser cats rushed in, anxious, tails high.

I stumbled in the dark, in my own house. I had never done that before. Occam caught me, one hand under my arm, the other holding paper grocery bags. Stepping surely, lightly in the shadows. Cat eyes, seeing in the dark; had to be. "You okay, Nell, sugar?"

"I'm just peachy," I breathed. I flipped the switch and the lights blazed, the house looking unlived in, abandoned. The fire was out in the cookstove. Even the walls were cold to the touch. A fine layer of ash from the woodstove and dust coated everything. I had been home from Spook School for a week and hadn't dusted anything.

JoJo shut the door behind us all. I stood in the entry, exhausted, leaning against the wall, and watched as my coworkers carried groceries to my kitchen. Occam started a fire in the Waterford Stanley and added water to the water heater, just as if he lived here, as if he knew what to do. Feeling as if the earth had gained a few tons of gravity in the last hours, I made it to the couch and sat, clumsily pulling an afghan over me.

T. Laine pulled food from the grocery bags, which was a good thing, as there was no meat in the kitchen and nothing fresh to cook. Had I been alone, with my bandaged hands, I'd have made do with leftovers and water. Thankfully they had picked up a cooked turkey breast and raw veggies and a loaf of artisan bread. And some canned soup for me. I had eaten commercially canned food at Spook School, and most of it was nasty stuff, but the spicy tomato smell of the soup was pretty nice as it glopped out of the waxed-paper carton, into a soup bowl.

My teammates sliced meat, poured kibble for the mousers,

opened and washed the salad fixings, and nuked the organic roasted red pepper–and-tomato soup.

I kicked off my shoes as they made themselves at home. T. Laine knew where I kept the sheets, and while the bread toasted, she made up the guest beds. JoJo went to my room and got out my nightclothes. At home in my kitchen, Occam set the table, shooing the cats out of the way, talking to them with little bats and pats and hisses and vocalizings that the mousers seemed to understand. These were things that only the very best of friends would have been able to do.

I felt the tension ease out of my torso and limbs as my friends worked. Tears stung my eyes. "Thank you," I said, the words too loud, ringing in the tall ceilings and up the stairs. "For taking care of me. For proving what Rick said when I first met y'all. That I'd never have to 'go in alone.'"

From behind the kitchen table, Occam smiled, a crooked twisting of his lips, one dimple on his left cheek pulling in tight. "Nell, sugar, that's what this unit is all about. Teamwork. In everything." He poured four glasses of Sister Erasmus' wine into plastic wineglasses they had bought, and set two on the long, ancient, kitchen table, at the right of the plates. The two others, he brought over. "If you put your hands together, you can hold this."

"I need to go out into the woods," I said, taking the stem in my padded hands.

"After you eat, sugar. And rest a bit. You look a mite peaked."

"That's the way to make a girl feel pretty, cat boy," T. Laine called from the kitchen.

Occam stiffened, as if hearing his own words, and the dimpled smile disappeared. For a moment, he looked lost, uncertain. Then he leaned in closer, holding my gaze with his own and announced, "Nell is, hands down, the prettiest thing I ever saw, all bloody or all dolled up."

A blush flashed up my chest at the words, and my glass bobbled as his meaning ricocheted through my brain like lightning. He caught the stemware, straightened it before the wine spilled, and let me get a mittened grip on it again. The silence in the house assured me they had all heard his words. "Is that better, Lainie?" he asked, his eyes not letting me go.

"Only if you ask the poor girl out to dinner."

He tipped his glass at mine. The plastic edges met with a

low-pitched tap. "I'm getting there, Lainie. How 'bout you butt outta this convo."

"Ohhhhoooo," she said, as if this was an interesting development.

His voice dropped. "I'm not trying to stop you from getting to your woods. I'll help you do anything you want, Nell, sugar. Any way you want. Anytime you want."

My blush spread, as some strange part of me interpreted those words in a totally improper way for a widder-woman. "Ummm . . ."

"But I'd appreciate it if you would eat first. I was scared half to death when I saw you in the ER again, all bloody and bruised and mangled. And there wasn't a single person I could bite or claw."

Laughter tickled at the back of my throat, but I managed only another "Ummm . . ."

"And I'd like to take you to dinner. In a restaurant, like regular people do, instead of like weres do, over a bloody carcass."

"Ummm . . ." My brain clicked back on. That one I could answer. "I'm not regular people, Occam."

The dimple reappeared, and he eased back. "For which I am eternally grateful, sugar. Drink your wine." He stood and went back to the kitchen table.

I drank half the glass. The sugary alcohol slid down my throat and into my system. I knew I should drink a gallon of water before the wine, but I didn't ask for any. I just drank and watched Occam as he finished setting the table, wondering what all he might have meant about him needing to bite or claw someone. And me being pretty. And him wanting to take me to dinner. That sounded as if he was asking me on a date. Not now, not ever. I wasn't even sure if I liked men as friends. But Occam wasn't a human man, so . . . I pushed the thoughts away to deal with later, when I felt more myself.

The meal was simple, and though I had to sip my soup through a plastic straw, it was even more delicious than the scent had proclaimed, a far cry from the Spook School fare. As we all ate, the unit filled me in on more post-*Break* happenings. And I finished off two glasses of wine, which left me pleasantly tipsy.

Dessert was a cheese called Brie, heated on slices of the

artisan bread in the oven with a topping of my raspberry jam, and more wine. It was true what they said about alcohol. It gave a body false courage. And sometimes a big mouth. In a lull of the conversation, I said, "I feel a big-cat walking toward the house. Somebody has let Rick out of his cage."

"That would be Pea," Occam said.

"Why would Pea let a wereleopard outta his cage?"

"He needs to eat?" Occam suggested.

JoJo said, "Before she took off and left Rick high and dry, Paka had a long chat with Pea, at the end of Pea's claws. Pea seems to be of the opinion that you can fix Rick."

I laughed, but her expression said she was dead serious. "Pea talks?"

"Not to humans. Not to witches. Not even to whatever you might be," JoJo said, staring at a third bottle of wine in the glass-fronted cabinets along the back wall of the dining area. "But she talks to the werecats. Pea indicated to Occam that you had claimed Paka for your land, and through her you claimed Rick."

I didn't know how to respond to that. Truth was truth. "Paka took off, so I didn't too good of a job claiming her. Besides. I have no idea how to fix a werecat stuck in cat form, any more than I know how to fix a werecat stuck in human form."

"You know how to encourage a seed to sprout," T. Laine said. "You know how to make a tree grow fast and tall and straight. Maybe it's like that. Tell Rick to be what he already is."

JoJo got up and pulled the bottle from the cabinet. I was now down to four bottles of the rare sweet wine. I'd have to ask Sister Erasmus to trade me for more. Her sister-wife, Mary, had the gout. Maybe I could trade her some herbal tea for the wine.

"Nell?" T. Laine said.

I frowned and shrugged as JoJo opened the wine and poured us all more. "I'm willing to try, but who's gonna keep him from eating me while I'm working?"

"That, Nell, sugar, is my job," Occam said, toeing off his boots. "Let's get you outside and healed and then we'll see about helping Rick."

My hands ached, even after all the wine. Far more than I usually drank. The world spun, and I pressed down with my swollen hands, holding myself upright in a sitting position, on the roots of the married trees. I had never had a hangover, but I feared that would change come morning. I promised myself I'd drink a gallon of water before I turned in. But for now . . .

I took a calming breath and let my consciousness flow down into the ground, through the topsoil and the twined and twisted roots, past the rocks, broken and shattered. Into the deeps of Soulwood.

The wood was slumbering, the sleep of winter making it slow and lazy and peaceful. But it knew me, reached out to me, and coiled itself around me, making space beneath the ground for me. Around my body, the trees moved in the soughing breeze. The chill air wisped across my flesh, a swirling icy breath, stealing my body heat. I felt that part of me start to shiver.

As if it knew I needed something, the woods gathered warmth from deep and deep, from the center of the Earth's crust, and curled a tendril of that heat up. Up through the ground, into me. I sighed and relaxed.

My fingertips, frozen only moments before, warmed and dug into the wood of the exposed roots. Fingernails pressing in. Skin tightening on the stitches. Releasing micro-amounts of cells and serous fluid and blood to fall on the land. The earth saw my injury, knew the wounds. It sent tiny tendrils of vines up through the warm ground. The vines coming awake at the false spring of the ground heat. They feathered over my hands. Rootlets pressed against the unhealed wounds. Gently pushing into me. The invasion of the vines wasn't painful, just pressure, a persistent tingling, itching on my skin and inside, deeper, on my bones.

In my belly, the rooty scars moved. Coiled tight. Insistent and tenacious as they expanded their claim on me. After long minutes, the vines and roots inside me stilled. Healing me. A tightness I hadn't been aware of eased. I took a breath and let it out.

And remembered what I was supposed to be doing. *Rick.* And other things I had neglected to do. Rick was a thorny problem, one I had no idea how to handle. But the other things . . . those I could address.

I sent my consciousness back to the sapling I had killed, and the earth I had salted. The ground there was barren, hard as stone. It felt like an infection that had been encapsulated from the rest of the body by a membrane. Like a pocket of pus, one that had hardened and died. There was no indication of Brother Ephraim at the salted earth. No bloody darkness. Nothing of life or growth or goodness.

I left the salted earth and let my consciousness travel to Brother Ephraim, curled against the outer wall of Soulwood. Unlike Soulwood, Brother Ephraim wasn't sleeping. He was coiled like a venomous snake, rattles clattering, trembling with hate. The thread of himself to the salted earth had been cut. Severed. The wound on his side looking like a burn scar, keloid, puckered, and misshapen. I let the sense of satisfaction ripple off me and to him. A warning. I got the impression of a hissing reply, all anger and no words. I slipped beneath the space he occupied on Soulwood land and looked up, at the wall where he cowered, studying the trail of his essence, the one leading to the church compound and the tree there. The tree's energies were stronger than before, a reddish light of energies pulsing palely back and forth to the soil at the gate where I had splashed some of my blood. It almost felt as if the energies were considering a move there. I should go see the tree. Soon. And consider the opposite of a curse. I should consider blessing it and the ground where I wanted it to move.

I turned my attention to the coiled snake of Brother Ephraim's hate, and I imagined the border of Soulwood, envisioning it growing in thickness, in density, like stone beneath the ground. Stone that choked off all life and energy.

Ephraim's thread of power to the tree darkened, the pulse slowing to a trickle. I imagined enormous boulders crushing together, squeezing the power off. The thread had been there for so long that it had carved a pathway through the land, claiming part of it, but I tightened my hold on the land, and was gratified to see the energies slow, pale, and die. Ephraim howled in fury. I'd have to find a way to kill Ephraim. For now the narrow passageway to church land had been tightened, dammed, squeezed, and strangled. Ephraim was isolated.

Satisfied, I reached for the two big-cats on Soulwood, Occam and Rick. They were eating a deer, the fresh kill stretched out over a massive root system, the woods taking in the blood, drinking it down. The moon was no longer full, but it was only hours past, and the cats were contented in their cat fur. One of the two was mine, belonging to the land, to Soulwood. *Rick.*

I reached out and stroked the life force that was mine, much like I might stroke one of the mousers. A long mental swipe from forehead to tail tip. Rick purred. Occam went still. His claws squeezed out and scraped on a broken limb nearby.

I stroked again. Rick rolled over and lay with his head on the ground, his bloody paws out in front of him. He stretched.

I remembered what it had felt like to read a human, the incredible heat and wetness and noise and blood of the woman. The sight of the slime molds that had eaten into her, a darkness that didn't belong. I reached out and into Rick, reading him as I had the land, as I had the human woman. I sank into the heat, blood rushing like myriad streams. Thunder and wind, regular and even, filled my ears—the purring of a cat, so loud it hurt me, even so far away. The metronome of a resting, contented heartbeat, *thu-thump, thu-thump.* And lights like fireworks everywhere.

Magic. Rick had no slime-mold-damaged darkness; rather, he had magic, bright and sparkling, heated and steamy as a jungle night. Magic as strong as the *Infinitio,* the curse captured in the containment vessel. But this magic was claw and fang and blood and breath, each element that made him werecat glowing and pounding with life. With need. With hunger for the hunt, yearning for blood, and for the powerful desire to rend flesh and eat. And with a disdain for the human beneath. *Werecat.*

Hidden within and beneath the cat, was the human, much less dazzling, less violent in nature, but intense and sparkling, with a piercing, cutting energy. Fierce. Furious. Bitter at what his life had become. The things and people he had hurt and lost. By his mistakes. And by the magic that had snared him. Self-loathing so acute it was nearly incapacitating. The loss of lovers, friends, family, taken from him, first by the witch who had tattooed him with magic, then by the cat that had ensnared and ensorcelled him. And last, by the cat he had become.

Over it all was the glaring awareness of two strange things. The coloring and magic of the tattoos that bound Rick to his human form. Something in his magic was damaged. Ripped away. Torn and leaking and broken. The way a limb would look, tendons stripped and shredded, blood seeping, bone sharp and shattered. His magics had been cursed and then shredded away. I knew what was missing. The massive addiction that had been Paka's magic was gone.

There was nothing I could do about the self-loathing or the anger or bitterness. They were strictly human things.

But the tattoos and the addiction . . . those I could help.

I reached in and pulled on the tattoos. The bindings were threadlike, woven into the man's flesh, and I could see them even in the cat form. They stretched from his arm and shoulder into his human soul. Binding him into a here and now, inflexible and static. I searched within the inks and the magic, finding the blood that sealed him to a cat form and, unexpectedly, to a vampire. The working was maggoty with death, snarled and tethered, and I was certain that I'd never have been able to do what I intended had he still been human shaped and unchanging. I snipped the threads that were knotted there, that held the working to the ink that had been tattooed into him, comprehending that the spell had never been completed, but left unfinished. The magics fell away, leaving only the glowing of the cat eyes in the tattoos.

The leopard's heart rate sped, the thunder and wind of his breathing altered from purr to growl. Rick rolled to his feet. His screaming challenge slashed into the night. I felt him leap into a run. Coming for me. Occam on his tail.

The addiction I could heal the same way I might a sick tree or plant on Soulwood. I sent a tendril into the wound. Feeding it with my magic. Pulling together the broken strands, knotting them off. One, then another. Then dozens.

Rick stumbled and rolled. Down. Into a gully. Scattering fall's leaves, into a pile so deep it buried him. He writhed, fighting gravity, inhaling bits of leaves and dirt. Insects and small creatures skittered away. Fighting, he hit bottom and, in a sinuous move, brought his feet beneath him. He leaped straight up, hard and high. Erupting through the deep pile of detritus.

Within him, I mended the broken parts and rewove the fabric of completeness, gifting his soul with life and wholeness. I could do this because I had claimed Rick months ago, through Paka, when I claimed her for the land. While he was here, on Soulwood, he was mine to grow and heal. I boosted his werecat energies, adding to his magic and his power, but binding it back to his will, and his intellect.

Rick caught a root system with his claws and pulled-climbed up it back into the air. He shook and screamed his displeasure. His cat didn't like being shackled to the man as well as the moon.

I secured the last of the strands, smoothing them, stretching them into place. The magics that had been tied to him by the witch so long ago were gone. All that Paka had been and had ruined was gone. Now there was only man and cat. His will and the moon. Rick stopped, the sound of his scream echoing into the darkness. *Nell?* He thought at me. *What . . . ? What did you do?*

Not sure, I thought back. *I hope I helped.* I pulled away and back to my body. In the distance, I heard Rick scream, half human, half cat, full of agony.

I fell over, exhausted. My face landed on the ground, my hands near my eyes. Tiny green leaves were unfurling from the fingertips of my hand. Long and pointed at the tip, growing wide at the blade, rounding out and back to my nails. Which were green and veined.

That . . . that couldn't be a good sign.

Hands lifted me beneath my arms and at my ankles and carried me toward the house. My head flopped forward. My last vision was of my belly and the leaves and roots that grew there. Growing out of me. Again I heard Rick scream, before darkness claimed me.

EPILOGUE

Thanksgiving would be different this year. For all the years since John and Leah proposed to me and I had gone to live with them, I had celebrated every holiday away from the Nicholson clan. After John passed and I was alone, I had still kept away, believing that my family was a danger to me. Now my life had changed. I knew my extended family loved me, and had never stopped loving me. I was free to come and go from the compound of God's Cloud of Glory Church. I could visit with my mother, father, his other wives, and my full and half sibs, without fearing that I would be forced to stay there. Without the risk that my life would be stolen from me.

Many good things had happened over the last days since I'd left Spook School. I had learned that bloodlust could be controlled. I had learned that whatever the spirit of Soulwood was, it wasn't an Old One. I had found that I could survive a battle beneath the earth. I had grown, inside, where no one but me could see it. Good things I contemplated as I drove away from my woods, toward the lands of God's Cloud of Glory Church.

Thanksgiving Day, at eleven o'clock in the morning, I parked in front of my childhood home. I turned off the engine and removed my driving gloves, checking my fingertips. *No leaves.* They had withered and died within hours of my last communing with Soulwood, and the attempted healing of Rick. Which had been only partly successful.

I had a lot of things to address—the sentient tree near the sanctuary that hadn't yet moved to its new place. I still had the thorns from it and the option to have them analyzed, but that might bring danger to my door. I needed to deal with—kill—the dark blot of Brother Ephraim. I needed to visit with Dougie and her family in their home. Needed to force Daddy to the doctor, and probably back under the knife. Tell my sisters that we weren't human. That was not gonna be easy. Had to finish up my final classes and go for some additional certifications at Spook School. Winterize my garden. I also needed to consider Occam's interest in me, which made my middle feel all fluttery. Lots of things. But for today, I would be with my family for the first time in years.

A knock sounded and I couldn't help my flinch. I turned to see Sam, his face pressed to the window glass, squishing his nose. I stuck my tongue out at him and he laughed and opened my truck door. "Hurry up, Nell. Mama's taking the turkeys outta the ovens, and Mama Carmel has the casseroles cooked. And you got to meet my wife."

I slid out of the truck as Sam pulled a woman to me. "Sara-Bell, this is my sister Nell. You two got a lot in common. Nell used to steal my bubblegum. SaraBell stole my heart."

The woman beside him was tall and limber, with angular shoulders and long limbs. Not the tiny, delicate woman I might have thought a churchman would desire, but a Viking of a woman, blond and blue eyed and strong. A girl only a few years younger than me. Maybe twenty. I should remember her; it would be the socially correct thing to remember her, but . . . I didn't. She would have been nine years old when I'd left the church at age twelve. That was an eternity to a child. "My husband just said his heart was bubblegum," SaraBell said.

"I heard. And he said you'd stole it. Good for you," I said back.

SaraBell wrapped her arms around me in a hug. Sam gathered us both up and hugged too, a group hug, odd feeling and hooking into childhood memories like a crochet hook into yarn. Pulling. Tugging at a heart that had grown cold over the years.

"Welcome home, little sister," Sam said. "Hospitality and safety while you're here."

"Welcome, Sister Nell," SaraBell said.

"Peace be to both of you and to your home," I said, taking refuge in one of the many proper replies a guest would share. "I'm glad to have a new sister," I added. And then I teased, "And if this rascal ever gives you any trouble, you just give me a call. We'll gang up on him."

"Done," SaraBell said, stepping back. "Let me help you with the bread," she said.

And so my formal reunion with my extended family began.

The next weeks would be difficult. But for now, there was family. And that mattered.

Read on for an excerpt of the first book
in Faith Hunter's *New York Times* bestselling
Jane Yellowrock series,

SKINWALKER

Available wherever books are sold!

I wheeled my bike down Decatur Street and eased deeper into the French Quarter, the bike's engine purring. My shotgun, a Benelli M4 Super 90, was slung over my back and loaded for vamp with hand-packed silver fléchette rounds. I carried a selection of silver crosses in my belt, hidden under my leather jacket, and stakes, secured in loops on my jeans-clad thighs. The saddlebags on my bike were filled with my meager travel belongings—clothes in one side, tools of the trade in the other. As a vamp killer for hire, I travel light.

I'd need to put the vamp-hunting tools out of sight for my interview. My hostess might be offended. Not a good thing when said hostess held my next paycheck in her hands and possessed a set of fangs of her own.

A guy, a good-looking Joe standing in a doorway, turned his head to follow my progress as I motored past. He wore leather boots, a jacket, and jeans, like me, though his dark hair was short and mine was down to my hips when not braided out of the way, tight to my head, for fighting. A Kawasaki motorbike leaned on a stand nearby. I didn't like his interest, but he didn't prick my predatory or territorial instincts.

I maneuvered the bike down St. Louis and then onto Dauphine, weaving between nervous-looking shop workers heading home for the evening and a few early revelers out for fun. I spotted the address in the fading light. Katie's Ladies was the oldest continually operating whorehouse in the Quarter, in business since 1845, though at various locations, depending on hurricane, flood, the price of rent, and the agreeable nature of local law and its enforcement officers. I parked, set the kickstand, and unwound my long legs from the hog.

I had found two bikes in a junkyard in Charlotte, North Carolina, bodies rusted, rubber rotted. They were in bad shape. But

Jacob, a semiretired Harley restoration mechanic/Zen Harley priest living along the Catawba River, took my money, fixing one up, using the other for parts, ordering what else he needed over the Net. It took six months.

During that time I'd hunted for him, keeping his wife and four kids supplied with venison, rabbit, turkey—whatever I could catch, as maimed as I was—restocked supplies from the city with my hoarded money, and rehabbed my damaged body back into shape. It was the best I could do for the months it took me to heal. Even someone with my rapid healing and variable metabolism takes a long while to totally mend from a near beheading.

Now that I was a hundred percent, I needed work. My best bet was a job killing off a rogue vampire that was terrorizing the city of New Orleans. It had taken down three tourists and left a squad of cops, drained and smiling, dead where it dropped them. Scuttlebutt said it hadn't been satisfied with just blood—it had eaten their internal organs. All that suggested the rogue was old, powerful, and deadly—a whacked-out vamp. The nutty ones were always the worst.

Just last week, Katherine "Katie" Fonteneau, the proprietress and namesake of Katie's Ladies, had e-mailed me. According to my Web site, I had successfully taken down an entire bloodfamily in the mountains near Asheville. And I had. No lies on the Web site or in the media reports, not bald-faced ones anyway. Truth is, I'd nearly died, but I'd done the job, made a rep for myself, and then taken off a few months to invest my legitimately gotten gains. Or to heal, but spin is everything. A lengthy vacation sounded better than the complete truth.

I took off my helmet and the clip that held my hair, pulling my braids out of my jacket collar and letting them fall around me, beads clicking. I palmed a few tools of the trade—one stake, ash wood and silver tipped; a tiny gun; and a cross—and tucked them into the braids, rearranging them to hang smoothly with no lumps or bulges. I also breathed deeply, seeking to relax, to assure my safety through the upcoming interview. I was nervous, and being nervous around a vamp was just plain dumb.

The sun was setting, casting a red glow on the horizon, limning the ancient buildings, shuttered windows, and wrought-iron balconies in fuchsia. It was pretty in a purely human way. I opened my senses and let my Beast taste the world. She liked the smells

and wanted to prowl. *Later*, I promised her. Predators usually growl when irritated. *Soon*—she sent mental claws into my
soul, kneading. It was uncomfortable, but the claw pricks kept me
alert, which I'd need for the interview. I had never met a civilized
vamp, certainly never done business with one. So far as I knew,
vamps and skinwalkers had never met. I was about to change that.
This could get interesting.

I clipped my sunglasses onto my collar, lenses hanging out.
I glanced at the witchy-locks on my saddlebags and, satisfied, I
walked to the narrow red door and pushed the buzzer. The bald-
headed man who answered was definitely human, but big
enough to be something else: professional wrestler, steroid-
augmented bodybuilder, or troll. All of the above, maybe. The
thought made me smile. He blocked the door, standing with
arms loose and ready. "Something funny?" he asked, voice like
a horse-hoof rasp on stone.

"Not really. Tell Katie that Jane Yellowrock is here." Tough
always works best on first acquaintance. That my knees were
knocking wasn't a consideration.

"Card?" Troll asked. A man of few words. I liked him already.
My new best pal. With two gloved fingers, I unzipped my leather
jacket, fished a business card from an inside pocket, and extended
it to him. It read JANE YELLOWROCK, HAVE STAKES WILL TRAVEL.
Vamp killing is a bloody business. I had discovered that a little
humor went a long way to making it all bearable.

Troll took the card and closed the door in my face. I might
have to teach my new pal a few manners. But that was nearly
axiomatic for all the men of my acquaintance.

I heard a bike two blocks away. It wasn't a Harley. Maybe a
Kawasaki, like the bright red crotch rocket I had seen earlier. I
wasn't surprised when it came into view and it was the Joe from
Decatur Street. He pulled his bike up beside mine, powered
down, and sat there, eyes hidden behind sunglasses. He had a
toothpick in his mouth and it twitched once as he pulled his
helmet and glasses off.

The Joe was a looker. A little taller than my six feet even, he
had olive skin, black hair, black brows. Black jacket and jeans.
Black boots. Bit of overkill with all the black, but he made it
work, with muscular legs wrapped around the red bike.

No silver in sight. No shotgun, but a suspicious bulge beneath
his right arm. Made him a leftie. Something glinted in the back

of his collar. A knife hilt, secured in a spine sheath. Maybe more than one blade. There were scuffs on his boots (Western, like mine, not Harley butt-stompers) but his were Fryes and mine were ostrich-skin Luccheses. I pulled in scents, my nostrils widening. His boots smelled of horse manure, fresh. Local boy, then, or one who had been in town long enough to find a mount. I smelled horse sweat and hay, a clean blend of scents. And cigar. It was the cigar that made me like him. The taint of steel, gun oil, and silver made me fall in love. Well, sorta. My Beast thought he was kinda cute, and maybe tough enough to be worthy of us. Yet there was a faint scent on the man, hidden beneath the surface smells, that made me wary.

The silence had lasted longer than expected. Since he had been the one to pull up, I just stared, and clearly our silence bothered the Joe, but it didn't bother me. I let a half grin curl my lip. He smiled back and eased off his bike. Behind me, inside Katie's, I heard footsteps. I maneuvered so that the Joe and the doorway were both visible. No way could I do it and be unobtrusive, but I raised a shoulder to show I had no hard feelings. Just playing it smart. Even for a pretty boy.

Troll opened the door and jerked his head to the side. I took it as the invitation it was and stepped inside. "You got interesting taste in friends," Troll said, as the door closed on the Joe.

"Never met him. Where you want the weapons?" Always better to offer than to have them removed. Power plays work all kinds of ways.

Troll opened an armoire. I unbuckled the shotgun holster and set it inside, pulling silver crosses from my belt and thighs and from beneath the coat until there was a nice pile. Thirteen crosses—excessive, but they distracted people from my backup weapons. Next came the wooden stakes and silver stakes. Thirteen of each. And the silver vial of holy water. One vial. If I carried thirteen, I'd slosh.

I hung the leather jacket on the hanger in the armoire and tucked the glasses in the inside pocket with the cell phone. I closed the armoire door and assumed the position so Troll could search me. He grunted as if surprised, but pleased, and did a thorough job. To give him credit, he didn't seem to enjoy it overmuch—used only the backs of his hands, no fingers, didn't linger or stroke where he shouldn't. Breathing didn't speed up, heart rate stayed regular; things I can sense if it's quiet enough.

After a thorough feel inside the tops of my boots, he said, "This way."

I followed him down a narrow hallway that made two crooked turns toward the back of the house. We walked over old Persian carpets, past oils and watercolors done by famous and not-so-famous artists. The hallway was lit with stained-glass Lalique sconces, which looked real, not like reproductions, but maybe you can fake old; I didn't know. The walls were painted a soft butter color that worked with the sconces to illuminate the paintings. Classy joint for a whorehouse. The Christian children's home schoolgirl in me was both appalled and intrigued.

When Troll paused outside the red door at the end of the hallway, I stumbled, catching my foot on a rug. He caught me with one hand and I pushed off him with little body contact. I managed to look embarrassed; he shook his head. He knocked. I braced myself and palmed the cross he had missed. And the tiny two-shot derringer. Both hidden against my skull on the crown of my head, and covered by my braids, which men never, ever searched, as opposed to my boots, which men always had to stick their fingers in. He opened the door and stood aside. I stepped in.

The room was spartan but expensive, and each piece of furniture looked Spanish. Old Spanish. Like Queen-Isabella-and-Christopher-Columbus old. The woman, wearing a teal dress and soft slippers, standing beside the desk, could have passed for twenty until you looked in her eyes. Then she might have passed for said queen's older sister. Old, old, *old* eyes. Peaceful as she stepped toward me. Until she caught my scent.

In a single instant her eyes bled red, pupils went wide and black, and her fangs snapped down. She leaped. I dodged under her jump as I pulled the cross and derringer, quickly moving to the far wall, where I held out the weapons. The cross was for the vamp, the gun for the Troll. She hissed at me, fangs fully extended. Her claws were bone white and two inches long. Troll had pulled a gun. A big gun. Men and their pissing contests. *Crap.* Why couldn't they ever just let me be the only one with a gun?

"Predator," she hissed. "In my territory." Vamp anger pheromones filled the air, bitter as wormwood.

"I'm not human," I said, my voice steady. "That's what you smell." I couldn't do anything about the tripping heart rate, which I knew would drive her further over the edge; I'm an animal. Biological factors always kick in. So much for trying not to be nervous. The cross in my hand glowed with a cold white light, and Katie, if that was her original name, tucked her head, shielding her eyes. Not attacking, which meant that she was thinking. Good.

"Katie?" Troll asked.

"I'm not human," I repeated. "I'll really hate shooting your Troll here, to bleed all over your rugs, but I will."

"Troll?" Katie asked. Her body froze with that inhuman stillness vamps possess when thinking, resting, or whatever else it is they do when they aren't hunting, eating, or killing. Her shoulders dropped and her fangs clicked back into the roof of her mouth with a sudden spurt of humor. Vampires can't laugh and go vampy at the same time. They're two distinct parts of them, one part still human, one part rabid hunter. Well, that's likely insulting, but then this was the first so-called civilized vamp I'd ever met. All the others I'd had personal contact with were sick, twisted killers. And then dead. Really dead.

Troll's eyes narrowed behind the .45 aimed my way. I figured he didn't like being compared to the bad guy in a children's fairy tale. I was better at fighting, but negotiation seemed wise. "Tell him to back off. Let me talk." I nudged it a bit. "Or I'll take you down and he'll never get a shot off." Unless he noticed that I had set the safety on his gun when I tripped. Then I'd *have* to shoot him. I wasn't betting on my .22 stopping him unless I got an eye shot. Chest hits wouldn't even slow him down. In fact they'd likely just make him mad.

When neither attacked, I said, "I'm not here to stake you. I'm Jane Yellowrock, here to interview for a job, to take out a rogue vamp that your own council declared an outlaw. But I don't smell human, so I take precautions. One cross, one stake, one two-shot derringer." The word "stake" didn't elude her. Or him. He'd missed three weapons. No Christmas bonus for Troll.

"What are you?" she asked.

"You tell me where you sleep during the day and I'll tell you what I am. Otherwise, we can agree to do business. Or I can leave."

Telling the location of a lair—where a vamp sleeps—is information for lovers, dearest friends, or family. Katie chuckled. It was one of the silky laughs that her kind can give, low and erotic, like vocal sex. My Beast purred. She liked the sound.

"Are you offering to be my toy for a while, intriguing nonhuman female?" When I didn't answer, she slid closer, despite the glowing cross, and said, "You are interesting. Tall, slender, young." She leaned in and breathed in my scent. "Or not so young. What are you?" she pressed, her voice heavy with fascination. Her eyes had gone back to their natural color, a sort of grayish hazel, but blood blush still marred her cheeks so I knew she was still primed for violence. That violence being my death.

"Secretive," she murmured, her voice taking on that tone they use to enthrall, a deep vibration that seems to stroke every gland. "Enticing scent. Likely tasty. Perhaps your blood would be worth the trade. Would you come to my bed if I offered?"

"No," I said. No inflection in my voice. No interest, no revulsion, no irritation, nothing. Nothing to tick off the vamp or her servant.

"Pity. Put down the gun, Tom. Get our guest something to drink."

I didn't wait for Tommy Troll to lower his weapon; I dropped mine. Beast wasn't happy, but she understood. I was the intruder in Katie's territory. While I couldn't show submission, I could show manners. Tom lowered his gun and his attitude at the same time and holstered the weapon as he moved into the room toward a well-stocked bar.

"Tom?" I said. "Uncheck your safety." He stopped midstride. "I set it when I fell against you in the hallway."

"Couldn't happen," he said.

"I'm fast. It's why your employer invited me for a job interview."

He inspected his .45 and nodded at his boss. Why anyone would want to go around with a holstered .45 with the safety off is beyond me. It smacks of either stupidity or quiet desperation, and Katie had lived too long to be stupid. I was guessing the rogue had made her truly apprehensive. I tucked the cross inside a little lead-foil-lined pocket in the leather belt holding up my Levi's, and eased the small gun in beside it, strapping it down. There was a safety, but on such a small gun, it was easy to knock the safety off with an accidental brush of my arm.

"Is that where you hid the weapons?" Katie asked. When I

just looked at her, she shrugged as if my answer were unimportant and said, "Impressive. You are impressive."

Katie was one of those dark ash blondes with long straight hair so thick it whispered when she moved, falling across the teal silk that fit her like a second skin. She stood five feet and a smidge, but height was no measure of power in her kind. She could move as fast as I could and kill in an eyeblink. She had buffed nails that were short when she wasn't in killing mode, pale skin, and she wore exotic, Egyptian-style makeup around the eyes. Black liner overlaid with some kind of glitter. Not the kind of look I'd ever had the guts to try. I'd rather face down a grizzly than try to achieve "a look."

"What'll it be, Miz Yellowrock?" Tom asked.

"Cola's fine. No diet."

He popped the top on a Coke and poured it over ice that crackled and split when the liquid hit, placed a wedge of lime on the rim, and handed it to me. His employer got a tall fluted glass of something milky that smelled sharp and alcoholic. Well, at least it wasn't blood on ice. Ick.

"Thank you for coming such a distance," Katie said, taking one of two chairs and indicating the other for me. Both chairs were situated with backs to the door, which I didn't like, but I sat as she continued. "We never made proper introductions, and the In-ter-net," she said, separating the syllables as if the term was strange, "is no substitute for formal, proper introductions. I am Katherine Fonteneau." She offered the tips of her fingers, and I took them for a moment in my own before dropping them.

"Jane Yellowrock," I said, feeling as though it was all a little redundant. She sipped; I sipped. I figured that was enough etiquette. "Do I get the job?" I asked.

Katie waved away my impertinence. "I like to know the people with whom I do business. Tell me about yourself."

Cripes. The sun was down. I needed to be tooling around town, getting the smell and the feel of the place. I had errands to run, an apartment to rent, rocks to find, meat to buy. "You've been to my Web site, no doubt read my bio. It's all there in black and white." Well, in full color graphics, but still.

Katie's brows rose politely. "Your bio is dull and uninformative. For instance, there is no mention that you appeared out of the forest at age twelve, a feral child raised by wolves, without even the rudiments of human behavior. That you were placed in a children's home, where you spent the next six years. And that you again vanished until you reappeared two years ago and started killing my kind."

My hackles started to rise, but I forced them down. I'd been baited by a roomful of teenaged girls before I even learned to speak English. After that, nothing was too painful. I grinned and threw a leg over the chair arm. Which took Katie, of the elegant attack, aback. "I wasn't raised by wolves. At least I don't think so. I don't feel an urge to howl at the moon, anyway. I have no memories of my first twelve years of life, so I can't answer you about them, but I think I'm probably Cherokee." I touched my black hair, then my face with its golden brown skin and sharp American Indian nose in explanation. "After that, I was raised in a Christian children's home in the mountains of South Carolina. I left when I was eighteen, traveled around a while, and took up an apprenticeship with a security firm for two years. Then I hung out my shingle, and eventually drifted into the vamp-hunting business.

"What about you? You going to share all your own deep dark secrets, Katie of Katie's Ladies? Who is known to the world as Katherine Fonteneau, aka Katherine Louisa Dupre, Katherine Pearl Duplantis, and Katherine Vuillemont, among others I uncovered. Who renewed her liquor license in February, is a registered Republican, votes religiously, pardon the term, sits on the local full vampiric council, has numerous offshore accounts in various names, a half interest in two local hotels, at least three restaurants, and several bars, and has enough money to buy and sell this entire city if she wanted to."

"We have both done our research, I see."

I had a feeling Katie found me amusing. Must be hard to live a few centuries and find yourself in a modern world where everyone knows what you are and is either infatuated with you or scared silly by you. I was neither, which she liked, if the small smile was any indication. "So. Do I have the job?" I asked again.

Katie considered me for a moment, as if weighing my responses and attitude. "Yes," she said. "I've arranged a small house for you, per the requirements on your In-ter-net web place."

My brows went up despite myself. She must have been pretty sure she was gonna hire me, then.

"It backs up to this property." She waved vaguely at the back of the room. "The small L-shaped garden at the side and back is walled in brick, and I had the stones you require delivered two days ago."

Okay. Now I was impressed. My Web site says I require close proximity to boulders or a rock garden, and that I won't take a job if such a place can't be found. And the woman—the vamp—had made sure that nothing would keep me from accepting the job. I wondered what she would have done if I'd said no.

At her glance, Tr— Tom took up the narrative. "The gardener had a conniption, but he figured out a way to get boulders into the garden with a crane, and then blended them into his landscaping. Grumbled about it, but it's done."

"Would you tell me why you need piles of stone?" Katie asked.

"Meditation." When she looked blank I said, "I use stone for meditation. It helps prepare me for a hunt." I knew she had no idea what I was talking about. It sounded pretty lame even to me, and I had made up the lie. I'd have to work on that one.

Katie stood and so did I, setting aside my Coke. Katie had drained her foul-smelling libation. On her breath it smelled vaguely like licorice. "Tom will give you the contract and a packet of information, the compiled evidence gathered about the rogue by the police and our own investigators. Tonight you may rest or indulge in whatever pursuits appeal to you.

"Tomorrow, once you deliver the signed contract, you are invited to join my girls for dinner before business commences. They will be attending a private party, and dinner will be served at seven of the evening. I will not be present, that they may speak freely. Through them you may learn something of import." It was a strange way to say seven p.m., and an even stranger request for me to interrogate her employees right off the bat, but I didn't react. Maybe one of them knew something about the rogue. And maybe Katie knew it. "After dinner, you may initiate your inquiries.

"The council's offer of a bonus stands. An extra twenty percent if you dispatch the rogue inside of ten days, without the media taking a stronger note of *us*." The last word had an inflection that let me know the "us" wasn't Katie and me. She meant the vamps. "Human media attention has been . . . difficult. And the rogue's feeding has strained relations in the vampiric council. It is *important*," she said.

I nodded. *Sure. Whatever. I want to get paid, so I aim to please.* But I didn't say it.

Katie extended a folder to me and I tucked it under my arm. "The police photos of the crime scenes you requested. Three samples of bloodied cloth from the necks of the most recent victims, carefully wiped to gather saliva," she said.

Vamp saliva, I thought. *Full of vamp scent. Good for tracking.*

"On a card is my contact at the NOPD. She is expecting a call from you. Let Tom know if you need anything else." Katie settled cold eyes on me in obvious dismissal. She had already turned her mind to other things. Like dinner? Yep. Her cheeks had paled again and she suddenly looked drawn with hunger. Her eyes slipped to my neck. Time to leave.

Also From *New York Times* Bestselling Author
FAITH HUNTER

. . .

THE JANE YELLOWROCK SERIES

SKINWALKER
BLOOD CROSS
MERCY BLADE
RAVEN CURSED
DEATH'S RIVAL
BLOOD TRADE
BLACK ARTS
BROKEN SOUL
DARK HEIR
SHADOW RITES

. . .

"Faith Hunter has created one of my favorite characters, ever.
Jane Yellowrock is full of contradictions . . . Highly recommended."
—Fresh Fiction

"Jane Yellowrock is smart, sexy, and ruthless."
—Kim Harrison

faithhunter.net
facebook.com/official.faith.hunter
penguin.com